A Second Chance

C. L. Rose

A Second Chance

Olympia Publishers
London

www.olympiapublishers.com
OLYMPIA PAPERBACK EDITION

A CIP catalogue record for this title is
available from the British Library.

ISBN: 978-1-80439-512-7

This is a work of fiction.
Names, characters, places and incidents originate from the writer's
imagination. Any resemblance to actual persons, living or dead, is
purely coincidental.

First Published in 2023

Olympia Publishers
Tallis House
2 Tallis Street
London
EC4Y 0AB

Printed in Great Britain

Acknowledgements

Thank you to my family and friends who have supported me throughout the entire process and saw faith in me when I didn't always see it in myself. Thank you for reading the manuscript and giving me the confidence to get it published. I love you all. Thank you to Mum and Dad, for always helping and supporting me in every way imaginable. It wouldn't have been possible without you. To my husband and to our kids, there are no words to express my love for you guys. Thank you for being my anchor and my drive to finally do this.

CHAPTER ONE

Gemma hated football. Everything about football she hated. And it wasn't because it took over her day-to-day life while she worked at her mum's pub. It wasn't even that fact that it infuriated her how much a single person could be paid for kicking a ball up and down a pitch.

No.

It was because of him.

She looked up disdainfully at one of many TVs along the pub walls and the news broadcasters were *still* discussing the upcoming World Cup. Yes, it was probably exciting to everyone, even for those who didn't care about football. The World Cup was to be held in England, so everyone was jumping on the bandwagon.

Getting behind our lads, as some were saying.

Some were just enjoying having a few beers and joining in with it at all in the pubs.

Suppose that was a good thing for Gemma and her mum, Linda. This would make them huge revenue. And they both needed the money. The pub wasn't doing as well as it had done in the past. So Gemma grinned and bared it. Just because she didn't like the World Cup, or anything football, didn't mean they wouldn't be showing every game.

Which meant, every shift, guaranteed, Gemma would have to watch *him* play. There was still a bit of time until the World Cup, weeks really, but the team had just been announced and the

7

friendlies were underway. So fans started to pile in, filling all of the pub's tables and stools. The kitchen was flying out fish and chips and gammon and eggs left, right and centre. Pints were being pulled one after the other, trays of shots and Jägerbombs leaving the bar every few minutes and there was a loud buzz with people laughing and clapping each other on their backs. There was a sea of white and red England football shirts, mostly of the older kits but some had spent a few bob on the new shirt.

It took all of Gemma's effort not to roll her eyes at them.

A group of lads in the newest England shirts rocked up to the bar to Gemma, headed by one of the cockiest, 'thinks himself a big shot' man known to man.

Matt Clark.

Who happened to also be Gemma's below-par boyfriend.

Gemma had known Matt for many years, she had grown up with him and she never thought she would end up with him. Matt wasn't an ugly man, he was fairly tall, but at only five-foot-ten, he was only a couple of inches taller than Gemma. He had light brown hair which would have been nice if he didn't also have black eyes. His light hair and dark eyes almost made him look even paler and washed out. He kept himself in fairly good shape, with his manual job of being a car mechanic, but wasn't ripped or massively toned.

Matt had been one of those popular guys in senior school and college who had had the world as his oyster. But he peaked. Peaked and when all of his gang moved on, growing up and moving out of the small north west town of Netherby, it had just been Gemma left.

She hadn't moved on either, she still worked in her mum's pub, like she had done when she was fifteen. But since her granddad had died two years earlier, she had become joint owner with her mum. Those around her had grown, moved and got these amazing careers, but she was still working in that pub.

Gemma was tall, she got her height from her dad who wasn't on the scene and didn't care to know her. She had her mother's long dark brown hair and blue eyes. But Gemma's eyes weren't twinkling like her mother's. They were dull and almost colourless. Though people commented (generally her mother's friends and older customers at the pub) that Gemma was pretty, she didn't believe them. Gemma wasn't a skinny girl either, though she was tall and her pudginess was a little more distributed over her body, she was still a size sixteen (in a decent shop) and larger than other girls she knew. She was fat and plain and there was nothing remotely interesting or special about her. To put simply, Gemma absolutely hated how she felt about her appearance.

With no self-confidence or self-worth, it was easy for Gemma to blend into the background, for her to go unnoticed. No one had ever flirted with her, asked for her number or on a date. Matt had shown some interested at first but never made her feel special and as Matt said, he was all she had. No one else was interested. So Gemma had to take what she could get. She had been a virgin until she had got with Matt two years before, when she was twenty-three. Nearly completely untouched by another. Well, not fully untouched if she was completely honest with herself, but she didn't allow her thoughts to stray to *him*.

"Roly-Poly, get us some drinks," Matt demanded, not even pausing to say hello to Gemma before he turned his back to her and started talking to his little posse of younger, more impressionable boys who worked in the garage with him. A very clever nickname Gemma had gained during her school years, due to being about two or three stone heavier than all the skinny girls in her year. Also, Gemma's surname was Walker, which was another amusing irony for all the bullies that came up with the nickname. Matt had been a contributor to that nickname and sometimes Gemma thought it was probably the only "funny" thing he'd ever come up with.

Even if it was at Gemma's expense.

The lads with Matt were fresh out of school or college trying to learn a new trade, hoping that it might be their key out of that hellhole of a town. And Matt enjoyed being able to try and mould them into little minions that followed him around and made him feel like the "boss" until they finally came to their senses and left. Then he would recruit and the process would start all over again. But Gemma never left. He always knew that Gemma wouldn't go and he could always control her.

So Gemma never spoke back, she ignored how he spoke to her and just poured them some pints. They were grouped around the bar as she put down the pints and they were discussing the World Cup with great enthusiasm. They were talking about each of the players in turn, saying what they liked and disliked about each.

Apparently, each of them should have been the manager, thought Gemma with a roll of her eyes as she turned back from them.

"But that Robbie Wilson man," Ethan said and Gemma froze, unable to pull herself away. "He is class man, you have to admit. Love or hate him, he is fucking class. He'll win this World Cup for England." Ethan was the oldest in the posse but was still only about eighteen. He had a baby with a local girl, who again was only seventeen or eighteen. Ethan, out of all Matt's "friends", was the one most likely to stay in Netherby. Matt would be happy, he had someone to boss around at work on a permanent basis. And Ethan would stick it out, because he needed money to provide for his kid.

They all murmured in agreement to what Ethan said, drinking their pints and puffing out their chests.

"I went to school with him," Matt said, taking a huge swig of his pint and belching. "Fuck off!" and Matt nodded importantly, taking another gulp.

"Yeah, used to do all sorts together. He ended up going into the academy before we finished school, but he's still my mate."

Bullshit.

Matt hadn't been in contact with Robbie for the best part of ten years. Robbie Wilson hadn't been back to Netherby since he got scouted and went to an academy in the nearest big city and become one of the most successful football players that England had ever had.

He was their star player, all of England's World Cup dreams were on him. He was also Gemma's first love.

See, Gemma and Robbie actually grew up together. Their mothers had met at the school gate on their very first day at the local primary school. Soon after that, their mothers became best friends so they were always chucked together at social events. Left to play together with his younger sister, Pip, who still to this day was one of Gemma's closest friends and Gemma's childhood best friend, Abi. But she was also someone Gemma didn't allow herself to think about too much either. Abi had died just before Robbie went off to the academy and even ten years later Gemma found it extremely difficult to accept. Gemma had always felt guilty about the night of Abi's death, feeling responsible for it. So, Gemma didn't allow herself to live a happy and fulfilling life.

If Abi couldn't do that, then Gemma wouldn't either. She owed her at least that much.

So, it had always been the four of them, Gemma, Abi, Pip and Robbie. When they were young enough to be dragged to parties by their parents, the four of them would take themselves off and play games like murder in the dark or hide and seek, or even just hang around outside talking and joking.

It was some of the happiest memories Gemma had, before they got old enough when hormones made things awkward and complicated. That was when Gemma really started to fall for Robbie. Before he started to get more into his online chat rooms and his friends, he would hang out with them and make her laugh until her cheeks and stomach hurt. They would also go trick-or-treating with each other and do stupid pranks on the adults and run for their lives, howling with laughter. Gemma would go to Robbie and Pip's house at the weekend and have a sleepover with Pip and all the while, she just wanted to be around Robbie.

But the older they got, the more Robbie wasn't there. Robbie was immensely popular and would often be out all weekend. He would be at parties every weekend and during the day he was out with his friends, often just hanging around shopping centres or parks. His group of friends started to include girls who were all so pretty and skinny, the complete opposite of what Gemma was.

One of these girls included Miranda Johnson who, put simply, was a bitch.

She used to make it her life goal to bully Gemma whenever she was around her, making snide remarks about Gemma's size, what she was wearing and sometimes even her smell. So she used to make Gemma feel absolutely awful about herself constantly during their school days.

And to break Gemma's heart even more, Robbie then went on to date her in their final year at school. So not only was Gemma pinning hard after Robbie, but Robbie also had a girlfriend that he would constantly be snogging all over the school and Gemma just seemed to always stumble upon them.

To make matters worse, Gemma's mum gave Robbie a weekend job at the family pub with Gemma, so Gemma was forced to spend a lot of time alone with Robbie on a Friday night.

Robbie was so different when they were alone, that Gemma couldn't help but totally fall head over heels for him. She would look forward to every Friday night when she would get a snippet of Robbie's full attention, they would joke and talk about everything and anything, which made it all so much worse when he then would go on to ignore her totally in school. She supposed it was better than him saying cruel things like Miranda and Matt had done, but to completely change was just so heart-breaking.

So once Robbie had left, Gemma tried so hard to get over her feelings, putting it down to a childhood crush and she thought she had got over it, until a couple of years later. She was working in the pub again, fresh out of college. It had been a slow midweek shift. Football had been on and Gemma had been serving a customer, when he suddenly shouted out and pointed at the screen.

"There he is! That's that Robbie Wilson! He was a kid from around here! His parents still live here. I forgot it was he's debut!"

Gemma's head had shot around so fast, that she felt a crick in her neck. Rubbing her neck, she looked at the screen, just in time to see the camera zooming into a figure in a red football kit. The manager was shouting in his ear, showing him some paper and Robbie was nodding and concentrating hard.

He had changed a lot.

He was no longer skinny; he had filled out even though he was clearly still lean. He looked much taller, though it was hard to tell on the telly but he looked at least half a foot taller than when Gemma had last seen him. His hair was still dark but he was also sporting a fashionable haircut and a lot more tattoos. But looking at his face, Gemma's heart went into overdrive and all her feelings came rushing back in a huge wave of emotion. It was like he was right there behind the bar with Gemma, like she could almost see straight into those deep brown eyes that make her knees weak.

It had completely rattled Gemma and it was from then on, Gemma hated football and couldn't bring herself to look at any matches, especially the ones with his team. Because, if she let her mind wonder, it would take her back to those quiet Friday evenings when those eyes had been on her, almost surveying her. But in her dreams, she imagined the grown-up Robbie. He was so much taller and full of muscles, but his warm brown eyes and his face was still the same as it always had been. The way she would watch his lips moving and how, more than anything at the time, she wished she could reach out and run her hands through his thick, brown hair—

"Gemma? Hello? Earth to Gemma?"

Gemma was suddenly thrown back out of her fantasy of Robbie Wilson's full, kissable lips and back to the pub with the loud buzz of a busy shift.

"Gem? Are you okay?" Gemma looked up and saw the beautiful brown eyes that she knew so well and fantasied about so often. Yet they were not the brown eyes of Robbie Wilson, but it was his younger sister, Pip. Gemma couldn't help but smile, she had missed his sister while she had been away at university.

"Pip? Oh my God, what are you doing here?" She leaned over and pulled Pip into a one-armed hug over the bar. Pip had the same brown eyes as Robbie, but her hair was more auburn like her mother's. She was tall, but not as tall as Gemma. She also had one of those bodies that Gemma was envious of, that she seemed to effortlessly keep slim and in shape. Gemma may have been envious of Pip's figure, but Gemma was envious of most girls' figures. She loved Pip like a sister and there was no malice in Pip.

"I've come home early for the summer, to see Mum," Pip said, her expression turning sadder.

"Ah," Gemma said and she squeezed Pip a little harder for a moment. "I'm sorry." Pip did a little shrug and a sad smile.

"Yeah, it's shit."

"How is she?" She shrugged. Rose, Robbie and Pip's mum, had a cancer scare. She had had an operation to remove a significant growth in her breast. They were waiting on the results of the removal.

"They've done everything they can now. We just got to see what will happen now." Gemma felt a pang through her heart to think what they all must be going through, it was sickening. She couldn't imagine her mum sick, she was all Gemma had in the world.

"I'm so sorry," Gemma said pointlessly, as she didn't know what to say really, but Pip still smiled and squeezed her hand appreciatively. "How's uni?" Gemma asked because she just couldn't stand the look on Pip's face any longer and she wanted to distract her. It worked because Pip's sad face was taunted into a grimace.

"Argh, so happy this year is over; four exams in two days? No thank you."

"Sounds grim," Gemma admitted.

"Understatement."

"Want a drink?"

"Cider please," she said as she scooted into the only free bar seat. Gemma didn't bother asking what flavour and she grabbed Pip's favourite one and gave it to her, with the ice and pint glass. "Thanks," she said and poured it out and drank a few deep mouthfuls before smacking her lips and sighing. "Ah, lovely."

"Do you still want those hours over the summer then?" Gemma asked, knowing the answer but wanting to double-check.

"Yes, I'll need the money for next term."

"But I'm sure—" but Pip cut her off.

"I don't want Robbie to pay for everything, he already sends me money every month to make things easier. Plus, working will help keep me preoccupied. I can't be cooped up in the house all the time, I'll go insane."

Gemma nodded and was being called over by another group just arriving at the bar.

Things were really starting to pick up and people were coming in for the late-night match. Robbie's team wasn't playing, Gemma has already checked. But it was a friendly between two European teams and the pub was packed. Gemma generally preferred doing the bar to the floor, but when it was busy like this, she would have much rather been waiting tables. At least she wasn't stuck listening to drunk people going on and on about how great the game was and how brilliant Robbie Wilson was and how amazing it was that he was a local boy.

He was one of them, they would say.

It didn't help Gemma, who was trying to not think about Robbie. But with Pip home and the match on, it was inevitable.

Gemma was pouring a load of pints for Matt and his cronies when she heard them talking about Robbie again.

"Have you seen that bird he's with now?" Matt was saying and Gemma had to roll her eyes. "The supermodel? Mate, I'm telling you, I wouldn't say no." Gemma coughed back a laugh and Matt glared at her. "What?"

"Well, not being funny Matt. But don't think a supermodel like that would A, be seen dead in this town and B, say yes to you." They all burst out laughing, excluding Matt who glared at Gemma with a sick sort of smile on his face. Gemma didn't know what made her say it and she regretted it the second the words left her lips. He wouldn't take it lightly and he would make sure she knew behind closed doors later tonight when they were alone in the flat above.

It had been all the talk about Robbie Wilson all night; it had messed up her whole façade and she hadn't been paying attention to her words.

She quickly turned her back, feeling her skin going hot and prickly. Her heart beat nervously as she chanced a glance at Matt in the mirror, who was still smiling slyly behind her.

Shit, she thought, she was in for a bad night.

"And do you think anyone remotely famous would even glance in your direction?" Matt asked quietly and the lads behind him went very quiet. Gemma swallowed, thinking about her answer. She was already in trouble, so there was no need to be cautious.

"Well," she said, with her back still to them, "No one famous ever visits this town, so I doubt I would ever be in that situation. But I can assure you, anyone who kicks a ball around for a living and gets paid a ridiculous amount every year is not worth my dying breath."

"Wow. Well, it's nice to see you too, Gem," said an achingly familiar voice behind Gemma, she swung around and pretty much screamed as she dropped the glasses that she was carrying. They went cascading to the floor and shattered, spraying

17

everyone in close proximity with gin and tonic. There was the usual cry of "Weyhey!" From the usual dickheads in the group and accompanied by a feeble round of applause, but Gemma couldn't focus on them in that moment.

Standing next to Pip, leaning casually on the bar, was a man. He was breathtakingly handsome in his expensive polo shirt, with his big, flashy watch and tattoos covering both his arms. He was looking at Gemma with those deep brown eyes that so often haunted all of Gemma's thoughts and dreams.

It was Robbie Wilson.

CHAPTER TWO

Ten Years Earlier

Argh, the weekend again. Gemma hated the weekend. The weekend meant people at school would be going to parties and hanging out at the skate park, but for Gemma, it meant one thing. Working.

So, Gemma found herself standing awkwardly by the kitchen pass, waiting for table eight's food order. The heat of the lamps was making her even warmer than she already was. Something about her polyester black pants and top made her sweat so much during her work shifts. She could physically feel her fat rolls doubling in size as the unflattering fabric clung to them.

She pulled at the fabric to try and release it from tucking underneath the roll. Her skin got constantly prickly and hot as she tried to subtly fan herself as she waited for the chef. Her new pants were itchy and digging into her waistline and the apron didn't help as it bunched along her waistline. She tugged at that as well, really wishing she could just shrink and disappear.

"Table eight, Gemma, please." The new head chef smiled at her, as he passed her the plates.

He was nicer to her than anyone else and Gemma did know it was because she was the owner's granddaughter and daughter, but it still made Gemma blush and get a little flustered. He did have lovely blue eyes, with a very cool eyebrow piercing.

Gemma fumbled with the plates for a second and she chanced a glance at him again. He was smiling slightly as he observed her, which made her more flustered.

"Ah," she said awkwardly, "thanks, Jake."

"You're very welcome, Gem," he said smoothly and quietly nearly making Gemma drop the plates in surprise.

She never had anyone flirt or even be remotely nice to her and it was a confusing feeling.

She stumbled off and she swore he chuckled.

Back out in the dining room, Gemma quickly went to table eight, slightly thankful that the order was small enough that she didn't have to return to the kitchen and gave them their meals before returning to the safety of the bar. She started polishing some of the glasses (it was still early on Friday night) when a familiar voice shouted at her.

"Gemma!" It was Pip, who was running towards the bar, her face flushed and excited.

"Hi, I didn't know you were eating here tonight."

"I didn't either. But Mum said your mum wanted to speak to Robbie."

Gemma's heart dropped with sickening speed. "Robbie's here? He never comes to dinner with you guys any more." Gemma could hear the slight panic in her voice and knew full well Pip could too. She looked at Gemma for a moment before saying.

"Yeah, he's here. Your mum wanted to ask him something." What on earth could Gemma's mum want to ask Robbie?

Before Gemma could reply, she saw him. He was walking in with his mum and dad. He was wearing his football tracksuit; obviously, he had come straight from training. The three of them approached the bar and smiled at Gemma.

"Hi Gem, is your mum here?" Rose asked. Gemma's voice was slightly stuck and she stared at her. Rose was slightly "hippyish" in her fashion. She always wore neutral colours with paisley patterns and flowing fabrics. She had auburn hair that was short and styled, heavy eyeliner and a nose stud.

She was beautiful and Gemma's mum's best friend. And pretty much a second mum to Gemma.

"Hi," Gemma said, smiling at her and trying to ignore the fact that her eyes were the same shade of brown as Robbie's. "Um, she's in the back if you want to go see her."

"No, no. We'll just take a seat and talk to her soon, come on you two, let's grab a table."

"Do you want any drinks?" Gemma asked, still averting her gaze from Robbie.

"Kids?" she asked, looking at each in turn.

"I'll get a coke please, Gem," asked Pip and Gemma started getting it ready.

"Yeah, me too, please, Gem," said Robbie and she chanced a glance at him and saw him smiling at her. "Thanks."

"N-no p-problem," she stammered and when everyone but Robbie went to sit down, Gemma continued, "I-I'll bring them over."

"I can help," he said and he grabbed one out of Gemma's hands as she walked around, holding the two pints. Gemma shivered as his hand brushed hers and she looked into his eyes. They stared at each other for a moment, before Gemma pulled her eyes away, looking at his feet.

"So, ah, what does my mum want to see you about?" Gemma asked, just more for something to say as they walked back to the table with the rest of his family.

"Ah," Robbie's voice sounded croaky and he cleared it

21

before attempting to answer again.

Gemma glanced at him quickly, noticing he looked a little confused.

"Um," he croaked again, "I think she wants to offer me a job, on a Friday night." Gemma stopped in her tracks. Robbie stopped too and looked back at her. "Everything okay?" he asked.

"Ye—" it was Gemma's turn to be croaky, she coughed, "yeah, but—" she cleared her throat again. "Surely you've got better things to do on a Friday night than work here."

"Well," he said and looked down at his feet. "Mum says it'll be good to get out and get some responsibility. Plus, I need the money if I want to get into the academy."

Gemma nodded, but her heart was pounding uncomfortably in her chest. She didn't think she could bear the thought of having to be around Robbie every Friday night, but then at the same time, she was beyond excited to have some time with him.

Alone.

"Gem?" They had reached the table in an awkward silence and Pip was holding out her hand waiting for her drink that Gemma was still holding. Gemma shook her head and passed her the drink before uncomfortably excusing herself and fleeing back to the bar. On the way, the kitchen bell rang so instead of the bar, Gemma headed back towards the kitchen instead. The chefs were talking among themselves, and Gemma waited quietly for the final bits of the order.

"So, who's this lad your mum's taking on then, Gem?" Jake asked and he smiled suggestively at her again. Gemma felt her cheeks flush again and she grabbed the plates, without answering. And as she walked away again, she could hear them all laughing.

Brilliant.

Everyone already knew that Gemma was madly in love with

Robbie, but Gemma just hoped above all, that Robbie would never know too.

Present Day

"R-Robbie?" Gemma said lamely, staring at him for far too long but unable to stop herself.

Robbie Wilson was in the pub again, after nearly ten years.

And he was still as breathtakingly handsome as Gemma remembered.

He had changed, obviously. He had grown up. He was no longer the skinny sixteen-year-old that Gemma remembered, though still slim and athletic, he had filled out a lot. His skinny arms were now full of toned muscles and tattoos. His face looked less hollow and his jawline was straight and solid. And he was taller.

A lot taller.

He used to be about the same height as Gemma, but now, even across the bar and when he was leaning easily against the bar, he was much taller than Gemma's five-foot-eight frame.

Gemma guessed he was now at least six-two. It was obvious he also had a lot of money since Gemma had last seen him. He had a diamond earring in one of his ears, an expensive-looking watch and even his teeth looked whiter and straighter. But under all those changes, there was one thing that hadn't changed.

His eyes.

His deep, brown eyes that made Gemma's legs turn to jelly as she looked into them.

Looking into those eyes, it was almost as if they were transported back to when they were fifteen and those secluded hours in the same pub together.

"Hey, Gem, long time no see." He smiled a crooked smile and held onto Gemma's gaze for a moment before someone came over to him and clasped his shoulders.

"Fuck off! Robbie? Robbie fucking Wilson?!" Their gaze broke as Robbie looked at who was grabbing hold of him and Gemma saw that it was Matt.

"Matt? Jesus. I wasn't expecting to see you! You still live around here then?" They shook hands and clapped each other on the back and Gemma realised how much Robbie had really grown. Matt was only a couple of inches taller than Gemma and he barely made it to his shoulders.

"Yeah, fuck man, you've grown! You look so much smaller on the TV." Gemma snorted and both Robbie and Matt looked at her. Robbie looked like he was trying to hide a smile and Matt was glaring. "What?" he said shortly, "Something funny, Roly-Poly?"

Robbie's smile instantly dropped at Matt's words and he was looking at him. "Roly-Poly?" Robbie asked, very quietly.

"Yeah, he still calls me that. Thanks for the ingenious nickname by the way."

"You still call her that from when we were stupid kids?"

"Name kind of stuck," Matt said, shrugging his shoulders arrogantly. "Anyways, you don't mind do you... babe?" That caught Gemma's attention and she looked at him suspiciously.

But Robbie was the first to ask, "Babe?" He moved his eyes back and forth between them, waiting for them to speak. Matt spoke before Gemma could think of an answer.

"Yeah, we're together." He shrugged nonchalantly. "You know how it is, pretty small population here, you can't be picky and definitely no supermodels! You sly dog! Heard about that French supermodel! Jesus, you are one lucky fucker."

It no longer bothered Gemma how Matt spoke about her, it happened so frequently she was used to it. But Matt speaking about the supermodel... it made Gemma so unreasonably jealous. The thought of Robbie with her was enough to make her stomach squirm bitterly. Someone was signalling for Gemma a little further down the bar. As she walked away, she felt Robbie's eyes on her, following her.

"Matt, don't talk about her—" but Matt cut him off, asking him another heinous question about one of the many women Robbie had been rumoured to be dating. Gemma was out of earshot of them so she served the man who signalled her and took his payment before he turned to walk away. As he did, his position was filled with Pip again.

"Where did you—" but Gemma was cut off.

"I'm sorry, but I hate the way he is with you. I know you don't want me to say anything, so I walked away. Why do you let him speak to you like that, Gemma? He's a dick!"

"Like he said, you can't be choosy here. There isn't a huge selection of men... or women for that matter. Why didn't *you* tell me Robbie was coming home? I feel like a right dick."

Pip laughed a little and shook her head.

"That was brilliant!" She then proceeded to speak and sounded near enough exactly like Gemma, "Hem, hem: 'anyone who kicks a ball around for a living and gets paid a ridiculous amount every year is not worth my dying breath.' Brilliant! That was so funny!"

"Ha, ha." Gemma's cheeks reddened again. "Hilarious."

"It was, and to answer your question, he only told me a couple of hours ago he was coming home, to spend some time with Mum. He's got some leave before the World Cup. Plus, you always get weird when Robbie is mentioned."

Gemma spluttered, trying to remain suave but failing miserably. "I don't get weird. I don't care whether or not your older brother comes home or not. It's no skin off my nose. He's going to cause quite a stir... er, in the pub I mean." And she waved randomly at the air around her, "like, everyone is going to know he's here and flock to try and shake his hand like he's God's gift to women... and men I suppose... and anyone who likes football or anyone who..." Gemma trailed off, not quite knowing what she was saying, and Pip was watching her, with an amused expression and her eyebrows raised very high.

"See? Weird," she said simply and grinned again as Gemma spluttered non-communicably. "Anyway, I don't know how much he'll actually be about in the town. He'll probably just stay with Mum mostly." And her expression was so disheartened, that Gemma instantly forgot she was being awkward and flustered over Robbie and she reached out and grabbed her friend's hand.

"Oh Pip, I don't know what to say." She sniffled and shook her head.

"There's nothing you can say." And they held each other's hands for a moment, sitting in a heavy silence. Gemma was about to try and say something supportive, but she jumped as a pair of long, tattooed arms wrapped themselves around Pip's shoulders and squeezed her.

"Are you okay, Pip?" Robbie asked quietly, looking down at hers and Gemma's entwined hands. Pip nodded but seemed unable to speak so Gemma tried to for her.

"Ah, we were talking about your mum... Robbie."

Robbie seemed to take in a sudden breath and bit his lip as he looked down at his younger sister. "I see, it's all right, Pip. I'm here now. Do you want to go see her now?"

Pip nodded and sniffled again before wiping the tears off her cheeks.

"Okay, let's go," Robbie said and he kept his arms around Pip's shoulders and as they turned, Robbie looked at Gemma and they held a gaze for a moment. "It was good seeing you, Gem." He glanced her up and down and looked back into her eyes again, a little something suggestive gleaming there. "I hope we can meet up properly while I'm home, I'd love to catch up. You..." He stumbled again and Gemma looked at him, quite confused about how it was acting.

"You look good, Gemma."

And he left with Pip, turning to look at her (who was stunned into a gaping silence) one last time before he pushed open the pub door and it swung shut behind him, leaving Gemma extremely confused about what had just occurred and what he meant by "You look good."

CHAPTER THREE

It was late when Gemma finished and closed up the pub later that night. There had been a big party of more football fans who were clearly coming in to try and get a glance at the well-known Robbie Wilson. Yet, they were all left disappointed to learn that he had left hours previously. But no one was more disappointed than Gemma. She was desperate to know what Robbie had meant by "You look good".

Was it a compliment? Was he just being polite?

Gemma didn't want to stretch her fantasy so far to think Robbie Wilson had actually complimented her and found her attractive.

No, that would surely not be the case.

People like Robbie Wilson didn't find people like Gemma attractive.

Well, according to Matt, no one really found people like Gemma attractive. They'd do, but they weren't breathtakingly beautiful. They had to settle for what they could get.

Matt had always made that clear for Gemma.

He had settled for her and she should have been grateful. She wasn't alone, she wasn't a virgin any more and she had someone to be with outside of work.

Yeah sure, conversations weren't exactly riveting and the sex was okay, but she wasn't alone. Gemma was no longer the single, fat girl who people felt sorry for.

It also brought her great comfort to know her mum would

think she wasn't alone any more.

Gemma knew it had been so hard for her mother to watch her for years being alone. She knew Gemma wanted the whole "old fashioned" family life with a husband and a couple of kids.

And Matt was the only man in Gemma's life who could give that to her.

Did it matter that she didn't love him? If she was being completely honest with herself, she felt like she didn't deserve to be happy. Abi wasn't there with her. If Abi couldn't live a full happy life, then Gemma wouldn't either.

So as she put the pub alarm on and went out into the warm, late spring air and around to the flat entrance, she put Robbie Wilson to the back of her mind. There really wasn't any point wasting any more energy on the matter. As she went to the flat entrance outside on the street, she ran into the young couple that rented the other, small one bedroom flat next to Gemma's and Matt's. Gemma's mum owned the whole building, it had been left to her by Gemma's granddad who had owned the pub and flats before her mum. Gemma had been brought back to the flat when she was first born, but her mum had moved out a few months later when her dad had left. Gemma's granddad had then rented both flats out and gave the extra income to Gemma's mum to help her when she became a single parent.

So, a few years back, when the previous tenant had left, Gemma's mum had offered it to her, which she gladly accepted as it was conveniently situated above the pub where she worked full time and it was much cheaper than market rentals. Matt moved in a couple of years after Gemma and the young couple not long after that.

Even though Gemma lived next to them, she still wasn't completely sure what their names were, she thought maybe Jenny and Michael but she wasn't brave enough to call them by it just in case it wasn't right.

"Hi," Gemma said, opening the door with her key and indicating them through first. "After you."

"Thanks," possibly Jenny said. "Busy night?"

"Oh yeah," said Gemma as they passed her into the hallway that led to the stairs to lead to the two flat doors on the next floor. "The World Cup is apparently very interesting, even for those who don't like football normally."

"Yeah, even I watch it when the World Cup is on and I don't even know what's going on," Jenny joked and Michael shook his head.

"It's seriously embarrassing," he grinned down at her, "I can't take you anywhere." And he wrapped his arms around her quickly and kissed the top of her head affectionately. "Good job you're fit and I'm bonkers about you." Gemma looked away as she giggled and they embraced. She went up the stairs, leaving them snogging in the doorway and shouted "Night" over her shoulder before unlocking her flat and shutting the door swiftly behind her. She took in a deep breath and tried to swallow the bubbling envy in her stomach.

Even though Gemma knew she didn't deserve a relationship so loving as Jenny and Michael's, Matt would never be like that with her. Whenever Gemma saw couples being affectionate, she couldn't help but feel a little bitter.

No one was bonkers about her.

And rightly so, she thought, Abi's face flashing into her mind. She sighed, closing her eyes to the sudden tears, and resting her head against the front door.

"What took you so long?" A hard voice came from behind her and she spun around, pressing herself to the door. It was Matt and he was sitting on the couch, his face was hard and cold and he surveyed her across the room, his bottle of beer in one hand and his other hand clenched into a fist.

Oh no, thought Gemma, this wasn't going to be pleasant.

"There was a group that wouldn't shift, had to ask them to leave a couple of times," Gemma said quietly and she averted her eyes from him and looked down at her feet as she took her shoes off. She didn't even hear him approach, but suddenly she saw his feet and she straightened up and looked up at him. The look in his black eyes stopped Gemma's speech, she knew remaining quiet was the best way to deal with the situation.

She was almost scared of him at that moment.

"What," he said, deadly quiet, "the *fuck*," he really emphasised that, "was that tonight?"

Gemma's silence was obviously not adequate because he shouted so much louder that Gemma jumped.

"Well?"

"Wh-what was what?" Gemma asked quietly, shrinking against the wall as he glowered down at her.

"What you said before."

Gemma's stomach dropped. She knew he'd be angry but he looked mutinous now.

"You made me look a dick in front of those guys."

She wanted to say, "You're already a dick, I didn't do anything." But she held her tongue. It wouldn't be worth it.

"I-I," she stammered, trying to think what to say, but then realised only one thing could make it all right. "S-sorry, Matt." She whispered quietly, looking back down at her feet and hoping she looked sorry. Matt moved so quickly it took Gemma's breath away, with one hand, he grabbed her shoulder and forced her into the wall, slamming her back against the wall with a sickening slap. His other hand went to her chin and gripped her so hard, it was impossible to open or close her jaw. He forced her to look up at him and he bared his teeth and pressed his body to hers maliciously. His breath with sickly, hot and smelling of alcohol.

"What did you say?" he murmured, smiling at the fear in her expression. "Didn't quite catch that."

"I'm sorry, Matt," Gemma squeaked and she fought back the tears burning in her eyes. He stayed like that and she felt him press his hips closer. With a nauseating realisation, Gemma realised that he was aroused. She could feel him pulsating against her hip and she squirmed and shivered against the wall with fear.

He was turned on by Gemma's terror and submission.

He held her for what seemed an eternity. She kept her eyes averted and tried to steady her breathing. Matt knew she was petrified, but he was dragging it out for as long as he could. He sucked his teeth and bit his lip as he looked into Gemma's face. She felt him rub his thumb along her cheek and jawline and turned her head suddenly, so she looked into his once more.

"Good." And he slapped her cheeks lightly, before planting a single kiss on her lips, before he ran his hands over her bum and squeezed her cheeks, pulling her closer and pressing himself more into her. "Right, let's go to bed then."

Gemma exhaled and sagged slightly as he turned and walked away, into the bedroom. Gemma took some deep breaths and put her hands on her knees as she tried to calm her heart rate. A few moments passed in silence, but then Matt called out from the bedroom. "Gemma!"

And Gemma instantly stumbled forward and went into the bedroom. Matt was waiting for her, standing by the bed and he put his hands on her face and pulled her face to his and kissed her. It was quite a gentle kiss, which confused Gemma after what had just happened.

"Matt?" she whispered as his mouth moved from hers and he was pulling at her pants.

"Shhh, shhh, shhh," he said, almost soothingly. "Lay down," his voice was coming out a little rougher and more desperate. Gemma did what he asked and he ripped the pants off her before he placed himself between her legs. He pulled his own pants down, not fully, but enough for him to expose himself to her. He pushed his way between her legs and put himself into her within a second of springing free.

Gemma wasn't ready, or even remotely turned on, so it hurt a little but she sucked in her breath and didn't say anything. She wanted to forget what happened before, so she tried to immerse herself in the heat of the moment too. Trying to participate and moving her hips with the rhythm of him, but Matt had one goal in mind. He was already speeding ahead of Gemma, thrusting and grunting with little consideration for Gemma, so Gemma gave up. By the time he finished, she would still be miles off.

And sure enough, a couple more thrusts later, Matt exclaimed and collapsed on top of her, panting and sweating. He didn't pause long before he rolled off and literally climbed into the bed without a second glance at her. Gemma got up and decided a shower was in order. She stood underneath the hot, beating water, fighting back tears, and scrubbing herself clean, trying not to think about what had just occurred. After a much lengthier shower than normal, she got dressed into her pyjamas and brushed her teeth. She felt out of her body, it was almost like she was watching someone who looked exactly like her brushing her teeth, getting dressed and putting cream on her face. She walked back into the bedroom and climbed into the bed, next to Matt who was already snoring and stared up at the ceiling.

Gemma felt hollow and empty.

Almost like she didn't belong to herself.

She knew she should have left him. She didn't want to be the pitied fat girl again. She didn't deserve anything better than this. So she lay there, finally letting the tears flow freely as she accepted her life.

That would be as good as it gets.

Gemma closed her eyes and listened to Matt's rhythmic snoring as she tried to drift off. But then, through the night air, another noise reached Gemma in her dozing state. At first, she thought she might have been dreaming about Robbie, with his deep, brown eyes and muscular, tattooed arms around her. Yet, as Gemma woke and realised it wasn't a dream, she groaned and put her hands over her temples and pressed.

It was next door, *again.*

Gemma could hear the pounding rhythm of their love making, on full volume. Michael was most definitely making sure that Jenny reached the height of pleasure, by her moans and noises. Faster and faster, her cries got louder and louder until they both seemed to reach this pinnacle of pleasure. And Gemma could imagine their bodies entwined as they revelled in the euphoria of their coition.

And as all was silent again, Gemma felt that bubbling sense of animosity about her relationship with Matt. And though she felt she didn't deserve it, she found herself wishing that he was that tall, handsome football player whom she tried to never think of.

The next day, Gemma had left the flat early, before Matt had awoken from his stupor. It was early morning and Gemma was back in the pub, preparing for the opening. She still had a good couple of hours, but she took her time. She had to keep busy, and preferably, away from Matt. She knew the pub wasn't in a terrible state as she had closed, but as it was so busy, a few cleaning jobs needed to be done before opening. So she swept and mopped sections and stretches of the bar. She restocked the fridges and crisps ready for another busy weekend shift. She went through and emptied all the bins, which had to be left the night before and grabbed three or four bags in each hand and hauled them through the doors going to the back, through the kitchens and to the backdoor, to where the big bins were on the back alley.

It was quite warm already and Gemma groaned. She hated the heat, it always made wearing her uniform uncomfortable and she felt like she just tripled in size and her clothes felt stupidly tight.

"Goodness," said a voice from behind her and Gemma dropped all the bags with a little squeal. "We are gloomy on this fine spring morning."

"Robbie!" Gemma exclaimed as she spun around and gaped at Robbie, who was standing behind her, leaning against the half wall on the side of the pub.

"Good morning," he said and he grinned at her flustered appearance.

"Wh-what are you doing here?" she asked shakily, rubbing her hands awkwardly down her thighs for some unknown reason. Robbie raised his eyebrows at her and watched her rubbing her legs. That made Gemma feel even more hot and flustered and she put her hands behind her back to cease any attention being drawn to them.

"I came to see you, I wanted to ask you something."

"Here?" Gemma asked, looking around at the secluded alley, what could be so important that it couldn't wait until later?

35

"Well, I did knock on the front door but you didn't answer."

"I was putting the bins out," she said, rather pointlessly. Robbie chuckled as her cheeks burned more.

"Yes, hence why I am out here."

"Obviously," she muttered, inwardly kicking herself. Robbie laughed again before going on.

"Well, my mum was wondering if you guys might be up for a little dinner, like old times?"

Gemma's heart sank a little, she didn't know what she had been expecting, but it hadn't been that.

"Sure, that sounds good," Gemma said swiftly, hiding her disappointment. "When?"

"Well, in a few days? We'll do it at ours and I'll get a cook in as mum isn't up for any cooking and cleaning these days."

"Of course, I don't mind cooking," Gemma said and instantly regretted it. She couldn't bloody cook, so why was she offering? Robbie raised his eyebrows questioningly and Gemma understood why.

"I didn't know you could cook?"

"I can't... but I can try?"

And Robbie just laughed as her words came out like a question. "Thanks for offering, but maybe next time." Translation: maybe never.

"I'll get someone in and then you can relax and join in with us then. We don't want you cooped up in the kitchen all evening, it would sort of defeat the purpose."

"Yeah, sure."

"Plus, food poising while training for the World Cup doesn't sound the best combination."

Gemma looked at him and saw his eyes were gleaming with mischief. "No, you're quite right. Would you like to come in and

I'll cook you some breakfast?"

He laughed and so did Gemma. "I'm not that terrible. But suppose, cooking for so many could really go wrong."

"Yeah, let's just leave it to the professional, eh?"

"Fine, but I make a mean beans on toast."

"Oh, I don't doubt it." Gemma laughed again and then there was a little silence. Gemma shifted from foot to foot awkwardly.

"Um, so get Pip to text me the details?"

"Or I could just grab your number and text you myself."

"Oh," Gemma said, feeling slightly giddy about having Robbie's number again after so many years. "Oh yeah, sure." So Gemma got her phone out and handed it to him and he put his number in the keypad and rang it. Gemma heard his phone ringing and he hung up. "Thanks," she said as she took it back and rolled back and forth on the balls of her feet.

"So…" Gemma said and when Robbie didn't say much, "I've got to get back in, we'll be opening soon. See you." She threw the bags of rubbish into the skip before turning back and smiling at Robbie. She went to move past him when he reached out and grabbed her hand and stopped her from going any further.

"What time do you finish? I was wondering if you wanted to meet up, have a good catch-up. It's been so long." Gemma looked up, which was a mistake because she looked straight into his eyes again and she felt herself melting into his gaze.

"I-I should finish about four."

"Perfect, I can pick you up and maybe we can get a drink, maybe some food?" Gemma found herself agreeing and Robbie's face broke into a wide smile.

"Brilliant," he said and he let go of her arm. "I'll see you later, Gem." And with that, he turned and walked away, leaving Gemma feeling very flustered and confused.

CHAPTER FOUR

Gemma spent the rest of her shift literally being a bag of nerves. Every time a man came into the pub that was tall and lean (which, she supposed, wasn't that often as Netherby was short of tall and lean young men) she would jump or drop what she was holding.

"What is the matter with you today?" asked Pip, when Gemma dropped yet another pint glass that luckily bounced but caused a huge racket. After another chorus of "weyhey!" for the eighteenth time that day, Gemma swooped down and snatched up the glass and threw it back into the glass washer, mortified. It was nearly four and Gemma knew Robbie would arrive any moment.

"Nothing," Gemma said, keeping her eyes away from Pip.

"Are you tired or something?"

"Why would you say that?" Gemma asked, still not looking at her and busying herself.

"Because you are being weird!"

"I'm not!"

"Did you have too much sex last night? Is that why you're tired?"

"Who's had too much sex?" And this time, Gemma really did drop a full pint of beer, which sprayed all over her.

"Robbie!" she exclaimed and standing before her with his eyebrows raised was Robbie.

"Hi, everything okay?" He leaned down and hugged Pip fleetingly in greeting and looked back at Gemma, eyebrows still raised.

"Oh yeah, Gemma's just a little tired. Someone had too much action last night."

Gemma's cheeks burned as Robbie looked at her. He was smiling, but it seemed to be frozen on his face and didn't quite reach his eyes.

"I see, Matt's that good, is he?"

Gemma spluttered. "I didn't get action last night, trust me. That's not it."

"Then what is it?" Pip asked innocently, but she had a cheeky grin on her lips.

"Nothing." Gemma mumbled.

"Are you ready then?" Robbie asked after a moment surveying the two girls.

"Where are you going?" Pip asked sharply, now looking between Gemma and Robbie.

"Gemma and I are just going to catch up." Pip's eyes flew at Gemma and she looked down again, starting to clean up the spilt beer.

"Really?" Her eyes grew wide and she jumped up. "Go then! I'll clean this up, Gem, go, go!"

"Well," Gemma said, looking down at her soaked uniform. "I might have to get ready quickly, have a shower—" but Pip cut her off. "Then go! I'll clean this up."

"Are you—"

"No, I'm not sure. That's why I bloody offered! Go! Gemma, you never get to go out anywhere, you're always here. So go and I'll take over until Harry comes in to switch. Go!" Gemma looked up at Robbie, who was smiling and shaking his head slightly.

"Do you mind waiting? I'll have a quick shower and get dressed?"

"Sure, go. I'll help Pip."

"You're going to help Pip, behind the bar?"

"I have done it before," he reminded her.

"Ten years ago. And you weren't that great, to be honest," Gemma admitted and Robbie faked offence.

"How dare you, I was very good." And Gemma had to laugh, which made Robbie laugh. "Right, fine, I was terrible. But I can still help for half an hour while you get ready."

"Thank you," Gemma said and she smiled at them before she turned to leave, not without hearing someone say. "Hey, are you that football player?" Gemma shook her head, still smiling. Robbie definitely would bring in a lot of revenue.

Gemma was showered, dressed and even put on a little makeup, before she came back downstairs and into the pub. Gemma had opted for a nice-ish top and jeans and boots. She didn't know how fancy she would need to be. So, she had to opt for smart casual. She didn't have time to panic or choose loads of outfits; Robbie was still waiting in the pub for her.

When she entered the pub again, the crowd that was gathered by the bar shocked her. At first, she thought they had had a random influx of customers and she was fully prepared to jump back behind the bar. But as she approached, she realised it was Robbie who had attracted the crowd.

They were all waiting their turn to talk to him, some getting him to sign their shirts or pictures. Gemma rolled her eyes, before making her way through the crowd to the bar. Robbie was signing a picture and getting his photo taken with someone when he spotted her.

"Gem! All ready?"

The crowd all spun around to stare at Gemma. "Er, yeah."

"Great, right. Got to go everyone." There was a general

complaint and he waved them off good-naturedly. "Can't keep the lady waiting." Gemma felt her cheeks flush with a little thrill. He extracted himself from the group and walked back over to Gemma, smiling almost sheepishly. "Quick, let's get going." And he placed his hand on the small of her back and started to lead her out of the pub. They were just about to go out the door when another group came in through it. This time it was a group of lads and bringing up the rear was Matt.

Gemma's heart sank instantly.

"Robbie, mate," he said, completely ignoring Gemma. "Back again?"

"Yeah, mate," Robbie said, shaking Matt's outstretched hand, not fully reciprocating the excited tone that Matt had. "Just going to have a catch-up with our Gemma here." Matt then looked at Gemma and took in their stance. His eyes fell on Robbie's hand that was still on the small of Gemma's back, then back up at Gemma's face.

"I didn't know you were hanging out." Robbie withdrew his hand and Gemma wrapped her arms around her chest.

"We bumped into each other this morning and I asked if she wanted to catch up. It's been nearly ten years after all." Robbie said evenly, surveying Matt, who was still staring at Gemma.

"I didn't realise you were so close."

Gemma could sense the danger underlying his words.

"Well, a lot has happened in ten years." Matt then looked up at Robbie and for a moment, no one said anything. Matt's eyes just moved between them suspiciously, keeping that thin and almost frightening smile on his face.

"Come with us," Gemma blurted out and Robbie looked down at her confused. "It's just old friends hanging out and catching up. Come."

41

Matt pouted his lips in thought, before he nodded. "All right."

So the three of them then left the pub, Gemma feeling a lot less excited and a lot more apprehensive about the whole ordeal.

Robbie led them to his car and Gemma physically stopped and took in the sleek, sexy car parked in the pub car park. Gemma wasn't a car enthusiast, she could just about differentiate between logos and makes but that was it. But even Gemma knew this car, which definitely didn't fit in with the sea of Ford and Vauxhalls, was an exquisite sports car. Gemma didn't know the logo so it wasn't one she had ever seen before.

Matt whistled in appreciation.

"Yeah, she's a beauty," Robbie said and he caught Gemma's eye and smiled.

"Fuck, I'm so jealous. Everything I have is shit."

Robbie looked at him for a moment. "Not everything," he replied quietly. But Matt wasn't listening, he was still looking at Robbie's car with envy. Gemma looked at him, about to question his meaning when she caught his eye. He was staring at her so intensely it shocked her for a moment. His eyes were boring into hers and she felt the whole world melt away. Robbie was looking at her so warmly and whole-heartedly, Gemma had a sudden urge to run over to him and through her arms around him.

"Hey! Hello!" Matt was shouting and they broke their gaze. It took a second to realise that Matt was talking to Robbie, asking him questions about the car and Gemma shook her head.

What had that been? What did he mean by "not everything"? Gemma chanced another glance at him and he was looking at her again. She glanced at Matt too, but yet again, he was just more interested in the car, firing Robbie all sorts of questions.

42

Gemma had to turn her back for a moment because she was feeling a little overwhelmed. She had tried for years to not think or fantasise about Robbie. They had history, yes, but that's what it was. Just history. So why had he come back and was saying all these things? It hurt her heart too much to even consider the possibility that Robbie liked her in any other way than an old family friend.

It just wouldn't be possible.

And the heartache of the probable rejection was too much.

Her heart had barely recovered last time. And Robbie being back was bringing up all the emotions like it was fresh again.

Seeing Robbie, being around Robbie, was causing Gemma such emotional turmoil. But the moment she allowed herself a small glimmer of hope or happiness, she was crippled but a much stronger emotion.

Guilt.

It was because of Gemma's obsession with Robbie when they were younger that Abi and Gemma even went to that party on that night. Gemma felt another ripple of guilt quivering through her stomach as she tried not to remember that night.

"Gemma?" Robbie asked and her eyes snapped up as she was jolted out of her thoughts. "Ready to go?"

"Uh, yep," she said and she stumbled forwards to the car, walking towards Matt and trying to avoid any contact, eye or physical, with Robbie.

"In the back, Roly-Poly," Matt said, shoving her forwards and tapping his toe impatiently as she clambered into the small, leather-smelling backseat. Matt flung the chair back as far as it would go. Rather unnecessarily as he was a good four inches shorter than Robbie, who climbed in gracefully and fitted comfortably in the driver's seat. Gemma gnawed at her bottom lip, feeling Robbie's eyes on her every so often in the rear-view mirror. She kept her gaze out the window and watched Netherby fade away as Robbie sped down the country lanes and to the larger, surrounding city. They didn't drive long and about ten minutes later (ten minutes Gemma and Robbie sat in silence and Matt constantly asked questions about the car's performance) they arrived.

It was a little, casual bar that Gemma had known but never visited. Once Gemma unfolded herself out of the backseat, they started to head to the entrance. Matt walked along ahead, like usual, he didn't bother waiting for Gemma. But Robbie hung back and walked beside her.

"Sorry about the room. I thought it would just be us. I would have brought a bigger car." That caught Gemma off guard.

"How many cars do you have?" she asked before she could help herself. "Sorry," she said instantly, "that was rude, you don't have to answer that."

"It's fine," he laughed, "I have five." Gemma stopped in her tracks and stared opened-mouthed at him.

"Five? Sorry, you have *five* cars?"

"Well yes, I have—" but Gemma cut him off.

"Don't bother with brands or names. I won't have a clue." And he laughed again, actually throwing his head back.

"Right well, I have two sports cars—"

"Wh—"

"Don't interrupt, let me finish!"

Gemma mimed zipped her lips and threw away the key.

He nodded approvingly, "right, so I have two sports cars. This one and a..." He seemed to consider something for a moment, "A *red* one." And Gemma nodded appreciatively so he continued. "I have an SUV... um, a big four-wheeled drive?"

Gemma nodded and he laughed again. "Good, well, I wasn't even sure you knew what that was." Gemma punched him and pointed her finger in warning. "Right, sorry. Ah, so two sports cars, an SUV and an old, classic convertible and a limo."

"A limo?" Gemma exclaimed, stopping and staring again. "Why do you have a limo?"

He shrugged his shoulders, "I use it a lot, you know, for going to events or parties."

"Oh," Gemma stopped and started to think how different Robbie's life was from hers. He was being invited to big events with celebrities whereas she was being invited... nowhere.

"You all right, Gemma?"

Gemma looked back up and him and smiled slightly. "Just realising how much your life has changed, that's all."

"Yeah, well," he said and he nudged her with his shoulder and smiled brazenly, "Some things never change." Then he winked. He actually *winked* before he turned and walked to catch up with Matt who was still going on about one of Robbie's sports cars. Gemma brought up the rear on her own, more confused than ever.

The boys waited for Gemma at the door and when she reached them, Matt went straight in and Robbie held the door open, indicating that Gemma should follow. Robbie holding the door meant that Gemma had to brush past him. There seemed to be this electric charge between them and Gemma felt breathless and jittery as she glanced up at Robbie and saw he was looking intently at her. She wasn't used to any attention really, let alone being from the boy (well, a man she supposed) that she had been in love with for over a decade. Once inside, Robbie went up to the host, who was waiting by the door, and spoke to her quietly. Gemma looked around and it was a nice, quiet bar with many booths and stools with high tables.

"Thanks," Robbie said and looked over his shoulder at Gemma and Matt, "They've got us a bigger table." And they followed the host to a secluded booth, away from the main entrance. "I needed somewhere more private, so we can be left to talk." They slid into the booth and Gemma found herself between Robbie and Matt. Robbie passed Gemma a menu and she gazed down at it.

"Do you guys want anything to eat?" Robbie asked as he gazed down. Gemma looked at the food, her stomach rumbling slightly.

"Roly-Poly will probably eat," Matt said and he rolled his eyes at Robbie and smirked.

Gemma felt her stomach twisting as the bile rose in her throat. Gemma cleared her throat. "I'm not hungry," she said quietly. She could barely eat in public, let alone in front of Robbie.

"Are you sure? You've been at work all day," Robbie said gently, ignoring Matt completely. Gemma opened her mouth to reply but Matt cut across her again.

"Not hungry?" Matt scoffed, "You're always bloody hungry. She's not a cheap date."

Gemma watched Robbie turn to Matt and glare at him. He opened his mouth but Gemma reached under the table and squeezed his leg. He turned to her, surprised. She shook her head slightly and he frowned.

She didn't want anything to set Matt off. She was still frightened in case he turned again.

Robbie physically swallowed, clenched his jaw and nodded once. "Thank you." Gemma mouthed and she lifted her hand off his leg. The waitress come round then and asked for their order.

Matt ordered a pint, Robbie a soft drink and Gemma just went with a safe fruit cider.

"You not drinking then?" Matt asked as the waitress walked away.

"No, I don't drink when I'm training," Robbie said flatly.

"Not even one?"

"Not even one."

"Fuck, that's commitment, I couldn't give it up."

Robbie didn't answer, he just looked at him and looked as if he was chewing his tongue. The waitress returned with their drinks.

"Thank you," Matt said, in what must have been an attempt at charm because he smiled suggestively at her. The waitress looked taken aback and smiled at him awkwardly before turning to Robbie.

"I'm sorry to ask, I know you probably don't want anyone bothering you. But are you that Robbie Wilson? The football player?" Gemma scoffed a chuckle that wasn't quiet enough because both Robbie and Matt looked at her.

Robbie was smiling, trying to fight off a laugh too, but Matt, well Matt looked furious.

Gemma's stomach instantly dropped and she found nothing funny about the situation. She glanced at Matt, whose face was now masked in that sickly smile, that didn't reach his eyes.

She looked up at Robbie, who was watching her again, now with a frown. The waitress cleared her throat, as they all had quite forgotten she was there.

"Oh yes, sorry," said Robbie, flashing the most charming smile that Gemma's breath faltered. She had no idea how the waitress remained standing, seeing as she had been the one receiving the full force of Robbie's attention. "Yes, I am," he said smoothly and Gemma could actually see the waitress's eyes blinking rapidly. It would appear she wasn't so averse to his charm as Gemma had once thought.

"Oh, ah, erm," she stammered and Robbie waited patiently for her to speak again. He was apparently used to this reaction to him. "Well, ah, good luck for the World Cup," she blurted out and rushed off, her cheeks red and acting a little flustered.

"Poor girl," Gemma said, after a minute of loaded silence.

"Why?" Robbie asked, turning to her.

"Well, she's probably really embarrassed. She didn't expect your charm to be so full on I don't think."

"My charm?" he asked, raising an eyebrow.

"Well, charm, money, fame," Gemma said, waving her hands, "whichever you want to say. She probably hasn't spoken to someone so famous in all her life. It can be quite intimidating."

"You're not intimidated," he pointed out.

"Oh please," she said, feigning nonchalance. "How can I find you intimidating when I've seen you sing on singastar when you went through your 'Mum, I'm going to move to America and make it as a singer' phase?" It was a lie obviously, Gemma was constantly flustered around him but hopefully she wasn't as obvious as the poor waitress. Robbie laughed nonetheless and took a swig of his drink. Matt spoke then, asking Robbie all sorts of inappropriate and slimy things about the women he knew and Gemma didn't bother listening really. Robbie was just answering, being polite, but Gemma could see he didn't really want to discuss any of that. After ten minutes of Matt boring everyone about some car crap or about how brilliant he was, he announced that he was going to the bathroom. When he was out of earshot, Gemma turned to Robbie.

"I'm sorry Matt crashed our drinks," she said, not really

knowing what to say.

"Why did you stop me before, Gem?"

Gemma bit her lip, wondering how much she should divulge. "Well," she said carefully, "sometimes Matt can get a little upset if I undermine him."

"Because he's a dick?" Gemma laughed. "Seriously though," said Robbie continued, "I forgot what a total arsehole he is."

"Yeah, he is," Gemma agreed before realising what she was saying.

"Then why are you with him, Gemma?" Robbie asked and he turned to her, his eyes boring into hers. "Why do you stay with someone like that?"

"Because…" Gemma bit her lip, trying to hold back the words but she couldn't. "There is no one else."

"What do you mean? Of course there is."

"No, Robbie, there isn't. I'm not the usual standard of beauty, am I? I'm not skinny or pretty. That's fine. We can't all be like that and I have accepted that. A girl like me in Netherby has to take what I can get. I… I…" Gemma trailed off, her mind on Abi again. She couldn't say it. She couldn't tell Robbie that she was riddled with guilt and unable to allow herself to have happiness. They were silent for a couple of moments, as Gemma couldn't speak again.

Robbie looked as if he was going to talk but then Matt returned and nothing else was said on the matter. The rest of the afternoon was passed in small talk and a few reminiscences of their childhood, mostly about Gemma being such a loser when Matt talked about anything. But a few looks were passed between Gemma and Robbie and Gemma knew Robbie wanted to say more but wouldn't with Matt around.

So the rest of the evening was uneventful and when Robbie dropped Gemma and Matt back off at the pub, Matt went in for a drink while Gemma snuck off upstairs and into her bed, under the covers as she tried to think about what had happened that day and what all of Robbie's comments *could* have meant.

CHAPTER FIVE

The next day in the pub was another busy one. Gemma had a strong suspicion that word had spread enough for everyone to know Robbie was back. And everyone wanted to see him; everyone wanted to shake the hand of one of England's best football players, ever. There was always a little hum of excitement as groups of fans would chat to one another but constantly looked over their shoulder in the hope that someone might catch a glimpse of the celebrated local lad. Gemma couldn't help but smile and shake her head at all the nonsense. It even got to the point that Gemma excused herself and pre-warned Robbie. Ducking into the back office for a few seconds, she pulled out her phone and sent the message.

Just a heads up, it's mental here! Everyone's waiting for the prodigy child! Gx

She laughed and put her phone in her pocket but before she had even stepped out of the office, her phone pinged. She frowned, she rarely got any messages and she doubted Robbie would reply that quick.

But it was Robbie.

Christ, I'm going to need your help! Don't leave me alone and then fake an emergency or something, please! I'll owe you xx

God, Gemma felt like a giddy schoolgirl. With a grin she replied.

Fine, but I want something good in repayment. I'm talking

51

like sports cars and diamonds if I'm going to have to stand around and listen to everyone talk about how brilliant you are all evening xx

"Who's making you smile?" Gemma's mum, Linda, walked into the back and eyed her suspiciously. Gemma blushed, putting her phone in her pocket as it pinged again.

"No one."

"Shut up, I haven't seen you smile like that for a long time."

"No one, now stop being nosey."

Linda laughed and shook her head. "Fine, keep your secrets, but we need you back out here, please. If you can pull yourself away from your phone." She laughed again and left, Gemma went to follow, but she checked her phone again.

You don't want much then? xx

Gemma smiled, bit her lip and replied as wittily as she could in her giddiness.

Well, I could have asked for two sports cars, but that seems a little extravagant, doesn't it?

See you later then xx

Ping.

Oh no, I think it's rather understated personally. See you soon xx

Gemma's heart started beating faster.

See you soon xx

It was amazing how much just a simple phrase could send Gemma's heart and nerves into overdrive.

She pocketed the phone and returned to the bar, throwing herself into serving and trying to distract herself from the nervous squirm in her stomach. It was almost surreal that feeling; she could have been fifteen or sixteen again, working at her mum's pub on a Friday night waiting for Robbie to walk through those doors. But she wasn't sixteen, she was in her mid-twenties, an adult. Pint after pint went out and Gemma was just as nervous as ever. It didn't subside. If anything, she got more nervous as the night went on. She had her back to the bar, reaching up to grab a liquor that was hardly ever ordered (thanks to the customer who was being extra difficult in his order) when she heard him.

"So these sports cars, what are we talking? Lamborghini or Porsche?" Gemma jumped and nearly sent the very old and very dusty bottle of liquor to the ground. She steadied herself in time however and spun around.

"What?" she asked confused, unable to think clearly for a moment. He seemed to look more achingly handsome than usual. He was wearing a fitted, white T-shirt and fitted jeans with white trainers on. Gemma suspected that Robbie would have looked handsome wearing an unflattering bin bag. Gemma really had to focus on not physically drooling after him and tried to look into his face instead. But that was just as attractive, so Gemma tried to look around for something to say, wringing her hands as she held tight onto the ancient bottle.

"The cars? You said they would be repayment," he added, grinning at Gemma's distress.

"Ah," She cleared her throat and looked at him again. "Whichever, I don't even know what you said anyway," She admitted, deciding it was feeble to lie. "I'm crap with cars."

"Yeah, I've realised. It'll have to be diamonds then," he said with a shrug, he was leaning over the bar as he looked at her, a devilish smile playing on his lips.

"I'm crap with that as well, to be honest," Gemma admitted, shrugging and finally putting the bottle down. "You could get me cheap, fake stuff and I couldn't tell the difference. Go to Primark and save yourself a few bob." He laughed and Gemma laughed.

The likelihood that Robbie even knew where the nearest Primark was, was extremely slim. They fell into a silence as they gazed at each other for a moment. Robbie was looking at Gemma intently, making Gemma feel slightly self-conscious (well more so, she always felt self-conscious).

"What?" Gemma blurted out, unable to stand his surveying look any longer.

"Your laugh—" but what Gemma's laugh was, she'd not find out, because, at that moment, a tall, blonde, beautiful girl slid next to Robbie and squealed.

"Robbie Wilson?" Robbie jumped, breaking his gaze with Gemma, and turned to the girl.

Both Gemma and Robbie's faces masked the same expression of surprised… and horror.

It was Miranda. Miranda Johnson. She was Robbie's ex-high school girlfriend and one of Gemma's high school bullies.

"Ah," said Robbie, glancing pleadingly at Gemma. "Oh, Miranda, um, how are you?"

She swung her slender arms around him brazenly and pulled him in with surprising force. "Robbie Wilson," she exclaimed again and when he pulled away, she grabbed either side of his face and pulled his face to hers. Gemma watched in horror as it looked like they would kiss there and then, but at the very last second, Robbie turned his head to stare at Gemma (looking rather fearful, Gemma noted) and she kissed him on the cheek. Robbie chuckled forcibly and grabbed her hands that were still around his neck and pulled them off him, putting them on the bar in front of them.

"What, ah, what you are doing here?"

"Well," she said, flashing him a dazzling smile and stroked his arm with her finger. "I heard you was back in town and I couldn't believe how long it had been, Robbie." She spoke in a low purr, her words dripped with seduction. Gemma's throat felt tight and it was hard to watch her trying evidently hard to flirt with him. Gemma looked at Miranda, for the first time taking in her physical appearance. She was still tall and slim, but with age she had become curvier. She was still slender however, with a perfect figure. She was tanned, but Gemma suspected it was fake. She had done work to her face, her lips were much fuller than before, unpleasantly so Gemma thought. She was very dolled up, with heavy, contoured makeup, with chiselled cheekbones and heavily highlighted nose and cheekbone tips. Her eyebrows were darkened by the makeup and her lids were thick with smoky, glittery makeup. Her heavy makeup made her sparkling green eyes smaller and almost duller. She had a lot of big, blingy jewellery on with long, manicured nails and a big, expensive-looking bag. She was smiling suggestively at Robbie, still stroking his forearm with her long-manicured fingers.

Gemma bit back a laugh as she thought about trying to manoeuvre day-to-day tasks with claws like that. Even something as simple as using the toilet must have been a dangerous task. Obviously, Gemma hadn't hidden her amusement as well as she thought, because Robbie turned to her with his eyebrows raised in question. She shook her head, smiling and nodded towards Miranda. She was still waiting, fluttering eyelashes and suggestive smile, for Robbie to respond to her.

"Er, right. Yes," Robbie said tightly and he pulled his arm away and let it hang by his side. "It has been a long time, ten years?"

"Yes, ten years. Just before you left for that camp or whatever it was for football."

"Academy," Robbie supplied politely and he looked at

Gemma with wide eyes. Gemma interpreted that as "help me" but Gemma felt herself feeling anxious being around Miranda again. Her palms were sweating and her throat felt dry.

"Yeah, I'm back seeing my mum, before the World Cup starts."

"Oh God, yeah, I heard about your mum. I hope she's okay."

"Thank you," Robbie said stiffly and he looked at Gemma again, hoping she would talk at some point during the conversation. Miranda noticed Robbie looking distracted and followed his gaze to Gemma. Gemma's heart plummeted when Miranda's eyes met hers. Miranda's green eyes looked into Gemma's blue ones and Gemma was overcome with mixed emotions.

She was anxious, she was angry, she was envious, she was self-conscious, she was self-loathing and so many more than Gemma couldn't even articulate.

In that moment, Gemma wasn't twenty-six-year-old Gemma, she was awkward and fat, fifteen-year-old Gemma who wasn't looking at Robbie, superstar football player or Miranda who was stylish and sexy.

No, she was looking at Robbie, long-time love interest who was popular and cool and Miranda, who was Robbie's girlfriend, skinny and pretty but who also terrorised Gemma.

Ten Years Earlier

Why was it so hot? It was the end of September and Gemma had been back at school for nearly two weeks. England was having a "last hurrah" attempt of summer, with a mini heat wave stretching over four days. Everyone else at school loved the heat; they loved rolling up their skirts and tanning their legs during breaks. The girls loved undoing the bottom half of their shirts and hitching them up so their flat stomachs were out for all to see, showing off their last-ditch efforts of tans before the autumn took over and plunged them all into dark mornings and freezing winds.

Gemma loved the autumn and the winter. She didn't feel so out of place in jeans, jumpers and coats. She wore pants to school, you'd never catch her in a skirt, let alone a skirt without tights, but they were unflattering and uncomfortable to wear. They dug in at her hips and clung to her thighs so much that she thought she might burst out of them.

She absolutely hated how she felt. And even going two sizes bigger, they were just such an unforgiving material. The heat made everything worse, all her clothes clung to her and she could feel the sweat droplets on her forehead and neck. Since going through puberty, Gemma had also struggled with finding a deodorant strong enough to help her stay smelling fresh each morning. She was on her fifth different deodorant her mum had bought her and she hoped it could stand up to the heat wave.

Gemma was walking down the hallway before first period, trying to dash to her locker to freshen up before heading to class. Abi was already there and waiting, wearing a short skirt, with her long legs on show. Gemma felt a ping of envy, wishing more than anything to have Abi's body. Abi wasn't cool by the school standards, she was geeky, pasty and enjoyed Japanese cartoons too much to be fit to classed be cool. But she was loyal and kind and a really good friend to Gemma.

"Morning," she said as she sipped what looked like an iced coffee.

"Morning, iced coffee?" Gemma asked, as she did her combination for her locker and swung it open. "How very mainstream of you."

"It's too hot for normal coffee, but it tastes like I've just licked a unicorn's arse."

Gemma stopped what she was doing and looked at Abi incredulously. "What the hell is a unicorn's arse supposed to taste like?"

"I wouldn't know, but I would guess it would be this drink. Want some?"

"Ah, no thanks. You keep the unicorn's arse for yourself thank you."

"Unicorn arse?" said a voice from behind Gemma and she spun around to see Robbie looking at her, a smile on his face and his eyebrows raised. Gemma still wasn't used to Robbie talking to her at school, before he started working with her, it was just the odd head nod and civil hellos. And with both of them having surnames beginning with 'W' their lockers were always right next to each other.

"Yeah," said Gemma, her voice a little squeaky and awkward, "Abi says her ice-coffee tastes like unicorn arse." And Abi held up her drink and shook it and Robbie laughed.

"Right. Well, I'm more into tea, to be honest. Can't drink the stuff."

"You don't drink coffee?" Gemma asked, shocked she didn't know this. He smiled and shook his head.

"Nah, tastes like shit."

"Well, I suppose it's an acquired taste."

"Maybe, but you know what's not an acquired taste? Jake's mac and cheese."

"Oh yeah, it's pretty good I guess."

"Pretty good?" Robbie said disbelievingly, "I've dreamed about that stuff."

"Oh wow."

"I know, lame but it's so good."

"Dream big, Robbie, dream big."

Robbie grinned at her for a fraction of a second before someone shouted for him. They both looked in the direction of the call and Gemma groaned. It was Miranda Johnson. She had her long blonde hair pulled back into a high ponytail and her skirt was hiked up so high that it was barely covering her privates. Gemma stuck her head back into her locker, trying to melt away into the background. She subtly tried to reapply her deodorant and spray her body spray without being detected by Robbie or Miranda.

"Hey Robbie," Miranda was saying and Gemma could hear the flirtation in her voice.

Gemma bit her lip to stop any tears from forming in her eyes.

"Hey Miranda," Robbie said softly and she could imagine him smiling lopsidedly. He would probably draw himself up to his full height and widen his shoulders in an attempt to show off how tall and muscular he was getting. He was as tall as Gemma now, so compared to Miranda, he towered over her petite frame.

"A little birdy told me it is your birthday this weekend."

"Yeah it is, it's Friday actually."

"What are you doing for it?"

"Well, I'm supposed to be working, but maybe I'll do something on Saturday. School's only just started, so not sure about a massive party."

"Screw work! Are you kidding? You only turn sixteen once! And you have to have a party! Come on! Please! For me?" Gemma glanced over at them quickly, enough time to see Miranda fluttering her eyelashes and pushing her chest out.

"Well, I'm not sure I can get out of work."

"Shut up, of course you can. It's only the pub." Gemma

didn't know what possessed her to talk and draw unwanted attention to herself, but it just sort of slipped out.

"You won't have to work Friday, Robbie; I'm sure Mum will let you have it off."

Both Robbie and Miranda looked at Gemma. Robbie was looking reluctant, which baffled Gemma because she assumed he would want to have a party for his birthday. Miranda just glared at her, pulling a disgusted face. Gemma wasn't someone Miranda socialised with, so to be seen doing it at school was very damaging to her reputation.

"Ah, well…" Robbie said reluctantly still looking apprehensively at Gemma. Gemma glanced at Miranda and saw her glaring at Gemma, then at Robbie then back again. Then, to Gemma's surprise… and dread, her face changed. This fake smile spread across her face, wide and ugly on her beautiful face.

"Aw, go on, Robbie. Gem's right," it was odd for Miranda to call Gemma by her name, let alone Gem which only her friends called her. "Her mum will be fine with it, I'm sure. And you only turn sixteen once." She fluttered her eyelashes at him and Gemma's stomach squirmed at her apparent want for Robbie. Gemma had to look away and she started to fiddle around with something in her locker to appear busy. As she rummaged, she heard Miranda's voice again, this time deep and dripping with desire.

"Please, Robbie? For me?" And Gemma put her head deeper into the locker, biting her lip and fighting back the apparent tears.

"Argh, yeah, fine." Robbie finally said and his voice was thick and croaky. Apparently, he wasn't as immune to Miranda's pleas and Gemma once thought. Another bubble of envy burst in her stomach and Gemma decided to grab her books and slammed her locker door before turning towards the couple and about to move past them to first period.

"Hey, Gem," Robbie said, side stepping Miranda and stepping in front of Gemma. "You should come too. Bring Abi if you want. I'm sure your mum can spare you, if she can spare me." Gemma blinked at him and stared at him in surprise.

"Me?" She said quietly, looking back and forth between them.

"Yes, you." Robbie cracked a smile, obviously finding her confusion amusing. "Um…" Gemma bit her lip and glanced at Miranda. Her face looked furious for half a second before she regained control of her face and smiled the sickly-sweet smile again.

"Oh my God Gem, yeah! You should totally come! It'll be so much fun." Robbie smiled down at her and she beamed back, with another little flutter on her eyelashes.

"We'll be there. I'll talk to Linda myself," Abi said before Gemma could sputter and try and weasel out of it.

"Great!" Miranda beamed, but it didn't reach her eyes. "See you there! Come on, Robbie, walk me to English?"

"Ah, sure. You coming, Gem?" Miranda glared at her and Gemma took the hint. "Um, go ahead. I'll catch up." Robbie nodded and they turned and walked down the hallway. Miranda was touching Robbie and evidently flirting with him again.

"Oh," Abi whispered, "she didn't like that! Robbie so wanted you to walk with them!" Gemma scoffed and sagged slightly against the locker as she waited for Robbie and Miranda to be out of sight before she set off towards English.

"Oh yeah, Robbie Wilson, the most popular guy in school is into me. That's likely."

"Why wouldn't it be?" Gemma smiled softly at Abi, appreciating her loyalty. "Because he is him and I am me."

"Meaning?"

"That's guys like him go out with girls like her, not girls like me."

"Why would he want you to go to the party then?"

"He was just being nice, his mum would be upset if he didn't invite me."

"Pfft, whatever. He was an eager beaver." Gemma laughed and they started walking towards English.

"Shut up, eager beaver. It's Robbie Wilson—"

"Who've you've known since you were five."

"But we're in different circles. Robbie Wilson would never fancy someone like me."

"Whatever."

Gemma laughed and they walked off together down the hallway. They reached the classroom and Gemma and Abi went to their usual table. Gemma made eye contact with Robbie who was at the very back and he nodded and smiled at her. She smiled awkwardly and went to her seat, keeping her head on her books as she got her notes out. It was then, Gemma heard her.

Miranda was whispering loudly to her friend and looking at Gemma with malice. "Yeah, her, Roly-Poly. Yeah, I have no idea. Why the hell does he want her there? Oh my God, she's so fat and seriously have you smelled her today? Like, have you heard of deodorant? Oh my God, you stink!" There was a ripple of giggling and Gemma sucked in her breath.

"Gemma?" Abi asked, "are you okay? What's the matter?" Gemma got up, tears streaming uncontrollably from her eyes. She felt like her whole insides were screaming and on fire. She bit back a sob and turned around, looking at Miranda and seeing their mocking watching her with glee. Gemma felt the sobs bubbling up inside and her face brimmed with tears and she looked at Robbie. He was looking at her, confused, then at Miranda, then back to Gemma.

"Wha—" he said, but then he looked into Gemma's eyes and his eyes wide with confusion. "Gemma?" He asked quietly, "What's wrong?" But Gemma just shook her head and a sob rippled through her mouth, as she put her hand over her mouth and fled from the classroom.

Leaving them all behind.

CHAPTER SIX

Present Day

"Oh my God," Miranda said in her drawling tone, "Gemma? Gemma Walker? Shut up! How are you doing girl? You look fabulous!" And she smiled her sly smile that Gemma didn't believe it. "Are you still working here? Wow! Some things never change!" There was an awkward pause where Robbie looked back and forth between the two girls before Gemma found her voice.

"Gee, thanks, Miranda. Yeah, still working here."

"Aw, well, moving out of Netherby isn't for everyone." She smiled and Gemma smiled back.

"Haven't you just moved back?" Gemma asked innocently, "After your third divorce?"

Miranda's face dropped and Gemma bit back a laugh.

"Third divorce?" said Robbie, raising his eyebrows, "You have been busy."

"Well, Robbie," she said, regaining her control and smiling at him again. She touched his arm flirtatiously again. "Sometimes you just know when there's something better out there. There's been no one like you." Gemma watched her bitterly and saw someone trying to get her attention to be served, so she walked off down the bar to serve him. As she served him, she heard Robbie again.

"Yeah, you're right. Sometimes you just know there's

someone better out there. And sometimes, Miranda, you have regrets about those you chose over them." Gemma looked up then and saw Robbie watching her and her breath caught as their eyes met.

"Oi, hello? Oi? Roly-Poly?" Matt's voice shattered their gaze and Gemma's head snapped up to him. He was leaning on the bar, frowning. "This bloke's still waiting for his pint."

"Oh sorry!" she said, flapping slightly before handing him the pint. "On the house. Sorry for your wait."

"Thanks, love," he said, smiling kindly and he dropped a load of coins into the tip jar.

"What the hell is wrong with you?" Matt demanded when the man had left.

"Nothing," Gemma said, keeping her eyes averted from both Robbie and Matt. But Matt looked to the other end of the bar and saw Robbie sitting there, watching them both.

"Is that Miranda Robinson? Fuck me, she looks great." Gemma gave him a non-communal shrug, still avoiding looking at Robbie. "What's going on with you and Wilson? Why won't you look down there?"

"Nothing!" Gemma said, "I'm just working."

Matt frowned at her again and then looked back at Robbie, then back again. And as Gemma had her back to them, refilling the crisps, she heard Matt call out.

"Robbie! Miranda! Come down here!" And Gemma groaned, she couldn't help it. They came to stand by Matt, who was grinning at Miranda in a blatantly pervy way. Miranda pulled a disgusted face at him and rolled her eyes.

"Looking good, Miranda. Shit, what's it been? Ten years?"

"Not long enough, Matty." She then turned her back to him and to Gemma's surprise, he laughed.

"Still uptight I see, Miranda."

"Not uptight, just with standards." And she smiled at Robbie and winked and then it was Robbie's turn to pull a disgusted face. Gemma couldn't help but try and stifle a laugh but everyone looked at her.

Miranda was glaring, Matt was tight-jawed and clearly angry and Robbie was smiling.

"Something funny?" Matt asked and Gemma could tell by his tone that it was a rhetorical question. She just shook her head and went back to busying herself with serving customers. As she did, she heard Matt trying to spark up a conversation again. "We should all catch up properly. Go out or summit."

"Yeah, Robbie, what do you say? For old times' sake?" Robbie paused and Gemma glanced at him and saw that he was looking at her.

"Well, I suppose I could. I've got some time off next week before I have to go back down to London for the World Cup."

"Yes, Robbie!" Matt called, clapping his back, "Fucking can't wait. Like old times but fucking better! Buzzing!"

"Well, we can't tomorrow, Gemma and I have a family meal." Matt's head snapped to Gemma and his nose was flaring as he was surveying her.

"What family dinner?" he asked quietly and the noise in the pub seemed to quiet instantly.

Miranda and Robbie were looking back and forth between them. Apparently, it was obviously that Matt's demeanour and tone had changed.

"Just our mums wanting dinner," Gemma said quietly.

"When was this decided?"

"Today," Robbie said loudly and he stood up and stood to his full height, towering over Matt. Matt raised his eyebrows at him as he still leaned cockily on the bar. "Is there a problem?" Robbie asked and Matt seemed to assess him for a moment, with half a smile before he shrugged his shoulders defensively.

"No," and he broke into an easy smile, which didn't seem to reach his tight eyes. "Just wondering if *my* girlfriend was going to tell me about it."

"It's only just been arranged," Gemma said quietly and Matt just smiled at her.

"I know," was all he said as he smiled.

"Well, how about next weekend?" Miranda said chipperly as the silence grew awkward, but no one was paying her any attention. Gemma was looking at the floor again, Matt was looking at Gemma while Robbie watched Matt, his jaw clenched. "Um…" said Miranda again, looking between them all. "Hello?"

"Next week is fine for me," said Matt, snapping back and grinning lazily. Robbie was still tight-jawed and looking at Matt when he answered.

"Yeah, fine with me," he said quietly, "What about you, Gem?"

Miranda had to physically hide her annoyance that Gemma was even included.

"Yeah, I should be able to get it off."

"Are you sure?" Matt asked and Gemma looked at him. There was something in his expression that told Gemma that defying him was probably a bad idea, but Gemma felt brave with Robbie there.

"Yep, should be fine. Pip is wanting more hours anyway. I'm sure she'll work."

"Really? That is good news." And his tone was light, but Gemma knew well enough he wasn't as happy as he was making out. Robbie didn't look like he believed him either. "So that's settled," Matt said jollily. "The four of us again, like old times."

"Yep," was all Robbie said, as he kept eying Matt.

"How exciting!" said Miranda and she was flashing Robbie her most dazzling smile, which he didn't see, as he never took his eyes off Matt.

"This should be interesting," Gemma said under her breath. Gemma was going to go on a night out with her boyfriend who was, to put it bluntly, a controlling narcissist.

And with the girl who was not only the girl who caused most of Gemma's insecurities growing up but who was also Robbie's ex-girlfriend.

And with the man whom Gemma had been in love with for over a decade, who had been dropping these confusing and suggestive signals. Signals that made Gemma want to burst with joy and excitement and guilt all at the same time.

Gemma had never felt so confused. It was like she was fifteen again.

Ten Years Earlier

Robbie's birthday party approached with staggering quickness and Gemma found herself walking home from school the afternoon of it. Abi was walking along beside her, the sun still abnormally warm for the beginning of September.

"I've decided what I am going to do at university," Abi announced randomly. Gemma turned to her with her eyebrows raised in question, so Abi continued. "Well, I'm still going to become a vet. And I am going to do it at Liverpool University, it's not too far away but far away enough to live on campus and enjoy university life."

Gemma nodded approvingly.

"You can still come and see me some weekends!" Abi sighed, almost exasperatedly. "Or," and Gemma noted the annoyance in her voice, "you can just come with me? Oh come on, Gemma, you should come to Liverpool with me!"

Gemma chewed on her lip, she really didn't want to have the debate again.

"I can't. I'm not made out for university, Abi."

Abi scoffed at that. "Well, I know that isn't true. You get better results than me!"

It was true, Gemma most certainly was an achiever when it came to her grades. No one ever knew, however; Gemma couldn't face the negative attention that she would receive for being smart as well as all that she already received. Not only would she be labelled the sad, fat loser, *nerd* would be added to her title too.

Also, if Gemma was being honest with herself, she was petrified by the idea of university. Gemma suffered from crippling social anxiety when she was in a place she knew, to be somewhere new. Gemma shuddered at the thought.

"Are you cold?" Abi wrapped her arm around her shoulders (well, she attempted as she was about half a foot shorter than Gemma). But Gemma smiled at the gesture anyway. She looked at Abi, who smiled warmly at her and released her slightly awkward one-armed hug.

The idea of going to university with her, living in a dorm together and tackling the experience of university together... it actually sounded pretty appealing. But then Gemma realised that they wouldn't be doing the same course. There was no way Gemma could manage being a vet, she'd break down every time she saw a sick or dying animal. She couldn't even watch nature programmes without getting upset for the prey. And then, if the prey got away and the predator went without a meal, she would feel awful for the predator. There was no way she could cope with being a vet. But she would love to do something with her life that made a difference. To be the one that helped others who were struggling… that would be pretty amazing. But then her stomach squirmed with the idea of actually attending university classes. Her heart beat erratically and Gemma's throat felt tight.

How could she even set foot inside a university classroom?

Then there was college, Gemma realised. Her breath was coming in thick and fast, yet she felt like no oxygen was getting into her lungs. How could she manage either one when the mere thought of it started off a panic attack? Gemma closed her eyes and took in some deep calming breaths. College was a year off and she would have Abi with her. Pretty much everyone went to the same college, there was only one in the nearest big town. It wouldn't be as much of a change as university. And if she could manage that, then maybe she could manage university with Abi. Her breaths seemed to calm slightly. Everything was still a while off; she still had another year at school to get through first.

"Gemma?" Abi asked gently and Gemma's eyes flew open. She only realised then that they had stopped walking. Gemma swallowed, trying to wet her dry throat. "Are you okay?" Abi asked and she put her arm on Gemma's, squeezing gently.

"Yeah," Gemma croaked and she cleared her throat before continuing. "It's just… I just get a little overwhelmed thinking about the future. That's all."

Abi nodded kindly. "I'm sorry, I won't mention it again." She smiled and tipped her head to the side to indicate that they should keep walking. "Come on, let's get going. I'm starving and I want to eat before we go to Robbie's party."

Gemma had to laugh. "You're always hungry." Abi nodded

in agreement.

"Yeah, that's true. But seriously, I've been thinking about your mum's banana bread all day. Toasted, oh God, with butter..." Abi mimicked loud salivation, tipping her head back and letting her tongue lollop out the side of her mouth.

"I don't know where you put it all," Gemma laughed, but there was a tiny stab of jealousy hidden beneath her words. Abi never skipped meals and regularly snacked on sugary foods.

Gemma didn't eat at school and only ate fruit when she got home, yet still she was fat and Abi was perfectly thin. It was a good job Gemma loved her so much; otherwise, she wouldn't be able to stand being her friend.

They walked on with renewed vigour, Abi leading the way to Gemma's house. Gemma's mind drifted back to their previous conversation about university. They remained silent for a little while until Gemma finally spoke.

"I'll think about Liverpool," she said quietly and Abi spun around, all thoughts of banana bread disappearing from her mind.

"Really?" She beamed up at Gemma and then threw her slim arms around Gemma's neck and pulled herself to Gemma for a hug. "Oh, Gemma!" she exclaimed, pulling back and jumping up and down. "Gemma that would be amazing! We'd have so much fun!" Gemma couldn't help but smile and nod along.

"But we're going to have to get jobs as soon as we get there."
"Why?"

"Because it's going to take two incomes to keep you fed!" And Abi laughed, Gemma joined in along.

And they walked back to Gemma's house, laughing and discussing possible jobs they could have at university.

They spent the remainder of the afternoon hanging out, eating banana bread and looking up courses for Gemma at

Liverpool University. They had enjoyed their afternoon so much, that Abi glanced at the clock on Gemma's bedside table and gasped.

"Oh! We should get ready!" Gemma glanced at the clock.

"Oh crap, I forgot all about it." Gemma's inside were suddenly squirming with nerves. "Do we have to go? Let's stay here and watch *Harry Potter* or something."

"Oh wow, that's a crazy Friday night. Yes, we have to go! Robbie asked you!"

Gemma rolled her eyes. "Not this again, Abi, he only invited me because his mum would have asked him to."

"Come on, Gem! He didn't want to have a party, he wanted to be at work, with *you*. But then he felt pressured into having one, so he practically begged for you to come."

"Stop it." Gemma blushed, shaking her head and turning her back to Abi. "Let's just get ready and get it over with."

"That's the fighting spirit!" Gemma didn't see, but she was certain that Abi rolled her eyes at her. They got ready anyway and Abi into black jeans, a strappy top and her Doc Martins.

Gemma was searching through her wardrobe when Abi came and stood next to her.

"Are you not dressed yet? I'm going to have to get your makeup done soon, your granddad will be here in an hour." Gemma stressfully tugged each item hung up on the metal bar from one end of the bar to the other. It made a shrieking scraping noise as if it was screaming at Gemma to just pick something.

"I have nothing to wear!" Gemma cried, pulling the clothes back the other way, researching the same five outfits as if something was going to magically spring out at her.

"Well," Abi said, pushing her gently to the side and having a look at the clothes hung up. They were a couple of tops, a couple of work and school shirts and two dresses. One of them was dark and florally with material that was light and flowy.

It had been something that Gemma's mum had bought for her in the summer in the hopes that Gemma might actually get her legs out and soak up the sun for once.

It didn't happen and it went straight into Gemma's wardrobe, with the tags still on. "Oh, Gemma!" Abi sighed, pulling the flowy dress out and holding it to herself. "You'd look beautiful in this. You should wear this." Gemma chewed at her bottom lip as she looked at the dress.

"I don't know…" she said, looking at how short it looked. "I don't like having my pasty legs out."

"Wear tights and some boots. It'll look stunning. You can even wear your black denim coat." Another one of her mother's buys over the summer.

"Well…" Gemma looked at the dress again. They were really running out of time and she needed to get her makeup. "Right, fine. I'll wear it." She held out her hand and Abi handed over the light dress.

"Good! Now quickly, I need to do your makeup." So Gemma got herself into a dress and tights, something she normally wouldn't be caught dead in. She didn't get time to self-loathe in the mirror for long because Abi forced her into a chair, brandishing a makeup brush.

About twenty minutes later, Abi dragged her to floor-length mirror.

Normally, Gemma tried to avoid looking at herself in any mirror, especially full-body ones.

But Abi dragged her in front of it before she could protest.

"See? You look beautiful." And Gemma was shocked about her appearance. The dress actually looked nice on and Gemma felt really grown up and sophisticated in it. The tights made her legs look smooth and slimmer. The small boots she borrowed from her mother topped off the entire outfit. For once, Gemma felt fairly comfortable in something.

And Abi's makeup!

Gemma turned to Abi, her mouth open in shock.

"What?" Abi asked, her face dropping slightly at Gemma's expression.

"*When* did you learn to do makeup like this?" Gemma turned back to the mirror and took a closer look. Abi had done everything so delicate and soft; it was the opposite of her usual harsh, black makeup. Abi shrugged, grinning modestly.

"I like makeup. Just because I use black doesn't mean it's the only colour on the eye pallet." She turned back to Gemma, beaming up at her. "Do you really like it?"

"Thank you, Abi, it's amazing."

"Now do you see what I see? You're beautiful, Gemma! With or without makeup."

Gemma blushed and looked down at her booted feet and shook her head. Gemma might feel okay in what she was wearing, but she still couldn't take a compliment.

"Right," Abi said, taking her arm. "Let's go show Robbie Wilson what he's missing." And before Gemma could splutter and gasp, Abi dragged her out of Gemma's room and out to the waiting car. Gemma's granddad beamed at Gemma from the front seat, gushing about how beautiful she looked. Gemma again just blushed and shook off the compliment. Gemma's granddad then pulled out of the driveway and off towards Robbie's house.

Gemma's stomach was twisting, and her heart was beating uncomfortably fast. Abi was babbling away cheerfully to Gemma's granddad while Gemma chewed the inside of her cheek.

This was a bad idea, she decided. She shouldn't be going. She didn't belong with Robbie and his friends. And there was a horrid gnawing sensation in the pit of her stomach that something was going to happen tonight.

And Gemma knew it would be something to do with Robbie.

All too soon, they pulled up outside Robbie's semi-detached home. It was obvious by the thumping base of music and lights in the windows that the party was already in full swing.

Gemma swallowed as she looked at the house she knew so well.

It was too late now to turn back.

"Right," Gemma's granddad turned and looked at the girls, face serious. "Have fun but be safe!" He pointed a long, thick finger and both girls in turn. "No drugs or anything. Call me when you're ready for picking up."

Abi smiled and Gemma rolled her eyes. "Yeah, okay, Granddad. Thanks for the lift." Gemma sat up and kissed her granddad on the cheek quickly before pushing Abi out of the car. "See you later."

"No drugs!" her granddad shouted one last time before Gemma slammed the door behind her. Abi was laughing as Gemma huffed exasperatedly.

"Seriously, who does he think we are? Like we'd be doing any of that," Gemma said gruffly but Abi shrugged.

"I'm not opposed to it. Not that hard stuff like," she added quickly, "but I wouldn't mind trying a bit of pot."

Gemma rolled her eyes at her. "Well, maybe tonight will be your lucky night. I heard that Matt Clark is a bit of a pothead. Maybe he'll share some with you."

Abi physically gagged. "Ew, Matt Clark. I wouldn't share a

spliff with him, it would be like kissing him. God, could you imagine?"

Gemma shuddered at the thought. "I'd be rather caught dead than snog that idiot."

"Hear, hear!" Abi turned and smiled at Gemma, "Are you ready?" Gemma took in a deep breath and squared her shoulders towards the house. "Right, let's go," she said and they linked arms and headed for the buzzing house ahead of them. Abi excited and beaming and Gemma anxious and self-conscious.

Inside, the music was blaring and there were so many people crammed into the party, it seemed to spill outside in the garden as well.

"Let's get a drink," Gemma said to Abi, pulling her towards to kitchen and drinks counter. Gemma's throat was dry and felt thick. "I need one." They made their way to the kitchen to get a drink. They managed to find themselves some beers and even though Gemma hated the taste of it, she drank deeply. She felt like there was a spotlight on her and everyone was looking at her.

It wasn't really the case, in all honesty, no one was looking at her.

Gemma took a massive glug of more beer. Gemma was about to turn to Abi when a shrill voice rang through the air.

"Oh. My. God. What the hell are you doing here?" Gemma knew instantly whom the voice was coming from behind Gemma. Gemma took a deep breath and turned slowly to face Miranda. She was looking amazing obviously, in a mini-denim skirt and a short, tight top that showed off her toned mid-drift.

Gemma suddenly felt like her entire body triple in size. Gemma's eyes looked over Miranda's small and petite body with jealousy bubbling in her stomach. Gemma's eyes flitted to the floor as tears sprung up in her eyes and burned at the rims of her eyes. Gemma felt Abi swelling with rage next to her.

"And what the hell are you wearing?" There was a ripple of sniggering and Abi stepped forward. Gemma grabbed her arm and Abi's furious face turned to Gemma. All fury instantly melted from her face and Abi looked up at her, her eyes wide.

"Gemma?" she asked quietly, but Gemma just shook her head, the tears clouding her vision. She pushed past the cackling Miranda and her friends and out of the kitchen, towards the bathroom. The tears streaming down her face, she ran down the hallway towards the bathroom. The toilet was in sight, but then someone side-stepped and stood in her way.

Matt Clark.

Gemma groaned internally at the sight of him. Matt was one of Robbie's friends. Friends said loosely as Matt followed Robbie around like a lovesick puppy. Matt was one of those short-skinny kids when they were younger who had suddenly shot up over the last summer. He was getting as tall as Gemma but still a couple of inches shorter. He hadn't started to fill out and was still scrawny. His black eyes gleamed with malice as they racked over Gemma's body and face, sneering.

"Fuck me, Roly-Poly." His eyes lingered a little too long on Gemma's chest. Gemma felt herself hunching over and wrapping her arms defensively across her chest. "Who invited you?"

Abi caught up to Gemma, panting slightly and glared at Matt.

"What's it to you, Clark? Fuck off."

Matt glared at her before his face broke into another sneer. He didn't say any more, just stalked past them. As he passed, Gemma's nostrils filled with a sickly mixture of weed, cigarettes and Lynx Africa. When he was gone, Abi turned to Gemma, her anger melted straight away.

"Don't listen to that bitch, Gem," Abi said softly, rubbing

her arms up and down affectionately. Gemma sniffed and blinked back her tears. She did not want to cry at the party. She didn't want to give Miranda the satisfaction. She nodded as she steadied her breath, wiping under her eyes.

"I'm just going to go and check my makeup." She glanced down the hallway as she saw a group of girls gathering around the door to the toilet. She groaned and added, "I'll go to the upstairs one. Go find Pip and I'll come find you in a minute."

"Are you sure? I could come with you."

But Gemma shook her head. "No, I'm fine honestly. I'll just got sort myself out and come find you."

Abi nodded and Gemma scooted around her and headed for the stairs. She reached the familiar landing and started to fumble for the door. Gemma knew the layout well, even in the fading evening light. Gemma's hand found the door of the bathroom and it turned. Gemma sighed in relief about it being unlocked, but as she turned her head to glance up the corridor, she noticed a door ajar with streaming, orange light. Gemma frowned and glanced around the rest of the hallway; every other door was shut apart from the room that was situated at the very end of the corridor.

Robbie's room.

Gemma was frozen, curiosity threatening to take over. She gnawed at her bottom lip, listening for any sound coming from the room. All she heard was the thumping of music from below. Gemma decided she should just check and then she could shut the door again. So Gemma stepped quietly down the hallway and reached Robbie's door. She hadn't ever been inside Robbie's room, only gazed longingly at it whenever she had gone into Pip's room. Gemma poked her head around the door and glanced about the room.

It was a typical teenage boy's room.

It was dark, blue and messy. There were posters of bands and bikini-glad women on the walls. There were piles of clothes scattered about the room and a guitar propped up in the corner. There was a general smell of Lynx Africa and CK-One. Gemma breathed in deeply.

It was bigger than Pip's room, with a large window framing the setting sun. Gemma pushed herself further past around the door to look in the far corner, behind the door.

There was a double bed pressed up against the far wall, with the window at the base of the bed. Sitting there, perched at the end of the bed and looking out of the window, was Robbie. The orange tones of the sunset made his olive skin glow. Gemma gasped at the sight of him, surprised to see him cooped up in his room and not at the centre of the party below.

Robbie must have heard her because his head suddenly turned to face the door as Gemma tried to pull her head back and leave the room undetected.

"Gemma?" Robbie called out and Gemma paused. Robbie had obviously seen her. It was embarrassing to think she'd be caught snooping, but it would be even more awkward and embarrassing if she just left. With her heart beating, she opened the door slightly and looked at him sheepishly.

He didn't look mad; he was smiling gently at her, an eyebrow raised in question.

"S-Sorry," Gemma stammered, looking at the ground as her excuse tumbled awkwardly from her lips. "I was just using the toilet and I saw the door was open and I was just checking..." Her lame excuse trailed off and was met with a slightly awkward silence. "Sorry," she mumbled again, glancing up at Robbie through her eyelashes quickly before returning her gaze to the floor. "I'll just go." She turned and started to leave when Robbie called out again.

"Don't go!" he practically shouted after her and Gemma turned back to him, surprised by the slight desperation in his voice.

"W-What?" she said, confused.

"D-Don't go," he stammered and Gemma noted his cheeks almost looked flushed in the setting sun. "Come and sit down," he said after a few more awkward moments.

"Um…" Gemma glanced down the hallway before turning her head back to Robbie. He had turned his whole body towards her, one hand on a space next to him on the bed and the other held onto a can of beer. Gemma thought she should decline and leave, but she couldn't do it. So she stumbled in, tripping over various items on the floor as she passed the room. Robbie looked as if he was fighting off a smile, to be polite, but Gemma blushed all the same. She lowered herself as delicately as she could onto the bed next to him. She was silently mortified at how much the bed dipped beneath her large frame compared to Robbie. Robbie seemed to almost dip slightly more towards her.

Gemma sat awkwardly, trying to hold in her stomach and wanting the ground to open up and swallow her whole.

There was another awkward silence and when Gemma really thought she couldn't take any more, Robbie moved. He was leaning back on the bed, looking out the window again and seemed at ease with the whole situation. He took a swig of beer and held it out for Gemma. With a shaking hand, she took it and took a swig, trying to not grimace at the taste. She tried to not put her hands to her lips and savour the fact that she had just drunk from Robbie's drink.

Gemma felt Robbie's eyes on her back. Her skin prickled and felt really hot, but she couldn't look at him. She just looked awkwardly out of the window at the setting sun.

"Ah, beautiful view," Gemma croaked into the silence. She groaned internally at her lame attempt to strike up a conversation. It wasn't like she hadn't been alone with him, she had numerous times when working at the pub on a Friday night. But that was different. Something felt very loaded about sitting so close to Robbie, on his bed, in his bedroom, with a romantic sunset setting in front of them.

Of course, Robbie wouldn't see anything romantic about the whole situation. He wouldn't see Gemma in that way. But the way he was watching Gemma made her feel so hot and flustered.

"Ah," Gemma attempted to strike up another conversation but it died in her throat. She had chanced a glance at Robbie as she fumbled with her words, but their eyes had met and all the moisture had evaporated out of her throat. She swallowed but it felt like sandpaper lined her throat. Robbie held out the can of beer again to her but never took his eyes off her. Gemma grabbed it gratefully and took another swig, using it as an excuse to break the contact between their eyes.

"Do you ever wish your life could be different?" Gemma's head spun around at the random and somewhat loaded question. Robbie's big brown eyes were wide and full of questions. Is that why he was up in his room? Pondering life?

Gemma swallowed and looked down at the can of beer that was still in her hand. Did she ever wish her life could be different?

Every second of every day, she wished her life could be different.

How many times had she gone to bed, squeezing her eyes tight and wishing that she would wake up a different person? She didn't wish for different friends or family; she wished her body would be different. She longed to wake up and have a small, petite body like Miranda. She longed to wake up skinny and with Robbie as her boyfriend. She longed to be able to wrap her slender arms around his neck and press her bony body against his. She longed for him to be able to wrap his arms around her willowy body and place his head on the top of her head, lovingly.

But it never happened.

She always awoke the next morning, bitter and disappointed that her wish hadn't come true. But what could Robbie wish for? Surely he was happy with his life?

"Sometimes," Gemma lied, swallowing the bitter feeling of wanting something so badly.

"Do you ever think things aren't fair?" he murmured again, his eyes still on her face.

"Sometimes. But isn't that what they say?"

"What?"

"That life isn't fair?"

Robbie didn't answer, he just watched her.

"Have you ever wanted something so badly, but you couldn't have it?"

Gemma's mind pictured herself, but slim and beautiful with Robbie's taller frame draped over hers affectionately. "Yes," she whispered and her eyes met his. Their eyes locked and Gemma was suddenly aware of Robbie's entire body. From the knee and thigh that was pressing lightly against hers to the pure heat radiating off his entire body. Gemma felt the lightest of touches on her thigh, above her knee. She looked down to see Robbie's hand lightly on it.

"You…" Robbie said as his eyes went up and down Gemma, taking in her appearance. It wasn't in a creepy way, the way Matt had done. It was kinder. He seemed to swallow before bringing

82

his eyes back to hers. "Gemma, you look…" He trailed off again. The hand that was on Gemma's knee moved to her face, his fingertips light and gentle against her skin. He gently took a strand of her hair between his fingertips and played with it gently before tucking it behind her ear. His fingers then trailed lightly down her cheek and jaw. "Gemma," Robbie whispered and Gemma watched him with bated breath, her heart pounding uncomfortably against her chest.

"Gemma, I wish—" but then a voice sounded from the hallway that made them jump apart. Gemma realised with sickening jolt to her stomach, that the voice was Miranda.

Robbie leaped off the bed, looking at the door and then Gemma and back at the door. His face was horrified and anxious as his face flicked back and forth between Gemma and the door.

"Stay here! Don't move!" he hissed and ran to the door and threw himself out of the door. Gemma ran to the door and pushed herself against the wall behind the door in case it flew open. She could hear Robbie and Miranda just outside the door.

"Where have you been?" Miranda was asking.

"Just grabbing something from my room, come on. Let's go back down."

"Or maybe we could hang out in your room? I'd like to see it." Gemma's stomach lurched as she looked around for places to hide in the messy bedroom. Thankfully, Robbie redirected Miranda.

"Maybe later, I need another beer."

"How come Roly-Poly is here?" Gemma could practically hear the eye-roll and hatred in her voice. "She is so lame."

"Ah, well, you know what it's like. My mum wanted me to invite her to be nice. She hasn't got a lot of friends." A blow struck Gemma's gut at Robbie's words. After how he had just been with her in his bedroom, he wasn't defending her to Miranda. He was just as bad as the rest of them. Tears stung at Gemma's eyes as her stomach gnawed at her stupidity.

Of course Rose had asked him to invite her. There wasn't any other reason why he would invite her. Gemma heard them leaving and she waited a couple of minutes before fleeing Robbie's room. The smell of Robbie was making her feel very sick. She ran down the hallway and down the stairs, not seeing Robbie or Miranda again. When she reached the bottom of the stairs, she ran into Pip and Abi.

"Hey, you okay? I was about to come up," Abi said, Gemma just nodded and walked past them towards the front door.

"Let's just go, yeah? I've had enough of these dickheads."

"Can I come?" Pip asked, running along behind them. Gemma just nodded, she just had to get out of that house. "Brilliant. Thanks, Gem! I'll go pack a bag quick. Meet you up on the road. I can't stand being here." Pip rolled her eyes at both Abi and Gemma before disappearing back into the swelling crowd.

"Come on," Gemma said, restarting her attempt to push her way to the front door. The alcohol had been flowing a few hours by that point and there were many couples entangled up against the wall towards the front door.

"Nice," Abi commented as they pushed past a particular enthusiastic couple. Gemma thought she recognised the back of Matt's head but she didn't pause long enough to look. There was just one more couple in their way. Gemma couldn't see who it was, just someone tall entangled around such a small figure, she wasn't visible at first. Just as Gemma was passing them to pull herself through the front door, Abi's foot tripped over a dislodged shoe from the knocked-over shoe rack. Obviously, this couple had been very fervent when they began their make-out session. Abi went flying into Gemma's back and knocked her off course and sent her flying into the back of the tall boy and tiny girl by the door.

"Shit," Gemma gasped as her face hit between the boy's shoulder blades. Her nostrils were suddenly filled with a very familiar scent. A scent she had just smelt upstairs in a bedroom she had never been in before. The figure had turned to reveal Miranda, who was clutching at this body for dear life. Her lips were swollen with kisses and her eyes were dazed. Then her eyes turned mutinous as she spotted Gemma was the reason for the disturbance.

"You!" she spat, still clutching at the boy for dear life. Gemma's eyes left Miranda and up to the figure in question, who she was still leaning against. His big brown eyes found hers, wide. They weren't angry. They almost looked shocked and upset. His mouth was open as if his voice had failed him as he tried to talk. They stared at each other for a moment. Then Abi pulled Gemma back so she wasn't leaning on Robbie any more.

"S-Sorry," Gemma mumbled, but her voice sounded distant as if it was another from far away saying the words.

Robbie's mouth was still open as he stared at Gemma. Gemma thought he might actually finally speak, but then Miranda did.

"Well, you fucking should be. You creep!" Robbie blinked down at Miranda, almost forgetting she was there even though his arms were entangled around her.

"It was an accident! I didn't see you! I didn't know it was you!" Gemma felt tears prickling in her eyes again as she looked at Robbie, begging him to believe her.

All the while, inside, her heart felt like it was breaking.

Robbie had been kissing Miranda.

It had finally happened and Gemma had seen it.

Gemma blinked back the tears from the confrontation and the absolute heartbreak happening internally. She needed to get away.

Thankfully, at that moment, Pip joined the group. She looked around, eyes furrowed. Her eyes finally settled on Robbie and Miranda's entwined figures and her face glowering at them.

"I'm going to Gemma's," she announced, glaring coldly up at Robbie. "All these people are dicks, Robbie. I don't know why you've changed to be like these arseholes. So when you're done sticking your tongue down this cow's throat" — Miranda gasped and Robbie's jaw tightened as he locked eyes with his sister's — "tell Mum where I am. Can't believe you, Robbie." Pip turned to Gemma and Abi, her bag over her shoulder. "Let's get out of here. I don't want to be here a minute longer."

And with that, the three girls turned on their heels and turned their backs to Robbie and Miranda. They left through the open front door and escaped. And even though Gemma was heartbroken and replaying seeing Robbie and Miranda in her mind the entire way home, she couldn't help thinking something: that Pip was spot on.

CHAPTER SEVEN

Present Day

The next night, Gemma found herself on her way to Rose's house in a taxi. To her dismay, Matt, who seemed to think the invitation had stretched to him as well, also was accompanying her.

He hadn't come down hard on Gemma the night after they had all met in the pub. Gemma was obviously relieved, but it made her uneasy. It was almost like he was plotting something and Gemma was sure Matt enjoyed the torture of it all. It was likely. The car ride was silent and Gemma played with the creases in her skirt nervously.

"You seemed to have put in a lot of effort for this *family* meal," Matt said, looking her up and down uncomfortably.

Here we go.

"You think? It's just a skirt—"

"Who do you think you're trying to be? Something you're not? All a skirt does is bring attention to those tree trunks you call legs." Gemma bit her lip and looked out the window as she tried to compose herself.

Thankfully, before Matt could open his mouth again and say anything else hurtful, they had pulled up at Rose's. Gemma could see a flashy sport's car outside and she sighed with relief.

"What did you say?" Matt barked and he was glaring at her.

"N-nothing."

"Good. Let's get this over with." He got out of the taxi,

leaving Gemma alone. Gemma sat for a moment, trying to regain her control. Suddenly her door flew open and Matt's angry face came through it. "Move!" he barked and Gemma felt herself scrambling out of the taxi, turning back to pay the driver before she stood before Matt. He looked at her and Gemma felt her stomach churning, waiting for another round of criticism and snide comments. But nothing happened, Matt just looked at her then suddenly turned on his heel and stalked off towards the front door. Gemma blinked then she scurried after him and reached him just as he knocked on the door. He stepped back so as the door opened, Gemma was in his eye line and Matt stood behind her. His hand rested at the small of her back, but not in an affectionate way. It was more of a controlling gesture, like Matt was going to dictate all of Gemma's movements. The door opened and Gemma found herself looking straight into the eyes of Robbie. They stared at each other for a moment. Suddenly, Gemma felt hands on her waist, wrapping around her and felt Matt pressing himself into her back. It might have looked like an affectionate notion to anyone else, but Gemma knew better. It was another possessive and controlling notion.

Matt was giving her a warning.

Robbie didn't believe Matt's sudden act of affection either.

He looked them up and down for a few moments, before his eyes reached hers again. There must have been something in Gemma's eyes, because Robbie held his tongue and invited them inside without any other comment.

"Would you guys like a drink?" he asked as they followed him down the hall, towards the kitchen. Gemma inhaled and smiled to herself for a moment.

The air was heavily-scented and Gemma could even smell incense burning. It just smelled of Robbie's childhood home. The smell of Robbie's home always brought back a lot of memories for Gemma.

She remembered the times she and Pip would have sleepovers in her room, giggling away until the early hours of the morning.

She remembered Rose making them enchiladas, which was something Gemma never ate before.

She remembered Rose and Arty (Robbie's dad) throwing their annual Halloween party and Gemma would go trick-or-treating with Pip and Robbie and they were some of the happiest times she would have.

She remembered staying over at the weekend and being with Pip but always hoping for a look at Robbie. She hoped to run into him in the hallway to Pip's room or the bathroom. Or just hoped that he would stay in on that evening and eat dinner with them, instead of going to hang out with his friends.

She remembered being able to hear Robbie and his band practising their music (during their short rock-band phase) and really wishing that she could be on the other side of the door and watch him.

Gemma found herself smiling slightly as the memories kept flooding back to her. "What's so funny?" Robbie asked, smiling lopsidedly.

"Just remembering your grunge-rock phase."

Robbie groaned. "God, don't remind me. We thought we were Fall Out Boy."

Gemma laughed. "Suppose it was better than your 'rapper' phase. With you hats on the side, chains and baggy, low-riding jeans."

"Hey, that was a big look back in the day."

"Oh I know, I loved it back in the day too." And Gemma

grinned at him, before catching Matt's eye and stopping instantly. Robbie looked at her, then Matt then back at Gemma.

"Do you want a drink?" he asked again, as they didn't answer the first time. Gemma opened her mouth but Matt took it upon himself to answer for both of them.

"I'll have a beer and Gemma will have a *diet* coke." Robbie stopped and looked at Matt with raised eyebrows. He then looked at Gemma, completely ignoring Matt.

"Do you want a *diet* coke, Gemma, or would you like something else?"

Gemma considered just taking the coke and keeping the peace, but there was something about Robbie's presence that sparks a bit of bravery in her. "Do you have any flavoured gins?"

"Of course, would you like one?"

"That would be lovely."

"Lemonade okay?"

"Perfect." And Gemma smiled at Robbie, who smiled back. They had reached the kitchen, where Arty was pouring a couple of glasses of wine and putting the bottle back into the fridge.

"Gemma! Hello darling!" He embraced her, giving her a quick kiss on the cheek before squeezing her again. "Still as beautiful as ever." There was a scoff from Matt, which could have been disguised as a cough if he had really tried, but Matt didn't care about etiquette. Arty looked at him for a moment, before plastering a friendly smile on his face and outstretching his hand.

"Ah, Matt, it has been a while." They clasped hands and let go very quickly. "Rose is through there. Go ahead, Gemma, she's missed your beautiful face."

Another scoff from Matt and Gemma was sure Robbie's jaw would break because it was clenched so tight. She caught his eye and indicated he follow her down the hallway, leaving Matt in the kitchen, stuck in conversation with Arty. Gemma suspected Arty was trying to distract Matt and Gemma smiled to herself and thanked him internally. Gemma intended to move to the living room and see Rose, but Robbie's hand wrapped around her arm, above the elbow and pulled her into an adjoining room. As Gemma blinked against the bright light and looked around, Gemma realised it was the downstairs toilet.

"Robbie?" Gemma asked, but Robbie was already speaking.

"Why the hell are you with him? He talks to you like shit." The anger in Robbie's voice was very apparent.

"I—"

"I'm serious, Gemma, I don't understand it. And when I want to say something, you signal to me not to. Why not? I don't think I can hold my tongue any more."

Gemma stepped towards him, panicked.

"No, Robbie, please!" She placed her hands on his chest and looked up into his eyes. "Please don't say anything. Please."

Robbie looked down into her eyes, seeing the panic in her wide, blue eyes. He placed his hands over hers and stepped closer so there was only mere centimetres between them.

"Why Gem?" he whispered, his eyes gazing into hers. "Are you scared of him?"

Gemma just looked into his eyes, struggling with her breath. The moment was so intense and being so close to Robbie was literally taking her breath away. Robbie lifted one of his hands off hers and touched her cheek with the lightest of touches. Gemma's breath caught and she closed her eyes for a moment, savouring such a gentle touch. No one had ever touched her so.

"Has he done something, Gemma?" Robbie whispered and Gemma's eyes flew open and she looked into Robbie's, who had moved even closer to her. Both of his hands now cradled her face as he looked into her eyes. Gemma felt her lips quivering and tears burning into her eyes. Robbie's expression quite literally broke in front of her eyes. The pain was evident on Gemma's face and it made Robbie want to double over. "Oh Gemma, it's okay. I'm here." And Robbie pulled her to his chest and wrapped his arms around her, holding her tight. And Gemma couldn't hold it in any more, a sob ripped through her mouth.

She tried not to let out the sobs too loudly. Matt was still only in the other room, but Gemma clutched onto Robbie, burying her face into his chest.

They didn't know how long they were embracing for, but after some time, Gemma's sobs slowed and eventually ceased. They just held onto each other for a while longer. After some time, Robbie spoke. Gemma kept her head on his chest, feeling the rumble of his voice through his muscly torso. "You've got to break it off, Gemma," he said softly and Gemma's stomach dropped. She pulled back from him and ran her hands through her hair then kept them over her face again.

"It's not that simple, Robbie."

"It is."

"It's not, Robbie!" Gemma fought back more sobs.

"Why not?"

But just then Gemma heard someone shouting. It was Matt. "Shh!" she said to Robbie and put her finger to his lips, straining to listen.

"Gemma—" he breathed, his breath hot on her fingers. But Gemma was too panicked to be thrilled by the sensation.

"Shh! Please, Robbie! Please! He can't find us together… *here*."

"Why not?"

"Just because! Please, please stay hidden! Please? For me? I'll go out and pretend I've come out of the bathroom and you join us in the living room, please, Robbie?" Her eyes were wide with pleading and Robbie looked into her eyes for half a second before he reluctantly nodded and stayed quiet. Just because Gemma moved her finger from his lips and cupped his cheek for a moment and whispered, "thank you".

She then turned her back to him, but not before she saw his expression soften and he nodded softly once. She opened the door, a little less than she normally would but she was trying to conceal Robbie in case Matt was waiting for her in the kitchen.

Luckily he wasn't and she made her way down the hall without being detected and walked into the living room. There on the couch was Linda and Rose, both talking and laughing lightly with a glass of wine in their hands. For a moment, Gemma thought Matt had left, but to her dismay, he materialised by the door and snaked his hand around her elbow and tugged her unceremoniously to the side.

"Where the hell have you been?" he hissed and his expression was mutinous. Gemma swallowed the fear bubbling up in her and tried to act nonchalantly.

"Toilet? Why? What's happening?"

"Nothing! That's what! I want to get this over with and go home!" He glared at her, then at the empty hallway behind her. "Where the hell is Wilson?" Gemma shrugged coolly (she hoped).

"I don't know. Haven't seen him since we left the kitchen. He was on the phone." And Gemma hoped that Robbie would say that as an excuse. At that moment, Robbie came into the living room and smiled easily.

"Sorry about that," he said. "Manager just wanted to discuss training."

"That's okay love," Rose said and she beamed proudly at him. "The World Cup is quite a big deal."

Robbie laughed lightly. "Yes, you could say that. Did Dad get you a drink, Gemma?" he asked politely and acting as nothing had passed between them since they entered the kitchen, what seemed like hours ago.

"Ah, no. I was just using the loo."

"God, he's useless, isn't he? I'll get you that drink." And he smiled at her and turned, leaving the room once again. Gemma walked over and greeted Rose while she waited for her drink.

"How are you?" Gemma asked and sat down next to her.

"Like a million bucks," she joked and it was obvious she was trying to not complain.

"It's okay to say you feel like crap, it would be acceptable."

She laughed and shook her head. "I'm still here. And I hope to be for a long time yet."

Gemma looked at her mum, who was smiling rather sadly at her. "Of course," said Gemma, with as much enthusiasm as she could muster. "You can't go anywhere. Who on earth would do all of Robbie's washing for him?"

Everyone (besides Matt) laughed and chuckled. Robbie came back into the living room and handed Gemma her drink. She took a sip and it was a delicious, fruity taste.

"Yes, I suppose. He is a bit of a mummy's boy."

"Bit of a mummy's boy?" Gemma scoffed, "If he wasn't so rich, I'm sure he'd still be living here."

"Um, yeah," said Pip and Robbie rolled his eyes.

"You can talk, who still drives you places?" Robbie jabbed at Pip.

"Well," said Pip, puffing out her chest, "Who still rings

Mum every night at—"

"Look what you've started." Rose rolled her eyes but was smiling warmly at her two children. "There just as bad as they were when they were kids."

"Oh no," said Gemma, shaking her head. "No way. You didn't know half of that stuff they got up to. Chinese burns and flour in beds was only the beginning."

"Oh I knew," said Rose all-knowingly, "I just ignored them half the time."

"They would have been permanently grounded," said Arty, "And we never would have had the house to ourselves at the weekends," he added, shooting Rose a wicked smile and winked.

"Argh," said Robbie and Pip together, forgetting what they were spatting about.

Everyone else laughed (excluding Matt again) before Arty announced dinner should be ready and they made their way into the dining room. They all sat down and Gemma found herself sandwiched awkwardly between Matt and Robbie. The table wasn't huge so there was a lot of elbow and leg brushing. Into the middle of the table went a couple of trays of enchiladas, some Mexican rice dishes and some nachos.

"You found a chef that would serve Mexican food?" Gemma asked, smiling at all the familiar foods before them. It was just like when they were kids.

"Actually," Robbie glared slightly at Rose. "*She* wouldn't let me get one in."

"You cooked all this?" Gemma asked Rose, slightly exasperatedly. "You are meant to be taking it easy."

Rose just shrugged her slim shoulders, feigning innocence. "Arty did most of it. I only supervised."

Gemma rolled her eyes but was smiling. Rose made the best

enchiladas.

"Who serves Mexican food at a dinner party?" Matt said snidely, only really quiet enough for Gemma to hear.

"Mexican food at a *family* dinner actually," Robbie said, looking at him. Gemma looked between them as they both eyed each up for a few minutes.

Gemma cleared her throat and tried to move the conversation onward. "Enchiladas? I haven't had these for years."

"They were our favourite." Robbie smiled at her and she knew that they were both remembering all those family dinners all those years ago. "Do you remember when mum introduced you to mac and cheese?" Robbie asked her, smiling broadly at the memory.

"Oh shut up," Gemma said, smacking his arm.

"That's my fault," Linda admitted, pulling a face. "I wasn't really adventurous with food."

"You didn't have time, Mum, you were always working at the pub."

"Still, I can't believe you didn't have mac and cheese until we were twelve. It's still one of my favourites. Not as good as enchiladas though." He winked at Gemma and Gemma felt her cheeks burning as she looked down at her plate.

"Well—"

But Matt decided he had had enough and spoke over Gemma. "So Robbie, seeing as you're so *rich* how come you haven't bought your mum and dad a big fancy house?" he said, indicating the cramped table and small kitchen-diner.

Gemma gasped. "Matt!" she exclaimed. "You can't ask that!"

"Why not? We're all friends here aren't we?" And he smiled and put his arm around Gemma, squeezing her shoulder much harder than affectionately.

Another warning.

Robbie looked at Matt and his arm around Gemma. He smiled and looked like he was calculating his next answer, but before he could even open his mouth, someone else answered Matt.

"Actually, Matt," said Pip, her tone hard and unfriendly, "if you must know, as we're all *friends* here, Robbie has offered to buy my parents a new, bigger house but they refused. They love this house as it is our childhood home, with lots of memories. So instead of buying them a new house, he paid it off."

"And he's bought them new cars," Gemma added and Matt glared at her, so she put her head down, intending to keep herself quiet. There was an awkward pause.

"And he bought the pub," said Linda and Gemma's head snapped up to her and she was looking sheepishly at her. Gemma looked around the table and the only other person who was surprised by this news was Pip. Gemma turned to Robbie and he smiled shyly.

"You own the pub?" Gemma asked, looking into his eyes.

His eyes were soft and hesitant. "No, Gemma, your mum owns the pub. I bought it for you both, so you don't have to worry about paying the lease on it."

Gemma's eyes welled up and she looked at her mum, whose eyes were swimming with tears also.

It had been common knowledge that the pub had been struggling. Financially, it had been really tough for both Linda and Gemma. They had worked all hours and sacrificed so much just to try and stay afloat. Could it really be possible that they didn't need to struggle any more?

"When?" Gemma asked quietly, looking back between

Robbie and Linda.

"The paperwork all went through this morning, my lawyer said," Robbie said quietly, as he surveyed Gemma and watching her reaction. He looked a little worried like Gemma would have been upset by this news. "I'm sorry, Gemma, if I intervened. I just knew things were tough and I didn't want you guys to struggle and have so much financial worry. It seems so selfish of me to have so much while—"

But Gemma had thrown off Matt's arm and pulled Robbie into a tight embrace, as the tears flowed freely down her face.

"Thank you," she whispered as she held onto him, her tears soaking his expensive shirt. She gave him a quick squeeze before starting to release him, she patted where her tears had stained his shoulder. "Argh, I'm sorry, Robbie."

"Don't worry about it," he said gently and she looked into his eyes. Gemma felt all her repressed feelings for Robbie bubbling up. She wanted, more than anything in that moment, to reach out and pull his face to hers. She wanted to feel his lips on hers and to put all her pent-up feelings into a single kiss. But a rude awakening stirred her suddenly from her fantasy and it came in the form of Matt.

He pulled on her arm and jolted her back to the present moment.

"For God's sake, Gemma. Hello? Pass the rice!" Gemma shook her head and looked at him confused, then at the table of food in front of them.

"Right," she said, reaching for the rice. "Sorry."

The conversation was slow and consisted more of small talk for a few moments and Robbie and Gemma both served themselves. There seemed to be this electric charge pulsating between them. Their elbows would brush together and Gemma felt like an electric shot had shot through her body. She could just feel Robbie's every move and breath. Gemma felt something else stirring within her, bubbling away alongside the strong desire she felt for Robbie.

It was guilt.

Guilt, because she still wanted Robbie so badly, even after so long. That she was still so in love with him, that she was forgetting all her reasons for pushing aside her own wants and desires. Forgetting about her beloved best friend and what she promised her memory the day of her funeral. Gemma battled silently for a few moments with her conflicting feelings. She was so engrossed, that she lost the flow of the conversation for a bit.

Absently, Gemma reached for another serving of enchiladas and rice and she felt Matt's eyes on her. She looked at him, just after she had just scooped the second spoonful of rice onto her plate.

His eyebrows were raised in question and judgement.

"What?" she asked quietly, feeling self-conscious under his unrelenting gaze.

"Another serving?" was all he said and Gemma felt her stomach drop as she looked at her plate. All her appetite had disappeared instantly.

It was like her body grew five times bigger than she was. Her clothes suddenly felt tight and clingy. The prickling she felt before was a now hot stabbing all over her skin as she felt all the fabrics of her clothes digging into her fat.

"I didn't realise," Gemma said quietly and put down her fork and crossed her arms across her chest.

"That's a lot of carbs. You don't need all them," Matt said and he reached over and grabbed her plate off the table and pushed her rice off her plate and onto his. "I'll just take this." She could see out of the corner of her eye, Matt was smiling.

He was sitting straight and practically beaming after putting Gemma down.

It seemed to make him grow ten feet taller.

Gemma swallowed back the bile now bubbling in her stomach.

"And," he said, not quite finished with his snide comments, "we both know you don't need the extra carbs... do you, Gemma?" Gemma didn't reply, she just sat with her face down and so Matt persisted vindictively. "Do you Gemma?"

"No," she whispered and he nodded.

"That's right." He scooped an overflowing forkful of rice into his mouth and smacked his lips approvingly. "God, this rice *is* good."

Out of the corner of her eye, she saw Robbie watching them. He was turning, face red with anger. His mouth was starting to open, starting to lean forwards around Gemma, his eyes on Matt. Matt had turned back to his food, a smug smile on his face, so Gemma glanced up at Robbie.

She was pleading with him, she just couldn't face the repercussions if Matt and Robbie came a to a head. Matt would surely punish her extensively. Robbie looked at her for a moment and then sighed and nodded once.

He was holding his tongue and Gemma was extremely thankful.

The rest of the dinner passed with little more happening and a couple of hours later, Gemma and Matt were packed back into the taxi (leftovers in Tupperware boxes) and waved off by the Wilsons. Robbie just watched, grimly, and didn't look happy about Gemma being back in the company of Matt. But Linda was sharing the taxi and intended to drop them off first, so it meant that Gemma wouldn't be alone with Matt until back in the flat. That gave her at least another fifteen minutes of reprieve.

Just as the taxi pulled up to the pub and Matt climbed out, Gemma's phone rang. She answered it without looking at it, as she was climbing out of the taxi.

"Hello?" Half a second pause followed.

"Gemma?" It was Robbie and he sounded extremely distressed.

"Robbie?" Both Linda and Matt looked at Gemma. Linda looked concerned and Matt looked annoyed but Gemma realised, she didn't care. "Robbie? What's the matter?"

"Mum's collapsed. An ambulance is on its way."

"Oh my God," and Gemma looked at her own mother, whose eyes were wide with worry.

"What?" she asked desperately and Gemma's throat felt dry as she said the words.

"Rose has collapsed, Mum."

Linda's face instantly whitened and Gemma reached out and grabbed her hand. She grasped it so tightly as she watched Gemma for any more information.

"The ambulance is here. Will..." Robbie seemed to struggle to formulate the words for a few seconds. "Will you come with me?" Gemma didn't even need to think, the words came to her lips without any consideration.

"Of course. We're on our way."

"Thank you, Gemma." His voice cracked and Gemma felt her heart physically breaking. "I'm coming. Hold on," she said quietly but determinately. The line went dead and Gemma started to climb back into the taxi, just as Linda was telling the taxi driver the new address again.

"What the hell are you doing?" Matt asked angrily and

Gemma turned to him, for once unphased about his anger. She looked him dead in the eye and held her head up.

"I'm going to the hospital to be with Robbie."

"No, you're not," he hissed and grabbed the door. Gemma grabbed the handle, looking him in the eye again, her face full of determination and confidence.

"Yes, I am. Goodbye, Matt." She grasped the handle and swung the door with such force that Matt was shocked and lost his grip on the door. She then locked it in case he attempted to throw it open and drag her out. But Matt seemed so surprised with Gemma's sudden confidence, he didn't even try to stop her. However, when the taxi started to take off, he must have realised Gemma had defied him and he smacked the side of the door in frustration. Both girls jumped in the back, but the taxi driver kept driving and sped off.

The taxi sped off toward Robbie, leaving Matt glaring after them in the road.

CHAPTER EIGHT

As Gemma and Linda pulled up at Robbie's childhood home, they could see the flashing blue lights of the ambulance lighting up the street. Gemma flew out of the taxi and she could see the front door was open. Standing with his back to them was Robbie. Even though he had his back to her, Gemma could just see, by the way he was bent over, his head in his hands, that he was a broken man.

And it broke Gemma's heart.

"Robbie?" she called out and he spun around. If Gemma had thought he looked broken when he had her back to him, it was nothing compared to his face. His face was completely shattered with pain, his eyes red and swollen and his lips were turned down into a miserable grimace. His eyes met hers and Gemma opened her mouth to say something (what she didn't know) but then Robbie just strode towards her. He cleared the space between them in two huge strides and he wrapped his arms around her, crashing her into his chest and burying his face into her neck. His body shook with sobs as he held onto her. Gemma wrapped her arms around him and held him tight, trying to comfort and soothe him.

"Oh Robbie," she said, the tears streaming down her face. "What happened?"

"It was literally just after you left," he said between sobs. "She just said she felt ill... we tried to get her to sit down... and she just... just... collapsed."

103

"Oh my God," Gemma said and she squeezed him tighter. "I'm so sorry."

"Excuse me," someone said behind them and they jumped back. It was the paramedics wheeling Rose on a portable bed and rushing her to the back of the ambulance. Arty was running along behind her, his face pale and drawn. Behind him, holding his hand, was Pip. She saw Gemma and threw herself at her. Gemma grabbed her with one arm, while the other was still gripped around Robbie's waist.

Pip was crying incoherently into her neck.

"Are you following?" someone asked Robbie and he spun to see the paramedic.

"Yes."

"Okay, well, we're going now."

Robbie grasped Gemma's hand and pulled her towards the car. So Linda, Pip and Gemma all got into Robbie's car and he raced behind the ambulance as it blue-lighted to the hospital. Robbie reached across to Gemma and grabbed her hand. She looked up at him and his face was so drawn and broken. So Gemma squeezed his hand with both of hers.

Robbie drove close to the ambulance and within minutes they were at the hospital. The ambulance went off straight to the A&E drop off and Robbie went into the adjacent car park and pulled into the first spot he saw. They all vacated the car silently and made their way to the entrance. As Robbie came around the car, he reached for Gemma's hand again, holding it close to his chest as he started walking to the entrance.

"Please stay with me," he said so quietly that only Gemma heard him. The breath escaped Gemma's lungs and she stopped and looked up at him as Linda and Pip ran on ahead. He was looking at her in such a fearful way, it reminded her almost of a child. She reached out and cupped his cheek for a moment.

"Always, Robbie. I'll always be here for you." She thought for a moment, then added, "For you all." To try and sound a little less intense but Robbie didn't notice.

"Thank you," he whispered and he looked relieved and less frightened. Their fingers entwined and they ran off to the entrance behind Linda and Pip.

What happened over the next few hours was a bit of a blur.

Sometime later, after spending what felt like hours waiting, Gemma found herself waiting in some sort of waiting room, alone. It was seemingly a private room off a ward where Rose had vanished into hours earlier. Robbie and Pip were in the room with Rose and Arty and Linda was off trying to find a café or coffee vending machine. Gemma could feel her phone buzzing in her pocket and she didn't need to look at it to know who it was.

It would be Matt.

She had already seen that he had rung her eleven times. Why she decided to finally answer it, she wasn't sure but she found herself swiping the screen and bringing it to her ear.

"Hello?"

"Hello? Hello? That is all you are going to say? What the fuck is going on? Where are you?"

"I'm at the hospital."

"Who's there with you?"

"Well, no one right now."

"Where the hell is Wilson?"

"With his sick mum, in her room. Is that all right with you?"

Matt wasn't used to hearing Gemma being defiant but Gemma just didn't care.

"What the fuck did you just say?" he said quietly and in a

deadly tone. Gemma swallowed, feeling her braveness falter.

"Matt, I am in the hospital because the woman I grew up with, basically my second mum, is so ill that she collapsed. We don't know what's happening and whether she'll pull through it. I am here for Rose and I'm here for the rest of the family—"

"Robbie you mean."

"Yes, Robbie as well—"

"Get your fat arse home right now."

"No."

Matt was shocked into silence for a moment.

"No?" he said quietly and Gemma's heart beat uncomfortably.

"No," Gemma said.

"What do—" But Gemma had had enough.

"For God's sake, Matt, no means no. I am not coming home. Not until I know that they're all okay and don't need me any more. Okay? Goodbye."

"Do not hang—" But Gemma had already pressed the red button. She took in a deep breath and realised that she was shaking. She put her head into her shaking hands and tried to steady her breath.

"Gemma?" someone said softly and Gemma's eyes whipped up to look into Robbie's.

Though his eyes were still a little bloodshot and drawn, his complexion was much better. "Oh, Robbie!" Gemma said quickly and she stood up and gazed into his face. "How is she?"

"She's awake, still a little weak. It's the chemo, it just weakens her heart so much."

There was a pause and then Robbie sagged, looking so broken again. Gemma gasped and put her hands around him, pulling him to her. Robbie wrapped his arms around her and pressed his face into her neck as the tears came again.

"Oh Robbie," Gemma said as she rubbed his back. "It's okay. She's in the best place. She's okay now."

"Yeah, but for how long?" he said as he pulled back and took a deep breath. He smiled sadly at her and nodded to her phone still in her hand. "Was that Matt?" It was Gemma's turn to sigh and sag. She sagged back into the chair and sighed as she nodded. "Is he pissed that you're here?"

"Yeah." And there was silence again and Robbie seemed like he wanted to say something but held it back. Gemma raised her eyebrows at him. "What?"

"Why are you with him, Gemma?"

"Argh, Robbie. Please don't."

"I'm serious, Gem, what the hell are you doing with him? He treats you terribly and with no respect. He's constantly putting you down. He controls you. You deserve so much better."

Gemma couldn't help but scoff slightly. "You wouldn't get it, Robbie."

"Why not? Why do you think I wouldn't get it?"

"Because you are attractive and well-liked." Gemma hadn't meant to say it, but it had just slipped out.

"You don't think people like you?"

"I think people feel sorry for me. There's a difference."

Robbie was frowning at her, clearly confused, so Gemma sighed and tried to explain more. "People feel sorry for me because I am the fat girl who never really caught anyone's attention. And I'm not just talking about interested in me romantically, just in general. I just blend into the background and am easily looked over."

"That's not true."

"It is, Robbie," Gemma said simply and she smiled a little.

"It doesn't matter, I am used to it. And that is why it's not so simple to finish with Matt. Yes, maybe he doesn't treat me that well all the time, but he is the only person that has ever shown the slightest bit of interest. I know I don't need a man to be happy, but I don't want my mum to worry about me any more."

"What do you mean?"

"Well, I knew my mum was worrying because I got to my early twenties and never had a boyfriend or any love interests. Not many friends, only really Pip, but she was off to uni and had all that going on. All the while, I was still at the pub working all weekend, every weekend. I had no social life and no direction in life. My mum was petrified that I was going to just be alone. Having someone means a lot to my mum. She just doesn't want me to be alone."

"I'm sure your mum would rather you be alone than be with Matt. Gemma, surely there would be someone else. *Anyone* else. Someone who would treat you the way you deserve."

Gemma surprised him by laughing. "But that's it, Robbie. There is no one else." She looked into his eyes again and smiled, a little sadly.

Robbie sat up straight, turning himself to Gemma and grabbing her hands in his.

"Well Gem, I—" but he was cut off by Arty, Pip and Linda coming into the waiting room.

Gemma snatched her hands back and stood up, looking at each of them in turn.

"What's happened?" Robbie joined Gemma, standing and looking at the group. Linda held up her hands and smiled slightly.

"Nothing, nothing. We've just all been talking with Rose and we've made a bit of a plan to run by you both."

"Okay," Gemma said, waiting for her mum to continue.

Robbie crossed his arms and nodded, giving her his full attention.

"So, Robbie, first things first, Rose wants to talk to you, if you don't mind going in to her now, then she wants to talk to Gemma, alone. When you get back, if you don't mind taking us all back to your house? Your dad needs to pack a few things for her and then come back and drop it off. Do you think you could maybe give Gemma a lift home when you come back? There aren't any taxis available for hours because it's a Saturday night." Robbie frowned and glanced down at Gemma for a moment before deciding not to question Linda and nodded.

"Of course." Linda nodded her head towards the door and Robbie shot Gemma another questioning look. Gemma raised her eyebrows and shrugged, also confused with the whole inconspicuousness of the conversation. Robbie left then and Linda turned back to Gemma.

"Right, so Pip and I are going to head back and sort out the house for Arty, Arty is coming back to quickly bring some stuff for Rose and then Robbie can take you back home after. That sound okay?" Gemma gnawed at her bottom lip for a moment, her phone was buzzing in her pocket again. "Gem? What's wrong?" Her mum asked, her blue eyes soft.

"Can… can I stay at yours tonight?" Her mother looked at her for a moment and Gemma waited for her to say anything about Matt, but she never did.

"Of course, you don't need to ask. It will always be your home."

"It's just late and I don't want to wake…" Gemma trailed off.

"You don't need to explain," Linda said softly, grabbing her arm and squeezing it affectionately. "You are always welcome home."

"Thanks, Mum." Gemma wrapped her arms around her quickly, giving her a squeeze. "Okay, so that's the plan," Linda said again and they all sat back down, waiting for Robbie to return. No one really spoke, Pip just lay her head on Gemma's shoulder and closed her eyes while Arty and Linda spoke quietly between each other. After about twenty minutes, Robbie returned. Gemma looked up at him and saw his jaw was tight with his eyes lit with a fiery determination.

What Rose had said, Gemma couldn't even begin to guess but whatever it was, it seemed to have an effect on Robbie. His bright eyes met Gemma's and Gemma could see something going on in his expression.

It was some sort of debate but before Gemma could query him, his decision was made and his head snapped to Linda.

"I'm taking you back now then and coming back for Gemma?"

"Please, Robbie, if that's okay? There aren't any taxis available."

"No problem. Ah…" Robbie turned to Gemma again, "She's erm…" Gemma frowned at Robbie's sudden awkwardness. "Ah, she's waiting for you." He nodded towards the door and corridor leading to Rose's room.

"Okay?" Gemma said, confused by Robbie's whole demeanour. "I'll ah, just go see her then." Robbie nodded.

"So, I'll, ah, be back for you soon."

"See you."

It was all so awkward.

And Gemma had no idea why.

So she hugged Pip and her mum quickly goodbye and left as quickly as she could muster without actually physically running.

She went down the corridor and arrived at Rose's room. She

110

knocked gently and waited for Rose to quietly invite her in. Inside was a typically cold, sterile environment of a hospital room with strong clean smells and beeping machines.

"Gem," Rose sighed, looking tiny in the hospital bed with clean white and blue sheets. Gemma's eyes filled with tears and ran to Rose when she outstretched her arms for Gemma's embrace. Gemma hugged her, probably a little too roughly for her delicate state, but Rose didn't complain. She hugged her so tightly, and for just a couple of moments, they embraced in total companionable silence. Gemma sniffed and pulled herself back, still perching on the side of her bed and taking Rose's cold hand in both of hers.

"You feel cold. Do you need another blanket?"

Rose just smiled and reached up with her free hand and rubbed Gemma's cheek affectionately. "Such a caring girl. You've always cared so much for those around you."

"I love you," Gemma said, pushing her face more into her chilled touch.

"I love you too, Gem. You know you're like a daughter to me."

"I feel the same about you too. I see you all as my family." Rose smiled softly.

"Except Robbie," Rose said bluntly.

Gemma was so shocked by her statement that she coughed and spluttered on the sudden intake of air into her lungs as she gasped. And she did that for several, long, painful moments.

It must have been a good five minutes before Gemma was actually able to respond. And when she did finally get her breathing back to a semi-normal rate, she was flabbergasted.

How the hell did she reply to that? So she went with, "W-W-what?" That was all she managed.

111

Rose smiled again. It was strange, serene and knowledgeable. Like she was some sort of superior monk who know all the world's secrets on peace and love.

"You don't love Robbie the way you love all of us. I am not saying you don't love him," Rose said, holding her hands up as Gemma tried to interrupt. "You are *in* love with him."

Gemma felt her stomach dropping out from beneath her as she stared at Rose. Gemma's jaw swung open but she couldn't close it. Dread started to seep into every fibre of her body. If Rose knew, surely everyone did?

Including Robbie?

"W-w-what?" Was all she managed again.

"Please don't deny it. We haven't got time for that."

"Got time?" Gemma mumbled but Rose was already speaking over her. "Robbie will be back soon. Look, I know you're in love with my son."

"Does he know?" Gemma whispered, her voice so quiet and scared. Rose reached out and took her hand, squeezing it affectionately.

"Don't worry about Robbie. This is more of a conversation about your happiness. Gemma, you cannot be happy with that imbecile?" Rose didn't need to say his name, but Gemma had a clear understanding of who she meant.

"Matt is…"

"He's a dickhead, Gemma."

Gemma spluttered out a laugh, shocked by Rose's lack of tack. "And you deserve to be with someone who treats you much better." Gemma sighed, her shoulders sagging.

"It's complicated," Gemma mumbled, placing her head into her hands.

"I think it's very simple. Dump him and get with someone

who will make you happy."

"And that would be? Tell me. Because I don't know about any young, attractive, kind, caring men who live in Netherby, let alone any that would date someone like me."

"Someone like you?"

"The fat girl, with no interesting qualities or any direction in her life."

"Gemma, don't talk like that. You are beautiful, smart and funny. If a man can't see that, then he isn't worth your time." Gemma couldn't help but roll her eyes at the typical 'mum' response.

"It's not just that though Rose."

"What is it?"

"It's… it's…" Gemma took in a steadying breath and forced her eyes to look into Rose's kind, loving face. "It's her."

"Who?"

"Abi," Gemma whispered and Rose gasped quietly. Her bony hands flew to her face in an attempt to cover the shock. They were silent for a few moments before Rose spoke again.

"Abi? What does Abi have to do with your relationship with Matt?"

"I don't deserve happiness," Gemma whispered, her eyes brimming with unshed tears.

"Why ever not dear?" Rose pulled her hands from her mouth and reached out for Gemma. Gemma walked over and Rose took her hands in hers, looking up at her with those huge brown eyes that Gemma knew so well. They were full of sympathy and pain at Gemma's revelation.

"Because she's not here with me," Gemma breathed, her voice so low and full of emotion, it was hard to speak. "I can't be happy without her, Rose. I just can't. It was my fault. She wouldn't have been there if it hadn't been for me being selfish."

"Oh, my dear." Rose gasped and she brought her in for another tight hug. Gemma began to weep, letting out nearly ten years of pent-up emotions.

"I miss her so much." Gemma was sobbing. "I need her with me. I don't know how to do it without her."

"I know, dear, I know," Rose soothed and Gemma could feel her tears sliding down her own neck. "God, you poor thing. Keeping all of this in for all these years."

That made Gemma sob even harder as she clutched to Rose's slim frame. When Gemma's sobs faded and she was left with her erratic breath, Gemma pulled back from Rose, feeling so hollow. She thought if she had maybe let out the emotions the guilt wouldn't weigh so heavily on her chest.

But it still did. Maybe not as much as it had done previously, but it was like her heart was encased in solid stone, stopping her heart from beating to its full potential.

"Gemma," Rose whispered, taking her face into her hands again. Gemma looked at Rose again and her expression was so kind and full of love. "You deserve to be happy. What happened to Abi was an accident. It wasn't your fault. She wouldn't want you to be unhappy. She loved you so much. She would want you to be happy, Gemma."

Gemma bit down on her lip, she didn't have the energy to contradict her.

She felt so emotionally drained, so she just nodded and Rose smiled softly. She leaned forward and kissed her on the cheek.

"Now, go home darling. Get some sleep. And please," she emphasised that last one, "please, please, please. Please think about your own happiness. You deserve it, Gemma."

Gemma half-heartedly smiled and nodded. She stood up,

kissing Rose on the cheek quickly before leaving the room, feeling oddly disembodied.

She staggered along the corridor again and back into the waiting room, where Arty and Robbie were waiting for Gemma. Gemma found herself unable to look at Robbie, almost scared that he would discover her apparently poorly kept secret also. Both boys left Gemma in the waiting room quickly as they dropped off supplies and clothes for Rose and said a quick goodbye. What seemed about two minutes after, they both rejoined her in the waiting room.

They then left, saying little between them as they made their way back to the car park near the entrance and out into the chilly spring night air. Gemma wrapped her exposed arms around her middle, shuddering at the sudden chill in the air. It was late spring and nearly summer but apparently still cold.

"Are you cold?" Robbie asked her suddenly and her eyes snapped up to his. His face was only lit slightly by the orange light from a nearby streetlight. But even in the semi-darkness, Gemma knew his face so well. She could see every contour of his face. She knew every shade of brown in his big eyes. She knew his jaw was straight and strong. And when he was angry or upset, you could see the muscles visible tightening. She knew that he had one protruding vein on the left side of his neck that stuck out when he spoke or laughed. She knew every curve and line on his Adam's apple when it lifted and fell whenever he swallowed or spoke. She knew absolutely everything about his face and body in excruciating detail that it haunted all her thoughts and dreams.

Gemma found herself looking at every inch of his features in turn, marvelling at the sheer beauty that an individual could possess.

And her insides burned and yearned so much for him, that it

made Gemma physically sick.

Another shiver ricocheted through her body, but this time it was nothing to do with the chilly night air.

"A little," Gemma finally replied, licking her drying lips and trying to line her dry throat more. She watched Robbie's eye track the movement and she felt her heart rate picking up slightly at the sight. Gemma watched his Adam's apple bob up and down for a moment before he started to shrug off his jacket and pass it over to her.

"Oh no, Robbie, I'm fine honestly."

But Robbie had already pushed it into her hands. "Take it, please." Gemma mumbled a lame "thanks" and started to shrug on the jacket. It was large, warm and smelled divine. Gemma pulled it around her closer, taking a deep, secret breath. Her clothes would smell of Robbie when she had to return the jacket and something about that made Gemma's heart race with excitement.

"Come on," Robbie said, a little gruffly as he watched Gemma for a couple of moments, looking at her wrapped in his jacket. He cleared his throat and started back towards his car. Gemma stumbled along behind them and finally caught up with them. She went to go into the back seat, but Arty reached out and covered her hand with his as she grabbed the door handle.

"I'll sit in the back dear, Robbie said he's going to drop me off first, if that's okay? I'm exhausted and your mum's on the way back to his."

"Of course. I don't mind trying—" but Robbie cut her off.

"Don't even say the word 'taxi'."

Gemma smiled, glancing up at him. But Robbie wasn't smiling, he was watching her intently, his jaw tight. Gemma's smile faltered and her throat dried instantly. The intensity that

Robbie was looking at her made her whole being stutter and falter under his gaze. Then he suddenly turned on his heel and walked a few more steps to his car.

Confused again by Robbie's whole behaviour, Gemma followed and slid into the slightly awkward, silent car.

They continued to drive on in silence.

Gemma's mind was full of Rose's words. She was repeating them over and over in her head as she pictured Abi's face.

Would she really want Gemma to not be happy? The short answer was no.

Abi was incredibly selfless and loved Gemma, she would want her to be happy. But could Gemma allow herself to be?

Suddenly, Gemma looked out the window and noticed Robbie had pulled up outside his parent's house. Arty was getting out of the back, saying his goodbyes as he clasped onto Robbie's shoulder, then Gemma's before he left the house. Both Gemma and Robbie watched his retreating figure. He looked physically and mentally drained and that was just by looking at his back.

Gemma glanced up at Robbie, who still had his eyes on his father's retreating back. "Do you think he'll be okay?" Gemma asked softly and Robbie's eyes snapped back to Gemma's face. Gemma's breath caught by the intensity of his stare. All thoughts of Arty or Abi suddenly vanished from the forefront of her mind. All she could see Robbie. All she could feel was Robbie in that small, slick sports car.

Robbie broke the gaze again, turning his head suddenly to the front and the car purred back to life again. Gemma blinked stupidly, looking away, trying to gather her scattered thoughts once more.

Gemma couldn't keep up with the constantly changing moods.

They drove in another awkward silence and Gemma chewed her bottom lip. Robbie glanced at her out of the corner of his eye. And a few times, Gemma thought he might break that awful silence. But his mouth snapped shut as he gripped the steering wheel with white knuckles. Gemma nearly cried with relief when they pulled onto her mum's street, her hand braced on the door handle so she could fling herself from the car as soon as they stopped. Robbie pulled up and Gemma turned to him quickly. She didn't look him in the eye as she didn't want to be locked in that intense stare again, to only be dropped, confused and perplexed.

"Well," Gemma said, painfully awkward. "Thanks for the ride. Let me know how she is in the morning?" Gemma watched as Robbie's Adam's apple bobbed as he swallowed. He nodded and Gemma sighed slightly. "Well, um, goodnight, Robbie." And with that, she pulled the door handle and stepped out into the night. She walked up the small path that led to her mother's snug two-up-two-down and rummaged in her pocket for her keys.

It was then she realised that she was still wearing Robbie's coat. She spun on her heel, Robbie's name on the tip of her tongue but words failed her.

Robbie was striding up the path, with a determined glint in his eyes.

"Robbie?" was all Gemma managed because, in a couple of long strides, Robbie had cleared the space between them. He wrapped one long arm around her waist, pulling Gemma to him while the other went to the back of her head and into her hair. Robbie closed his eyes and pulled Gemma's face up, so that she was looking up, watching his face coming towards hers.

It was like it was happening in slow motion. Gemma watched as Robbie's full lips came down to hers. His breath was hot on her face as he closed the gap between them.

And so, nearing midnight on a Saturday evening, on the street outside her mother's house, Robbie Wilson kissed Gemma Walker. And with the words of Rose still ringing in Gemma's ears, she let go of all her pain and guilt for a night and kissed him back.

And it was not for the first time during their nearly two-decade acquaintance.

CHAPTER NINE

Ten Years Earlier

Gemma had spent the rest of the term trying to avoid Miranda and Robbie. It was made even more difficult by the fact that Miranda and Robbie's new favourite make out spot was Robbie's locker. Their antics often meant that they sprawled over Gemma's locker too. So Gemma took it upon herself to pack her school bag with all the books and equipment she would need each day and only visit her locker as school finished. This had worked; Gemma didn't stumble upon the couple as much as she had once done, but it also meant lugging a huge rucksack with all her books in. The term finally ended and with Christmas and New Year to look forward to, the school bell finally rang for the last time that year. There was a general cheer from all the students and a buzz that meant holidays were finally upon them. Gemma was just happy to not be lugging around six textbooks all day and she wouldn't have to stumble upon Robbie and Miranda any more.

Gemma and Robbie still worked on the weekends together and Miranda often came in to visit Robbie but she would have to remain at her table and wasn't allowed out back. There, in the seclusion of the back and away from Miranda's eyes, Robbie would be tentative and kind towards Gemma. They would talk about anything and everything. And all the while they talked, Robbie's eyes would be on Gemma like she was the only one in the world. To say it was confusing for Gemma was an understatement. The second they were out the front and in the public eye again, Robbie would change.

He near enough ignored Gemma.

Gemma knew she shouldn't entertain Robbie if he could talk to her in private but not when they were in public. She couldn't do it. Having Robbie's sole attention for those few secluded moments each week made her feel on top of the world for a short while.

So that's how they had continued, week after week.

One Friday night, in those weird few days between Christmas and New Year, Gemma and Robbie were working their usual Friday shift. It was a strangely quiet shift so Gemma and Robbie were taking extra time to sort out cutlery pots and condiment stands.

"How was your Christmas?" Robbie asked as the cutlery thumped rhythmically into the pots.

"Ah," Gemma shrugged, "all right. Mum and Granddad got a bit drunk and the roast was ruined. But it's all good because the pudding was lit... literally."

Robbie laughed. "Your mum is always drunk."

"Not always! Just Christmas mostly." And they both laughed. "How was your Christmas?"

"All right. Mum still can't get over the fact that Pip has stopped believing in Santa so she's gutted that we don't get excited any more. It's been bloody years and she still hopes that we'll get all excited again."

"Aw, poor Rose. I miss the magic of Christmas, to be honest."

"Yeah, I used to love waking up and going through my stocking that Santa had left."

"I never had a stocking really. Just a present at the end to

121

keep me busy until my mum got up because I wasn't allowed to get up until at least six."

"Pip and me used to get up about four. It's disgusting thinking about it now."

"You're such a Grinch."

"Hey, don't mock *The Grinch*. That's a boss film."

"True, true. One of my favourites." They fell into a companionable silence and just the *thud, thud, thud* of the cutlery filled the air for a few moments.

"What are you doing for New Year?" Robbie suddenly asked into the silence and Gemma looked at him surprised.

"Ah, nothing. Probably working, why?" He seemed to be debating something internally. "I'm having a party at mine. You should come. Bring Abi again if you want." Gemma blinked at him, still surprised. Anxiety started to ripple through her stomach, squeezing her insides and making her chest feel tight. She had sworn she wouldn't go to another of Robbie's parties and over the past few weeks, he had had a few and she was never invited.

It was painful, but she would tell herself it was for the best. She didn't want to face humiliation again. But as her eyes met Robbie's her breath faltered. His huge eyes were wide and he looked so vulnerable. It looked like Robbie actually wanted her to go and he was nervous about asking her.

Why would Robbie ever be nervous about asking Gemma anything? "You want me to come to your New Year's party?"

"Ah, yes? That's why I asked. If you're not doing anything." His attempt at a joke was poor and his words awkward and clumsy.

"I'm not doing anything," Gemma said quickly, frowning slightly at the strangely flustered Robbie. He was fidgeting and tapping his fingers on his legs repeatedly.

"Good, good." He nodded, averting his eyes from her and nodding. He repeated what he said again and Gemma just frowned at him again. There was another silence that followed, but this one was awkward. Robbie cleared his throat and Gemma shuffled on the balls of her feet.

"Um, so what time?" She hadn't meant to ask such a lame question, but the awkward silence made her panic.

"What?"

"What time is your party starting?"

"Oh…" Robbie said and he half smiled. "There isn't really a start time. Guess when people finish turning up. It's not an official thing."

"Oh… well… what time is that?" And Robbie laughed and Gemma swatted his arm. "Hey, I don't go to these things."

"What, parties?"

"Yes!"

"What about my birthday?" There was another awkward silence as their eyes met. Gemma didn't reply and Robbie cleared his throat. He turned his eyes back to his lap and swallowed a couple of times. Gemma watched his Adam's apple quiver and bob up and down. Robbie must have sensed she was looking at him because his eyes suddenly shot up. Gemma managed to avert her gaze to her own lap, but it had been obvious that she had been looking at him. Her cheeks burned under his gaze, but she didn't dare look back up.

"Okay, come about eight. Everyone will probably be there by then."

"Thank you," Gemma said and she let out a sigh of relief. And just then, Linda called them back out to help out the front as it had got busier. Nothing else was really discussed for the rest of the shift, but Gemma kept watching Robbie. She was confused as to why he had invited her at all. Her stomach twisted and turned with nerves. Why had she agreed?

Surely Robbie had to like her a little to invite her along?

Gemma tried to not hope too much, but as the shift came to an end and Robbie waved to her goodbye, Gemma couldn't help but feel a little hopeful and excited.

Robbie had left with a babbling Miranda on his arm, beaming up at him and throwing herself all over him. Yet Robbie had stopped before they left, turned and looked for Gemma. He had looked for her and Gemma was sure his face broke into a smile at the sight of her.

And he waved and smiled.

It was enough to send Gemma's heart speeding.

Yes, it was just a smile and a wave, but to a girl like Gemma, when the boy you've been in love with for years seeks you out for a wave and a smile, you get a little bit excited. Even if you suddenly remember you agreed to go to another party that Gemma knew would surely end with her crying over him yet again.

A couple of days later, Gemma and Abi were in the back of Abi's dad's car, on the way to Robbie's party. Even though Abi was reluctant to go to another one of Robbie's parties, she didn't complain. She even did Gemma's makeup nicely again. Gemma was wearing a flattering dress, though maybe a little older in style compared to the fashion trend for young women at that time, but Gemma felt pretty good.

"Here we are, girls. Now have fun. Abs, call me when you're ready for picking up. Yeah? See you girls later."

"Thanks, Dad," Abi said and she leaned forward and kissed

her dad on the cheek before getting out of the car. "I can't believe we're invited to *another* Robbie Wilson party." Gemma tumbled out of the car and joined Abi on the other side. "He must be so into you," Abi said and she grinned at her. Gemma's cheeks flushed scarlet.

"Shut up, he doesn't fancy me. Bet his mum asked him to invite me again."

"Pfft... whatever!" And Abi strolled ahead, taking Gemma's hand.

Abi went through the front door, as it was already propped open, and down the hall towards the kitchen. There was music pumping and Gemma could literally feel the beat of the music pumping through her feet. It was one of the latest pop songs blasting and Abi turned to her and rolled her eyes.

"Argh, is Gaga playing? Vom."

"Oh, it's the Emo and Roly-Poly," said Matt, who just seemed to materialise out of nowhere. He looked Abi up and down with a disgusted look before he turned his attention to Gemma. Gemma felt extremely self-conscious as Matt's eyes seemed to survey her much longer than he did with Abi. There was an expression behind his eyes that Gemma wasn't familiar with. Gemma could only describe it as hunger. But that was stupid because Matt would never rack his eyes over her body... *hungrily*.

It wouldn't have made sense.

So whatever Matt was doing, he did it for a few more moments before he spoke again. "Jesus, Roly-Poly. Why are you wearing my nan's curtains? Fuck me." But as he threw his insult at her, he kept looking her body up and down with his unknown expression.

It made Gemma very uncomfortable.

"Gemma," a voice said behind her and she spun around. It was Robbie and he, too, looked her up and down.

Why was everybody looking at her that way? She glanced at Abi and she was smiling to herself as Robbie ignored her.

"You came," Robbie said quietly and his eyes finally made it back to hers. Gemma's breath caught as she was lost in his eyes for a moment.

"I said I would…" she said, a little lamely, but thinking was becoming difficult.

"Do you have a drink?" he asked and he indicated to the kitchen bench behind them that was piled with many bottles of alcohol and mixers.

"Ah no, how did you get this past your mum?" Behind her, Matt scoffed meanly but Gemma ignored him.

Her cheeks were already flushed with embarrassment about asking such a lame question.

Robbie took pity on her. "What she doesn't know won't hurt her."

"Where is she?"

"At the pub, I think. She said if your mum couldn't go to a party, she'd bring the party to her." He rolled his eyes, shaking his head. Gemma smiled as he poured her an alcohol that was dark and almost looked like rum and mixed it with coke. He handed it to her and she took a sip. She coughed and Robbie laughed. "Sorry, too strong?" But Gemma shook her head, trying to be suave about the whole situation. She looked at Abi (with slightly watering eyes) and passed her the drink. Abi took a swig and didn't even blink.

"Perfect," was all Abi said and she drank some more.

Gemma laughed and shook her head. Robbie had already made her another and when she drank again, it was less strong and much more pleasant.

"So you've been spared at the pub tonight then?"

"Yeah, the cutlery can wait a night."

"Mate, that place would fall apart without us." Gemma laughed.

"Yeah, we keep that place going. Not a single table without condiments or cutlery on our watch." Robbie threw his head back and laughed and Gemma couldn't help but smile. Robbie's laugh died off and they both looked at each other for a moment. It was a loaded moment and Gemma felt her heartbeat in her throat as Robbie's eyes bored into hers. A few loaded moments passed as they stared at each other.

Should she be the one to break the stare?

Could she break the stare?

She seemed to be frozen in time. They both did. Whatever was happening between them, they were both frozen in place.

"Um, hello? Robbie? What's so funny?" A loud and slightly annoyed voice finally broke their gaze. Robbie was blinking and frowning down at the voice. Gemma looked down and her heart immediately sank.

It was Miranda.

She was dressed in a crop top that showed off her entire toned midriff and tight, well-fitted and very low-rise jeans. Gemma felt something between envy and insecurity rise up within her.

"Uh," was all Robbie managed before Miranda shrugged, obviously deeming whatever Robbie was going to say as unimportant and pulled him towards her and kissing him right on the mouth.

Gemma looked away, trying to swallow the bile that was now in her mouth, but before she fully turned away, she saw Miranda looking at her while she was kissing Robbie.

And while Robbie was somewhat preoccupied, Gemma slipped away, looking for Abi. She found her in the back garden, sitting on a low wall. Gemma sat down too and passed an hour or so watching their surrounding classmates, laughing and drinking.

An hour and a decent amount of alcohol consumed later, Gemma groaned as she watched Matt make his way to them, swaying as he went.

"Evening ladies," he hiccupped, clearly a lot more buzzed than either Gemma or Abi.

They glanced at each other and Abi had a slight grimace on her face.

"What do you want, Matt?" Abi asked, not hiding her irritation in the slightest.

"Nothing from you, Abigail, that's for sure."

Abi looked at Gemma for a moment, with raised eyebrows. "What do you want?" she asked again.

"Wanted to see if Roly-Poly wanted to get a drink."

Gemma just stared at him. "A drink?" she said after a few moments of silence.

"Yes," he said slowly and looked at Gemma like she was stupid. Gemma certainly felt stupid.

"Uh…" Was all Gemma managed before more of Matt's cronies quite literally dived on top of him and he was swallowed in a testosterone sea of yells and friendly punches.

"Saved by the brainless jocks," Abi muttered and she indicated with a nod that her and Gemma should make their escape. Gemma was more than happy to. Just as they were leaving, Miranda intercepted them.

"Hey! Roly-Poly!" Gemma physically sagged, before she took in a deep breath and turned back to Miranda. She was grinning but Gemma saw the malicious glint in her eyes. "Where are you going?"

"Um," Gemma said and she glanced at Abi, who was glaring at Miranda, before she continued. "Just back inside."

"To find Robbie?" And there was a snicker from the sea of meatheads behind her. "N-no. I don't know where he is."

"Sure you don't," she said and there was another snicker behind her. "You should just leave. You know that you don't belong here. He only invited you because his mum asked." There was a stab in Gemma's chest, but she kept her head high.

Gemma wanted to say some sort of witty remark, but she wasn't brave enough. Abi, apparently, was though.

"Oh yeah? Is that really why he asked or do you suspect something else? You must see what we all see. That's why you're always such a bitch to Gemma."

Gemma watched Miranda's face turn mutinous and the crowd behind her was thickening. Gemma couldn't cope with everyone pointing and staring at Gemma. She simply couldn't cope with the attention.

"Abi," Gemma said quietly, grabbing her arm. "Stop, please." But to Gemma's horror, someone else had joined the crowd of people now.

Robbie.

No, no, no, no, no.

This couldn't be happening.

"Well," said Miranda in a menacing tone, "why don't we ask him then?"

"Abi!" Gemma squeaked and she looked at her, panicked like a caged animal.

"Yeah, do that! Then we'll see who's really right!" Abi said, ignoring Gemma's pleas.

"Hey, Robbie!" Miranda shouted and waved him over. Gemma's heart sunk at the sight of him, looking between Gemma and Miranda.

"What's up?" he asked.

"Well, we just wanted to settle a debate. Didn't we, Gemma?" Miranda said sweetly, fluttering her eyelashes innocently.

"About what?"

"Nothing!" Gemma said quickly, before turning to Abi and adding, "We were just leaving." She grabbed Abi's arm forcibly and tugged her back to the house. "Call your dad Abi."

"Well," Miranda said loudly, ignoring Gemma completely. "We wanted to ask you, once and for all," and Gemma gasped as Miranda steam rolled on, "Do you want to be with Roly-Poly over me?"

Silence.

A deafening, painful silence.

Robbie was looking at Gemma, then Miranda, then the crowd behind them, then Gemma and repeating again and again.

Gemma didn't know how long had actually passed but the longer that silenced dragged out the more dread filled Gemma. She wished Robbie would say something, even if he just laughed it off in usual Robbie style. But he then looked at Gemma, just for a second and Gemma could see something flitter across his face.

Pain?

Asking forgiveness?

Now Robbie was the caged animal, panic all over his face. Then he finally spoke. "What?" He scoffed, as he started to laugh. It wasn't his usual light, infectious laugh. It was strained and fake. Gemma's stomach dropped. She knew what he was going to do and she couldn't bare it. Her eyes filled with tears as she bit her lip and watched Robbie. She just couldn't look away. "Me?" He said sneeringly, "And Roly-Poly?" He cackled again and Gemma could feel the tears rolling down her cheeks. "Yeah right!" Everyone behind then laughed and jeered before he added menacingly.

"In her dreams."

Gemma felt the air being sucked from her lungs. She was looking at Robbie, who was avoiding her gaze. Everyone else seemed to fade into the background and all she could look at was Robbie. This wasn't someone she knew, she didn't recognise the boy standing in front of her. He was still avoiding her eye and the background started to come back into Gemma's peripheral vision. Gemma went to leave, but before she could flee, she saw Abi step forward her eyes on Robbie.

"You absolute coward," she said, quietly but everyone was looking at her silently. "You fucking coward. How dare you—"

"Abi, just drop it," Gemma said and it was much harsher than she had planned. Abi turned to her confused.

"But he *is* a coward!" she yelled and Gemma felt herself getting angry and defensive. "He doesn't like me! He's just made that abundantly clear."

"You're seriously defending him?"

"Not defending, Abi, just talking the truth. Boys like Robbie do not go out with girls like me. Everyone knows it, Miranda knows it, Robbie knows it and even *I* know it. Why can't you?"

"Because he's clearly got feelings for you!"

"No, he doesn't! He's just said so!"

"That's because—"

"Enough, Abi! Just shut up!" And there was a collective gasp and even some jeering from the jocks again. Gemma couldn't help it, she didn't want to be humiliated any more. "I am humiliated, are you happy now? Everyone now knows, with stunning clarity, that Robbie Wilson does not fancy me. Robbie Wilson would never go out with Roly-Poly, Gemma Walker."

"Gemma…"Abi said and she stepped forwards.

"Just stop Abi! Drop it and leave me alone!"

"Gemma—"

"No! I've had enough! You've fucking done enough! Just leave! I don't want to see you again!" She didn't want to see anyone ever again. The look of hurt on Abi's face didn't register to Gemma at that moment, but it would be etched in her memories for the rest of Gemma's life. "Leave!" Gemma shouted again. Deep down, she knew it wasn't Abi's fault, but it was easier to blame her than Robbie.

It was easier to blame her best friend than the boy she loved. That was just too painful. So Abi, after one final glare at Robbie, turned and left. Gemma was shaking, the tears were brimming up in her eyes and she was really trying to hold it together in front of half the school.

When Abi's retreating figure had disappeared, Gemma made off up to the house as well, heading for Pip's bedroom so as to avoid Abi while she waited for her dad out front.

It took Gemma a moment to realise that it wasn't silent. There were shouts and jeers from people, all shouting out things to her and smacking their lips and making kissing noises as she passed. She must have drowned out the noise during her fight with Abi.

How could she do that to her? Put her on the spot with Robbie like that?

She must have known Gemma would have been humiliated when he rejected her in front of all those people. Gemma finally

132

made it to the safety of Pip's room. She was out at a friend's house for the night, she didn't want to be present for another one of Robbie's "dickhead filled parties" as she so plainly said. Gemma should have followed her lead. She should have said no to Robbie, once and for all. She slid into Pip's room and she shut the door firmly behind her.

She called her mum, and to her dismay, a ride home wouldn't be at least until after midnight.

"They were swamped," was all she said. At the pub, her mum and granddad were working flat out, so Gemma had to hide in Pip's bedroom for at least another hour. Though it was near midnight, it would take a while for last orders and the clean-up before one of them was freed up to come and get her. Gemma threw herself onto Pip's unmade bed and buried her face into her pillow as the sobs threatened to overcome her. Some time passed and Gemma's sobs seemed to slow down until she was able to breathe more evenly again. Gemma then turned over and looked up at the ceiling, as silent tears flowed down her face.

How could she have allowed herself to hope? How could she even consider a possibility? Stupid, *stupid* girl.

She could hear the party still going on around her and she just prayed that her granddad would be there soon. She was listening to the steady beat of the music when she heard a slight tapping on the door. She bolted up and her heart quite literally jumped up into her throat. Before she could enquire who was knocking, the door opened and to Gemma's shock and horror, Robbie slid through the little gap he had made. Gemma leaped up and moved to the far corner of the small, crammed with crap, room.

"Gemma," Robbie said, once he had shut and *locked* the door behind him. Why hadn't Gemma remembered the lock? She kicked herself internally. "Gem…" Robbie said again, looking hesitant and almost anxious as he stood by the door.

"Oh," said Gemma quietly, shocked she could actually speak through the shock of seeing Robbie. "Oh, it's *Gem* now, is it? Not Roly-Poly? Now that you're not in front of your goonies, you can call me Gem again?"

Robbie cringed at the venom in her voice. Gemma kept her head high and tried not to think of the irony of her bravery now she too, wasn't in front of said goonies.

"I'm—"

"Sorry?" Gemma scoffed. "No, you're not, Robbie. You just said what everyone else knew."

"No!" he said quickly and Gemma just frowned at him.

"Yes, you did. Now, please, leave me alone. I've done enough crying over you today." Robbie seemed to flinch at her words but Gemma realised she didn't care any more.

She was done with it.

"I'm done." She said quietly, "I'm done with it all. I'm sick of hoping that you'll smile at me at school. I'm sick of wishing that you would talk to me in school like you do in the pub. I am sick of thinking I am seeing something that clearly isn't there."

"I—"

"No, Robbie, I'm serious. I have had enough. Go back to your party and I'll leave when my granddad arrives. I won't embarrass you any more."

"You don't embarrass me."

Gemma actually laughed at that. "Yeah, okay," she said and she sat back down on the squeaking bed again, her head in her hands and her eyes on the floor. It took Robbie less than two strides to cover the room and found himself kneeling in front of Gemma. He grabbed her wrists and pulled her hands from her face until she was blinking wide-eyed at him. Neither Robbie nor Gemma could have guessed what would happen next but within half a second, Robbie had thrown his face forward until his lips were pressed against Gemma's. It wasn't the slow head-bending manoeuvre that Gemma had always imagined. It wasn't the slow, seductive fusing of lips she had so often fantasised about.

Robbie was kissing Gemma with an urgency that she could have never imagined. His hands were on the sides of her face as he held her face to his, clearly not wanting her to pull back.

Gemma wouldn't have done anyway.

Though Gemma had no experience, she knew she was lost within his kiss. Robbie was leading the kiss, he was tilting his head this way and that as his lips moulded and moved with hers with such a determination that Gemma felt light-headed. Gemma could feel his tongue licking her lips for entry and when Gemma obliged and opened her mouth, Robbie's tongue darted into her mouth and led the way. Robbie had moved from the ground to sit next to her on the bed.

Gemma could hear something outside, but it felt like it was reaching her through a tunnel filled with water. Almost off in the distance somewhere, not there, in Pip's bedroom with Robbie's lips on hers.

The muffled noise at the party sounded like... counting?

Robbie must have heard it as well because he pulled back and glanced at the door for a moment before he looked back at Gemma. His gaze was warm as he gazed into her eyes as the counting continued. Gemma had never seen him so flushed as his gaze so alight with something Gemma had never seen before.

There was a blazing fire in his eyes that made Gemma feel weak. She just wasn't used to being looked at like that. Like she was the most beautiful person in the world.

There was still a murmur of noise outside and as Gemma stopped and focused on the noise she realised they were counting.

"Three, two, one!" then there was a general cry of "Happy New Year!" and whistles and shouts. Gemma looked back at Robbie and he was looking at her again with those blazing eyes.

"Happy New Year, Gem," he whispered and he brought his face back to hers and kissed her again. The kiss depended and Gemma could feel Robbie's body pushing into hers so that she came to be laying back on the bed, with Robbie beside her.

She couldn't believe how it felt. It was nothing she had ever imagined, and she had fantasised about anything and everything to do with Robbie.

At first, Gemma wasn't aware of her phone vibrating in her coat pocket. It was quite easy to ignore it when Robbie's mouth was on hers. But the vibrating seemed to jolt some sense back into Gemma. She pulled away and looked down at her pocket.

"What?" Robbie asked softly and she looked back at him.

"My... my phone. I think my granddad is here." Realisation seemed to flitter across Robbie's face, but he seemed unwilling to move.

They stayed like that for a moment, just holding each other and looking into each other's eyes. Gemma's phone went off again and this time Robbie could hear it too. He sighed and got up and pulled Gemma up with him. She pulled her phone out and saw three missed calls from her granddad and groaned.

"I better go, I don't how long he's been out there for." Robbie nodded and Gemma went to the door, Robbie followed her out of Pip's room, through the relatively quiet hall, down the stairs and out the front. They walked in silence up the path and in the dark, Robbie's hand found hers in the darkness and their fingers entwined. As they walked, Gemma's phone went off again.

"Argh, sorry," she said as she reluctantly let go of his hand. "Better answer before he comes looking for me." And as she pulled it out, she grimaced because the name on the ID was her mother's.

Not a good sign.

"Hi," Gemma said, as she rolled her eyes at Robbie. "Sorry Mum, I've only just seen Granddad's calls. It was uh... loud in there. I'm coming now."

"Gemma?" Her tone instantly put fear into Gemma. "Oh Gemma, thank God! Thank God! Dad! She's okay!" Gemma could hear her granddad responding with his relief. He said something about going to pick her up. He hadn't even set off yet. Gemma's heart gave a sickening jolt.

Something was wrong.

"Of course I'm okay. Mum, what's wrong? I thought Granddad was already here?"

"No, h-he hasn't set off yet." She took a deep breath before continuing. "S-Something has happened..." And she stopped and Gemma waited with bated breath. "Something has happened to Abi."

Gemma's whole world started to crumble around her and she could feel herself shaking with such ferocity, her teeth clamped together. Before Gemma could speak, before she could even draw breath, Linda spoke again.

"They're at the hospital. There's been a car crash."

CHAPTER TEN

Present Day

Robbie brought his lips to Gemma's slowly and after a few soft, slow kisses, there was a sudden heat that seemed to spread from their adjoined lips. Gemma's hands seemed to move without conscious thought. They moved their way up his strong arms, up his neck and finally found his hair. Her fingers gripped into his hair and held onto him with all her strength. Robbie's hands moved from Gemma's face so that one entwined around her waist and the other on her bum. He pulled her to him so that there was no space between them. She could feel *all* of him pressed against her. Robbie seemed to push Gemma back, until she found herself pressed up against a cold wall, or possibly her mum's front door. Robbie's lips kissed the side of Gemma's mouth, down to her jaw and down to her neck. Gemma arched her neck as if to give him greater access. Her hands were still gripping into his hair as the thrill of his lips on her neck sent shivers through her.

"Robbie," she whispered and he moaned quickly before he moved back to her mouth again. Gemma felt a thrill of pleasure at the sound. It gave her pleasure to hear his groans of desire. Something stirred deep within Gemma's gut. It was like something had awoken in her and she was being consumed by the heat and passion. She couldn't believe how much she *wanted* Robbie. He was arching his body against hers and Gemma couldn't believe how right it felt. It was like they were meant to hold each other in this way. In that moment, everything in the world felt right for the first time in ten years.

Gemma was in two minds about dragging him into her mum's house. She was surprised she felt comfortable enough with him that she even considered it. But before she could make a decision, a car driving way too fast down the road, honked and someone shouted out the window to them.

They broke apart, looking at the car, full of young lads, wolf-whistling. They sped past and Gemma instantly snapped back to reality. She looked up at Robbie, not believing what she had just done. Yes, Matt was a controlling, unloving man, but he still was technically her boyfriend. But kissing Robbie had shown her how *good* he made her feel and what she was missing. She knew Matt didn't deserve her respect, but Gemma needed to finish things with him before she ever considered starting anything with Robbie.

"Robbie."

"No, don't say anything," Robbie half-heartedly begged.

Gemma had to laugh and she leaned forwards so that her head was resting on his. "I have to break up with Matt."

"Yes, yes you do."

"I'll do it tomorrow."

"Not right now?" Robbie pulled a puppy dog pleading expression. "Then maybe—" but whatever Robbie was going to suggest was interrupted by Gemma's phone. It vibrated and went off at full volume. Robbie sighed, "One day, I will get rid of that phone. Your phone is always interrupting us."

"Always interrupting?" Gemma looked up at him with raised eyebrows as she tried to fish it out of her small, compact bag. "Hardly, it's been ten years since the last time it interrupted us." Gemma glanced down at her phone. The phone stopped ringing just as she pulled it out.

"That's two times too many," he said under his breath and looked at Gemma, frowning. "Who was it?"

"Matt." Gemma sighed again.

"He doesn't deserve you, Gemma," Robbie said quietly and he placed his hand under her chin and lifted it so that her eyes met his. Gemma melted into his touch, shutting her eyes against his caressing hand. "You deserve someone who will make you happy."

Gemma's stomach suddenly jerked and her eyes flew open. A wave of guilt submerged her every cell as she remembered Abi. Could she ever really forget her reasons for not allowing herself happiness?

"What?" Robbie said, looking at her. He took her face in both hands, looking deeply into her eyes. Gemma took a steading breath, trying to think of the words.

"I don't deserve happiness, Robbie," was all she could muster and Robbie's eyes were wide with pain and shock.

"Yes, yes you do Gemma. Why would you say that?"

But Gemma shook her head, regretting being honest with Robbie. "It doesn't matter." She sighed, her eyes drifting down.

Robbie's hands found her chin again and he lifted her eyes again. This time, he smiled softly, leaning down to kiss her again. It was a long, delicate and gentle kiss. It made Gemma sink into Robbie's chest and sigh happily. Gemma's arms wound around Robbie's neck as he pulled back slightly.

"I suppose I should head in." She didn't want to, she wanted Robbie to come in with her, deep down. But she just didn't feel brave enough for that just yet. Robbie smiled too and he leaned forwards and placed a kiss on her forehead. He kept his lips resting against her head for a moment, shutting his eyes and taking a deep breath. They were silent for a few moments, embracing.

"You have no idea how long I've wanted to do this," Robbie murmured against her forehead, squeezing her closer.

Gemma couldn't help but smile. "Probably not as long as I have wanted to do this."

"You have no idea."

"I would invite you in…" Gemma trailed off, looking down at her feet again, feeling the heat rising in her cheeks. She felt brazen suggesting it, but Robbie made her feel so comfortable she almost didn't feel scared.

Standing with Robbie's arms around her, she felt comfortable. Robbie smiled gently at her blush, caressing her reddening cheeks.

"As much I would like to go inside," he leaned down and rubbed her nose with his, placing another sweet kiss on her lips, "and you have no idea how much restraint it is taking, by the way," Gemma flushed even deeper, "when I do finally get to make love to you, I want it to be a fresh start. For you to be all mine."

"I will break up with Matt tomorrow." Gemma sounded slightly desperate as she very much wanted Robbie to make love to her. "I will."

"Good. Then I'll see you tomorrow?" Robbie's eyes were wide and shinning in the darkness. Gemma couldn't speak, she was mesmerised by them so she just nodded. Robbie's face broke into a breathtaking smile. "Good. Now, one more kiss before I drag myself away." And without any more words, Robbie leaned down and they kissed again. It was another passionate, warm kiss that made Gemma's toes curl with anticipation.

Then after a few more kisses, Robbie pulled away. They said

their goodbyes and Gemma watched him pull off in his sports car while she opened the door. She slid in, snuck upstairs and into her childhood bedroom. She threw herself on the bed, looking up at the ceiling, smiling uncontrollably.

And not for the first time, Gemma was lying in her old bedroom, in her old bed, thinking about Robbie Wilson and remembering the feeling of his lips on hers.

The next morning, Gemma and her mum went to open the pub. She still hadn't seen Matt and her stomach was turning over with anxiety. She knew she had to break up with Matt, but the nerves were starting to really build. She wanted to get it over with. She assumed Matt would be waiting for her at the pub entrance, but he wasn't. Then he didn't come in when the pub was opened and even a couple of hours later. His absence might have once been a comfort to Gemma, but it made her uneasy.

Gemma even tried to call him a couple of times, but both times went through to voicemail. By lunchtime, Gemma's nerves were shot.

Gemma was bending down behind the bar after the lunchtime rush, her mind still on what she was going to say to Matt when someone called her name. She jumped because the voice that had called her name wasn't Matt as she expected.

It was Robbie.

"Robbie!" she called out, feeling her cheeks flushing as she remembered their kiss the night before. "How... how is your mum doing?"

"She's better thank you. They still want to keep her in to monitor her but she's much better."

"Oh, that's brilliant news! Oh, Robbie! I'm so happy for you guys!"

"Thanks again for coming last night, I couldn't have got through it without you."

"Oh," Gemma said as she shrugged off his praise, "Oh Robbie, it's nothing. I didn't do anything."

"You did more than you could ever know." And at that, he reached across and squeezed her hand in thanks. She squeezed it back and their eyes locked for a moment. It was only a short moment however because Linda decided it was a good time to come back to the bar. Their entwined hands dropped instantly and Gemma felt her cheeks beginning to flush again.

"Robbie! How's Rose? Your dad sent me a message this morning but nothing since."

"She's much better thanks, think she'll be up for another visit today if you're up to it?"

"Of course! I was planning to swing by later this afternoon."

"You can go now, Mum," Gemma said and she looked at her with raised eyebrows. "Lunch rush is over and I've got Tilly in as extra anyway so there's no rush to come back."

"Are you sure?"

"No, that's why I offered." Gemma rolled her eyes at Robbie who laughed. "Yes, of course I am sure. Go be with Rose. It'll cheer her up and you need it too."

Linda smiled and she leaned in and kissed Gemma on the cheek. "Thanks, Gem, you're a..." she trailed off.

"A gem?" Gemma supplied and Linda laughed.

"Yes, I suppose. You are an amazing girl, don't know what I'd do without you."

"Oh, Mum," Gemma said, blushing as her mum hugged her.

"I'll be back to take over the night and you can have the night off."

"Mum—"

"No, I'll hear nothing of it! Pip is wanting more hours, I'll message her and see if she wants to work. I'm sure she will when she finds out it's for you. You deserve a night off."

"I agree!" Robbie said and he lifted his soft drink in a toast. "To Gemma, the gem of our lives! Hear, hear!"

"Hear, hear!" A few people with pints toasted Gemma along with Robbie and Linda and Gemma thought her face might set alight.

"Stop it!" Gemma hissed and pulled Robbie's glass down to the bar. He chuckled and shook his head but did no more toasts. Linda said her goodbyes and left. When she had gone, Robbie turned back to Gemma.

"Have you spoken to Matt yet?"

Gemma's stomach turned nastily. "No, he's not answering my calls."

Robbie frowned. "How weird, after being on you all night?"

"I know. I'm suspicious."

Robbie stared at her, then his face seemed to darken. "Suspicious? Why? What would he do?"

Gemma shrugged. "What wouldn't he do at this point? He was pissed at me last night."

"You probably shouldn't see him alone then." Though it was said suggestively, Gemma could hear the serious tone. Robbie didn't want Gemma alone with Matt.

"Don't worry—" But Gemma stopped, she had just seen who had walked in through the door behind Robbie. Robbie saw Gemma's face change and spun around to follow her eye line. Matt has walked in, but not alone. Miranda was with him.

Gemma groaned.

Besides Matt, she was the last person she wanted to see.

"Robbie!" she said vibrantly, as she threw her arms around

his neck and kissed him on the cheek. Gemma suspected she had aimed for the lips but Robbie jutted his head to the side and couldn't move away in time to avoid a kiss altogether. Before, it may have made Gemma's stomach squirm with envy, but seeing Robbie's disgusted face and the events of the previous night, Gemma actually found it pretty amusing. She tried to hide a smile as Robbie looked at her with a disgusted look as he untangled himself from Miranda. Gemma's smile was instantly wiped from her face as Matt slid himself onto a bar stool and casually leaned against the bar. He looked at Gemma, smiling placidly. Then he was looking at Robbie with the same smile and then back at Gemma. It would appear as if he was feigning nonchalance, but Gemma could see the slight pull at the corner of his eyes. The slight tightness that meant the placid smile didn't reach his eyes.

He was furious.

Gemma's heart started to beat uncomfortably in her chest. He was planning something, but before Gemma could try and signal to Robbie, Matt spoke.

"So, Robbie," he said, his tone light so Gemma could hear the edge to his voice ever so slightly. "I ran into Miranda before and we were just talking about that night out you promised us."

"That *I* promised?"

"Well, we did say we would all try and get together. I know we said next weekend but I just thought maybe tonight would be good."

As far as Matt knew, Gemma was supposed to be working.

"Tonight?" Robbie asked with a raised eyebrow and he looked at Gemma. Gemma was frowning at Matt and Miranda.

"We thought it might be a welcome distraction after everything that happened last night with your mum, didn't we Matty?"

"Oh, yes," Matt said quietly and he was looking at Gemma now. He was watching her and Gemma looked at him. He was waiting for her reaction, to see if she'd stand up to them again. "It's a shame, Gem," he said quietly, "that you're working tonight then. Next time, eh?"

Gemma knew that was his way of saying no. It was a no to her going out with them, he was forbidding it and his eyes were hard as they looked at her. Gemma could feel herself shrinking back. That look was a warning.

Gemma finally understood his agenda. Matt would go along with pretending to go out, but Gemma knew he wouldn't actually do it. He would wait for the other two to make the plans to go out then withdraw at the last moment. Meaning Miranda would get what she wanted, a night alone with Robbie to try and rekindle their old flame. And Matt would get what he wanted, Gemma alone and back under his control.

"Well, it's a good thing her mum is giving her the evening off then, isn't it?"

Gemma had almost forgotten they were all standing in the pub. She was so trapped under Matt's gaze that she couldn't look away. Her eyes snapped to Robbie, who was looking at her with an encouraging expression. He was trying to help her stand up to Matt. He was reassuring her that he was still supporting her.

"Oh?" Matt queried and his eyes were on Robbie now. As he turned his head to the side, Gemma could see his tight jaw.

"Her mum thought she deserved the evening off. So Gemma can join us. She is more than deserving of a break, wouldn't you say?"

Matt's head moved slowly to look at Gemma, that tight smile back on his mouth. "Oh yes, I would agree."

"Perfect!" Miranda said jovially, though when Gemma

146

looked at her (she had quite forgotten she was there in all honesty) she didn't look so pleased that Gemma was coming along. The only one who did look happy about Gemma coming was Robbie. He was smiling at her, but she saw too, that his eyes were tight. He kept glancing at Matt, who was also looking at him.

There was a silent fight going on between them and for once, Gemma seemed to be the one that everyone was fighting over.

Linda arrived just before the teatime rush and took over Gemma. Gemma wanted to double-check check she would be okay on the Saturday evening shift. Linda assured her she would be fine. Pip was coming in to cover, so it meant Gemma had the afternoon to shop. Gemma generally hated shopping for clothes. The whole experience caused Gemma anxiety. She hated trying to find clothes in her size and then having to try them on while she got uncomfortable and sweaty in the changing room was another stress.

After a few hours of stress, Gemma was back in her flat (it was easier than carting everything she needed to her mum's) and standing in front of her dirty, wonky full-length mirror. She was dressed in something she wouldn't normally dare to wear. It wasn't a tight-fitting bodycon dress; she wasn't even going to try and slither herself into one of those. The amount of spandex needed for a dress like that was unfathomable. Gemma didn't want to be sweaty and tugging at her undergarments unnecessarily. But the dress, though still floaty on the bottom half, was much more fitted and strappy than she had ever dared to wear. She was showing much more skin with her back and arms than usual. What had possessed her to buy it, she hadn't a clue. She had panicked as she had moved from shop to shop

147

without any success. So she decided to brave it.

Her hair was curly and pulled back in places. Her makeup was simple but looked okay in Gemma's opinion. She'd never been great with fashion or makeup so she just tried her best. With a pang, she remembered Abi and how she used to do her makeup which always made her feel beautiful.

Gemma tried to swallow the rising guilt within her. Though Rose's words were still swirling around her head, she couldn't fully suppress the guilt she felt about Abi. Gemma tried to think about the impending task at hand. She flattened her skirt with shaking hands. It was going to be hard enough trying to blend into a club with skinny supermodels with their backless dresses and sleek hairstyles.

Argh, clubbing.

She'd been once or twice with Pip in her early twenties but she always ended up standing around, looking after every else's belongings while they all danced on the dance floor. Though she knew Robbie would be there (her tummy did a little flip every time she thought about him) but she knew he'd be magnetic for attention. There was going to be no blending into the background while Robbie was around. She heard her phone ping quickly and she pulled it out of her small clutch bag.

It was a message from Robbie which brought a smile to her lips.

Setting off now, be there in fifteen mins. How's Matt been? Rx

Gemma sighed, she glanced at the door before replying.

Still weirdly fine, he's kept himself away. He's in the living room while I've got ready in the bedroom. Don't know what he's up to xx

Gemma sent the message and went to examine her makeup

again and do touch-ups when her phone went off again.

Good, at least he's left you alone. Just try to keep to your room until I get there. See you soon. xx

That was fine with Gemma, she didn't want to speak a second longer with Matt than she had to. Gemma and Robbie had decided it would be best to postpone the break-up with Matt until their little reunion was over. It was only one more day, they had waited ten years and they could wait one more day surely? So Gemma did the finishing touches on her outfit, putting on her shoes and doing the final touches to her makeup. About ten minutes later, when Gemma was out of things to do to pass the time, her phone pinged again.

I'm outside. R xx

Gemma's heart started thumping with anticipation. She had only said goodbye to him a few hours ago but she was already excited to see him. She tried to not actually run out of the room and when she reached the living room, she saw Matt standing by the window. He turned to Gemma silently and looked her up and down, very slowly. His face was emotionless and cold, yet the way he surveyed her made Gemma feel extremely self-conscious.

"That's what you're wearing?" was all he asked and his eyes went back to roaming up and down her. Gemma looked down at her dress, trying to swallow her disappointment. She didn't care if Matt found her attractive, but she was hoping that she might have looked nice enough to stand next to Robbie.

"Well," said Gemma, hoping her voice didn't sound too upset, "well, yes, that's why I am wearing it."

He raised his eyebrow at her and his jaw tightened. There was a loaded moment while they both stared at one another.

"I don't think it's wise that you should come tonight," he

149

said in a low voice.

"Well, I don't really care what you think. I'm going." Gemma could see the colour changing in his face. He was going redder and redder. Gemma swallowed and took a step back. She knew that Robbie was just outside, but there still were two doors and a flight of steps in between them.

"What did you say?" he said, so quietly yet commandingly that Gemma's bravery wavered.

"That I am going," she said quietly and less defiantly. Matt took a step towards her, but then, thankfully, there was a knock on the door.

"Who let him in?" Matt hissed, glaring towards the door. Gemma didn't answer and she almost ran to the door. Her hand was on the door when she felt Matt's hand snake around the top of her arm and his finger dug painfully into her flesh. "What are you doing?" he breathed into her ear and she physically shrunk back from him.

"Just opening the door."

"Well don't! I'll get it." He tugged her back roughly and positioned himself in front of the door. He glared back at her for a moment before he threw the door open.

"Robbie, Miranda," Matt said and he nodded, stepping aside to let both into the small living room.

Gemma was surprised to see both Robbie and Miranda together. But before Gemma could ask Robbie, Robbie turned to her and started to say something. But he stopped. He looked her up and down and Gemma could see him physically swallowing. It wasn't like when Matt had looked her up and down, his eyes didn't make her feel self-conscious. Instead, Gemma felt a heat that she had never felt before prickling through her skin. She almost shivered at the sensation. His eyes went wide and for a moment, he literally just stared at her, opened mouth. She looked him up and down as well. He had light jeans on that fitted him very, very well. He had branded, smart trainers on, and guessing by the logo, a light, fitted and expensive button-up shirt on.

Gemma could also smell his cologne as he stood in front of her and she felt another shiver ripple through her.

She couldn't believe how weak she felt, like she could melt into a puddle on the floor in front of him.

Matt was watching the interaction between the two with his jaw tight. When he realised that they weren't going to saying anything, he cleared his throat. Gemma blinked and looked at Matt, who was glaring at her. Gemma's eyes instantly went to the ground and her cheeks burned.

"Who let you in?" Matt asked Robbie rudely.

Robbie raised his eyebrows at him. "When I arrived, Miranda was already waiting by the door. Then the couple next door were just leaving when they saw me outside. They're fans."

Gemma bit her lip, trying to hold back her smile.

"Are we going or what?" Matt demanded after a moment and they all murmured in agreement and moved towards the door. As they were filling out, Gemma was last to leave. She turned to shut the door as the rest made their way down the stairs. She fumbled, looking for her keys in a clutch bag for a moment and when she found them she went to lock the door.

"Hey," a voice said from behind her and Gemma jumped and her keys went flying. "Oh," Robbie said, laughing, "I'm sorry." He bent down and picked up the keys and placed them back in her outstretched hands.

"God, you're so quiet," Gemma said and she looked over her shoulder and realised that they were alone in the hallway. "Where are Matt and Miranda?"

"They're distracted outside," he said quietly as he reached out and touched her arm lightly. His light caress went up her arm to the straps on her shoulders. Gemma could feel goosebumps rising in the trail of his fingers.

"Robbie," she breathed and she looked up into his big, dark eyes.

"You look beautiful," he whispered and Gemma's breath caught. His fingers were feather-light as he flittered them up her arm, to her neck then up her neck to her cheek. Gemma's breath was coming out embarrassingly loud and fast, but she couldn't help it.

"So beautiful," he murmured again as he trailed his fingers across her cheek, putting a strand of loose hair back behind her ear. He then moved his fingers again to trace the outside of her lips. "You have no idea how much I want to kiss you right now."

Gemma thought she did if it was anything compared to how much she wanted to kiss him. For a fraction of a second, she thought he might lean down, but he held himself back. "But I won't, not until things are finished with Matt. I want you, but I want to do this the right way." Gemma caught his hand with hers and kissed his fingers.

"Me too and I will end it with Matt. Hopefully, we get this night over and I can."

"Good," said Robbie, a little raspy. "Because I can't wait much longer." And Robbie watched as Gemma bit her lip and looked up at him with those big blue eyes. His restraint nearly dissolved there and then. But he held on... just. "Come on, let's get this horrid night over and done with. And stay with me, I really can't be bothered fighting off Miranda's attentions all night."

Gemma had to laugh at that. "Deal." And she squeezed his

152

hand for a moment before dropping it. She finally got around to locking the door and they went back down the stairs and out onto the street. There, parked up outside by the kerb was... Gemma gasped at the sight of it.

It was a long, slick, black limo.

"Wow," Gemma gasped and she turned to Robbie with raised eyebrows. "One of your thousands of cars?" Robbie chuckled.

"One of my *five* cars. And really, it doesn't really count. Not like I can pop to Asda in this."

"No, I suppose not. Imagine trying to park it? Yikes." Gemma giggled at the image of Robbie trying to park it in a small parking bay.

"You know I don't drive it right?"

She didn't but she wasn't going to tell him that. "Of course I know. I'm not an idiot."

Robbie laughed again. "No, you're definitely not that." He beamed at her, making Gemma slightly breathless for a moment. She wasn't used to receiving compliments and praise. She didn't know what to do with it all.

"Oh, for Christ's sake! Move your arse and get in!" Matt yelled and Gemma jumped back from Robbie and looked at the limo. Matt was standing through the roof window and glaring at her. *That* was how Gemma was used to being addressed. Matt disappeared back into the limo and she glanced up at Robbie. He was clenching his jaw and he was staring at the spot where Matt disappeared, standing very still. Gemma reached out and touched his arm.

"Don't worry about it. He'll be gone soon. Just one more night." Robbie turned to her and nodded, but he was still clenching his jaw and fists.

"Come on, let's get this over with," she said and she walked towards the limo. As she walked towards the limo, the chauffeur went to get out of the limo but Robbie stepped forwards and waved him off.

"I've got it, Jim," Jim nodded, smiling at Gemma and dipping his head, before getting back into the driving seat again. Robbie stepped forwards and grabbed the handle, opening the door for Gemma. "After you." And he flashed her a cheeky, side grin and held out his hand to help her in.

"Thank you, sir," she giggled and climbed into the limo.

The inside was beautiful and very posh. There were four large, black leather seats on each side of the car, making a square shape. The carpet in the middle of the square was plush and thick.

There were lights on the ceiling and doors, the polished wood between the seats each with ice buckets with champagne in and platters with fruit and tiny foods on. Gemma climbed in and was closely followed by Robbie. They both sat on the same row of seats, both Miranda and Matt on the two seats running parallel to their seat.

"Are we ready sir?" Jim asked, rolling down the screen between him and the cabin.

"Yes, thank you, Jim," Robbie said lightly and he reached for the champagne and poured Gemma a glass. Their fingers brushed as Gemma took the offered glass and their eyes locked for a moment before Gemma's gaze dropped to her champagne. Then, just to be polite, he poured Matt and Miranda one too. They all took a drink and Gemma was surprised she liked it.

"Oh, that's nice," she said and she smiled at Robbie. "I don't normally drink champagne."

"No, you don't really drink do you, Gemma? Prefer the food normally, don't you? I'm surprised you haven't dived straight into that platter. We better get some quick Miranda, there won't be much left once Roly-Poly is through with it."

Gemma's cheeks flushed and she felt extremely self-conscious again. Matt turned and was looking out the window (both he and Miranda looked out), so he didn't see Robbie open his mouth, about to argue with him, but Gemma caught his attention. She shook her head and grabbed his thigh quickly. He looked down at her hand and she quickly pulled it back.

"It's fine, it's not worth it," she whispered and he looked at her for a moment. Gemma could tell that he wanted more than anything to say something but after a second look at Gemma, he clenched his jaw and nodded. Both Miranda and Matt turned their attention back to Robbie (pretty much ignoring Gemma).

"I'm so excited we're doing this again, Robbie," Miranda said, fluttering her eyelashes and playing with her hair. "It's been so long since we did anything together. Remember what we used to get up to at all those house parties?" She giggled and Robbie's jaw seemed to clench even tighter. Clearly, he didn't want to remember as much as Miranda did.

"Well, I was a stupid kid back then."

"Oh," she chuckled, "I don't know about that, Robbie, you most definitely *felt* like you knew what you were doing."

Robbie, clearly disgusted, didn't answer but chugged down his champagne in a couple of mouthfuls. He then poured himself another and drank that too. Gemma bit her lip to try and smile her smile. Robbie looked at her, his eyebrows raised but she just shook her head.

For years, she had been jealous of Miranda and her history with Robbie. But since Robbie had come back and their kiss the night before, things had changed.

It might be because Gemma now knew what it was like to be

155

really wanted by Robbie. Since he returned, he had made his feelings clear. Though Gemma still struggled to believe that someone like him could want someone like her, his past relationship with Miranda didn't bother her any more.

"Sir?" Jim said from the front. "We're here."

CHAPTER ELEVEN

"Thank you, Jim."

That was much quicker than she had expected and Robbie smiled softly down at her. "Shall we?" Gemma nodded and Robbie opened the door. She scooted along, but before she could go too far, she felt a tight hand snaking around her arm tightly holding her back. Miranda smiled spitefully at Gemma as she scooted out first and Matt held her in place, sneering down at her.

"Robbie! Wow! Oh my God!" Miranda cried as she grabbed his outstretched hand and hauled herself out of the limo.

"Don't fucking embarrass me. I mean it," Matt hissed in Gemma's ear, breathing, hot champagne-smelling breath over her face and neck. She swallowed as she bit back a cry out of pain. He was digging his fingers into her flesh so hard; she was sure he would leave bruises. "Don't fucking embarrass me. Do you understand? Keep your fat lips shut."

Gemma nodded and fought back the tears pooling in her eyes.

"Gemma?" Robbie asked and as he bent down to look back into the limo, Matt stood up and got out, blocking the view of Gemma as he exited. When he finally got himself out of the limo, Robbie bent back down again and looked at Gemma. "Gem?" he asked quietly and he leaned half into the limo, placing one of his hands on the leather seat and the other on Gemma's thigh.

"Are you okay?" Robbie's touch seemed to wake Gemma up and she shook her head quickly and sniffed quickly before putting the best smile she could manage on her face.

"Fine, Robbie." And she put her hand over his. She knew he didn't believe her.

"What did he say?" He was still talking gently, but there was more of an edge to his tone now. But Gemma shook her head and quickly touched his cheek before dropping it back down again.

"Nothing, honestly, let's just go in."

Robbie sighed and looked her straight in the eye. "Gemma, I am going to really struggle not saying anything."

"I know," she sighed too, "but it's only tonight. Please, Robbie?" And he sighed and nodded again. "Thank you," she said quietly and touched his cheek again before continuing.

"Right let's go." Robbie grabbed her hand as she stood up and helped her out.

It was everything you'd imagine an A-list club to be. Cool lighting, big bouncers in front of huge queues of hopeful nobodies, all leaning over the velvet drapes trying to get an A-lister's attention. There were elaborate decorations and water features and even a couple of palm trees thrown in for good measure. With the cool lighting, there were also lots of sudden, bright white flashes.

Gemma's stomach dropped. Flashes of cameras could only mean one thing. Paparazzi.

Instinctively, she tried to hold her head up slightly higher and sucked in her stomach.

Knowing her luck, she'd be on the front page of a tabloid by the morning. She felt Robbie straighten up and the cameras went wild with flashes. Robbie fell into place next to her and he seemed totally oblivious to them as he looked down at her as she took in the whole scene.

Matt and Miranda seemed to be off, talking to some reporter

and they were turning back and pointing back at Robbie.

"Jesus, I can't wait to read what they said about me tomorrow."

"It won't be anything bad," Gemma said as she dragged her eyes away from flashing lights and constant shouts of "Robbie! Robbie Wilson! How's training going? Prepared for the World Cup?" It was so easy to forget that Robbie was actually a very famous football player and a multi-millionaire. When they were together, he was just Robbie. Robbie Wilson whom Gemma had been in love with for over ten years. Robbie wrapped his hand around hers and she looked up at him as the flashing intensified again. She looked up at him with questioning eyes, but he just shrugged.

"They will write that we're a couple anyway, so might as well act like one." And he beamed down at her, before glancing over at Matt and Miranda. They were still busy with the reporter and not even glancing their way, so Robbie lifted Gemma's hand and kissed the back of it while he looked into her eyes. Gemma laughed, embarrassed and flushing bright red. She would look awful in these photos, but she didn't seem to care for once.

Robbie always made her feel like it was just the two of them, even when there were packs of paparazzi. Robbie dropped Gemma's hand but reached around her and pulled her to his side. He guided her past all the paparazzi, some were calling out "Is this your girlfriend? What's her name?" but Robbie ignored them, holding Gemma tight. He leaned down and whispered in her ear.

"Just ignore them. I do." That seemed easier said than done, but Gemma just stuck close to Robbie and put her face partly into his chest for shelter. He guided them right passed the queue of hopefuls wanting entry. Some of them shouted out to Robbie and he smiled and waved a couple of times at those who were apparently fans before cocooning Gemma in his arms again as he made his way to the entrance.

The paparazzi and fans seemed to instantly vanish past a certain point. Gemma looked around and Robbie dropped his protective hold on her. They were under a shelter above the entrance where two huge bouncers were waiting. Matt and Miranda seemed to have beaten them there and Robbie released his hold on Gemma's hand as well, but he stayed close.

Matt, who was raising his voice, seemed to be arguing with one of the bouncers. "No, we're not on the list! We are here with Robbie Wilson!"

"Sure you are mate, get in the queue."

"But we are!" Miranda shrieked. "He's behind us! We arrived with him; we're all old mates! I'm his childhood sweetheart." Robbie scoffed and both Miranda and Matt spun around, red in the face. "See!" Miranda shrieked again, "he's here! Robbie! Tell these imbeciles that we're with you!" Robbie considered lying and only taking Gemma inside, but he knew he couldn't do that… as much as he *really* wanted to.

"Robbie Wilson, as I live and breathe," one of the enormous bouncers said, his extremely serious face cracking into a genuine smile. He extended a huge arm and greeted Robbie in a one-armed hug and a clap on the back. "How you been, man? Not seen you around here for a long time."

"Hey, Ralph, yeah I know, man. I'm too old for this club shit these days."

Ralph barked out a laugh and shook Robbie's shoulder jokingly. "Mate, shut up. You are in your prime! When you have kids, I'm telling you, you age about three decades overnight."

"How is Daisy?"

160

"Teenagers man," he shook his head grimly, "It's like overnight, they go from these sweet kids to these moody, hormonal monsters. Good job I love her, and I'm soft." Robbie laughed and Gemma had to smile as well. "Seriously man, if you ever have a daughter one day. You will know what I am talking about." Something obviously was said over his radio because he listened for a moment before opening the door. He murmured something into the speaker and then smiled at Robbie.

"Go right ahead. You and your friends enjoy your night."

They moved into the club and there was a low rumble of a beat bouncing off the walls as they walked down the hallway. When they reached the end of the hallway, there was another door with a host waiting at the end. He was a kind-faced man and he looked generally happy when he saw Robbie, like they were friends.

"Ah, Mr Wilson. How are you this evening?"

"I'm good, thank you, Milo." They shook hands and clapped each other on the back. "How are the twins?"

"Keeping me on my toes, walking has suddenly turned to running so both the wife and me are kept very busy."

"Walking? Wow, that's gone so quickly. It only felt like yesterday when you told me Maria was pregnant!" Milo laughed and Gemma looked up at Robbie and smiled. Robbie was genuine and cared about those around him. He looked down at her and saw Gemma looking up at him.

He smiled one-sidedly at her and Gemma felt her cheeks burning.

"Fuck sake, Gemma, move your arse," Matt growled in her ear and Gemma jumped forwards. Milo opened the door and started to lead Robbie throughs. Gemma stumbled forwards and followed Milo and Robbie through the doors. When Milo escorted them through the doors and the low rumbling became a loud, heart pounding beat. There were flashing lights, mirrors and wait staff all walking around with expensive bottles of champagne and amber liquors. There were no paparazzi or flashing lights (other than those from the dance floors).

There were many flashy-looking men with tight shirts and big, expensive gold watches and very skinny women with very tight, backless dresses, strappy heels and high ponytails. Gemma swallowed, sucking in her stomach a little more.

There were some very beautiful, *skinny* girls in here.

Gemma felt enormous compared to them. They were even smaller than Miranda's slight frame. It was clear that these people *really* looked after themselves.

The instant they moved into the dance space, eyes began to look their way. Gemma knew who they would be looking at. It wouldn't be little, scrawny Matt on her left. It would be the famous, insanely handsome, six-foot-two football player on her right. The same insanely handsome football player who had just rubbed the back of his hand against Gemma's and was looking down at her smiling. Why would he want her when there were many beautiful girls around, all looking longingly at him?

A pang of jealousy rippled through her chest and Gemma sighed, deflated.

She most definitely didn't belong there and it was becoming more obvious how much she didn't belong in Robbie's world.

Gemma felt Robbie clasp his hand around hers and squeeze. She looked up and him and he raised his eyebrows in question. Gemma just smiled sadly and shook her head.

They followed Milo and even as they made their way to their private booths at the back, Gemma could see women (and men) all gawking at Robbie. Miranda apparently noticed this too because she stepped ahead of Gemma and wrapped her arm around Robbie, giggling disgustingly. Gemma rolled her eyes. She glanced at Matt, who seemed too distracted by the crowd of beautiful women.

Gemma hoped tonight that he might be distracted enough to leave Gemma alone and maybe even alone with Robbie. But Gemma wasn't holding her breath about that, it was already obvious Robbie was the catch of the night. Gemma sighed sadly again and looked down at her feet as she walked. It took her a moment to realise there were figures standing around her. She looked up and saw three suited men that seemed to walk on the outskirts of the group. Gemma frowned, when did they get there? Were they Robbie's security?

Matt had vanished into the crowd, obviously the call of so many beautiful women was stronger than his need to control Gemma. Maybe he assumed Gemma wouldn't stray out of the booth, which was probably correct, Gemma thought dully. No one was going to be paying her any attention all night and as she watched Miranda walk along with Robbie, she saw that Robbie was going to get a lot of attention. That wasn't including all in the club either.

Gemma watched Miranda attempt to link her arms with Robbie's again (he'd shrugged her off the first time) but Robbie was obviously losing patience. He said something to one of his security, who nodded and then went over to Miranda. After a moment, he walked her off somewhere. She didn't look unhappy, so obviously she was going somewhere she wanted. As Miranda walked away, Robbie stopped to face Gemma, waiting for her to catch up with him. He then fell into step beside her and glanced around. Obviously happy about something, Robbie smiled and wrapped his arm around Gemma's waist and pulled her to his side.

"Finally," he whispered in her ear as they reached the booth.

"Fi—" But Gemma stopped; Milo had turned to speak to Robbie.

"How's this, Mr Wilson?" he asked smoothly, indicating the big, roped-off booth behind him.

"Perfect, Milo, thank you. Get the twins something from me, yeah?" Robbie shook Milo's hand and money was smoothly exchanged. Gemma couldn't see the full amount, but she knew it was pink and red in colour which was the largest note that the UK has. And she would bet by their relationship, there was more than one note exchanged. Gemma suddenly thought about how rich Robbie must be. He was a successful football player, with nice cars and a lot of cash and credit cards. So must have earned a lot.

One year of Gemma's wages was probably less than what he got a week.

Another thing that made Gemma feel inadequate for someone so high flying and achieving as Robbie. Gemma slid into the booth with sagging shoulders and reached to take the champagne that Robbie was holding out and took a big swig.

It was cool and crisp and clearly, Gemma guessed by the label, very expensive. Robbie poured himself one and slid into the booth next to her. He put his arm on top of the booth, above Gemma's shoulders. He held out his glass and Gemma clinked hers with his.

"Where did Miranda go?" Gemma asked with raised eyebrows and she drank her drink and Robbie smiled lopsidedly at her.

"Well, apparently Denise Dickinson is here. And Miranda is a big fan."

"*The* Denise Dickinson? Where?" Gemma said as she scanned the crowd. Robbie laughed and squeezed her shoulder, bringing her attention back to him.

"Hey, she's doing me a favour, she owed me."

"Denise Dickinson owed *you* a favour?"

"She's an old friend." He shrugged and laughed at Gemma's open-mouth expression. "Well, at least we know Miranda is going to be distracted for a bit."

"And Matt?" Gemma asked, looking at the dance floor for him.

"She has some very lovely backup dancers that love to party too." He flashed a grin and Gemma continued to stare at him, open-mouthed.

"You've thought of it all." He shrugged and winked at her.

"I knew if they came, they wouldn't give us a moment's peace. This way, we are left alone." The hand that was draped over Gemma's furthest shoulder from Robbie, started to caress her neck and then her cheek and hair as he leaned closer. "*Alone*," he breathed and he was so close now that Gemma could feel his breath on her face. Her eyelids fluttered as she drank him in. She could feel all her rational senses turning to mush but she had to understand what was going on.

"Well, not totally alone." She glanced at the moving dance floor and even then, a couple of beady eyes were watching them.

"I don't care about them," Robbie murmured, not taking his eyes off Gemma. Gemma looked into the crowd, biting her lip.

"There are some beautiful girls out there, Robbie. I wouldn't hold it against you. I'm very good at holding drinks and minding coats, I've had years of practice," she jested, but there was an element of truth there.

Robbie pulled his arm back and for a moment, Gemma

165

thought he might get up but then she felt his hands on either side of her face and pulled her face to look at his.

"There is only one beautiful girl in here tonight Gemma and she's sitting right here." His eyes were alight with a fire that Gemma wasn't accustomed to seeing. It made her hot and tingly, it made her throat dry and her legs shake. Robbie brought his lips to hers and Gemma felt as if she had been set alight. There was a heat, spreading from their lips that made her shiver with desire. It wasn't a lingering kiss, it was a quick passionate one and as Robbie pulled back, he rested his forehead on hers. "It is, always was and always will be you, Gemma. Just you." He kissed her quickly again before he pulled back and kissed her nose and the top of her head. He leaned himself back slightly but kept a hand rested lightly on the inside of her thigh, by the knee.

Robbie's hand rested on her bare skin and on skin that was slightly more intimate than previously. He was caressing the skin absent-mindedly, but Gemma felt every movement. She felt her breath coming in a little faster, so she decided to calm herself down by questioning Robbie more.

"What if they came back?" she asked and when he looked at her confused, so she reiterated, "Miranda or Matt."

"Ah," Robbie said, understanding, "Well, Marcus and his fellas needed to spread out to do surveillance anyway. So they've just taken them with them, they'll keep them away from us and keep an eye out at the same time."

"'Marcus and his fellas?' Who are they?"

"My security team," Robbie shrugged.

"You have a security team?" Gemma stared at him as he laughed.

"Of course I do. Have you never noticed them?"

Nope.

166

His face broke into a wide smile as he could physically see on her face the concentration as she tried to remember. But try all she might, Gemma just couldn't remember seeing any of their faces over the past few weeks.

"Well, that just shows how good they are. You've not even noticed them. I'd toot my own horn and say it was because you've been enthralled with me but I think they're just really good."

Yep. That is exactly why Gemma couldn't remember them. But she wasn't going to say that to him, she had some pride.

Gemma bit her lip and she *still* tried to remember, slightly horrified she had never noticed them before.

"And they have *always* been there? Every time we saw one another?"

"Yep, maybe not in the same room or right next to me." He knew she'd be remembering their kiss outside her mum's house the previous night, "But always close and always surveying. I have to have one. There are some nut jobs out there. Plus, my managers are insistent on it."

Gemma stared at him. "I think I just forget that you're this big-shot celebrity. This football God that is England's one and only shot at winning the World Cup." She shook her head and laughed shakily.

"Well, I wouldn't say one and only shot. That's unfair on my teammates, but—" Robbie reached out for her and took her face in his hands again. "I like that you don't see me like that, you don't see the money or the fame. You just see me. You're the only one that has ever seen the real me. I've known you my whole life and there is no one else that knows me better." His breath was hot on her face again and her mind swam with the intoxication of him again. She could just feel him *everywhere*. She could feel his thigh pressed up against hers. She could feel his strong, muscular torso pressed against her body. He had his hands on her face again and his fingertips seemed to leave a trail of heat going up into her hair. His breath danced across her face and she breathed in his warmth. The smell of cologne filled her nostrils and made something clench deep within her.

It just smelt so wonderfully Robbie.

"Robbie," Gemma breathed, her arms going up and holding onto his elbows.

"Gemma," he whispered and he rubbed his nose along the length of hers for a moment. "I know I said that I would wait until you finished things with Matt. And I really, really, *really*," he emphasised the last really like it was almost painful, "know I need to do that, but…" He looked into her eyes and Gemma could feel all her resolve melting away. "But," he ground out, trying to focus again, "I know I've messed this up before, Gemma. This is, hopefully, my second chance to do right by you. And I want to prove that I am someone you can trust and depend on."

"Robbie, I—"

"I know I've hurt you, I know things didn't go the way you wanted. And the way I wanted as well. I was a stupid kid who—" but Gemma cut him off this time.

"Robbie, stop," she said and he put a finger to his lips to silence him. "Please stop. We were just kids, I don't hold anything against you."

"I should have been braver," he whispered and his eyes were wide with regret.

"We were just kids," Gemma said simply and she moved her fingers from his lips to caress his cheeks. She could feel the slight stumble of hair under her fingertips and she smiled. "Sometimes, the time just isn't right," she said softly as she ran her fingers along the line of his jaw.

Robbie had closed his eye at her touch but then they flew open and looked deeply into hers.

"The time is right… *now*."

Gemma caught her breath as she watched him turn his face to the side and grab one of her hands in his large one. He brought her fingertips to his mouth and kisses softly each finger, then kissed the palm. He then moved from the palm to the inside of her wrist and Gemma could feel the soft tingles that his kisses were leaving on her body. Something was clenching again deep within her.

"Robbie…?" she breathed and he kept his lips on her forearm as he looked up with hot, blazing eyes. Gemma bit her lip as she watched Robbie kiss up her arm. It was so easy to forget that they were in a club, with a lot of people around, but with Robbie, they went into their own precious world. As he moved up her arm to her shoulder, the said arm being kissed, wrapped around his neck and Gemma's fingers found Robbie's hair. Robbie kissed up her shoulder, up her neck and kissed up to her ear. He was breathing quite heavily and it was obvious that he, like Gemma, was fighting exertion.

"Do… Do you want to get out of here?" He whispered in her ear and Gemma's stomach did a little flip. He pulled back, his face only inches from hers again. He was watching her expression closely. He was giving her the option. It was her choice. Gemma bit her lip and looked into Robbie's eyes.

There was no doubt what they would do once they left the club.

Was Gemma brave enough to expose so much of herself to Robbie? And as she sat, gazing into those deep, brown eyes, Gemma knew her answer.

"Yes," she breathed and she could see Robbie physically sag with relief. She hadn't realised he had been so tense waiting for her answer.

"Thank God," He laughed with relief. Gemma realised that Robbie wasn't as smooth as he normally was. He was *nervous*. Gemma couldn't believe it. Robbie Wilson nervous about going back home with her, Gemma Walker. It would have been laughable if the moment wasn't so intense. Gemma kissed his cheek and he looked at her smiling.

"What was that for?"

"Just because."

"Thank you," he murmured as he put one hand on her cheek again and kissed her on the lips quickly. Heat quickly took over, because the kiss deepened and it took Robbie forcing himself backwards to break it. "Let's go," he said shortly and he cleared his throat and quite literally dived out of the booster. Gemma had to laugh, she had never seen Robbie like that before. But as she slid out and took Robbie's hand, she remembered something with an uncomfortable thud in her stomach.

"Crap," she said as he looked up and Robbie and grimaced. He just raised his eyebrows in question; his body was angled as if he was ready to physically pull her to the door. "Matt and Miranda," she said simply and Robbie grimaced too.

"Well," he said as he took her hand as they both stood beside the booth. "Miranda is sorted, I'll have Jason to make sure she gets home safely."

Poor Jason, Gemma thought grimly.

"As for Matt…" he trailed off but Gemma knew what needed to be done.

"I'll deal with Matt," she said, lifting her chin up. But she still squeezed Robbie's hand for comfort and he looked down at her and smiled.

"Together?" he asked and Gemma nodded.

"Together."

Robbie turned to the nearest security and spoke into his ear. He nodded and stepped back, pressing something in his ear as he spoke. Gemma looked at him questioningly but before Robbie could open his mouth, the guard spoke into his ear. Robbie nodded and indicated that security should lead the way. So, with one guard in front and one behind, Robbie and Gemma were led off to another part of the club. Across the huge floor and up a couple of steps and levels, Gemma and Robbie found Matt. He was trying his utmost to impress a group of girls, all of whom were clearly not impressed in the slightest.

As they both approached, they caught sight of Robbie and immediately looked more alert and interested. Gemma tried to not to growl and hide Robbie from view. Then Matt turned and glared at her. Gemma stepped forwards, but still held onto Robbie's hand for support.

"What?" he barked at her, his voice full of malice. Robbie's hand tightened and she glanced up at him. He was glaring at Matt, very tight-jawed. But he didn't say anything. He knew that Gemma needed to speak to him but she could tell he found it very difficult. Gemma took a deep breath and turned her attention back to the spiteful face of Matt. She felt strong holding onto Robbie's hand and when she looked at his face, she didn't have any fear.

"It's over." The music was still loud and Gemma had to speak louder than usual, but she knew he could hear her.

"What?" His voice was low but Gemma heard him with startling clarity. Her bravery wavered slightly. She tugged Robbie's hand so he was pulled closer behind her. Matt hadn't seemed to notice Robbie's proximity yet. His eyes were set on Gemma as he moved closer.

"It's over, Matt."

"Fuck off," Matt seemed to swell and suddenly grew in height. He was leaning towards her, sneering in her face. Gemma felt herself step back into Robbie. He wrapped his arm around her waist and pulled her back so that he was standing between Matt and Gemma. Robbie was standing tall and strong and Matt, who had been looking at his chest after the sudden swap between Gemma and Robbie, looked up at him. He was a good head shorter than Robbie, but that didn't stop him from leering at Robbie too. Gemma squeezed Robbie's arm and he glanced down at her. She was looking up at him and he sighed and nodded once. He stepped back again, but kept a protective arm around her waist and watched Matt closely.

"No, Matt, you fuck off. I want you out of my flat. You have *one* day—" Gemma held up one single finger to emphasise her point, "to move your shit out of my flat and get out of my life."

Matt glared down at her, looking her up and down with a look of disgust on his face. His eyes then focused on Robbie's arm, still wrapped around her waist. The disgust turned to pure anger for a fraction of a second before a cool mask of indifference covered his face. He raised his eyebrows and looked between Gemma and Robbie, an arrogant expression on his face now.

"Pfft. You two?" he snorted and shook his head. "Fucking good luck to you, mate," he said, sneering at Gemma again. "You've got your work cut out there. She doesn't move her fat arse much... if you know what I'm saying. You got to do all the work."

Gemma gasped, but before she could respond, Robbie stepped forwards and grabbed Matt roughly by the shirt and hoisted him up by the collar so he was closer to his face.

"You listen to me, Matty, and you listen good. Don't you dare talk about her like that. *Ever*. If I hear as much as a peep from you, you'll have me to answer to, is that clear?" To Matt's credit, Gemma supposed begrudgingly, he didn't cower and shrink away. He just stared at Robbie with that cocky half-smile that Gemma loathed.

"Am I clear, Matty?" Robbie murmured, his voice low and dangerous. Matt's mask of bravado slipped slightly and Gemma could see him swallowing and licking his lips. Then the cocky slight smile was back and he glanced at Gemma.

"Oh, crystal clear, Robbie, my old friend."

"And you stay away from her." Matt turned to Gemma and slowly a smile spread across his lips again. "Oi," Robbie said and he shook Matt again, "eyes on me."

"Of course," Matt said silkily, answering Robbie. And Robbie dropped him and turned and took Gemma's hand and led her away from him. Gemma glanced over her shoulder at Matt. He was staring, but almost distantly. His smile was transfixed as he stared after them and Gemma felt a sudden disturbing feeling.

She didn't like the look on Matt's face.

She turned her face back to the front and Robbie put his arm back around her waist and pulled her close again. Robbie put his lips to her ear and Gemma felt a shiver pulse through her as his breath prickly across her cheeks.

"I'm sorry about that. I shouldn't have lost my temper, I just can't stand how he is or," he smiled at her, "should I say was? How he *was* with you. I couldn't stand it any longer."

Gemma smiled up at him, feeling a weight had been lifted from her shoulders. "Thank you," she said and she leaned up and kissed him on the cheek quickly. "I couldn't have done it without you. I would have been too scared."

Robbie smiled but shook his head. "No, I didn't do anything. You are so brave to do that, to stand up to him. You're amazing."

They were nearly out of the club; they'd just passed the entrance with all the bouncers. Gemma beamed at Robbie.

"I feel amazing. Like a huge weight is lifted."

"Good," Robbie said as he beamed back. "You deserve so much better than him Gemma, someone who is going to treat you right."

"Someone like you?" Gemma had never been so forward before but the champagne and her break-up with Matt made her feel fearless. It made her feel *alive*. She knew what she wanted and for once, she was going to take it. Gemma had stopped walking, just before they walked out of the building and into the open. They were still sheltered from the paparazzi and incoming guests. She looked up at Robbie as he stopped and turned to face her.

"Yes, well, I hope so."

Gemma smiled, it was almost like Robbie was nervous. "You hope so?" She raised her eyebrows.

"Well, obviously if it's what you want. But I would like to be that for you, Gemma. I want to make you happy and treat you with the respect and admiration you deserve."

"Really?" Her fearlessness was quickly replaced with absolute glee. "You want to be with me? You, Robbie Wilson?" Robbie closed the gap between them and grabbed her hands in his, pulling them to his chest.

"I want you in every way and every aspect of my life Gemma. If you'll have me, I'll do everything in my power to make you happy."

"Oh, Robbie," Gemma blushed and turned her head away for

a moment. Robbie dropped one of her hands and gently pulled her face back to look at him.

"It's true, Gemma. It's always been you. And I would be honoured if you let me show you how much I care about you. How much I worship you."

Gemma's lips felt dry, so she licked them and chewed her lip in thought. Robbie ran his thumb over her bottom lip until her teeth released it. He ran his thumb back over her lips again, moving closer until his body was nearly pressing hers into the wall behind.

"So beautiful," he murmured and Gemma could feel herself melting at his words. "So, so beautiful." He was lowering his lips to hers, slowly and tantalizingly. He did so until his lips were an inch from hers and he looked into her eyes. Gemma held his gaze for a fraction of a second before he bent further and kissed her.

This kiss was nothing like any they had shared over the years. It wasn't surprising and confusing, like those they shared so many years ago. It wasn't a desperate or forbidden kiss that they shared the night before.

That kiss was leading to something. And it made Gemma's stomach clench with desire and also a bit of fear. But Gemma didn't want to be scared any more. She pulled back and looked into Robbie's (slightly confused) eyes. She was searching for something in them, something to give her that final bit of courage that she needed. Robbie was looking at her so warmly and lovingly, that Gemma realised what she needed to do. She reached up and kissed him quickly on the lips before grabbing his hand and literally pulling him through the final doors and out into the open. For a couple of steps, he was stumbling along behind her and she laughed. Robbie then fell into step with her and looked at her before he laughed as well.

"Jesus!" he exclaimed. "Where's the fire?"

"No point waiting is there? We've done that for the last ten years."

Robbie stopped suddenly and the hold he had on her hand pulled her back as well.

"What?" she asked and looked up at him, feeling a little apprehensive for the first time. Had she misread the signals?

Robbie seemed to swell slightly before he roughly tugged her hand towards him and pulled her in for one, single, heated kiss.

The flashes of cameras went crazy. But they ignored them. In that moment, there was only them and their fused lips. They broke apart but Robbie kept his forehead on hers. After an indefinite amount of time, Robbie seemed to blink and frown, turning to look at the sea of flashing lights. His face broke into a huge smile as he turned back to her and then Gemma laughed as well.

"Shall we get out of here?" he whispered and Gemma's breath caught at the glint in his eyes. She couldn't speak so she just nodded. Robbie clasped her hand and quickly brought it to his mouth and kissed it (to another sea of flashes) before he turned and lead her back to the limo. Jim was waiting by the door and he opened the door so Gemma could scoot in. Robbie closely followed and the door was shut behind them. Gemma looked around taking in the empty cabin and turned to ask something of Robbie. But her question was lost in her throat because he was looking at her in such a way, Gemma's mind could only focus on his face blankly.

He didn't say anything, he just pulled Gemma towards him and kissed her again. It was a hungry kiss and as their mouths moved together, something was stirring inside Gemma. Robbie pulled back quickly and looked towards the front of the cabin. Gemma blushed and saw the shutter between the front and back was open. Even though it was only slightly opened and unlikely Jim could see anything, she hadn't even heard him speak. So God knows how long he had been trying to get their attention.

"Sorry, sir, but where are we going?"

Robbie looked down at her and Gemma knew he was asking her. She smiled up and him and put her hand on his thigh and squeezed, unable to speak. She was worried if she spoke, she would lose her nerve.

And she wanted this, more than anything.

Gemma was surprised when Robbie let out a breath he'd been holding. He kissed her quickly on the lips and said, without taking his eyes off Gemma.

"Home please, Jim."

CHAPTER TWELVE

"Yes, sir," was all Jim said before he closed the inch gap on shutter leaving them quite alone. Robbie's hand caressed Gemma's cheeks and he looked into her eyes again.

"Gemma," he whispered, one of his hands taking a loose strand of her hair and twiddling it in his fingers for a moment, before pushing back behind her ear and continuing to caress her cheek again. He brought his lips to Gemma's again as his hands continued to caress.

Robbie's hands moved from Gemma's face, down her shoulders and slowly moved down her back.

She arched her back, a shiver of pleasure pulsating through her. Even just Robbie's hands on her made her feel amazing. His lips moved from hers, grazing her cheek and down her neck. Gemma tried to catch her breath, but Robbie's caressing lips against her neck made her tingle and flutter deep within. A noise escaped Gemma's lips without any control. It was a sound she had never made before yet heard it before from others.

It was a moan of pleasure.

Robbie moaned against her neck and tightened an arm around her waist. He lifted her up swiftly and pulled her onto him, so Gemma was sitting on top of him and straddling him. She was taken aback at how easily he had been able to move her, like she weighed no more than a bag of flour. Robbie had an arm around Gemma's waist and another in her hair.

"Gemma," Robbie whispered, his voice almost purred and

she could feel that tingling sensation again. "You're so beautiful." Gemma felt her eyes swell as she looked into his. His eyes so were intent on her and she could feel his hands still caressing her body. He actually *wanted* her and she had never felt like that before.

It was empowering.

Gemma kissed him, so ferociously that she seemed to catch him off guard again. He responded quickly and with matching enthusiasm. Gemma wanted to strip him off, to have him take her on the limo floor, but just as she started to tug at the bottom of his expensive shirt, the car slowed. Then the car stopped and Jim knocked on the screen but didn't look through.

Robbie pulled her close for one last kiss before he helped her off him and made towards the door. Robbie kept hold of her hand as he pulled her out of the limo.

Gemma gasped at the sight in front of her.

The house, no *mansion*, in front of her was exquisite. It was elaborate, with marble arches and huge lit-up windows. It was beautiful... and humongous.

"Wow," she gasped again. "I thought it would be bigger."

Robbie laughed and pulled her to him and kissed her. "Come on," Robbie said after a heated moment under the lights on the mansion. "I'll give you a tour... but later." He grinned down at her and tugged her onwards. They entered through the double front doors into a beautiful foyer. Gemma literally only managed to glance around before Robbie pulled her towards the huge marble staircase in the centre and when they reached the top, Robbie pulled her to his chest and wrapped his arms around her. He kissed her again and Gemma could feel his arms as they move down her back, over her bum and to her thighs. He bent as he kept lowering his arms and Gemma pulled back looking at him questioningly. She didn't have a huge amount of experience, but this did seem a little strange.

"What are you…" She trailed off because Robbie stopped at the back of her knees and flashed her a wicked grin. He pulled and lifted Gemma up so she could wrap my legs around his waist.

"Robbie!" she exclaimed, half embarrassed, half exhilarated. "Robbie, I am too heavy for—"

"No you're not," Robbie grinned and he kissed her again.

Gemma wrapped her arms and legs around him and kissed him back. Her head was now slightly higher, so she pulled back and looked down at him. It did seem like he wasn't struggling, and he kissed her again as he walked down the hallway. So lost in the moment, she barely noticed where they were heading and in no time, Robbie pushed his way backwards through a door, still carrying her on his front.

Gemma broke away from him to gaze quickly around the room. Again, everything was elaborate and bright. Filled with glittering objects and expensive-looking furniture. In the middle of the huge room, was a massive double king-size bed. Gemma's heart suddenly jolted at the sight of it, like she was only just realising that in a matter of moments, she could be seeing Robbie naked.

And him… her.

Gemma felt like she had been plunged into cold water suddenly, just as Robbie set her down. He turned away from her for a moment, adjusting something to do with the lights because they flickered and lowered to a more romantic ambiance. The champagne and adrenaline from the club had seemed to wear off suddenly and she could feel the unpleasant thoughts seeping into her brain.

Gemma suddenly felt very uncomfortable and her clothes

felt tight. It was as if her rolls of fat had doubled in size and they had become more prominent.

And then there was Abi.

Gemma had tried to put the guilt about Abi to the back of her mind. She was trying to not let it control her life, because Gemma did agree with Rose. Abi wouldn't want Gemma to be unhappy. But now she was trying to go for it with Robbie, her mind was being cruel and hurtful. Gemma never felt comfortable in her own skin, but suddenly, at that moment, it was the worse it had ever been.

Robbie turned and faced her, smiling but when he saw her expression, his smile slipped. "Gemma?" he asked gently, "What's wrong?" Robbie wrapped his arms around her, looking into her face. "Gemma?"

She put her hands on his chest and could feel his chiselled muscles beneath her fingertips. If Gemma could feel his muscles through his clothing, he must have been able to feel her fat through hers. She stepped back and wrapped her arms protectively over her chest and stomach. Gemma sucked in and extended her neck to try and get rid of any double chins. Robbie took a slight step forward and she looked him in the eye. He looked upset, hurt almost. She felt a pang of guilt through her chest.

"Oh, Robbie. It's not you, it's me."

"What's you? What did I do?"

Oh, she thought, *he's so perfect.*

"You didn't do anything Robbie, I got cold feet."

"Cold feet?" Gemma wasn't explaining it properly.

"Look at you, Robbie," she said, trying to explain clearer. "Okay?"

"And look at me!"

"I don't know what you mean," Robbie admitted after a moment's pause.

"You," she said indicating his perfectly carved body, "look like you are carved from stone. A Greek god made from marble, without a single ounce of fat on you." Robbie stared at her, so she went on. "You are literally a Greek god, and I am Stonehenge!"

Robbie burst out laughing and she slapped his shoulder. "It's not funny, Robbie! You should be with... supermodels! Like all those girls back in the club! They were all so sexy and skinny, they were all perfect!"

Robbie stopped laughing instantly. "I don't want any of them," he said flatly, "I want you."

Gemma swallowed slightly at the desire thick in his voice.

"But—" But Robbie cut her off.

"Gemma," he said and he stepped forward and grabbed her hands in his, pulling them to his chest. "I want you and I've wanted you for over ten years."

"Robbie..."

"It's true, Gemma, why do you not think it?"

"Because... because I am fat and ugly and I've not done anything with my life. I've stayed in the same job and the same town. Stayed fat and ugly and watched as the world passed me by. Nobody has ever wanted me, which is fine. I am used to standing in the background. It's where I belong."

Robbie took a sharp intake of breath. Gemma looked into his eyes and could actually see tears glistening in them.

"Oh, Robbie," she said as she wiped his eyes. As she wiped his cheeks and he nuzzled his head into her hand.

"Why would you say that about yourself?" he whispered.

"Because it's true," Gemma said matter-of-factly. It was and she wasn't asking for sympathy. It just was true, and she knew it.

She had accepted it. Robbie stared at her again, his face a little broken.

"Any man would be lucky to have you, Gemma. *I* would be so lucky."

"You're much too good for me, you need to aim higher, Robbie. That's what I'm saying, you—"

"I don't deserve someone like you, Gemma. I blew my chance and I hope that if you gave me a second chance, I could prove to you how much you mean to me. How madly in love with you." Gemma gasped slightly, but he ploughed on. "And how madly in love I have been with you for the last ten years. And if I'm being honest with myself it's probably been longer than that. I have never known anyone like you, Gemma, I have never seen anyone as funny, kind and selfless as you."

"You…" Gemma started, a hint of a smile on her face now. "You love me?" she breathed, staring at him for a moment.

He nodded vigorously. "I have since I was fifteen. Maybe even before."

"Pfft."

"It's true and I would love to show you how much I love you. Obviously, if you're uncomfortable, we'll go no further, but I assure you, Gemma, I have never seen anyone so beautiful and sexy in my entire life."

"But… but…" she said, trying to formulate words.

"And it's my biggest regret, bottling it up all these years." He pushed her hair behind her ears and rubbed her cheek with his thumb slowly. "I tried to deny it, I tried to forget about you. I tried to date others," a pang of jealousy suddenly rippled through her at the thought, "but no one compared. I found myself thinking about you when I was with them and so I always ended it. There was no one else. I dated many girls." Another sudden urge to

183

literally growl and Robbie must have guessed her feelings, because he added. "There was no one I found more interesting, more caring or sexier," he added with emphasis and gripped her face with both his hands and boring into her eyes, "than you Gemma. No one."

There was silence as Gemma tried to process the millions of emotions she was now feeling, each as confusing and intense as the next. Finally, she managed to formulate words and asked the most pressing question Gemma could think at that moment.

"You think I am sexy?" She felt a burning in the pit of her stomach when he smiled back. There was a look behind his smile. It was almost like... want. He wanted her and it felt very exhilarating to be wanted so much.

"The *sexiest*," he breathed and she felt a shiver run down her spine. Gemma's heart began to beat faster and her breath began to speed up.

I am going to be brave, she thought, *for Robbie and for myself.*

And for Abi, she would have wanted Gemma to love herself enough to let herself have happiness.

So Gemma released Robbie's hands and pushed him back slowly so that he fell gently onto the bed. She stood in between Robbie's long legs, looking into his face. Robbie's eyes followed her every move and she felt a little blush and smile creep onto her face.

There was something so extremely empowering about it all. For the first time in Gemma's life, she felt *sexy* and *beautiful*.

Robbie's want for her made the fire in her belly roar with excitement.

Gemma stood in front of Robbie and he reached out his arms to touch her hips. He pulled her closer and still looked up at her face. Gemma bit her lip and took a deep breath. She grabbed the bottom of her dress, and after a second of hesitation, she lifted it quickly up and over her head. She closed her eyes, letting the excitement and fear wash over her for a second. Then she jumped when she felt Robbie's lips, kissing her stomach and hips. She looked down and watched him with ragged breath. Gemma watched as Robbie kissed his way up her torso and kissed her breasts over her bra. She took in a deep breath as the tingling got more intense and pleasurable.

She had *never* felt like this before.

She had never even done foreplay before.

Robbie stood up and leaned down and kissed her. Robbie's lips moved again from her mouth, down the column of her neck. Gemma arched her neck, trying to catch her breath again.

Another involuntary moan escaped from Gemma's lips, down Robbie's ear as she gripped his strong shoulders. Robbie pulled back and she looked into his eyes.

"Gemma?" he whispered.

"Yes?" she breathed, her heart still racing.

"I love you," Gemma felt her whole body stop as she stared at him open-mouthed. She couldn't believe those words were coming out of his lips.

"I love you," he said, "I always have, I always will."

Robbie Wilson, *Robbie Wilson,* loved *her... her, Gemma Walker.*

Gemma stared at him and stroked his cheeks and lips for a moment, unable to believe this entire night. After a moment, staring and caressing his face, she said something that shocked them both.

"I love you too, Robbie Wilson, always have, always will."

Robbie sucked in a breath. "You don't have to say it because

185

I did," he said, but the sides of his mouth were turning up. He was fighting a smile.

"I'm not," she said, reaching up and cupping his face in one of her hands and looking into his eyes. "I have always loved you. I tried to fight it, forget about you as well. But I never have."

Robbie smiled a one-sided smile and he rested his forehead against hers. They embraced for a minute before Robbie spoke again.

"I want to show you how much I love you." He was smiling and he started to kiss her neck. That tingling was creeping up through her entire body again. She felt herself arch her back instinctively and she dug her fingers into his back. He moved down her neck, down to her collarbone and she felt her heart start to race. He stopped and glanced up at her, checking that everything he was doing was okay.

It was more than okay.

"You're so beautiful," he whispered and Gemma could see, in that moment, the love in his eyes. She felt a blush creeping up her cheeks and she looked down.

Even without all the kissing, he made her feel amazing. He made her feel so sexy and wanted; it was hard to not rip his clothes off. He even made her feel so comfortable; Gemma could rip *her own* clothes off.

In a moment of braveness, Gemma reached back and undid her bra and tossed it aside.

Robbie caressed her face and kissed her again.

Robbie turned her around and she felt the bed against the back of her knees. Robbie laid her down on the bed, with him lying on top of her. He kneeled for a moment in between her legs and he unbuttoned his shirt. He took it off and threw it to the side. Gemma never thought she would see such a perfect body, especially such a one in between *her* legs. She couldn't help but gasp a little as she reached out to run her hand over his tattooed chest and down his abdomen.

Gemma sat forward and kissed him suddenly and the heat was back. She felt the fire burning away within her and the tingling moved up from between her thighs to the pit of her stomach. The feeling of both their bare torsos together made the tingling amplify ten-fold. He leaned forwards, leaning her back and laying her down on the bed. He resumed kissing her neck, her collarbone and then her breasts. Gemma gasped as he took her into his mouth. He kissed her so intimately that Gemma was arching off the bed, pushing more of herself into him.

The way it made Gemma feel literally made her soar into this realm that she had never experienced before. She didn't know having sex, no *making love*, could feel so good. Robbie then moved from her breasts to her torso and down to her belly button. Gemma was amazed at how comfortable she was with having him kiss her there. Before Robbie, she would have been so worried about someone being in so close proximity to her stomach and the fat that she had there.

But not Robbie.

He kissed until the top of her knickers and stopped. He raised himself slightly and looked up at her. She looked down and stared into his eyes. Though Gemma was a little nervous, she was exhilarated and didn't want him to stop.

"May I?" he breathed and she took in a sharp gasp of air.

She couldn't find her voice, so she just nodded and he smiled back. He looped his fingers into the waistline and pulled them off. It was quick, but he didn't rush it either. It was as if he was always giving her options to stop if he went too far.

That was it, Gemma was finally completely naked in front of

Robbie. And it felt incredible. She had never felt so empowered and sexy in all her life.

"Oh my God, Gemma," he breathed, leaning back and looking over her entire body. She fought the urge to cover herself with her arms or hide away.

"Um,' she said timidly, feeling her face growing hotter and hotter. "Oh my God... good or bad?"

"Good," Robbie said without hesitation, "very, very good." And he looked into her eyes and she felt a smile spreading across her face.

"Oh, good," Gemma said, feeling the craziest urge to laugh.

"Well, I'll tell you like this. I have pictured the moment a million times in my head. I've imagined you naked a thousand times over the last ten years and nothing, and Gemma I really mean, *nothing* compares to the real thing." He was looking over her with such pride that Gemma couldn't help but beam up at him. Robbie kissed her quickly on the lips, it was as if at that moment, he would expire if he didn't do so. Then he sat back up and moved down her body until he reached her feet.

He started to kiss from her ankles, up her legs and up the inside of her thighs.

If she thought him kissing her torso was exhilarating, it was nothing compared to that. Gemma felt her back arch as the tingling sensation pulsated through her. Gemma gripped the sheets and closed her eyes.

Robbie kissed all the way up, in between her legs until he reached her hips and started to move to the middle and he glanced up at her. He must have seen something in her face because he lifted himself higher and looked into her eyes.

"Is everything okay? Do you want me to stop?"

Gemma bit her lip and looked at him and decided honesty

was the best in that situation.

She trusted Robbie with her whole heart and she knew she could be honest with him.

"Are you going to..." She trailed off, her cheeks on fire.

Robbie's eye twinkled with this desire and his slight smile was small but *very* suggestive. It sent a thrill through her and she could feel all her muscles (and nerves) melting away.

"Well," he breathed, his voice husky. "I was going to. Unless you don't want me to?" Gemma shook her head quickly and his smile widened. "Good."

"It's just..." Gemma mumbled, looking down at him and chewing her lip thinking of how to word it. She felt Robbie move up her body and pull her face to look into his.

"It's just what?" he murmured. She took in a shaking breath and looked back up at Robbie's ceiling. It was easier to not look at him just then.

"It's just... I've... never... you know. Done... *that.*"

Robbie was quiet for a moment. "You've... never? *Ever*?" She could hear the disbelief in his voice, so she chanced a look at him. He was clearly shocked, but there was also something else in the depths of his eyes. Anger perhaps?

"Well... Matt never... and he's the only one I..." Gemma trailed off, the second she mentioned Matt's name, Robbie's jaw physically tightened so much she could see the muscles contracting under his ear. Robbie was obviously trying to calm himself and after a couple of moments he relaxed and the anger in his eyes is replaced by warmth.

"Well," he said gently, "if you're happy to, I would love to show you something." He smiled suggestively again and she couldn't help but smile back.

"Okay," she said, barely a whisper. Robbie kissed her again,

189

sending her heart racing again, before he slid down her body, kissing and nibbling her body on the way.

More moans escaped Gemma's lips and she felt herself arching and pushing her body more towards him. The empowerment Gemma felt was nothing compared to the pleasure she was about to experience. Robbie kissed her in her most intimate of places and the intimacy and *pleasure* that came with it was unfathomable. Gemma arched herself off the bed, gripping the bed sheets with everything she had. That is what *that* felt like? Gemma had known what had happened, she had seen it before but nothing compared to how it actually felt. Robbie did things with his hands and mouth she had never experienced before.

"Oh my God, Robbie," she moaned, arching and thrashing beneath his kisses. "Oh... my..." She couldn't finish coherent sentences, her words were lost as pleasure literally exploded deep within her and she felt herself bending off the bed and calling out to Robbie as she wound her fingers into his hair and gripped hard. Gemma felt like she was in this glorious realm, like she was almost floating above them in this parallel pleasure universe.

There was a moment of quiet as they paused, drinking in the moment.

Robbie loved that he had done that and he watched as she slipped into the little haze of pleasure and joy.

Gemma felt Robbie first, coming up the bed and covering her with his body. Her eyes fluttered open and she saw him smiling down at me.

"You have no idea how long I've wanted to do that."

"Oh my God," was all she managed. He laughed again and he inched closer so their foreheads and noses were touching. "What was that?"

Robbie chuckled and he kissed her quickly. "I think," he said softly as he caressed her cheek while she was still staring at the ceiling above, baffled. "I think you had an orgasm."

But Gemma shook her head slowly. "No, I've had an orgasm before. That was not an orgasm." Robbie cleared his throat and she looked back at him, still a little dazed.

"Um, has anyone ever *given* you one?"

Gemma thought for a moment. "No, I guess not. Wow, I can't believe how different that was." She looked back at the ceiling, still trying to ride the high of what Robbie just did.

"So beautiful," he murmured into the air and she felt her stomach tightening again.

Gemma looked back at him and reached up and kissed him. The feeling of the heat rose back up within her again and she gripped onto Robbie's back as he kissed her deeply again. She lowered her hands and realised he still had his jeans on. She could feel him pressing up against her stomach, even through his thick jeans.

"Robbie," Gemma whispered and he pulled back and looked down at her again. "I need you," she breathed and tugged on his belt. He understood her and he lifted himself off her and the bed. Robbie stood next to the bed, not looking away from her. He pulled down both his jeans and boxers and stepped out of them, standing completely naked before her.

Gemma wanted to keep his gaze, but it was too tempting to not peek at him. He kept her gaze, so she quickly glanced down and up before she doubled back and stared at his manhood, wide-eyed. She heard Robbie clear his throat and Gemma glanced back up at him quickly before looking back down again. She couldn't help it.

"Everything okay?" Robbie asked and she could hear him fighting a laugh. Gemma looked back into his eyes, unable to wipe the expression of shock off her face. She cleared her throat, trying to formulate words.

"You are... um... well equipped."

Any seriousness that Robbie was feigning was completely shattered. He laughed and Gemma felt herself chuckling too, even as her cheeks burned.

"Well equipped?"

"Well, I didn't want to say 'well hung!'" That made him laugh even harder and so did Gemma. He climbed back onto the bed and covered her body with his once more. He looked down at her and was still smiling.

Gemma might not be a virgin, but she had only ever been with the one man. Her experience was still minimal at best. Matt wasn't small by any stretch, he had often boasted about it, but Robbie was most definitely above average. "I don't think it'll fit," she admitted sheepishly because she couldn't help but feel nervous and unable to see how it'll work.

"It will," he said, quietly. And he kissed her again and she could feel herself getting lost in his kiss again. Robbie nudged his way in between her legs again and Gemma could feel him at her entrance. Robbie pulled back so he could look into her eyes and he smiled slightly.

"Relax, Gem," he breathed and looking into his eyes and face, she could feel herself relaxing. A thrill of passion and excitement raced through her as Robbie lowered himself into her, very slowly and he filled her with a delicious sensation.

"Gemma," Robbie gasped and Gemma felt herself curving off the bed and pulling him in deeper. He began to move more and more and she felt herself mirroring his movements with a flick of her hips. The tightening began again in the pit of her stomach and she could feel herself building to the pinnacle again.

She gripped Robbie's shoulders and neck, feeling her nails digging into his sculpted muscles. The movements went from a steady pace to a more frenzied rhythm. Something was building and building deep within Gemma and when she thought she couldn't possibly handle any more pressure, there was an earth-shattering release. She arched more into Robbie and she was gripping him so tightly she was sure she would draw blood. Her body stiffened as the release washed over her and Gemma heard herself calling out to Robbie again. He wasn't far behind her and after a couple more deep, delicious movements, Robbie collapsed on top of her, panting and saying her name.

Gemma smiled to herself as Robbie slumped over her. Never had a man said her name with such passion or pleasure.

It was the most loved, sexy and *pleasurable* she had ever felt in her life.

Robbie made love to her in such a way she had never experienced before. And she loved him even more for that. He made her feel so wanted and loved; it was the best she had ever felt about herself.

Gemma felt so connected to Robbie, it was like they were two final pieces of a puzzle that got lost long ago, but were found again and put back together. It felt so right, Gemma couldn't believe that they had waited so long and wasted so many years.

For a few moments, they stayed entangled on Robbie's massive, silky bed. Their breath was ragged and Robbie's head was resting on Gemma's chest while she lay with her arms around him. Gemma felt weak and shaky, she could feel her arms and legs shaking slightly as they wrapped around Robbie's body. Gemma couldn't help it, she just started to laugh and Robbie looked up at her face. It was a moment or two while he watched her uncontrollably laughing before he started as well. They laughed and held each other for a little while longer until she couldn't laugh any more. They lay there again and Gemma looked into Robbie's deep brown eyes. She couldn't believe that they had just made love and that she was lying, *naked*, in his arms. After all these years, Gemma would have never ever thought she would be there and with Robbie.

Robbie started to caress her cheeks and she smiled at him. "Wow," she whispered and he grinned back.

"Wow," he replied and he kissed her lips softly. "I've…ah, well. That was amazing."

"It was."

"I've never felt like that before. Never felt such… pleasure." Gemma looked away, biting her lip while remembering what had just happened. Gemma felt Robbie's hand on her cheek and he pulled her face to face him again.

"I'm glad I was able to show you how much you mean to me."

"Honestly, that was…"

Robbie laughed and kissed her again. "It was… for me too."

"Really? Was I okay? I've never done any of that before."

"You were more than okay, I don't know about you, but that's the best I've ever had."

Gemma was taken aback, all those famous models and sexy women she'd seen him with all over the tabloids and *Gemma* was the best he's ever had? "Pfft, come on."

"What?"

"I am really the best sex you've ever had? Really? Me?" She shook her head.

"Gemma," Robbie grabbed her face again and forced her to look into his eyes. "I have never done that before, I have never made love to anyone before."

194

Gemma suddenly realised that she believed him. "I haven't before either." Gemma admitted, "Normally for me, it was always lights off, quickie with no foreplay or pleasure. It was over in a minute or so."

"It makes me jealous that you were ever with him," Robbie said gruffly. "But I know we both have pasts."

Gemma raised her eyebrows at him, *his* past was significantly lengthier than hers.

"But it *infuriates* me that he never showed you the attention you deserve."

She smiled back at him and snuggled herself closer into him. "All I want now is you."

"That's all I want too," he said and he had a devilish grin on his face. Gemma raised her eyebrows at him.

"Are you serious? *Again*?"

His grin widened and he nodded before he kissed her again, pulling her towards him. "I want to make up for all that missed time," Robbie murmured against her lips and he kissed her again. Gemma laughed against his lips as he pulled her on top of him and she kissed him back. Their kiss deepened quickly and once again, they expressed their love for each other physically again. It was as if they were making up for lost time, all those years of being in love with each other and not being together.

When they were spent, they held onto each other on the bed, naked and breathing heavily. Robbie's eyes found Gemma's and she realised she felt so at home in his arms. Sleep eventually took them and they held each other close, legs and arms entwined in the low light.

And Gemma had never felt more comfortable and happier in her entire life. For the first time in ten years, she felt like her life had a purpose. She felt like her life had a direction. She had felt so lost since losing Abi, but maybe, just maybe Robbie could finally give her direction again. So, as she fell asleep, listening to Robbie's breathing and steady heartbeat, she felt completely at home and with herself.

For the first time in her entire life.

CHAPTER THIRTEEN

Ten Years Earlier

Gemma's heart thumped uncomfortably in her throat as she watched the clock. She would have to face Robbie again and very soon according to the pub clock. Her stomach twisted and knotted tightly, she was angry at him but there was a part of her, a shameful part at that, that *wanted* to see him. And really, her anger was more with herself than with him.

Gemma just kept thinking about that kiss.

The feeling of his lips to hers, his hot breath in her mouth. The sensation of his body pressing into hers as they kissed on Pip's bed.

Gemma could still taste the beer on his breath, was that the reason why he kissed her? Did he not remember? Surely not. Yes, they had drunk but Gemma didn't think Robbie was so drunk that he didn't remember what happened back in Pip's bedroom. Was he that embarrassed that he was pretending it didn't happen? Was she that bad of a kisser, that he just wanted to pretend it had never happened? That was more likely than Robbie being too drunk to remember, Gemma thought with a sagging disappointment.

He was still with Miranda, school had returned and he was still holding her hand around campus, kissing her in the hallways and generally everywhere she went. Gemma tried to forget it; it was just probably a drunken mistake and she should focus on Abi. Abi was still in hospital, although stable it wasn't looking

197

good. Gemma fought back tears as she remembered seeing her. She looked so small in the bed, full of tubes and hooked up to the machine, it had even been hard to even hold her hand.

In all honesty, Gemma hadn't even wanted to hold her hand. She was still so riddled with guilt, she couldn't stand being around Abi longer than a few minutes at a time. It was even worse seeing Abi's mum and dad (who had been released himself a couple of days previously) with his bandaged arm and head, crying in the seats next to her.

Gemma just couldn't do it.

She tried to not think about it too much, it was easier to not think about Abi than it was to think about her. So instead, Gemma found her thoughts being filled with Robbie as a distraction. But she didn't want to think about him either.

But it was hard to put Robbie to the back of her mind when she would find him and Miranda snogging in front of their lockers again. Gemma would often have to fight back tears and spin and run away before either noticed she was there.

But every now and then, uncontrollable thoughts would come into her brain. She would be walking and suddenly she would remember the feeling of his lips on hers. His breath in her mouth and his hands on her face. It was burned into her memories and she couldn't shift it.

Robbie hadn't been back at work since before New Year. There was a general lull after the celebrations and the month of January was always slow. So by the time it was busy enough for Robbie to be brought back in as extra, it had been a month since their New Year kiss.

Gemma was watching the clock the night she knew he was due back.

What the hell was she going to say? What would they talk

about? Would they just ignore the whole thing and go back to how it was?

Before could think any more about it however, Robbie was coming through the pub doors, shrugging off his thick, wet coat. The second Gemma saw him, she escaped into the back, diving into unsorted cutlery. Gemma decided to busy herself with that until the evening rush picked up and she was needed to be out front again. She was a coward, but she didn't care. Robbie didn't join her in the back of house. So that's where Gemma stayed until she was called to the front an hour or so later.

It was getting busy and the tables were all nearly full. Gemma went straight to the pass and started serving food, keeping her eyes averted from Robbie who was getting drinks behind the bar.

She might have been paranoid, but she swore she could feel him looking at her. She almost looked at him to check, but she kept her nerve.

If he didn't or want to remember, she was going to forget it all too.

Gemma went to a table that was right at the back of the pub. Gemma walked passed that horrible mirror that she despised and she served their food. Instinctively, Gemma looked up into the mirror and felt the usual rush of hatred rush through her as she caught a glimpse of herself.

But at that moment, there was something else that caught her eye.

Robbie was staring at her, through the mirror. He was carrying what looked like two pints of coke and was frozen to the spot. She caught his eye and for a fraction of a second, they stared at each other.

In that instant, Gemma knew that he remembered

everything. By the way he was looking at her, it was like he was looking at her completely differently. But how, Gemma couldn't say. Gemma broke their gaze first, heat creeping up her neck and filling her cheeks. She suddenly felt extremely self-conscious and she couldn't bare her reflection any more. Gemma could feel tears stinging in her eyes. She wished, more than ever she had her entire life, to shrink.

Gemma wanted to shrink not only her body fat but her entire body. She wanted to shrink so small that she could disappear forever.

She was unable to cope in the suffocating pub a moment longer. Gemma ran from the table as quickly as possible, through the pub and kitchen, through the back door into the freezing January air. She took in massive, shuddering breaths and felt the cold air slicing at her airways. But it wasn't enough, more breath, more cold slices down her trachea.

She needed the pain, more and more.

She could feel the shivers moving through her muscles and the goosebumps all over her skin. Gemma crouched down and could feel the damp, frozen tarmac beneath her fingertips.

What was she going to do? She couldn't face Robbie now. It was easier thinking he had forgotten the entire thing and she could have just ignored it.

But that wasn't the case.

"Gemma?" A voice whispered behind her and she jumped up and almost screamed.

Gemma spun around and nearly went flying onto the wet ground when she saw who had spoken. "Gemma?" Robbie said, who was looking at her in a way he never had before. "Are you okay?"

"Um," she mumbled awkwardly, "yeah."

"Are you crying?"

Gemma wiped her cheeks with her sleeve quickly. "No."

He rolled back on his heels as an uncomfortable silence fell between them. She had a feeling what he wanted to say, so she tried to be brave enough to say it for him.

"Look, Robbie," Gemma started and she looked at his feet. She couldn't say anything when she looked into his face. "I won't say anything about New Year." Robbie stopped rolling on his heels. "I get it, I would do the same if I was you." She chewed on her lip, trying to get the nerve to look at Robbie but she just couldn't master it. So she just kept staring at his feet, waiting for him to turn and leave.

Or should she just leave?

She decided that would be the quickest option, to remove herself from the situation.

Gemma went to pass Robbie and head back for the pub door, but as she walked past Robbie, he reached out and grabbed her arm. Gemma looked down at his hand on her arm, then into his face. The way he was staring at her, it was like he was debating something internally. Whatever it was, he seemed to decide and he pulled her towards him. One of his hands went onto her waist and the other cupped her face as he pulled her face to his. They were the same height now; Robbie may have been slightly taller as Gemma felt her face being pulled upwards towards his.

She hadn't noticed that last time they kissed because they hadn't been standing but Robbie had apparently grown a fair bit in the last couple of months.

He pressed his lips to hers and closed his eyes but Gemma just stared at him for a moment. He tilted her head to the side as he started to deepen the kiss and Gemma felt her eyes involuntarily shut and her hands ran up his arms. Even though he was still quite skinny, Gemma could feel his biceps and other muscles starting to develop. She could feel his protruding veins running up his forearms, threading this way and that way all the way up to his bicep. Gemma hesitantly moved her hands from his arms to his shoulders and neck, as Robbie pulled closer. If Gemma thought the New Year kiss had been passionate, she had been wrong. Robbie was kissing her with such enthusiasm and heat, that they both were running out of breath quickly.

Robbie's lips moved to her neck as Gemma struggled to catch her breath. Her head swam with the taste and heat of his breath in her mouth and on her neck. He didn't give Gemma long to catch her breath before his lips were on hers again. He was kissing her so passionately, Gemma really did think she might faint with lack of oxygen. It was like Robbie could read her thoughts because he pulled back and they both panted.

"Gemma," he whispered softly as he struggled to catch his breath too. "Gemma, I—" but they were interrupted.

"Gemma!" someone screamed through the back door of the pub. Her mum. "What the hell are you doing? Get in here and help us!"

Gemma jumped slightly back from Robbie, but he still held onto her. He was staring into her eyes, intently and was debating something again. He took in a deep breath and looked like he was about to say something when her mum interrupted them… again.

"Gemma!" This time, her scream was very angry and Gemma knew any moment she'd be out here.

"Coming!" she called and they untangled their bodies and she ran inside. Robbie didn't follow her straight away so she left him in the now freezing alleyway and ran back to the front of house. Gemma went straight on the pass again and was about to run a table when her mum caught up with her.

"Where the hell have you been? Oh," she said when she turned back to her, "Gem, are you okay?" All hint of anger was gone, was there a terrible expression on her face? She tried to smooth all emotions out and plastered a small smile on her face.

"Fine," she said quickly and turned back to the pass.

"Okay, table six please. Where the hell is Robbie?"

Gemma felt my hands shake as she balanced the plates. "Um, no idea. Toilet maybe?"

"For twenty minutes? The boy takes the piss if that's true."

Gemma just shrugged her shoulders and gave a shaky laugh and turned around to run the food. Gemma had taken two steps before she nearly crashed into Robbie. Their eyes met and they both stared at each other for a moment, the heat pulsating through her again. The taste of his breath in her mouth and the feeling of his lips on her neck still burned into her skin.

"Bloody hell, there you are. Come on, table eight please, Robbie. And quickly please, they've been waiting a while now."

Robbie glanced at Linda and she did the same double take she had done with Gemma. "Jesus, are you okay? What's the matter with you two?"

"Nothing," they both said too quickly and Gemma looked at the ground before she ran off with table six's food. Gemma could feel Robbie's eyes on her again but she couldn't bring herself to look toward him. None of it made any sense, why would he kiss her again and so passionately? Gemma placed down number six's food and glanced up and saw Robbie serving a couple of tables away. His eyes met hers for a second before she looked back to the floor and went back to the pass again. Gemma grabbed the next table's food and quickly left before she could run into Robbie again. Gemma went to the other side of the pub with the food, her mind full of Robbie.

He was looking like he *wanted* her… at least that what Gemma guessed by his expression. Nobody had ever wanted Gemma before.

Gemma's mind was racing. For the first time since New Year's Eve, she felt something else in the pit of her stomach.

Was it hope?

Could she and Robbie possibly be together? She was suddenly overwhelmed with the idea of kissing Robbie again, imagining holding his hand as they went to the movies and sitting with him in the grass patches in school. The thing with those images was that Robbie looked the same, maybe slightly taller so there was a noticeable height difference between them both but it was Gemma that looked completely different. She was skinny and petite and pretty. She looked like Miranda.

It most definitely didn't look how Gemma looked, in that moment. She shook her head, fighting back the tears.

It would never happen because that's all it was, just a fantasy.

"Excuse me, love?" Gemma snapped back to reality with a sickening jolt. A customer was staring at her, all of them at the table were.

"Sorry?" she said, her voice hoarse.

"Can we please have two more cokes? On our tab?" Gemma glanced at the children at the table. There was a pretty girl staring at her. Instantly, Gemma felt a pang of jealousy for this unknown girl. She was skinny as well and drinking full fat coke.

"Yes," Gemma said, hoarsely again. "Of course, I'll bring them right over." She left the pretty, skinny girl behind as she stalked off to the bar. What Gemma would have given to just close her eyes and wake up looking like her. She would have given anything in that moment for that. Gemma got on with making the two drinks and as she was scooping the ice out of the bucket when she felt him there. Gemma didn't look straight away, but she could feel him next to her, looking at her.

"Gemma?" he whispered and she closed her eyes for a second, remembering the last time he had whispered her name with staggering clarity. Gemma looked up at him and he his were burning into hers. There was a fire behind his deep brown eyes that made her heart race. Gemma could feel herself choking on the air she was trying to suck in.

"Gemma, I—" but what Robbie was going to say, Gemma would never know. At the very moment the words left his lips, she heard a squeal of delight.

Miranda ran into the pub and straight up to the bar where Robbie and Gemma were. They both snapped their heads and looked at her and the small group she had brought in with her. Matt was among them and Gemma felt a sinking feeling in her gut. Miranda went straight up to the bar, reached across and grabbed Robbie's shirt at his chest and pulled him over the bar. She kissed him confidently and they embraced for a moment and Gemma looked away, fighting back tears again.

"Miranda," Robbie said, annoyed as he pushed her back and wiped his mouth on his shoulder. "I'm at work. Stop it."

"So?" she said and she grinned mischievously, "That's not stopped us before and we've done more than just kissing."

"Shut up, now," Robbie warned and he glanced at Gemma.

Gemma swallowed her rising bile as she digested that new information. What else that they done here? Jealousy was one of the new feelings she had while she imagined them doing numerous things.

Miranda must have thought Robbie was pointing to Gemma, the owner's daughter and granddaughter. She scoffed and shrugged, laughing over her shoulder.

205

"What, Roly-Poly? I'd like to see her say something."

"Miranda," Robbie said pointedly and she glanced at him. She shrugged and walked off, like a model on the catwalk, to her friends.

"We'll be over here then, try and sneak us some drinks," she glanced over her shoulder at him and winked. It was Gemma's turn to look pointedly at him.

"Gemma, I'm sor—" But Gemma turned on her heel, leaving him at the bar alone as she stalked off towards the table, with the customers' drinks. She then went back to the pass, trying to ignore the loud laughing coming from Miranda and Matt. Gemma knew by the way they were snickering it was about her as usual. Gemma just kept trying to avoid Robbie and his friends for the rest of her shift, the best she could anyway.

It was almost working by the end of the night, as some of the last customers ordering food were served. The lights on the pass had just been switched off as Gemma was bringing back some plates from an empty table when Robbie snuck in behind her and followed her into the kitchen. Gemma nearly sent all the plates cascading onto the floor, but luckily, they only clattered into the sink with a slightly smaller crash. They were quite alone and Robbie moved closer to her, his fingers brushed her forearm.

"Robbie…" Gemma didn't know what she was trying to say, the sentence disappeared as soon as it started through her lips. Robbie's fingers touched her cheek lightly as he caressed Gemma's face and traced her lips.

"Gemma, I want—" but Robbie never finished his sentence. At that moment, someone interrupted them.

"Gemma?" It was her mum again, but this time, she wasn't angry. She looked tentatively around the corner as Gemma and Robbie jumped apart again. The expression on her face had me instantly worried and the red, swollen eyes added to Gemma's worry. "Robbie, I think you need to sort your friends out," she added, surprisingly sharp with him

Gemma looked up at him and noticed he picked up on her tone as well.

"Okay..." he said and he glanced back down at Gemma and mouthed, "Later."

Gemma smiled gently at him before he turned and walked out of the kitchen. "What—" but Linda cut Gemma off.

"In the office, come on," she said very gently to her and Gemma followed her through the rest of the kitchen, to the back room where she shut the office door behind them. She indicated that Gemma sit in the chair by the desk and her suspicion instantly grew.

"Mum?" But she held up a shaking hand.

"Gemma," she whispered, her voice so low, Gemma could barely hear her. She cleared her throat, "Gemma," she said slightly clearly but with a waver. "Dennis called."

Dennis was Abi's father.

Gemma's stomach dropped and her heart began to race. Dennis calling would have excited Gemma normally in the hope of good news, but how Linda was acting, it wasn't good news. She just knew it.

"Just tell me." She took in a shaky breath.

"Gemma, something happened. Abi took a turn for the worse... she... her organs... her body couldn't fight it any more. Oh, I'm sorry sweetheart, she's gone."

It was like the words were coming to her through a long tunnel. A tunnel that was filled with water that muffled Linda's words. Linda was in the distance as Gemma felt the ground vanish beneath her. It took a moment for Gemma to realise that

Linda wasn't speaking to her through a water-filled tunnel, it was the blood pulsating in her ears. The pressure in Gemma's head thrashed and throbbed to the point that Gemma was sure her head would implode. How long did she stare at her mother's mouth, which remained unmoving? How long did she sit in the squeaking chair, unable to remember how to walk? Or even how she got to sit in it in the first place? How long did her mum try and regain her attention?

Gemma didn't know and she didn't care.

Gemma found herself standing up, looking towards the office door.

Linda may have spoken, even tried to grab her, but none of it registered. Gemma walked towards the door, an unknown destination in her sight. She didn't know if she was walking fast or slow, nothing was important any more. Gemma didn't remember walking through the kitchen, Linda on her heels, or out to the front of the pub. Gemma thought she might have had the front door in her sights subconsciously and maybe the hospital thereafter, but Gemma wasn't sure.

She didn't even see the leg stuck out in her path (on purpose by Matt) until she nearly tripped on it. She stumbled and could hear their laugh through the tunnel. She turned slowly, towards them.

They all stared at her and somehow, Gemma's expression made their laughter die away instantly. Gemma could feel her hands clenching as she stared at each and every one of them in turn.

"Abi died…" Gemma muttered and instantly their whole demeanour changed. The entire pub's atmosphere was shifted in an instant. Miranda looked panicked. Matt's usual cocky face was unreadable. They all stared at Gemma, apparently unsure what to say. "Nothing to say?" Gemma said quietly, "You had a lot to say at New Year."

Miranda looked up her with wide, petrified eyes. Gemma obviously looked like someone who wasn't of a sane mind. "Thanks to you," Gemma said, nodding to Miranda, who flinched away, "My last conversation with my best friend was an argument."

"That's not her fault," Matt said and Gemma glared towards him. Everyone pipped down instantly.

"It is *all* your fault. If you had just left me THE *FUCK* ALONE," Gemma was now screaming at them. Miranda and Matt flinched, along with the rest of them. "I WOULD HAVE NEVER FOUGHT WITH ABI! SHE NEVER WOULD HAVE LEFT THE PARTY AND SHE WOULD HAVE NEVER GOT INTO THAT CAR!"

Gemma was in hysterics, but she didn't care. The hatred she felt so much for them was so strong, she had no other rash feelings within her. Matt was closest, so Gemma started to attack him with glasses and saltshakers.

Miranda flew her arms over her head and flew out of the booth and the others started to flee, leaving Matt stuck under Gemma's assault.

Hands and arms grabbed her, restraining her back. They pulled her away from Matt so he could stumble and scramble his way away from Gemma.

"YOU KILLED HER! IT'S YOUR FAULT!" Gemma kept screaming at the top of her lungs, as she was dragged to the nearest exit and out to the front of the pub still screaming incoherently.

"Gemma!" Her mum was sobbing, "Gemma, honey, please—" but Gemma beat her away from her too. There was a pair of long, thin arms around her, trying to restrain her. Gemma fought her way out of his arms, repulsed to be even touched by him.

Gemma turned on him, seeing red.

"YOU!" she screamed hysterically. "YOU! YOU ARE THE REASON WHY WE FOUGHT! YOU ARE THE REASON WHY SHE LEFT EARLY! BECAUSE YOU ARE A COWARD! AND I FELL FOR IT... AGAIN!" Gemma lurched at Robbie, hands in fits and punching the air.

"Gemma, stop!" People were trying to restrain Gemma, but Gemma could only see Robbie.

They pulled her back slightly and Robbie was looking at her, his face distorted and broken.

"YOU'RE THE REASON SHE'S DEAD! I SHOULD HAVE BEEN WITH HER! NOT WITH YOU! I HATE YOU! I *HATE* YOU!" Gemma screamed and screamed until it became huge, uncontrollable sobs.

"Gemma," Robbie whispered, his voice cracked and broken. "I'm so sorry, please Gemma. Please believe me, I am so sorry. Please." Gemma couldn't scream any more, the sobs were ricocheting through her so violently, it looked like Robbie was shaking. It took her a minute to catch enough breath to speak, her voice came out low and hard.

"Leave," she said, "and never come back. I want to never, *ever* see you again."

"Gem—"

"Go."

"I—"

"Robbie," It was now Gemma's granddad that spoke and his voice came out firm and hard. "Just leave please." Robbie looked at him, his face broken. He looked at her mum, before he looked at Gemma one last time. Gemma just glared back and could see, even through her rage, the heartbreak on his face.

In years to come, that look would haunt Gemma's memories, but in that moment, she felt nothing.

She was completely hollow. An empty, worn shell, ready to crumple at the slightest touch.

He straightened his face and took all emotion off it before he turn on his heel and walked off down the street. Gemma watched the figure of Robbie Wilson walking in the orange glow of the street lamps until he reached the end of the street and turned.

That was the last time Gemma saw Robbie until he came back through those pub doors, ten years later. Because, a few days after that night, Robbie was signed by a major city club, some fifty miles away and moved there to play and finish school in the academy. And where he had his debut and became one of the best footballers in that club's history.

Gemma's life too changed in the coming days after that fateful night. Gemma came to the realisation that she didn't blame Matt, Miranda, Robbie or anyone else that was at that party.

With a crushing realisation, she realised that it was only Gemma to blame.

And Gemma's alone.

Abi's funeral was a couple of weeks after that night and Gemma had made that final promise to her best friend. The promise that as long as she would live, she would not allow herself to be happy again. It was her fault her best friend had died, all because she was in love with Robbie Wilson.

CHAPTER FOURTEEN

Present Day

Gemma woke the next morning in the middle of Robbie's humongous and apparently empty bed. Gemma sat up and looked around her. There were clothes, pillows and duvets thrown all over the huge room. Gemma looked down and realised she was only wearing a thin silk sheet over her naked body. She put her hand over her mouth and fell back onto the pillow laughing.

It was one of those "awkward laughs in a serious moment" laughs. That uncontrollable laugh.

Gemma couldn't believe she was laying, *naked*, in Robbie Wilson's bed. Gemma had pictured and imagined that moment for many, many years but somehow, she hadn't quite imagined the room the way it was before her. Apparently, in reality, they had been a lot messier and more enthusiastic. There was a knock at the door on the far wall of the bedroom. Gemma jumped up, trying to cover herself with the ridiculously small bed sheet she had procured. She sighed and relaxed when she saw it was Robbie coming in, carrying two cups of steaming something and a plate of toast. Gemma smiled as he walked towards her, a little slowly.

"Do you need some help?" she asked, scanning the floor for her dress or Robbie's T-shirt or anything other than that tiny bed sheet.

"Nope, I'm good. I haven't lost the skills from the pub all

those years ago."

Gemma scoffed and shook her head at him. "Skills? You think highly of yourself."

Robbie stopped and feigned offence. "I'm wounded, Gemma, I was hoping my skills were very good last night."

Gemma blushed crimson at that and Robbie teased her further. "I was under the impression you enjoyed yourself. Looks like I'll have to step up my game." Gemma glanced at him and caught his eyes with their blazed expression.

"Step up your game?" Gemma repeated, unable to hide her disbelief. "Surely there isn't much more you can do." And Gemma blushed deeper at the memory of the previous night.

"You have no idea," he purred and Gemma felt her bones go mushy as a shiver of heat pulsated through her body. Robbie put the mugs and toast plate on the nearest bedside table and crawled onto the bed next to Gemma. "There is much, much more I want to show you." His voice was husky and soft and Gemma could feel herself literally melting into the bed beneath her. "Much, much more." His face was an inch from hers and his eyes were smouldering. He was lowering his lips to hers, but Gemma pulled back after a moment and covered her mouth. "What?" Robbie asked, confusion replacing the heat in his eyes.

"I haven't brushed my teeth," she muttered sheepishly. Robbie's face broke into a smile. "I don't care." And Robbie pulled Gemma's face to his and kissed her with a ferocity that Gemma was left breathless (morning breath or not). They pulled apart, hot and tangled. "I don't know if I'll ever get enough," Robbie murmured as he caressed Gemma blushing cheeks. "I don't know how I'm going to go back to training." Gemma's heart sank.

"Argh," she muttered, pulling a grimacing face. "Reality."

She sighed but kept her arms wrapped around his neck and placed her forehead on his. "I wish we could stay in this little bubble forever."

Robbie kissed the tip of her nose before resting his forehead against hers again. "We've still got a few days."

"Really?" Gemma felt the smile spreading across her face.

"And I was hoping…" he trailed off.

"Hoping what?"

"Well, I was hoping you might join me at some point during the tournament."

"Is that allowed?"

"Yeah, of course."

"Really? You want me there?" Gemma couldn't help but smile.

"Obviously." He looked surprised and he grabbed both of Gemma's hands from around his neck and pulled them to his mouth, kissing both hands in turn. "I'm going to need you there. I don't think I can do it without you. Will you come with me to London for the tournament?" Gemma chewed her lip.

"I'll have to check with Mum, it's going to be the busiest we've been in a long while."

"I am sure your mum will agree. She's wanted us to get together for years." This shocked Gemma and her hands dropped and she leaned back, questioningly.

"What?" Robbie laughed.

"Oh come on, you didn't see it? Our mums have been planning this for years. Your mum was the one that told me to pull my finger out and tell you how I felt."

"*What?*" And Robbie nodded solemnly.

"Yep, when I first came home to see Mum. I came into the pub one afternoon while you were out and she pulled me over and

214

near enough interrogated me." Gemma put her face into her hands, groaning slightly. She could very much imagine what he was saying, her mother wasn't one that was easily swayed. "She told me that Matt wasn't good enough for you. She was only putting up with him so she could support you, she knew you'd need a support network when things went... well when things were over." Gemma's eyes swam with tears.

"She knows her stuff, that Linda." Robbie chuckled too and wiped her tears away. "She sure does. I didn't even need to admit my feelings for you, she knew already."

"How?"

"She always saw me watching you when we would work together in the pub. I told her I wished I had been brave enough to tell you all those years ago and she told me to grow some balls and tell you now." That made Gemma laugh.

"Well, I'm glad you did," Gemma said and she wrapped her arms around his neck and pulled him towards her once again.

"Me too," Robbie said huskily and their lips met. Gemma pulled back, biting her lip, trying to decide something. "What?" Robbie asked, as he traced his finger along her bottom lip and pulled it so it was released from her teeth. Gemma laughed lightly before taking in a deep breath and replying.

"Well, it's not just my mum that interrogates."

Robbie raised his eyebrows. "Please elaborate."

"Well, that night. At the hospital, with your mum."

Robbie's eyes widened with realisation. "No!" Gemma nodded and Robbie shook his head. "The sly..." he murmured under his breath still shaking his head in disbelief. Gemma looked at him, waiting for *him* to elaborate.

"Well, also on that night, my sweet, innocent mother interrogated me as well. Seems that she and Linda have been sharing notes. Basically, it was along the same lines: 'Grow some balls and tell her how you feel, a beautiful girl like that won't wait around forever.' Or something like that."

Gemma blushed and shook her head.

"Sad thing was, I think I will be here forever. Or at least, I would have been, if it hadn't been for you." Gemma cast her eyes down, still feeling the prickling heat stinging her cheeks as she chewed her lip. Suddenly, there were hands on Gemma's face, causing her to jump. Robbie lifted up her face up so her eyes met his.

"You saved me, Robbie," Gemma whispered but Robbie was shaking his head slowly.

"No, Gemma, you saved me. I didn't know I could feel so happy, I always knew there was something missing. It was you."

Gemma didn't get to reply, she swallowed the lump that had risen in her throat just before Robbie brought his lips to hers. At first, it was a slow and almost sweet kiss but within seconds of it starting, the overwhelming heat and passion that pulsated out of them took over. They found themselves back on the bed, really kissing again. Robbie's mouth left Gemma's and moved down the column of her neck as she gazed, dazed at the ceiling.

"I just can't stop," Robbie was murmuring into her skin.

"W-what?" Gemma asked stupidly and Gemma could feel him smiling against her neck.

"I can't stop. I can't kiss you enough, I just need you so much." He was panting and Gemma was pleased to realise that he wasn't as cool and calm as she thought. He seemed to be as frenzied and affected as she was. He was tugging at the silk sheet with jerky, frenzied movements. Gemma had become wrapped up in it, so she helped him by twisting this way and that until the sheet was finally pulled away.

Gemma still took in a deep breath and closed her eyes as she was fully exposed. Even though Robbie had seen her completely naked and from every angle the night before, she was nervous again. Maybe it was because the alcohol had well and truly left her system or maybe because some time had passed while they slept. All Gemma knew was that her heart was beginning to beat uncomfortably fast. Gemma kept her eyes firmly closed, but she could feel Robbie beside her. Robbie was kneeling beside Gemma, gazing over her body.

"So beautiful," Robbie murmured and Gemma's eyes flew open. Gemma let out the breath she had been holding. Robbie heard her exhale and his eyes went to hers. They had nothing but love and admiration in them and Gemma felt herself feeling more and more at ease. "What is it?" He asked gently.

"It's just... I feel so at ease with you. It just surprises me, that's all."

"What do you mean?" And he came to lie beside her, pressing his body into hers. The moment was still hot and erotic, but Gemma could tell Robbie was also curious.

"Well, just that I feel so comfortable being... naked. And I have never felt that way. Even by myself." Robbie was caressing Gemma's whole body while she spoke and it was extremely distracting. He was doing circular motions on the back of her knee, to the inside of her thighs, to the sensitive parts of her hips onto her stomach then around her breasts. Gemma's whole body felt alight again and she was struggling to keep her breathing under control and not pant in his ear. "R-Robbie..." She whispered and he continued his sweet, sensual caresses.

"Mmmh?" was his response and he was looking at Gemma's body again, deep in thought.

"Robbie?" Gemma said again and this time, his eyes

snapped up to hers. He leaped up from beside her and covered her body with his.

"Sorry, I was thinking." And his devilish smile was back.

"About…?"

Robbie's face went more serious as he looked into her eyes. "I was thinking about how I think you're the most beautiful girl I have ever laid my eyes upon and you just don't see it." Gemma blushed. "See?" Robbie's fingers touched her cheeks. "This face and this body," he said and his hands, feather-light, moved down her neck leaving a trail of tingling heat behind his fingertips, "is so beautiful."

His fingers were back to her breasts and he started doing tantalising swirls on them, causing them to pucker and Gemma to arch her back off the bed. Robbie must have put some shorts on while he went to fetch (the very forgotten) drinks and toast. Gemma could feel the thin fabric as she pressed her hips shamelessly into his as he moved down and replaced his fingers with his mouth and kiss her so intimately. She could feel him pressing against her, his feelings of wanting her pulsating against her. It made Gemma shudder with pleasure.

Robbie moved back up to kiss her mouth again before he started to trail kisses down her body once more, getting closer and closer to her centre, to her very core. She was beginning to feel something winding up within her once more and felt herself pushing forward to that sweet release.

"Robbie…" Gemma moaned and he lifted his head and his brown eyes were burning.

"Yes?" he whispered and smiled when she seemed to go incoherent as he began to touch her in her most intimate place. She threw her head back and Robbie smiled even more. "Yes, Gemma?" he asked innocently again, enjoying the sight before him.

"I—" But Gemma stopped.

Robbie stopped.

They both stopped and listened. There were voices, some distance away and unclear, but there were voices outside of the bedroom where Gemma and Robbie were tangled in a hot exchange. The heat disappeared instantly and they both looked at each other, wide-eyed for a moment, before Robbie leaped up. He ran to the door and stuck his head out, listening to the voices again and swearing under his breath. He shut the door quietly before racing over to his wardrobe and pulling out a couple of T-shirts and another pair of shorts.

"Here," he said and he threw a T-shirt and the pair of shorts at Gemma, who was frozen on the bed and still very naked. "You can wear these if you want."

"B-But who is it?" Gemma whispered, panicked. She was shocked when Robbie actually *laughed*. "What the hell could be funny at this point?"

"My mother. That's who's out there."

Gemma felt the blood leave her body and Robbie must have noticed because he ran over to her quickly and kissed her quickly. "It'll be fine, Gem."

"But I'm naked!" Robbie couldn't help but laugh as he got back up and walked over to the door.

"You won't be if you put them on."

"Like that's not obvious what we've been doing when I come out wearing your T-shirt!"

"Gemma, you're here at nine o'clock on a Sunday morning. I think it's going to be obvious why you are here." Gemma blushed deeply, Robbie took pity and stopped teasing. "It'll be fine, Gem, she's wanted me to buck up the courage and ask you

219

out for years. She near enough orchestrated the entire thing anyway. She'll be happy, trust me. Now get dressed or it'll be *extremely* obvious why you are here... *naked*." He flashed her a cheeky grin and slipped back outside into the hallway. Gemma could still the muffled voices and heard the apparent exclamation from Rose when Robbie appeared. Gemma sighed and pulled on Robbie's T-shirt and slipped on his shorts.

She wasn't even going to attempt to locate any of her clothes. It would take too much time.

She quickly ran over to the long, floor-length mirror and gasped at her appearance. She was extremely flushed and warm looking with a bird's nest as hair. She groaned and attempted to run her hand through her hair, trying to flatten it slightly. She needed a proper hairbrush to look semi-decent, but her fingers would have to do. Not wanting to put it off much longer, she left the room.

Once out in the hall, Gemma realised that she had absolutely no idea which way to go next. It was a huge hallway with many doors, but Gemma could just make out noise, so she decided to follow that. The voices took her down the hallway, past some humongous windows that had some seriously breathtaking views of the countryside and down the massive staircase Gemma remembered from the previous night. Her heart was beating so erratically in her chest, Gemma was worried she might just faint.

How many times in her life had she seen Rose before? Never had she ever been scared to see her. The woman was like a second mum to her. But seeing her there, at *Robbie's* house, wearing *Robbie's* clothes, it was totally different.

Everything would be totally different from that day on.

The talking got louder as Gemma seemed to move through what must have been a dining room, with a massive, long table that looked like it could sit at least fifteen people and where obviously Robbie could have a lavish dinner party if he wanted. Gemma then moved through a lavish living room with huge, corner sofas and a floating fireplace with huge French doors that opened to a beautiful garden, even though it was more the size of a football pitch. Gemma couldn't take it all in, she just kept turning her head this way and that as she moved towards the voices. Through the living room, she walked down a couple of cool marble steps and into a cool, white, modern kitchen space. Gemma actually stopped in her tracks and took it all in.

It was absolutely stunning and huge.

Gemma couldn't believe the size of Robbie's house, she knew he would have to be rich to be such a successful football player, but it dawned on Gemma that she had no idea how rich he was. The kitchen was so light and Gemma saw why. The whole south-facing wall was floor-to-ceiling windows, with more double sliding French doors that opened into a lower-level patio and deck area of the beautiful garden. Gemma could also see a stunning pool and hot tub just beyond the decking. Gemma's eyes fell on the two people standing on the decking, looking out to the stunning garden beyond.

It was Robbie and Rose.

Gemma took a deep breath and hugged her arms tightly around her chest and stepped towards them.

"What do I owe the pleasure, Mother?" Robbie was saying, nodding towards her and smiling but Gemma could see he wasn't impressed. "I thought you were supposed to be resting?"

"I'll go crazy if I spend another day at home in bed. Your father is out, and as you so kindly loaned Jim to me, I thought I'd pop round and see my favourite son."

"I am your only son. And how can you be going crazy? You

came home from the hospital yesterday afternoon," Robbie pointed out with raised eyebrows.

"Yeah well, you're my only son and you've got a pool." She shrugged her shoulders and nodded towards the pool. "Think that hot tub might help me relax."

"You could have rung and said you were coming." Robbie's tone was light but still slightly clipped. "I was busy."

"Busy at nine in the morning? Whatever with?" And Robbie nodded towards Gemma, who was now standing behind Rose. Gemma blushed as Rose spun around, staring wide-mouthed at her. She was suspended in such a way Gemma may have laughed if the situation wasn't so pivotal in all their lives. Nothing was said for a few moments as they all stared at one another.

Rose shocked.

Gemma embarrassed.

Robbie amused.

Finally, Robbie broke the silence. "Mum, have you met Gemma?" The moment needed to be broken and thankfully, Robbie's joke did just that.

"Oh, Robbie," Rose said, laughing lightly and slapping him on the shoulder. "But this is brilliant." She beamed at Gemma and pulled her towards her for a rib-crushing hug. "He finally came to his senses, did he?" she said as she pulled back and wagged her finger at Robbie.

"Hey, I came to my senses a long time ago. It just took me some time to get the right moment. And plus, Gemma has already told me that you stuck your nose in her business as well."

Gemma's smile was watery as she watched the exchange and Rose brought Robbie in for a hug.

"Well, someone had to do something. It's been obvious for years. About bloody time." She added and she kissed Robbie on

222

the cheek. "This is the best news I've ever had."

"Even better than finding out you were pregnant with me?"

"God, not with you. You were an accident. But it's pretty close to how happy I was when I found out I was expecting Pip."

Gemma laughed and all was normal again. Gemma felt a weight being lifted off her as Robbie and Rose continued their jesting exchange.

The only difference was that Robbie's hand found Gemma's and their fingers entwined as he pulled her closer to his side. Rose decided not to stay and use Robbie's hot tub, she didn't even stay for a coffee. Gemma was surprised she was actually quick to leave.

As she left and Gemma was sitting out on the beautiful balcony, Gemma was thinking about the whole exchange. "Do you think it's odd your mum didn't interrogate us more?" Gemma called out to Robbie as he made another round of drinks and toast.

"Um," Robbie said as he finished buttering the last slice and placed it on top of the already tall mountain of toast. "No, I suppose she didn't want to feel like she was intruding."

"Are we talking about the same person here? Rose always likes to dig for details!"

"I suppose normally yes, but I don't think she wants to know all the details regarding her son's adult relationship. If you know what I mean." Gemma blushed, she did know what he meant and instantly was thankful Rose hadn't pressed for more details about how and what had happened the night before.

"She looks much better," Gemma commented as she watched Robbie, yet again, try and carry two drinks and a plate of toast. He was concentrating hard and didn't answer. Gemma had to smile as she watched him. His tongue was even sticking out with effort.

"Are you sure you don't want any help?" But Gemma already knew his answer.

"Nope," he said, as he put the drinks and food down on the table and beamed at his handy work. "I told you, I've got skills." And he flashed her a cheeky, suggestive grin. Gemma had a sudden flashback of memories.

"Yes," she said quietly, taking her coffee and trying to hide her smile behind her cup. "You definitely have skills." Robbie sat down in the chair opposite her and reached for a slice of toast. Gemma took a sip of the rich, creamy coffee and sighed. "Wow, do you have a barista hidden in there?" Robbie laughed but shook his head.

"I am the barista."

Gemma pondered that for a moment before remembering something. "Hang on, you used to hate coffee. Now you make barista-style coffee?"

"A lot has changed in the past ten years, Gemma, I'm not the same boy I was when I was sixteen."

"No, you're not. That's true. I'm just surprised you can make a decent flat white." Gemma took another sip and sighed again. "That's amazing."

"I think my coffee skills are getting higher praise that my skills in the bedroom. You sound like you're really enjoying that coffee." Robbie took a sip of his own coffee and failed to hide a slight grimace. Gemma frowned and he caught her eye. "What?"

"Can I have a taste of your coffee?" Gemma asked and narrowing her eyes slightly as she looked at him suspiciously.

"Why? You've got your own orgasmic coffee." He looked uncomfortable.

"Please?" They had a slight stand-off as Robbie clasped his coffee with both hands.

"Fine!" he suddenly cracked. "It's only got half a shot in and loads of sugar and it still tastes like shite!" Robbie hung his head in shame and passed over the coffee to Gemma. She took a sip and gagged. If you could even call it coffee, it was more sugary milk than coffee.

"That's vile! But why did you pretend to have coffee?" Robbie put his head in his hands, embarrassed and shaking his head.

"I wanted to seem grown up and sophisticated! I hate coffee, still. To this day."

Gemma burst out laughing, proper belly laughing. Robbie eventually joined in and they both laughed until their stomachs ached and tears streamed down their faces. "You're such an idiot," Gemma eventually gasped and Robbie nodded.

"It's the hold you've got over me. I become a bumbling, awkward teenager again."

Gemma scoffed at that. "Oh please, there is nothing bumbling and awkward about you!" Robbie didn't add any more on the subject, he just shook his head and held out the plate of toast.

"Toast?" he asked, still grinning as he grabbed himself a slice and bit off the corner. "I'll make you a proper breakfast in a bit, just thought you might need an energy boost. I know I need some, if I'm going to keep up with you."

Gemma laughed and looked down at the plate. She grabbed a slice and nibbled it. Robbie watched her for a moment and Gemma looked up into his questioning eyes. Her stomach was stirring as she held the toast in her hand. Gemma knew she wouldn't be able to keep it from Robbie, but she tried to ignore it. She took another small bite and kept her head up, just praying her double chin wouldn't wobble as she chewed.

"Gemma, what's wrong?"

Gemma glanced down; she'd been hoping to keep it from Robbie a little longer than that. Gemma sighed and put down the barely-eaten toast. She sipped her coffee and kept her eyes on it for a moment as she tried to formulate the words.

"I… don't like… *eating*," Gemma said the last word with such malleus, that Robbie looked a little taken aback, "in front of people." She finished and her stomach was flipping and twisting uncomfortably.

"Why?" he said and she glanced up at him at his tone. He sounded so sad and confused. Gemma looked into his eyes, hating the expression of pain on his face. Gemma looked back at her coffee cup, chewing her lip, as she thought of a reply. Gemma jumped at the feeling of fingertips on her cheeks suddenly, which moved to her chin and lifted her chin up slightly.

Robbie was looking into her eyes as he caressed her cheeks again as he whispered, "Please?" His plea gave Gemma the will, the will to try and explain her strange mind.

"I feel… like people will judge," she said and by his expression, he was confused, so she continued. "Like, if I eat healthy food, like a salad or something, I know they'll be thinking: 'Why bother love? Who are you trying to kid? Salads didn't make cause *that*.'" Robbie looked taken aback, so she tried to continue, "But if I eat something unhealthy, I know people will be thinking: 'Wow, are you really eating all that? No wonder she's that size!'" Gemma tried to smile slightly at him, but he didn't return it. He was staring, slightly open-mouthed.

"Do you think that I would think these things too?" he whispered finally and it was Gemma's turn to caress. Gemma's fingers trailed his strong jawline and she could feel how tense he was under her fingers.

226

"Everyone thinks that. I didn't get this size by eating salads. I wish I could be one of the girls that eats really healthily, goes to the gym or running a few times a week. But I'm not like that, so I deserve for people to think that of me."

"Everyone eats, Gemma, that's how we stay alive."

"I *know* that, but what I mean is, because of... my *size*, I feel people will constantly be scrutinising what I eat."

"But why do you care?"

"I don't know," she answered honestly, "I always think about what others will think. My whole life I have always thought like that."

"You shouldn't care what people think."

"That's easy for you to say, you've always looked amazing. You've never been fat, or constantly bullied for being fat." Robbie gasped and Gemma backtracked. "That's not what I mean Robbie, I'm sorry. I shouldn't have brought it up." She grabbed his hand and brought it to her lips, kissing the back of his hands. She didn't want to make Robbie feel guilty, that was never what she wanted.

"You are apologising to me, because I used to bully you because I was a shallow, spineless git?"

Gemma winced at his harsh tone. "Well, you didn't really bully me—"

"I never defended or protected you from Matt or Miranda."

Gemma just shrugged slightly and half smiled. "Robbie, we were just kids."

"I still should have known better. Stood up for you, been brave enough to admit my feelings for you. I'll always hate myself for it."

"Don't hate yourself, Robbie, I don't hate you."

"It still affects you though, how we treated you." Gemma bit

227

her lip, thinking about her response. She wanted to be honest with Robbie, but also didn't want to blame him any more.

"I would probably still feel the same, even without that. It's something that's in me Robbie, something I have to constantly battle. I have a lot of baggage; you should run while you got the chance."

Robbie quickly took her face in his hands and looked deeply into her eyes. "I will never run again, Gemma. I don't deserve your forgiveness, but I am going to try my hardest and prove my worth to you."

"You don't have to prove anything, Robbie."

"Yes, I do," he said certainly and he leaned in and kissed her across the table. They lingered for a moment and when they pulled back, Gemma's head was swimming with Robbie.

"See," Gemma said dazed, "totally forgiven." He chuckled against her lips before he kissed her again.

When they broke apart, panting slightly, he whispered, "I don't forgive myself." And she looked into his eyes, seeing the true pain and regret that filled his eyes.

"Oh, Robbie!" she cried and threw her arms around his neck and pulled him close. She kissed all over his face and his lips multiple times before she pulled away. "Enough of this! I love you and that's all that matters now." Gemma took a deep breath and picked up the slice of toast. She took one last breath before taking a bigger mouthful and chewing it slowly. At first, she didn't look at Robbie, but after a couple more mouthfuls, she glanced back at him. He was looking at her with such warmth and love. Robbie loved her, no matter what and that filled her with a new sense of braveness.

They continued to eat their toast and drink their coffee (well Gemma did, Robbie admitted defeat and made a cup of tea), on

Robbie's beautiful balcony, overlooking his stunning garden. The late spring sun was rising high in the sky while they spoke about small things and reminisced about the night before. It wasn't until Robbie laughed about Matt, that Gemma felt l sudden jolt back to reality. She groaned and covered her face with her hands.

"Argh, Matt. I had actually forgotten about him until now."

"Good, I should hope that you weren't thinking about Matt in the last twelve hours."

"You know what I mean. It's just going to be messy."

"Why do you say that?"

"Because I just know. He won't go quietly."

"He'll have to." But Gemma wasn't as confident.

"Argh, I bet he's called. I don't even know where my phone is."

"Must be in the bedroom. Maybe we should go and have a look." He grinned suggestively again and Gemma tried to roll her eyes exasperatedly, even though her cheeks prickled with heat.

"Again? Goodness me Mr Wilson. You did get your energy boosted. But I might have to have a shower before you get any ideas."

"Hmm, maybe I'll join you."

Gemma flushed scarlet at that. "I really need to find my phone…"

"Fine, first phone then we shower." Robbie grabbed Gemma's hand and kissed the back of it, then each of her fingers before standing up quickly. "Come on," he said, tugging her up quickly.

"What's the rush?" Gemma asked, slightly shocked by Robbie's sudden change in pace. "You want to find your phone and I want you in the shower." Gemma gasped as he pulled her against him suddenly and pushed his hips into hers.

"Robbie!" she exclaimed as she felt herself being pressed into the wall behind her. "Hmm?" Was all Robbie said as he lowered his face to hers. Gemma's breathing became uneven as she could feel Robbie pressed against every inch of her.

"What were we doing again?" he asked, his silky voice as he kissed Gemma's lips quickly before moving to her chin and moving down her neck. Gemma lost the ability to form words as Robbie was kissing a particularly sensitive part of her neck and collarbone. "Gemma?" he asked again and he pulled back, smiling at Gemma's dazed expression. "What were we doing?"

"No idea," Gemma said dumbly and Robbie was unable to remain serious. He laughed and put his forehead against hers.

"We were going to find your phone, I think. Then you distracted me."

"*I* distracted *you*? At least you could remember what we were going to do five minutes ago. Now all I can think of is that shower."

"Me too."

"I suggest we skip the phone search and just go straight for the shower. I won't be able to concentrate and look for it." Robbie grinned and nodded enthusiastically.

"I agree. Much smarter and more efficient in the long run."

And at that, Robbie swept Gemma up into his arms and pretty much ran back up the stairs and into his room. He put Gemma down and then the kiss began and there was absolutely no looking for Gemma's phone (or other personal items for that matter) for a good hour or so.

CHAPTER FIFTEEN

When Gemma got around to locating her phone and clothes from the previous night (sometime later) she groaned at the number of notifications awaiting her. After a considerable amount of time in the shower, Gemma found her phone in her bag which had been thrown, with quite a bit of force, into the far corner. When she finally pulled it out of the little clutch bag, her mouth fell open.

There were a few messages off Pip and her mum, Rose had already spread the news it seemed. But most of the hundred messages and notifications were just Matt.

"What is it?" Robbie asked. He crossed the room, picking up things as he went. He had stopped what he was doing, (fixing the bedsheets) and walked over to Gemma, wrapping his arms around her waist. "Oh my God," he said into her ear as she looked over her shoulder and Gemma's phone, which she had lifted up to show him. "He's blowing up your phone."

"That's an understatement. He's called me ninety times! And I've got about forty messages. Jesus, after how he treated me, you'd think he'd be happy to be rid of me."

"It's because he can't control you any more, you stood up to him and he can't stand it." The phone started buzzing again as he spoke and they both stared at the name that lit up.

Gemma's heart started to beat faster and her hand started to shake slightly. Robbie noticed the phone quivering slightly and grabbed it off her.

"Here, let me enlighten him." He swiped the phone and held

it to his ear.

"Matt," he said and Gemma waited with bated breath. After a second, she heard a muffled voice that was clearly irate on the other line. "Well, that's just charming, Matty," Robbie said after a second of muffled yells. "Well, you see, Matt, she doesn't want to see you. She doesn't want you and you don't deserve her—" More irate muffling. "No, I don't think I deserve her either, Matt. She is an amazing woman who deserves the best. If she has chosen me, then I will spend the rest of my life giving her the best. So I'm going to be around, hopefully," Robbie glanced at her, so Gemma nodded and he smiled before he continued, "for a long time and you're going to leave her alone."

Gemma could hear an end coming to the conversation and with a rush of bravery, she outstretched her hand and Robbie looked at it. "Gemma wants to speak to you, now keep that foul language to yourself." He handed her the phone and before she had the phone fully to her ear, Gemma could hear the abuse being shouted. It was a string of vile words, along the lines of "fat slut" and "fucking bitch".

"Matt," Gemma said loud and clear, keeping her nerve. She spoke over his abuse, "You have until closing tonight to get your stuff out of my flat and to leave the key. If you don't do it by tonight, the locks will be changed, and your shit will be in bin bags in the back street." There was more abuse, but Gemma spoke over him again. "Tonight. Goodbye, Matt." Gemma hung up the phone and threw her phone back into her bag. Gemma could feel the adrenaline starting to run around her body as she looked slowly at Robbie.

"I can't believe I just did that."

"I can," he said and he was looking at her with a fiery expression. "I love that you're standing up for yourself and not letting him treat you like shit any more." Robbie put his hands on her hips and spun her around, so she was facing him. He wrapped his arms around her and pulled her close to him. He kissed then kissed her so deeply that Gemma's head swam.

They lingered for a while before Gemma pulled away and laughed lightly. "I've got to go home, I need to get ready for work. I'm on the closing shift tonight."

"No," Robbie said and he pulled her back to his chest. "No, please don't go."

"I don't want to. But I will have to go home eventually. I have no clothes."

"I can get you clothes."

Gemma pulled back, looking at him with raised eyebrows. "What? You have a stash of women's clothes?" Gemma didn't like that, "That's creepy."

Robbie laughed and shook his head.

"Of course I don't have a stash of clothes."

"None from any previous overnight guests?"

"I've had no other 'overnight guests' as you put it." Gemma just kept her eyebrows raised. "What? I haven't! I swear!"

"You, Robbie Wilson? The Robbie Wilson who is a football god, probably one of the sexiest men on earth who has had many girlfriends in the past... has never had a girl stay here over night?"

"Well, thank you for calling me the sexiest man on earth, but currently I am sure that is Idris Elba or John Legend or someone like that. And to answer your question, no I haven't ever had another girl stay overnight here. And I haven't had girlfriends because I haven't ever been in a serious relationship. Nothing ever went further than a few dates and a couple of meetups. I've never wanted other women here. You are the first woman I've *ever* had stay overnight and in *my* bed."

Gemma just stared at him, open-mouthed.

"How is that possible? There's been so many... hasn't there?"

Robbie just shrugged. "None of them were you, Gem. You're the only one I wanted." He bent down and kissed her sweetly on the lips and rested his forehead against hers. Gemma felt herself smiling as she looked up into his eyes.

"Robbie," Gemma sighed as he pulled her hands up to kiss them. "Stay... just a bit longer. I can take you to work later."

"I can't go to work in this," she looked down at her dress. Gemma had been wearing it (and not wearing, she supposed) for over twelve hours. Not to mention a change of underwear and those horrible, impractical high heels. "I cannot work in those!" Gemma pointed at the shoes with a look of distaste.

"I'll sort some clothes... and shoes," he added as he watched Gemma grimace at the heels. "You don't need to start until later do you?"

"No, I guess not. But how will you sort clothes?" Gemma knew for a fact that she was at least two or three sizes bigger than any other girl Robbie would have dated or not dated.

"I've got a stylist. She'll get you some new clothes."

Gemma stared at him. "You've got a stylist?"

"Yes."

"And she what... buys your clothes?"

"Pretty much, keeps things updated."

"Updated?" Gemma shook her head and laughed slightly.

"What? It's not different to you going to buy clothes when you need them." He was a little defensive, but there was also a smile forming on his lips.

"It's nowhere near the same. I have clothes in my wardrobe

234

that are ten years old." Robbie laughed and so did Gemma.

"Just let her get you some clothes. Please?"

"Oh, fine," Gemma said, giving up.

"Praise the Lord!" Robbie exclaimed and he pulled out his phone. He then put it to his ear and rested his chin on Gemma's head as he waited for whoever to answer.

Two rings and a female voice answered. "Mr Wilson?"

Gemma looked up at him, grinning as she mouthed "Mr Wilson?" Robbie rolled his eyes but ignored her.

"Hi, Amy, I need you to pick up some clothing for my…" He looked at Gemma with raised eyebrows as he said, "Girlfriend please." Amy was obviously shocked by that (nearly as much Gemma) but she quickly recovered.

"Of course, Mr Wilson. What would you like?"

"Whatever you see fit. She's got to work in a pub later, so she'll need to be comfortable and practical."

"What size is she may I ask?" Gemma's stomach dropped; she'd been dreading this question. Robbie turned to Gemma.

"Gem?" he asked, but then frowned at her. Her anxiety must have been obvious because Robbie lowered the phone slightly and looked at her with worrying eyes. Gemma untangled herself from his arms and took a couple of steps away, wrapping her arms around her chest. "*Gemma? What's wrong?*" But Gemma couldn't speak so she just shook her head. It was silent for a moment before the voice on the other end of the phone spoke.

"Oh, is that Gemma, Gemma who went out with you last night? Old family friend?"

"Yeah, that's the one." But Robbie was still looking concerned at Gemma.

"I've seen her, she had a beautiful dress on. I'll just get a range of sizes to be covered. Leave it with me."

"Thank you."

"You're very welcome. I'll be back in a couple of hours, Mr Wilson."

"Perfect, Amy, thank you." They said their goodbyes and Robbie hung up. Robbie was watching Gemma pacing back and forth for a few moments, before deciding to close the distance between them in three long strides. "Gemma, what's happened? Did I say something?" Gemma sighed and looked up at him. His eyes were wide and warm that Gemma felt instantly more relaxed.

"Oh, Robbie. You didn't say anything. It's me, all me." And she buried herself into his chest and cried. Robbie instantly wrapped his arms around her and kissed the top of her hair and waited while she cried. After a few moments, Gemma pulled back and Robbie was still watching her with questioning eyes. Gemma decided it was best to be honest with Robbie.

"I just had a little… panic attack thing, I suppose."

"Did I say something that made you anxious?" he looked horrified.

"Oh, Robbie. No… yes, I suppose… Something was said that triggered me but it wasn't you. It's going to sound ridiculous," Gemma mumbled, her eyes moving down to her feet. She felt Robbie grip her chin with one large hand and he pulled her chin up gently so that her eyes met with his.

"What did I say, Gem? Please tell me. I never want to upset you."

Gemma took a deep breath, closing her eyes and resting her head against his chest once more. It was easier to say it to him without actually looking him in the eye.

"It was when… Amy was it? When she asked for my size."

Robbie said nothing, Gemma listened to his heart beating

evenly under her ear for a few moments before Robbie spoke again. "And why would that cause you such distress?"

"Because I am embarrassed. I hate how I look and I don't want anyone to ever know what size clothes I wear."

"Even me?" Robbie said softly and Gemma lifted her head off his chest and they looked at each other for a moment. Gemma really thought about it all. How wonderful, affectionate and tentative Robbie had been in the last twenty-four hours. She shouldn't feel embarrassed around him, but that horrible little voice inside her head was telling her otherwise.

"I am probably three or four sizes bigger than any other girl you've dated, Robbie."

"So? You're also three or four times more funny and smart and beautiful than them as well."

"Oh, Robbie," Gemma scoffed, but she felt a smile returning to her lips. Her anxiety and tension were slowly subsiding and she knew she had Robbie to thank. "Thank you. For making me feel better."

"Always. But it's all true, every word of it."

"Thank you."

He pulled her in for a tight hug before releasing her again. "Besides, even if you told me, I don't have a clue about what sizes women's clothes are anyway. It's too confusing."

Gemma opened her mouth to start explaining but Robbie put his finger on her lips to stop her. "Please, for the love of God. Don't explain it." They both laughed and after a moment they fell into silence.

"All this talking about clothes is making me want to grab this," Robbie's hands clasped around the hem of Gemma's dress and lift it up slightly, exposing more of her thighs. "And pull it up, over your head and throw it away." Robbie's fingers were grazing the outside of her thighs. Gemma's breath was coming in and out a lot quicker and heavier.

"Oh really?" Gemma said, trying to sound calm and collected but her voice was thick with anticipation. Robbie just nodded and his fingers were drawing delicious patterns on her thighs and moving up slowly towards her bum. "Maybe we should do something about that then," Gemma said and she was surprised at how bold she sounded. Robbie nodded in agreement and with a smile on his lips, he reached down and hoisted her up so her legs wrapped around his waist.

"We *really* need to do something about that. Right now." And Gemma laughed before she kissed him. He pulled back and was looking at her with such warmth and fire that Gemma shuddered. "Yeah, right now," Robbie said and he carried her back towards the bed. But they didn't even make it to the bed before they were overcome with passion and fire once more.

Sometime later, Gemma found herself laying across Robbie's bare chest as they both were panting, spent from their rigorous activity.

"Wow," was all Gemma said and Robbie just nodded in agreement. "I really, really, *really* don't want to go to work now."

Robbie chuckled and he stroked her hair. "Then don't."

"I have to."

"No, you don't."

Gemma sighed and with some effort, she pulled herself up into a sitting position. "Yes, I do."

Robbie sat up as well and wrapped his arms around her, resting his head on her shoulder for a moment. "Fine. It seems I am unable to tempt you into staying with me." He faked sniffed and Gemma rolled her eyes.

"Believe me, I would more than happily stay with you but I

have to close up."

"Fine, I believe you. But let me take you out tomorrow. You usually get Mondays off, right?" Gemma nodded, slightly shocked he was so aware of her shifts. "You pick it, I'll take you wherever you want. Where is somewhere you'd like to go?" Gemma thought quietly for a moment before answering.

"The zoo," Gemma said finally and Robbie stared at her. Then he threw his head back and laughed.

"The zoo? Seriously? Why? Of all the places!"

"I used to get jealous when you used to talk about going there."

"When we were what... fifteen?".

Gemma nodded, smiling shyly. "I used to get jealous because you used to go with a group of you, with loads of girls too. And there would always be loads of pictures on Facebook and stuff. I would just be really jealous."

"You should have said, you could have come." But Gemma looked at him with raised eyebrows and Robbie shook his head. "Your right. I was a dick back then."

"Not a dick, just a kid," Gemma said kindly and she kissed him on the cheek. "That doesn't matter now. You've more than made up for all that in the last twenty-four hours." Robbie smiled and kissed her shoulder, keeping his face pressed into her shoulder for a few moments.

Gemma could tell he was still feeling guilty. "Robbie," she whispered and she rested her head against his. His eyes looked up at her and he smiled, still a little sadly.

"The zoo, it's a date then." He kissed the tip of her nose before he stood up and walked across the room to their discarded clothing. He reached into his shorts pocket (as Gemma quietly enjoyed the view) and pulled out his phone. "Amy has left the

clothes in one of the spare rooms, you can pick what you like."
He grinned at her and raised his eyebrows. "Or you can skive off
work and stay with me… naked." Gemma lay back down and
laughed.

"For God's sake, Robbie, not again."

"Not again, me asking? Or not again… again, again?"

"Both, but mostly asking me again. You know I would rather
be here."

He sighed. "I know, it was worth a try. Come on, I'll show
you where they are." They dressed back into their screwed-up
clothing and Robbie took her hand and led her through the door.
They came out into a hallway with many doors off it.

Gemma tried to get her bearings or pinpoint where they were
with her little knowledge of the house, but she couldn't.

It was just too big.

Robbie led the way while Gemma just took in all her
surroundings. They didn't walk much further though before
Robbie pulled her into another room. Inside was a huge suite,
beautifully decorated with sofas, tables and a huge bed. It was
similar to Robbie's room, but it was apparent that that room was
a guest room and hardly occupied.

"This is a *spare* room? It's beautiful. Most spare rooms are
full of shite and with a couch that pulls out as a bed. Normally
from IKEA." Robbie laughed and pulled her into his side. "How
many guest rooms do you have?"

"A few," was all Robbie said and Gemma just shook her
head. "What?" he asked.

"It's just mind-boggling how big this place is. The pub could
fit into it three times over." Gemma looked towards the bed and
saw loads of clothes laying on it and even some hung up along
the wall behind it. "Oh my God," Gemma said as she walked over

to examine all the clothes. "How much did she buy?" Robbie shrugged.

"She said she got a few things so you can pick what you like." Gemma was walking around the bed, taking in all the clothing. There were jeans, tops, jumpers, dresses, leggings, coats, trainers, boots, pumps… the list was endless.

"Robbie, how much has this cost you?" Robbie just shrugged again, pulling a dress out and looking at it.

"This is too dressy for the pub, but you'd look beautiful in this."

Gemma walked over to him and touched the floaty material as well. It was a stunning dress, with flowing fabrics and subtle patterns. "Wow, that's beautiful," Gemma said and she grabbed the hanger and walked over to the floor-length mirror and held it against herself. "Oh Robbie, this is too much I can't—" Gemma saw the tag and her mouth dropped open and her words were lost for a moment.

"Gemma?" Robbie asked and he came up behind her.

"This dress is three hundred pounds." Her voice was low and strained. She held the dress out, almost scared to damage it in any way.

"Yes?"

Gemma stared at Robbie, shocked. "That's more than I have in my bank account currently!" Now it was Robbie's turn to be shocked.

"You have *less* than three hundred pounds in your bank?"

"Well, yeah, it's the end of the month. I get paid in a couple of days." Gemma said matter-of-factly. "The point is, Robbie, three hundred pounds is a ridiculous amount to spend on one dress. That dress I wore last night was twenty pounds!"

"It's Hugo Boss." Robbie just shrugged again, "Do you

seriously have less than three hundred in your bank?" They obviously had very different things on their minds.

"Yes, but seriously, Robbie! Three hundred pounds?"

Robbie held up another, a black cotton dress with buttons down the front and a belt around the waist. "This dress is fifteen hundred."

Gemma dropped the three hundred pound dress, gasped and picked it back up again. "*WHAT?* No way!"

"Gemma, I'll save you some time. There is nothing in this room that will be less than five hundred pounds. Well, except that three hundred pound dress you're, or *was*, holding. You might be able to find some jeans a little cheaper but that's it." Robbie had a smile on his face as he watched Gemma's open-mouthed expression as she looked around the room. There had to be at least fifteen items in that room. "Gemma, just pick something. You know I would rather you stay here and not need these clothes, but you need to go to work. It's getting late."

"I can't accept this Robbie, it's too much."

"It really isn't, Gem, please. This isn't a lot of money for me." Gemma's head was boggled, but Robbie was right, time was running out. So she put the three hundred pound dress down (very, very carefully) and walked over to the jeans. They weren't much cheaper than the dress, but Gemma managed to pick a pair of jeans, a light, buttoned up shirt and a pair of trainers. The entire outfit was around few hundred pounds, but it was the cheapest Gemma could manage.

"Have you picked these clothes because you like them or just trying to get the cheapest outfit?" Robbie asked, exasperated.

Gemma grinned at him and shrugged as she pulled on her new clothes and looked at herself in the mirror. It was all such beautiful quality and really flattering. Gemma felt really nice in the clothes. Amy had very good style. But it wasn't worth a few hundred pounds. It was an unfathomable amount of money to spend on clothing.

But it was time to leave.

Amy had also brought some clothes for Robbie apparently because he picked himself a pair of expensive pair of jeans and a shirt, along with some trainers. Gemma nearly gasped, nothing looked as good as Robbie naked, but those jeans were pretty spectacular. Robbie walked back over to her and took her hand and kissed the back of it before he turned to leave. Robbie took Gemma back, through the slightly more familiar route to the kitchen. In the far corner, hidden sleekly behind a wall with huge artworks on, was a lift.

"A lift?" Gemma asked, looking surprised.

"Yeah, it goes to the garage." Gemma just shook her head smiling, "What?" Robbie asked, but he was smiling too.

"Oh nothing, lead the way."

Robbie pressed the button for the lift and the door open straight away. Robbie led Gemma through the lift doors and as they shut, Robbie pulled Gemma close. He pushed her against the wall of the lift and Gemma gasped as he pressed himself to her.

He kissed her on the mouth and after a couple of seconds surprise, Gemma was kissing him back. She arched herself so more of her was pressed against his firm body. Her fingers ran up his arms and into his hair where they entwined in his hair and pulled him closer to her. There was a ping and the lift doors opened. Their lips parted, but they kept their heads resting against one another, breathing hard.

"What time will you finish?" Robbie breathed, his voice hoarse.

"About eleven," Gemma said, "I'll be kicking people out at

243

half ten." Normally Gemma wouldn't be so pushy with the customers, but needs must.

"Then you'll be coming back here."

Gemma thought it might have been a question originally, but she had to smile at the slight begging behind his words.

"If you want."

Robbie raised his eyebrows and pushed his hips against hers, showing her the evidence of his want for her. "I want it very much."

Gemma's breath caught and she nearly threw herself upon him again but she knew she was going to be late. Robbie seemed to know what she was going to say and he pressed himself to her for one more delicious moment before he sighed. "I know, I know. 'You need to go to work.'" Gemma raised her eyebrows at his interpretation of her voice. "It was worth a try." He sighed again and pushed himself off her. Gemma tried to not pout at the emptiness he left behind before he took her hand and led her out into the cool garage.

Gemma's mouth fell open as she looked around.

She knew Robbie had a lot of cars, but she could tell (she was no car enthusiast, but she knew some things) by all the logos that they were all extremely expensive.

"Not one Ford Focus in sight," Gemma mocked in disappointment and Robbie rolled his eyes as he pulled her over to the nearest SUV. He opened the door for her and she stepped up and slid onto the plush, leather seats. Robbie slid into the driver's side and the car purred to life.

"Wow." Gemma said as she looked around at the slick dashboard. "Nice."

"Thanks," Robbie said and he steered the car out of the highly secure garage. On the way out, Gemma noted the security guards outside it and then they drove up the long, winding drive and up to the gated front. The gate opened and again Gemma noted the security again.

"So much security," Gemma said and she noted another car following them. "Are they security too?" Gemma asked and Robbie looked into his review mirror for a second.

"Yeah. Jason and Marcus are on my watch today." Gemma nodded as she watched the following car for a moment. Robbie glanced at her, then reached for her hand and took it in his. He brought it to his mouth and kissed the back of it, keeping it resting on his cheek for a couple of moments before he rested his arm on the armrest, his hand still entwined with Gemma's. They didn't talk much, the radio played low in the background as they continued to just hold hands.

Gemma sighed, contentedly.

What a twenty-four hours she had had.

She couldn't believe that at the same time the day before, she was shopping for a dress for a night out that would change her life completely.

Gemma's contented sigh turned to a sad sigh as Robbie pulled into the pub car park. Never so much in her life, had Gemma really not wanted to go to work. Robbie pulled into a space smoothly and they both sat in silence for a moment.

"So…" Gemma said, trying to prolong the inevitable. "I'll see you back here at eleven?"

"I'm coming in."

Gemma's head spun around to him and she couldn't help but beam at him. "Really?" She tried to not sound so ecstatic but failed miserably.

"Of course." Robbie pulled her hand back to his mouth and kissed the back of it again. His breath was hot on her skin as he spoke. "If you can't be with me at home, I'll be with you at work."

"I might even put you to work," Gemma joked and Robbie chuckled.

"Yes, I told you I've got my skills."

"Yes, yes you do." Gemma blushed at more memories flooding back to her.

"My, my, Gemma, are you blushing?" That caused her to blush even deeper.

"Right," Gemma said, turning to open the door and putting her back to Robbie while her face burned. "Let's go." And as she clambered out of the huge SUV, shutting the door behind her, she could hear Robbie laughing. Robbie got out of the car and walked around the front to meet Gemma and take her hand again.

"Lead the way Miss Walker." He leaned down and kissed her quickly, before pulling back and waiting for her to walk. Gemma sighed and turned towards the pub. She started towards it, with Robbie by her side, hand in hand.

CHAPTER SIXTEEN

The shift at the pub dragged. Gemma wanted nothing more than to grab Robbie and go back to his house and back to the dream world that she had left a few hours earlier. Gemma had been expecting to see Matt throughout the shift, but as time went on, the more it seemed that he wasn't going to make an appearance. When closing finally drew closer, Gemma had decided that she would risk going up to the flat and checking to see if Matt had actually left. She could do with picking up a few bits anyway before going back to Robbie's again.

Gemma followed the last customer out and she went to lock the doors behind them. As she reached up to latch the lock, she jumped as she felt arms wrapping around her waist.

"Finally," Robbie whispered in her ear and a shiver ran down her spine at his words. She turned around and Robbie pressed himself into her, pressing her against the door. His lips went straight to hers with an urgency that took Gemma's breath, literally, away. He pulled back and started kissing her neck. "I thought they'd never leave. I've been desperate to do this for hours." His breath was hot against the sensitive skin of her neck. Gemma swallowed and stammered stupidly, unable to speak. She could feel Robbie smiling against her skin. "Unable to speak? I must be doing something right."

"You... you're always doing s-something right," Gemma managed to stammer out before Robbie brought his lips back to hers. They lingered for a moment longer before they pulled apart slightly.

"Are you ready to go?" Robbie asked and Gemma couldn't help but smile at the slight impatience in his voice.

"Nearly, I was just going to check upstairs and see if Matt's moved out."

Robbie pulled back and raised his eyebrows. "Oh yeah, I had actually forgotten all about Matt. We'll all go."

Gemma nodded, not refusing Robbie's offer. She knew that having Robbie there would give her more courage and she felt safer. Gemma looked around, frowning.

"Where were Jason and Marcus during that little rendezvous?" Robbie looked at her, his eyes ablaze with a fire that made Gemma feel hot all over.

"They make themselves scarce."

"But they're still here?" Gemma asked, a little mortified as she scanned the pub for them.

Robbie laughed and caressed Gemma's burning cheeks. "Don't worry, they don't listen or see anything."

"But—" But Robbie cut her off.

"I don't want anyone, but me, to see you like that," Robbie said and Gemma looked up at his serious tone. And Gemma bit her lip. Robbie's pride and desire were such foreign emotions to her, that it made her knees weak. The air between them seemed to heat up real quick and Robbie pushed his hips into hers for a moment before he brought his lips to hers once more. It was a quick, but very passionate kiss, which left them both breathless.

"Come on," Robbie said, almost desperately, "Let's run upstairs to check quickly. I want to take you home." Robbie grabbed her hand as Gemma led them back through the pub, turning things off as she went until she was finally outside and waiting for the alarm to signify the locking of the pub. They then moved to the side door that led to the flats above and Gemma unlocked the door and went to go inside when Robbie pulled her back.

"What's wrong?" Gemma asked, and Robbie nodded over his shoulder at something. For a horrifying moment, Gemma thought it was Matt but then she saw the two large security guards behind Robbie.

They really did just appear out of thin air. The bigger of the two (who Gemma thought was called Marcus) outstretched his hand, palm up. Gemma guessed he was silently asking for her keys, which she placed in his large palm.

They both went silently through the door and must have gone up to the flat.

"What are they doing?" Gemma asked, peaking up the deserted hallway and stairs. "Doing a sweep, just in case."

"A sweep?"

"Checking for anything that could be a threat to us."

"That seems a little extreme," Gemma said, looking up at Robbie, wide-eyed. "What are they expecting to find?"

"Hopefully nothing. But Matt is now a significant risk."

"I know Matt is..." Gemma pondered her words, "controlling. But surely now we've broken up, he's gone?" Gemma was more hopeful than certain, but she didn't want to convey to Robbie that she was still scared of Matt. Robbie reached out and caressed her cheek.

"Matt's lost control of you. He won't take it lightly. I can't take the risk. I won't let him hurt you, Gemma."

"Do you think he would?" Gemma breathed, her eyes wide. Robbie smiled a half-smile and shrugged his shoulders gently.

"I don't know. But I don't want to find out. I need to keep you safe."

"And you need to be kept safe too."

Robbie smiled and brought Gemma close to him, leaning down and capturing her lips with his. They pulled apart after a heated embrace and Gemma closed her eyes for a moment, trying to catch her breath. Someone cleared their throat. Gemma's eyes flew open and she leaped back slightly from Robbie. Robbie kept his arms firmly wrapped around her, chuckling at her mortified expression. They both looked to see Jason and Marcus standing in the hall that led to the stairs and up to Gemma's flat.

"All clear, sir," Jason said, holding out Gemma's keys. Robbie took them, smiling.

"Thank you, Jason." Robbie unwrapped his arms from around Gemma's waist but took her hand and led her through the door and hall. They descended the stairs, and to Gemma's front door.

"You know, for behemoth men, they move quieter than mice," Gemma mumbled as she unlocked her front door again. Robbie laughed but didn't comment further. Gemma was sure she could also hear Marcus and Jason chuckling too. Gemma swung the front door open and took in her flat. Gemma looked around and was surprised to see everything was still in its place. Matt hadn't thrown anything around and he had left it all neat and untouched.

This made Gemma suspicious.

She went towards the bedroom, hesitating at the doorway to turn on the light before walking in with Robbie on her heels. The bedroom looked the same, neat and untouched so Gemma walked over to the drawers and pulled them open.

It was empty.

She walked to the wardrobe and pulled it open. It was empty.

She went to the bathroom to see if his toiletries were there.

Everything was gone.

Gemma turned to Robbie, too shocked to speak.

"Gemma? Is everything okay?" But Gemma just stared at him for a moment before she found her voice again.

"Everything is gone," she said and Robbie could tell the uneasiness of tone.

"And?" he said, slightly confused by her reaction.

"It's just weird. That he would leave so easily."

Robbie frowned at her, then looked around at the room. "And he's left everything the way it was?" Gemma nodded slowly and she too looked around. It was extremely eerie.

"It's like he's cleaned up…" Gemma said, walking around and looking at everything. "I'm not this neat normally. And I had been on a stint of shifts, seven days on the bounce. I haven't had time to do much housework. He's actually been on my case about how messy the place was and that I should be tidying more. It wasn't this clean when we left yesterday."

Robbie looked at her, then he started to examine everything as well.

"Like this," Gemma said, pointing at kitchen table. "I've been meaning to sort the table out for weeks…" she walked over to the centre of the table and stared.

His key was on the table, along with something else stranger situated at the centre of the table, in full display.

There was a bunch of flowers in a vase.

Gemma reached out and touched one of the beautiful petals with her fingers. She must have stared at the flowers for a while, because Robbie wrapped his arms around her waist, making her jump.

"Sorry," he murmured into her ear, "I was talking to you but I don't think you heard me."

"Oh sorry," she said and she shook her head as she looked at him, over her shoulder. "It's just so weird. Why would he buy flowers? He's never bought me flowers."

Robbie looked at Gemma, frowning again. "I think you should stay with me for a few days. It's all really weird, I would rather know you are safe."

"I can't stay there forever," Gemma murmured, looking back at the flowers, lost in thought.

"Well, you can."

Gemma looked at him, eyebrows raised.

"Fine, maybe that's too soon. But I still think you should stay with me for a couple of days."

Gemma just nodded, an uneasy feeling in the pit of her stomach. "Let me just grab some stuff then, okay?"

"Okay," he said and he kissed her quickly and released her arms from around her.

Gemma had a quick run around the flat, grabbing clothes and toiletries to last her a few days and within ten minutes, they were leaving the flat again. Gemma was glad to be out of the flat. Gemma couldn't say why, but the way Matt had left made Gemma extremely uneasy. She felt instantly safer and at ease when she climbed into Robbie's SUV and started back off to his house again.

Over the next few days, when Gemma wasn't at work, she was with Robbie. They never made it to the zoo the day after Matt moved out. They hadn't been able to leave Robbie's bedroom. So they stayed in his house and most often than not, they were naked and making love.

Gemma didn't think she could be so happy.

She felt like she was walking around in a bubble of happiness.

But after a wonderful few days, Gemma found herself back in Robbie's bed, the night before Robbie was due to leave for the World Cup. Gemma was laying on his bare chest, eyes closed and listening to his breathing. She was so content and sad at the same time.

"I really don't want to leave you here," Robbie said quietly into her hair and he tightened his arms around her.

"I'm going to see you in a couple of weeks." Gemma lifted up her head and looked into Robbie's face, smiling softly.

"That's too long, can you make it a week? Please?" He caressed her cheek and Gemma sighed as she looked into his pleading eyes. She bit her lip and really thought about it.

"Well, I'm sure Pip will be happy to work some more shifts..." Pip had already said she would work more if they needed. She was ecstatic that Gemma and Robbie were finally together. The words "about bloody time" and "I knew it" had been used countless times since the news broke.

"I really think I'm going to need you with me, I'll be worrying about you. Not to mention how much I'll actually be missing you." He kissed her then, a quick, burning kiss. "I just don't want to be apart from you."

"I'll see." But Gemma knew that her mum would be fine with it, she knew she would be joining him in London in a few days' time.

"Anything from Matt?" Robbie asked and Gemma frowned at him. "You'd know I'd tell you if he contacted me."

"I know, I know. I just don't like leaving you alone."

"He's gone, Robbie," But Gemma still smiled at his protective words.

"Is he though? Or is he just waiting for me to be out of the picture?"

"I'll have Marcus." Robbie had insisted that Gemma had security as well. Only that morning, she was on another cover of another tabloid. It was becoming harder to hide from the paparazzi. Journalists were even coming into the pub to try and interview Gemma, one even shoved his phone in Gemma's face, shouting questions about her relationship with Robbie before he was escorted out by Robbie's hired security.

Gemma hated seeing herself in the tabloids.

She avoided it as much as she could, but friends and family would keep telling her (even though she asked not to) whenever her picture was in the paper.

Gemma would always find herself looking for the article, which was often headlined with a question of who Gemma was and how this mysterious woman stole the heart of the most loved football player ever.

That morning tabloid was a picture of Gemma and Robbie, holding hands as they were coming out of a shop (nothing exciting, just a supermarket). Gemma looked awful in the picture, at least she thought she did. She looked humongous, with a double chin and an unflattering baseball cap slapped on her head. Robbie ignored it all, he'd had years of practice; but Gemma just couldn't let it go. She found herself scouring the internet for any pictures of Robbie and this mysterious woman. She often found herself going through social media feeds, looking through comments and a lot of them weren't nice comments.

"Forget the trolls, Gemma, they're just jealous," Robbie had said before he had brought her closer for a kiss that did help her forget about the trolls, but only for a few moments. All the things they were saying were things Gemma thought about herself anyway, but having someone else say them, was just so crippling and painful to read. Many tears were shed after she read those horrible comments.

"Gemma?" Robbie's voice shifted her focus back to that moment, in Robbie's bed, the night before he departed for London.

"Oh sorry," Gemma said, giving her head a shake. "Just thinking about some things I read today." She smiled sheepishly at him, but Robbie sat up and looked at her. His face was serious and Gemma knew what he was going to say, he felt very strongly about it.

"Gemma, stop reading what those low-life's think. *Please.* Nothing they say is true."

"It's a little true…" Gemma mumbled and Robbie grabbed her face in his hands, looking into her eyes.

"No, it isn't, Gemma. I love you. I love everything about you. I don't want anyone else but you. I think you are the most beautiful and sexy woman I have ever seen. I have done nothing but think about you for the last ten years." Robbie definitely knew how to turn her bones to mush. Gemma couldn't speak, she just needed him close. She wrapped her hand around his neck and brought his face to hers quickly, her lips seeking his. Robbie responded with a passion that made her pant for breath when they broke apart and looked into each other's eyes once more.

"Right, now you definitely have to come with me."

Gemma laughed and then she nodded. "Yes, I think so too."

"Really?" Robbie's eyes lit up and Gemma could help but smile in return.

"I'm sure we can swing it." Robbie beamed at her for a moment then he kissed her again.

He wrapped his arms around her and pulled her against him as he rolled onto his back.

255

"I'm sure I need you again," Robbie whispered against her lips and his hands were on her bottom, pulling her closer and closer to him. Gemma could feel all of him against her and she couldn't help but gasp at his arousal.

"Robbie!" she exclaimed.

"Hhm?" was all Robbie said as he leaned forwards, towards Gemma's breasts. She knew what he was going to do, he had done it countless times over the past week, but it still made Gemma quiver underneath his mouth. Gemma's hands went into his hair and she cradled him to her chest as he continued his passionate kiss. One of Robbie's hands moved from her backside and moved down between their bodies. Gemma arched her back, pushing her more into Robbie's mouth as his hand found their destination in her most intimate place.

Robbie groaned and pulled Gemma closer to him. Gemma let her head fall back as she enjoyed Robbie's intimate caress.

"Robbie," Gemma sighed.

"I need you," he breathed and within seconds, they were stripped naked. They paused for a moment, looking at one another, breathing hard. Gemma was atop Robbie, with him looking up at her.

"So beautiful," he said, reaching up to caress her face and body again. Gemma leaned down and captured his lips in a searing kiss. The kiss deepened and became increasingly more passionate quickly. A few moments later, their bodies were joined as one once more. They were still kissing deeply as their body's started to move in rhythm with one another. And a few moments later, their bodies erupted with pleasure and euphoria as they held each other tight.

They held on to each other for a few moments as they both caught their breaths again, still tingling with pleasure.

At some point, they slumped back onto the bed, still holding on to each other tightly. "I love you," Robbie whispered into the night as they both started to dose off.

"I love you," Gemma said sleepily and she felt Robbie's lips on her temple and she snuggled herself closer to him.

The next morning, Gemma awoke to Robbie who was sitting next to her on the bed and stroking her face.

"Morning," Robbie whispered and he leaned down to kiss her softly on the lips. "I've got to go."

"No," Gemma complained and she wrapped her arms around his waist.

"I know," Robbie said as he kissed her hair and held her for a moment. "But it's only a week."

"Well, it might be two," Gemma teased but Robbie shook his head firmly.

"No, it's got to be just a week. I might just about manage that." Gemma laughed shakily and she pulled her head back and looked up into his eyes.

"We've done ten years apart, I think we might manage seven days."

"Just about." And then he kissed her, quickly but deeply and it was enough for Gemma to forget everything and anything apart from her lips on Robbie's. Robbie sighed and pulled back, keeping his head resting against hers. "I'll see you soon. Stay here if you want, Gem, you don't have to leave because I'm not here."

"I can't stay here without you."

"Yes, you can. I've told everyone to expect you. Come whenever you want."

"Thank you," Gemma said, knowing she wouldn't stay there without him. "Can I drive the Porsche then?" Robbie laughed and shook his head.

"I love you, but not that much." Gemma laughed too but then silence came over them as they just looked at one another.

"This is ridiculous," Gemma muttered, shaking her head and shocked she felt like tearing up. "It's only a week or two."

"A week," Robbie clarified, "I know, I just really don't want to leave." He kissed her again quickly before he finally stood. Gemma went to stand up but Robbie put his hands on her shoulders again. "Stay. Don't rush. I'll call you in a bit yeah?" Gemma nodded and tried to keep a pout off her face. Robbie quickly leaned down and kissed her one last time before he waved and left. Gemma waited for Robbie to be gone before she decided to leave also, feeling oddly claustrophobic in Robbie's mansion of a house.

Gemma mopped about for the next couple days, counting the hours and minutes until she would be reunited with Robbie again. The pub was busier than anticipated and with Linda going down with a sickness bug for a few days, it was obvious that Gemma wouldn't be able down to go down to London as early as she hoped. She called Robbie a couple of times a day and he understood her situation but they were both disappointed that it would be an extra few days until Gemma would be finally back in his arms.

Even though she had Pip, who was an enormous help, Gemma was still pulling open to close shifts at the pub to help cover Linda's absence during the World Cup build-up. Gemma managed to watch every game and she was screaming along with the fans as she watched Robbie play beautifully. After a particularly intense match (Robbie had scored a penalty with minutes left in the match to ensure England's win) Gemma was

258

locking up after finally getting the last straggling customers out. Marcus was with her. they had become quite good friends (being around each other for hours a day, it was impossible not to) and even though he was built in the typical form of a bodyguard, Marcus was a big softie. Gemma felt very comfortable and safe in his presence, so having Marcus escort her up to her flat for his final check-up before he headed home wasn't a chore.

"Honestly, Marcus," Gemma said to him as the pub alarm did its final beep, "this really isn't necessary. I know Robbie is worried and protective, but no one really knows who I am really. I'm in no danger."

"Mr Wilson still wants me to sweep the parameter every night before departing, ma'am." Gemma resisted the urge to roll her eyes.

"Please, Marcus, please call me Gemma. I feel ancient when you call me that."

Marcus chuckled and looked at her with his light, blue eyes. "Yes… Gemma. Apologies."

"And don't apologise, please. You're just doing your job."

He nodded his head graciously. "Thank you, I think Mr Wilson is just concerned with all the media attention of late."

Gemma nodded, there had been a new article published that morning. Gemma had been on the front page, alongside a picture of Robbie taken from the match previous to the article. It had been about guesses about their relationship and it had alluded to Robbie's sensational game record being down to their new relationship.

Robbie said as much himself, but they still weren't prepared for the public to know about their relationship. Robbie wanted to keep Gemma protected from the onslaught of paparazzi attention for as long as possible. She opened the door that led to the street first and Marcus went in before Gemma, sweeping the hallway and stairs that led to her flat door.

"I must repeat myself when I say that Mr Wilson reminds you that you are welcome back at his house." Marcus turned back to her with raised eyebrows, "We can protect you a lot better there," he added, his eyebrows crinkling with worry.

"Oh, Marcus, please. What's going to happen here? It's a second-storey flat with a locked entrance and I am only here alone a few hours a night. I have that panic alarm to wear at night also." She didn't, but it was only on the bedside table. Really, she felt like was a pensioner in a care home or something. "Then I'm with you back in the pub the rest of the time anyway."

But Marcus still wasn't happy about the arrangement. "But Mr Wilson—"

"You leave *Mr Wilson* to me. Honestly, it's fine. I don't want to trouble you having to stay here at night as well as the day."

Marcus didn't reply, he swept the hallway and stairs and then escorted Gemma back up to the flat and again, when she opened the door, he did a sweep of the entire flat.

It was deemed safe and there was no threat, so Marcus bid her goodnight and locked up the flat as he left. Gemma sighed and stretched, she was exhausted but she forced herself to have a quick shower before Robbie's quick nightly video call. He was getting up early for training, so it was a quick goodnight for them both and Gemma crawled into her empty, cold bed, exhausted. Sleep took her almost instantly and she fell into a deep sleep, so deep, that when she stirred a few hours later she was stuck in that slow stupor for a few moments.

She blinked, confused.

It was still dark outside and glancing at her clock on the bedside table, it was only three in the morning.

What had woken her?

She lay for a moment and tried to think if it was a dream that had disturbed her. But she was sleeping so deeply, she couldn't recall dreaming.

Then she thought about her bladder, but she hadn't woken up desperately to relieve herself. But something was different.

And it took Gemma a few groggy seconds to realise what.

There was a pair of arms around her waist, pulling her to someone who was in the bed behind her. Gemma smiled slightly, for a moment, snuggling into the warm heat of the person behind her.

"Robbie," she sighed as he tightened his arms around her, pulling her even tighter. "What are you doing here?" But as he pulled her against him, he felt different... but oddly familiar.

Had he lost weight? But before she could think any more, he replied. "Hello, Roly-Poly. Have you missed me?" And it was not Robbie's voice that rippled through the dark.

It was Matt's.

CHAPTER SEVENTEEN

"Matt!" Gemma exclaimed and she went to scramble out of the bed but Matt grabbed her and pinned her against the mattress.

"Good morning." He was straddling her, with his knee pressed on her windpipe. She spluttered and gagged, trying to bring in any air she could. Matt eased his knee slightly so Gemma could get a few gasps of air through her mouth. "Looks like you've been busy." Matt leered again and he pressed his knee to her throat once more as he sat up and reached into his pocket. He pulled a folded piece of paper and unfolded it and released Gemma's neck once more so she could breathe. "You've been really, really busy." His voice was a low and deadly whisper. He lowered his knee and shuffled down Gemma's body slightly until he was straddling her chest and abdomen rather than her neck. Gemma was trying to catch her breath and blink away the fogging that had started in the corner of her eyes. Matt bent low, his face inches from hers. She could smell his foul breath, there was a smell of alcohol and tobacco.

"Imagine my surprise when I went into the local shop this morning and saw *this*." His voice was deadly low and Gemma just looked him in the eye. If she had ever been scared of him during their relationship, it was nothing compared to that moment.

Matt looked... unhinged.

"Who's that on the front of the newspaper, Gemma?"

Gemma's eyes flickered to the paper that he was holding

near her face and back to Matt's cold black eyes. Gemma swallowed and decided keeping Matt talking was the best course of action, until she could figure out how to get a hold of her panic button.

"Me?" she breathed and Matt sneered and nodded.

"Yes and who else?"

"R-Robbie?"

"Yes. How do you think that made me feel, seeing your ugly mug on the front of a very known paper?"

Why do you care? But Gemma didn't say that, she decided to play dumb. "Bad?" Matt threw his head back and barked a hard, cold laugh.

"Fucking bad? I was furious."

"W-why?"

"W-w-why?" he copied, going high-pitched and mocking. "Because Gemma, you are *mine*," he scathed and he pushed his face to hers, his eyes glaring at hers. "Fucking mine, Gemma."

Gemma blinked and swallowed, confused by his sudden and random possessive words. "But we broke up, I broke up with you."

"No, you didn't!" Matt yelled at her and his hands were suddenly on her throat and Gemma spluttered and choked. "You didn't break up with me. You don't get to decide. You are mine. And no one else's."

Gemma didn't contradict him, not only because she could hardly breathe but also because she didn't want to anger him further. Gemma just kept him talking as she slid her hand slowly towards the panic alarm on the bedside table. She would be able to reach it without moving much but Gemma needed to keep Matt's eyes averted. Luckily for Gemma, Matt was looking at her with a crazed possession and wasn't noticing her hand inching towards the alarm.

"I'm sorry," Gemma said and she tried to make herself look scared and as submissive as possible. Matt's teeth bared again and he almost shuddered with pleasure.

"Yes," Matt purred, "you will be."

Gemma froze getting the alarm for just a second as she looked into Matt's eyes. There was a dangerous glint in it that made Gemma's stomach squirm with fear. "W-what are you doing?"

"Taking what's mine," he growled and he still straddled her as he started to shuffle down and down her body until he was straddling her hips.

"No!" she shouted and she started to try and buck him off her but with his weight sitting completely on her, she couldn't. She threw her arms up and try and smack him and hopefully unbalance him enough to throw him off her but his hands grabbed her wrists with a loud smack. He pushed her hands back to either side of her head, keeping them pinned against the mattress. Gemma had forgotten about the alarm in her panic to try and overthrow Matt and now there was no chance that she would be able to reach it. Her brain was trying to think, trying to think about a way out of this situation. The only thing she could think was to talk and distract Matt from what he intended to do.

"Robbie will kill you!" she blurted out and Matt looked up at her with a cocky and amused face. "He'll know you've been here."

"That's my intention."

Gemma's blood ran cold. "What?" Gemma said, barely above a whisper.

"I want him to know I am here. I want his money." Matt bore down onto her, his face nearly pressing up against hers as he seethed. "I'm going to use you to get what I deserve."

"Then you'll let me go?" Gemma whispered again and Matt's eyes crinkled with a malevolent mirth.

"No," he growled and Gemma's stomach dropped. He wasn't ever going to let her go, he was going to take Robbie's money and somehow keep Gemma locked up, she would never be able to see Robbie again. She would be trapped with Matt for the rest of her life, how long or short that would be. "You are *mine*. No one else's."

Gemma tried to struggle again beneath him but it was fruitless. Matt might have been skinny, but he was still much stronger than her.

"But you treated me like shit! You never loved me!"

Matt threw his head back and barked out a laugh before he sneered down at her again. "I don't have to love you to control you." Matt grabbed both of Gemma's arms and held them above her head as he reached into his pocket and pulled out what looked like rope.

Gemma's stomach dropped at the sight of it. Matt had obviously planned things meticulously. He tied her hands together and tied them above her head, to the metal headboard. Once he had secured her arms, he trailed his fingers along her face as he caressed her cheek and neck. She tried to pull her face away but he just kept trailing his fingers across her face as he looked at her. He was pressing his body onto hers, so he can look into her eyes and with another jolt of nausea; Gemma felt his arousal pressing on her stomach.

"Do you remember the last time I tied you up, Gemma?" Matt breathed into her ear, pressing himself more into her.

Gemma nearly gagged, a horrific memory swimming before her eyes. They had tried tying up intimately a few times before,

265

but the last time had been horrible. Matt had enjoyed dominating Gemma too much. She had sustained injuries, physically and mentally. She had sworn she wouldn't allow him to do it again. Robbie had come back into her life a few weeks later and it never happened again. But Matt was back, tying her up once more. And the look in his eye was enough to make Gemma's heart splutter with panic.

Gemma knew he was planning a similar encounter for her again.

She knew what he was going to do and tried as she might, she couldn't throw him off her. His knees were pressed tightly to her sides as he continued his cruel caress.

"Was he any good?" he said in a deadly low voice.

Gemma's eyes met his and she could see a smile forming on his lips, but fury in his eyes. She didn't answer him, but she didn't have to. He stopped straddling her and shifted position so that he was kneeling between her legs instead. Gemma tried to kick out and kick him off but then he was laying on her and pinning her to the mattress.

"Are you going to keep fighting or just accept this, Gemma? You are *mine*." He growled at her, as one hand held her down as the other pulled at his belt.

"I will keep fighting!" Gemma shouted, trying to throw him off again. Matt laughed and released her for a moment and his hands went to the waistband of her pyjama bottoms. Gemma screamed and kicked her legs out but he kept hold of the waistband and began to tug them down. Gemma could feel the fear starting to paralyse her and she thought about what she could do to stop him, but she couldn't see stopping him. She knew what was coming and she was unable to stop it. Gemma fought back a sob, not wanting to let Matt see her fear of him. He was still pulling down her pants, he was doing it slowly and cruelly. She could feel them slipping down to expose her most intimate area, but just before he managed to expose her fully, something happened.

One moment, Matt was there, the next his hands had been whipped away as he was tackled to the ground. Gemma blinked and looked around, confused by the sudden onslaught of noise filling her ears. There were a few people shouting and Gemma looked to the side and saw someone on top of Matt, on the bedroom floor.

Gemma watched the two bodies on the floor, rolling around and throwing punches at each other. Gemma finally realised that someone had come into the room and tackled Matt off her.

And that someone was Marcus.

Gemma instantly felt relief and a sob ripped uncontrollably from her mouth. Gemma turned her head to watch the two men fighting again. Marcus finally got Matt onto his stomach and pinned his arms behind his back.

"Fucking stay down," Marcus yelled and then he finally looked up at Gemma. "Are you okay, miss?" Gemma just stared at him for a moment, frozen in place. "Gemma?" Marcus repeated, looking at her worried. "Gemma?" But at that moment, there was a booming voice shouting from the door.

"Police!"

"In here!" Marcus shouted and two big, uniformed policemen came into the room and took in the situation. Both their eyes swept over Gemma's clearly shaken frame, tied to the bed and Matt being pinned on the floor by Marcus.

Gemma looked over them on the floor again as the police went to take over from Marcus, who must have been telling them what had transpired but whatever he said, Gemma didn't hear.

At that moment, Gemma's eyes fell upon Matt's face. He was looking at her and *smiling*.

He didn't seem concerned that he was being pinned down by two policemen and handcuffed. Their eyes were locked, blue on black and Gemma knew. Gemma knew that this wasn't the end. Matt smiled because he knew he would get another chance. Another chance to finish what he started in her small bedroom, which she once shared with him.

He wasn't going to let her go. And Gemma was petrified.

The police took Matt away moments after that and the entire time he kept his eyes menacingly trailed on Gemma. While the police were dealing with Matt, Marcus leaped up and instantly released Gemma. She sat up, pulling her clothing back into place and was helped to her feet by Marcus. She was shaking so much, the whole room seemed to swim before her eyes. When he was finally removed from the flat, Gemma sagged against the wall, sliding down it until she was sitting on the floor and her head pressed against her knees. Gemma didn't know how long she was locked in that position but after an unknown amount of time, she felt someone kneeling in front of her.

"Gemma?" Marcus said tentatively and Gemma's head snapped up. Her face was broken, and Marcus went to grab her hand but stopped just before he reached her. "Gemma? Are you okay?" Gemma swallowed, trying to find her voice. She stammered and spluttered but couldn't get any words out. "It's okay, Gemma, you're safe now," he said gently and Gemma felt the tears and sobs bursting through her stammering and she pushed herself into his chest. Marcus threw his arms around and held her as the uncontrollable sobs broke through. Her body shook with such a force she thought her teeth tumbled right out of her mouth. Gemma could see in Marcus's face the worry and pain he was feeling for her and tentatively, he brought her forwards for a hug.

Then Gemma just cried.

She cried and she cried and she cried.

She cried until her body could no longer produce any tears and the sobs ceased to ricochet through her body. Marcus continued to hold her until he was certain she had stopped and pulled back and looked into her face, smiling kindly.

"The police want to speak to you... when you're ready."

Gemma took in a shaky breath and nodded. Marcus stood up then bent down and helped Gemma to her feet. Her knees were shaking but she was steady enough to not need Marcus to hold onto her. Marcus led her back into the living room and she sat on the couch. A policewoman came and sat down at the far end of the couch.

"Hi, Gemma, my name's Nancy. How are you doing?" Gemma looked into her kind, gentle face and took a deep breath.

"I've been better," she said quietly.

"Yes," she said sympathetically, "Do you mind telling me what happened tonight?"

"I... I went to bed, not long after Marcus left."

"Marcus is your security guard, yes?" Gemma nodded. "And he checks the flat every night before you go to bed?" Gemma nodded again.

"Yes, he does one final sweep before I go to bed every night."

"Do you mind me asking why you have a bodyguard?"

"My boyfriend just wants to be sure I am safe. He's famous you see, so I have been getting some attention from the media and paparazzi."

"Who is your boyfriend?"

269

"Robbie Wilson."

"The footballer?" Her mask of impassiveness slipped then. She was surprised.

"Yep," was all Gemma said, her surprise was offensive, but Gemma just didn't care at that moment.

"So, the suspect. How do you know him?"

Gemma sucked in another breath. "He's my ex."

"And how long have you been broken up?"

"Um, a couple weeks? I broke up with him and then got with Robbie. Matt wasn't a kind boyfriend. He was controlling and mean."

"And has he ever forced himself upon you before?" Gemma thought back through their relationship. The intimacies they had weren't exactly pleasant, but none of them had been forced.

"No," she said, quietly. "He said…"

"Yes?" Nancy asked kindly.

"He said I was *his*."

"Okay," she said and she jotted down a few notes in her notebook. How long had she had that? Gemma hadn't even realised she was writing. "And did he force himself upon you tonight?" Gemma remembered with shuddering clarity, how close he had been.

"Marcus stopped him just before he could—"

"Gemma?" Someone suddenly shouted and Gemma jumped up and looked towards the front door. It was open and the voice was yelling from the hallway. "Gemma? Marcus?"

Gemma's heart thumped in her chest, she recognised the voice and she fought back tears as she scrambled from the couch to the front door.

"Robbie?" Gemma cried and then he materialised in the doorway. "Robbie!" Gemma was crying and she held her hands

270

up so she could wrap her arms around his neck and he cleared the space between them in seconds. He pulled her to his chest with a crushing force and Gemma buried her head into his strong, warm chest.

"Gemma?" he said hoarsely, burying his face into her neck. "Gem, are you okay?" He pulled back and lifted her head up to look at her. He was touching her face, neck and arms. He was touching to see if there was any damage, if anything was injured. But she was unscathed. At least, physically.

Gemma shook her head as tears and sobs took over her once more and Robbie pulled her to his chest once more, kissing her hair. "Oh, Gemma. I was so worried." Robbie was holding her so tight and kissing her, Gemma just felt herself melting into his chest. She was soaking him in, breathing him in, as if he was her entire life force. She clung to him with a desperation that if she let him go, she would surely expire. She just couldn't release him.

He cradled her to his chest. Robbie seemed to become aware of the outside presence before Gemma. Even though she clung to him and he held tight, he spoke to the policewoman who was still in the room.

"Can I take her away from here?" he asked and his voice was croaky with emotion. The policewoman must have nodded because she spoke.

"We just need to take a few pictures, if that's okay with you, Gemma?" Nancy asked gently and Gemma felt Robbie's arms tightening around her. "We have the pictures we need of the bedroom. We just need…" She nodded to Gemma, who looked down at her wrists. There were red rope burns forming on them. She didn't even realise they were sore until that moment.

"Right now?" Robbie asked, a little hesitant. "She's gone through a lot."

"I know," Nancy said sympathetically. "It's just the more evidence we have against him, the better."

Robbie began to speak, but Gemma spoke over him. "That's fine, let's just get it over with."

Nancy nodded, and they went off into another room. Nancy took pictures of Gemma's entire body, documenting every injury she had sustained. She hadn't realised she even had any, but apparently she did. And a lot. Once she was done, they went back into the living room, where Robbie was waiting with the other policeman.

Gemma went instantly to Robbie and he wrapped her up protectively in his arms. "I've got all I need for now, we will be in touch."

"We will be in London." Gemma glanced up at him and she watched as he spoke to Nancy, his jaw was tight and straight. "I need to keep her safe."

"Okay, we will do what we need to do here."

"Thank you," Gemma said quietly, not taking her eyes off Robbie as she spoke to the police. "Thank you for everything."

"You were very brave Gemma, you are safe now." Tears pricked her eyes again and she buried her head into Robbie's chest. Nancy must have left because Robbie looked down at her and their eyes met. His hands cupped her face, holding her tight as he looked into her eyes.

"Gemma," he whispered and Gemma could see in his wide eyes pain. And it broke Gemma's heart. Gemma reached up and grabbed his face and pulled it down to hers so he rested his head against hers.

"I'm okay now. I promise." Robbie let out a breath of relief and closed his eyes as he rested his head against hers.

"I was so scared... I couldn't... think...I can't..."

"Shhh," Gemma said, "Don't say it. I'm fine now. I'm with you."

"And I won't be letting you go either."

"Fine by me." Gemma pulled his lips to hers. She knew Robbie wouldn't have made the first move. He wouldn't have wanted to do such a thing after what she had been through that night but Robbie was her anchor, her saviour, her everything. And in that moment, she just needed him close, as physically close as two people could possibly be.

Gemma deepened the kiss and though Robbie was hesitant, he responded by pulling her closer. Gemma moulded and arched her body so that she was pressing her entire body against the length of his.

"Robbie," Gemma breathed and Robbie made a guttural noise that rumbled up his throat and pulsated through Gemma. Robbie reached behind her and pulled her legs so he lifted her up and she could wrap her legs around his waist. Gemma started tugging at his top and pulling it up over his head. Robbie grabbed her face with his hands as they were suspended in that position for a moment, breathing heavily.

"Gem," he panted, and his eyes were huge and loving. "Gem, are you sure? We don't have to do this now." Gemma just shook her head and brought his face to hers again in a hot kiss.

Robbie moaned as the kiss deepened but Gemma could tell he was still reluctant.

"I need you," Gemma whispered and Robbie walked back to the couch and lowered her onto it. He covered her body with his and a moment later and Gemma was pulling at the waistband of his jeans. "Please Robbie, I just need you. I need you close." Robbie resumed with a renewed vigour, slipping Gemma's pants and top off in quick succession. He kissed and caressed her body as he embedded himself within her. Gemma clung to his shoulders as he moved with the archaic rhythm of love, and he continued to kiss her and hold her tight. Gemma felt her body tightening and quickening and within a few moments, she was arching herself off the couch to meet Robbie as he too pushed forward towards her. Gemma clung to Robbie as she was overcome with pleasure and love for this man. Robbie's pushed forwards a couple more times before he, too, was overcome with the pleasure of the moment. He slumped down on top of her, breathing heavily as they both lingered in that post-coitus high.

Robbie's head was resting on Gemma's chest as they caught their breath. Gemma was stroking his head as she let her eyes close. She had no idea how late it was, but it must have been the middle of the night or the early hours of the morning. She could feel sleep taking her, she felt Robbie sit up and then a blanket fell upon her. She felt Robbie slide back behind her and between her and the couch, pulling her to his chest. He stroked her hair and kissed her cheek before he nuzzled into her neck.

"I love you," he whispered into the darkness and Gemma was so exhausted that all she could muster was.

"Hmmmm yewww." Robbie's laugh shook her for a few moments before he too fell into a deep sleep.

CHAPTER EIGHTEEN

Gemma woke the next morning warm and cosy, tucked in tightly to Robbie's body. She also woke with a very sore crick in her neck. As romantic as snuggling on the sofa would seem, it wasn't great for the posture. Gemma stretched and groaned at the general stiffness of her body.

"Argh," she muttered as she tried to sit up. Robbie's arm wrapped around her waist and she looked down at him.

"Oh, I thought you were asleep," His eyes were still closed, but he was frowning. "Couldn't really sleep on this couch. It was a nice cuddle though." Gemma laughed and nodded in agreement.

"Yeah, you never see how uncomfortable couples are after they've spent a night crammed on a couch."

"Reality." Gemma chuckled and reached down and kissed him quickly on the lips, "Good morning." Robbie smiled under her lips and tightened his arm around her and pulled her back onto the couch.

"Good morning," and he kissed her deeply. After a few moments, they pulled apart and Robbie was smiling slightly. "I much prefer this reality."

"Me too," Gemma whispered, smiling too.

"I don't want to burst our little bubble, but we will have to get ready to go soon."

"Go?" Gemma asked stupidly, blinking her confusion at him.

"Yes, to London?"

"Oh." She had forgotten. "Oh!" She sat up straight and looked at him wide-eyed. "Oh! You are supposed to be at training! Right now!" Robbie laughed and sat up as well, quickly pecking her on the cheek before he got up and pulled on his jeans.

"My manager knew what happened last night, he understood that I was leaving and nothing was going to stop me. But as everything is okay, I can return to training. With you with me of course."

"Okay."

"Okay? No fighting me on it? No 'what about the pub?' or something along those lines?"

"No, if it'll make you feel better, I will go with you."

"*Me* feel better?"

"I don't want you to be distracted at this important time of your career."

"Screw my career, screw the World Cup!"

Gemma jumped slightly at his sudden tone change, he was loud and slightly annoyed. "I just want you safe and with me so I can make sure you're okay. That's all I care about. You, Gemma." Robbie added, in a much softer tone.

Gemma felt her eyes stinging with unshed tears. She couldn't speak, she just nodded and Robbie continued. "Good, now that's all cleared up, we will have to go soon. Wheels up in an hour and a half." He said, glancing at his expensive watch. "Do you want to pack? I can arrange clothes for you in London but I know you're funny about— What?" Robbie said, just realising Gemma was gaping at him.

"You said 'Wheels up'? What wheels?"

"Um... a plane?" he said, clearly confused by her confusion.

"You can *fly* to London? You have a *plane*?"

Robbie chuckled and nodded his head. "Yes... to both

questions."

Gemma's head exploded with hundreds of questions, so she went with the first she thought of. "Can you even fly to London? What's the point? Surely you just go up and then come straight back down again."

"Yeah, you pretty much ascend and descend. It takes about forty minutes."

"So, really environmentally friendly then?"

"Well, I usually drive or take the train down, but I had to get here as quick as I could last night." Gemma decided to not continue the topic further. He had come when he needed, she needed him and she couldn't mock him for that, even if she didn't fully agree with his mode of transport.

"Okay, I'll go pack. You're right—"

"I usually am, continue."

Gemma rolled her eyes. "I don't like when you spent money on me." It was Robbie's turn to roll his eye then he continued to get dressed. Gemma stood, wrapping the blanket around her and going to the bedroom to get dressed. She walked into the room and caught sight of the bed, still messed and the duvet and pillows sprawled everywhere. Gemma's heart started to thump uncomfortably in her chest as she could still feel the mattress pressing around her and the rope on her wrists. Her breath was coming in thick and fast and not in a pleasant way. There was a darkness filling her peripheral vision that was growing and pulsating until Gemma only had tunnel vision with the bed in the centre.

"Gemma?" A voice sounded as if it was underwater. "Gemma?" The groggy voice asked again. Gemma was barely aware of a pair of arms wrapping around her. They seemed to be lifting her up off the ground.

When did she fall to the ground?

The blackness was fading and the world was coming back into view.

"Gemma?" the voice was Robbie's and her head snapped to the side. Robbie was looking down at her, his eyes wide with worry and pain.

"I-I'm okay. I just had a…" she trailed off and stared at the bed again. He was holding her tight, rubbing her arms and it was then Gemma realised that she was shaking.

"Let's get out of here."

Gemma nodded and walked over to her drawers and pulled out some clothes. She dressed in her usual top and jeans and she quickly packed some clothes and toiletries into a small bag, she would have to take Robbie up on more clothes in London.

She had to get out of that bedroom.

So within a few minutes of her entering the bedroom, they left Gemma's small flat, bag backed and hand in hand. There was a car waiting out the front and Robbie and Gemma slid in to the back of the slick, black car. The car purred to life and started the second Robbie shut the door behind them. Gemma looked to the front and both Jason and Marcus were in the front.

Gemma glanced through the back window and saw a black SUV following them. "Security?" Gemma asked, indicating the car following. Robbie nodded. "It's been increased."

"Oh, Robbie, that isn't necessary."

"Yes, it is." Robbie's jaw was tight as he looked at the front. Gemma followed his eye line and saw he was looking at Marcus.

Glaring might have been more accurate.

"Are you okay this morning, Marcus?" Gemma asked and Robbie's jaw tightened even more, if that was possible.

"Why—"

But Gemma cut Robbie off. "Shh, I was talking to Marcus. Marcus?"

"I'm fine, thank you, Miss Walker. How are you?"

Gemma frowned at his tone. It was tight and not his normal light, jolly voice. Gemma could see him peeking at Robbie in the rear-view mirror. Gemma frowned at him but turned back to Marcus.

"Marcus, please, call me Gemma. And thank you for last night." Gemma could see Marcus' jaw tightening. He nodded once but didn't say anything so Gemma continued. "I just wanted you to know that I am grateful. I can't even think what would have happened if you hadn't got there when you did. You saved me." There was a loaded silence and Gemma looked at Marcus to Jason to Robbie and back again.

What was going on? "You're welcome, ma'am."

"Gemma, *please*, Marcus—" But Robbie cut her off.

"You wouldn't have needed to thank him if he had done his job and *stayed* with you." Gemma was taken aback by the ferocity of Robbie's tone. He was glaring at Marcus and Gemma looked back at him.

"Sir, it was agreed—"

"I don't care what was agreed."

"Robbie!" Gemma exclaimed but he ignored her.

"He could have *killed* her!" Robbie seethed and the atmosphere went from tense to explosive in a matter of seconds. No one uttered a word, the only noises were the car purring and Robbie's breathing. Robbie's ragged, angry breaths going in and out were as loud as someone shouting. Gemma kept looking back and forth and finally, she put her hand over Robbie's.

He was shaking but didn't move his hand from hers. Gemma squeezed it and then looked at him. Gemma had never seen him

279

so angry; his brown eyes were ablaze with this fury that it actually scared Gemma.

"Robbie?" Gemma said quietly and tentatively. He didn't speak, he just glared at the back of Marcus's head. "Robbie, if it wasn't for Marcus…" She trailed off and everyone in the car shuddered at the thought. "I am thankful and grateful that Marcus came when he did. If he had been later… Well, we all know what could have happened. But it didn't."

"He shouldn't have been there in the first place," Robbie whispered so quietly, Gemma strained her ears to listen. He sounded angry but in control again.

"But that is not Marcus's fault." Robbie looked at Gemma, his jaw tight. His eyes met hers and Gemma smiled sadly. "It's not Marcus's fault Robbie." His eyes were hard, but Gemma could see them softening. "It's not his fault." Robbie swallowed and looked down at their hands, he turned his hand over and entwined his fingers through hers. He brought her hand to his mouth and kissed the back of it, his eyes back on hers. He held her hand to his face as he stared at her.

Gemma scooted nearer and touched her fingertips to his face and caressed under his eyes. "I'm okay," she whispered and Robbie closed his eyes. He opened his eyes and still with her hand pressed against his mouth and face, he nodded slowly. With the tilt of her head, Gemma nodded to Marcus at the front and Robbie sighed before he nodded again.

"Marcus?" Robbie said, his voice was tight but much lighter. "Sir?"

"I'm sorry. That was out of line for me to speak to you like that. I… It's just when it comes to Gemma, I see red."

"Thank you, sir," Marcus said and Gemma could hear his voice cracking under the emotion of it. "And thank you…

Gemma." He turned then, to look at Gemma and she was overcome with emotion. In his eyes, Gemma could see the gratitude. She couldn't reply, she just nodded and Marcus turned his head back to the front.

The rest of the journey was spent in silence. Gemma curled up next to Robbie and rested her head on his shoulder and soon enough, they arrived at a small airport.

"Is this an airport?"

"Yeah," Robbie said, sliding to the door and opening it. Gemma followed suit and Robbie came around to meet her, taking her hand and pulling her forward. "It's for private jets."

"Ah, the world of the rich and famous!"

"Well, it's your world now too. If you want it to be." He kissed her hand, flashing her a cheeky grin and a wink before he pulled her along. "Come on, we're on a tight schedule." They made their way through the small airport. Robbie showed the correct documents and IDs and Gemma found herself boarded onto the small, luxurious plane. Robbie sat next to her and an air host offered her drinks.

"Really?" Gemma said, with her eyebrows raised at Robbie. "Someone to serve you drinks on a forty-minute flight?" She scoffed and laughed, "You have way too much money." Gemma was sure anyone other than Robbie would take offence but he, in true Robbie style, threw his head back and laughed. Gemma had to laugh too because it was all so ridiculous. A few weeks ago, she never would have imagined that she would be sitting on a plane, next to Robbie Wilson, flying to London to watch him play in the World Cup with all the other spouses and partners.

Gemma's soft drink arrived and she and Robbie cheered (he was having a soft drink, he was training after all) and she sipped it, looking around once more.

"It's stunning. I can't believe you own this. It's like something out of a movie." She took another sip and shook her head in awe. "You really own this? How much did it cost?"

"Do you really want to know?" His eyebrows were raised and his smile mischievous. "No, on second thought, don't tell me." Gemma was looking around again, her mouth open. There was silence for a couple of minutes as Robbie watched her, stifling a laugh. "Well, if you're impressed with this, wait until you see my yacht." Robbie couldn't help himself. Gemma turned to him, her mouth wide open. "What yacht?"

"Are you still able to blink?" Gemma over-exaggerated a couple of blinks. "What yacht, Robbie?" Robbie chuckled and shrugged nonchalantly. "Maybe after the World Cup, we can take it out. I'm due some leave after it—"

"You own a yacht too?"

"Yes, yes I do."

"How much did that cost you?"

"You know, some people may think it rude to discuss such things. Let's just say a few bob." Robbie was trying (and failing) to fight a smile.

Gemma looked like a rabbit caught in the headlights. "B-B-But…"

"The plane was more expensive, if you must know. So a yacht isn't really that big of a deal."

"Not big of a deal? Robbie! Where is it? When do you ever use it?"

"Currently, it's in a dock in France. I use it a few times a year."

Gemma just stared. She couldn't muster any words. There was another silence as Gemma tried to process it all. She was really starting to feel below par. What could she bring to their relationship? How on earth could their relationship last when their life and lifestyles were so different.

"Are you okay, Gemma?" Robbie asked.

"Yeah, it's… it's just…"

"Just what?" Robbie probed politely.

"Just that… our lifestyles are the polar opposite. I can't help feeling like I am seriously punching above my weight here. I just don't understand how you can want to be with me when I literally don't bring anything to this relationship." Gemma wasn't looking at Robbie, she was cowardly looking at her fingers.

"I just want you to bring you, Gemma." Gemma glanced up at him and his brown eyes were tender. He took her head into his hands and held her gaze.

"Ask me what the yacht is called."

Gemma thought for a moment. "*The Rose*?" She knew Robbie loved his mother more than anyone so it would only be fitting to name it so.

"Yes, but her full name is the *Gemma Rose*." Gemma's eyes widened as she watched him nod and continue. "I named it after my mother, who I love dearly, but also the woman who I have been *in* love with for over ten years Gemma. It's you; it's always been you. It will always be *you*. No matter how much money you do or do not earn. No matter if you are a size six or twenty-six. No matter if we have a tribe of kids" — Gemma heart warmed at the image — "and your boobs go so saggy they're dragging on the floor and every inch of you is covered in stretch marks. No matter if you get dementia and forget everything, including me. Even if you decide you don't love me any more, I will always love you, Gemma. Always."

Gemma's eyes welled up with tears and she suddenly had to kiss him. She undid her seatbelt and Robbie opened his arms so she could sit on his lap. It was a passionate, emotional and because of Gemma's tears, very wet kiss.

"I love you," Gemma murmured against his lips and Robbie groaned, his hands in her hair as he pulled her even closer to him. His mouth barely leaving hers, he uttered "I love you" before neither of them could speak any more and they spent a considerable amount of time kissing and fumbling for the rest of the plane journey. Truth be told, their lips didn't part until there was an announcement to tell them to prepare for landing. Gemma moved back to her seat, hot, flushed and slightly embarrassed as the air hostess came back into the cabin and checked them for landing.

"Where was she? Was she in here the entire time?" Gemma asked, blushing even deeper as she once again left the cabin.

"Don't worry, she sits up front with the pilot unless we call for her and we have been too busy on this flight to need her." Robbie flashed her an extremely cheeky grin, "But as for Marcus and Jason..." Gemma gasped and spun around in her chair. Marcus and Jason were sitting at the back of the plane, both looking particularly busy with their heads down and looking anywhere but at Gemma and Robbie. But Gemma swore she could see Jason's ears turning redder by the second.

"Oh my God," Gemma said, putting her hands over her face. She was mortified, everything just disappeared and melted away when she was with Robbie. And when Robbie had his lips on hers, well... nothing could stop her, even if the fires of hell were burning at her heels. "I can't believe that," Gemma said, still horribly mortified. Robbie laughed and took her hand and kissed it.

"You're an animal," he said, but his eyes danced with a fire that made Gemma squirm.

"Stop it," she said and her voice was shaking slightly.

"Why?" His voice was low and daring.

"Because we are about to land." And Gemma sat herself facing forwards, putting her hands back into her lap and trying to keep herself in check. Robbie laughed, leaning back in his seat with ease as he watched her keep her sight forward. They descended and Gemma kept herself firmly looking forwards and tucked in so she wasn't tempted to touch Robbie in any way. She clearly couldn't trust herself around him and she wasn't going to embarrass herself again, especially in front of Marcus and Jason. The plane landed smoothly and Gemma sighed in relief and relaxed her extremely stiff limbs again. She glanced at Robbie, who was still stifling a laugh.

"You okay?" he asked and she nodded.

"I can't trust myself around you. I didn't even realise Marcus and Jason were—"

"That is their job, they're supposed to be inconspicuous."

"I know, but not on a private jet. They'd have to Houdini to disappear that much. It must have been very uncomfortable for them to be present when I acted so…" she trailed off and blushed.

Robbie chuckled but seemed to take pity on her embarrassment. He leaned down and pecked her on the cheek. He then grabbed her hand and pulled her towards the door. "Come on then, let's get back to the hotel where you don't have to be so well-behaved."

"Robbie!" They were walking past the air hostess. "I'm so sorry," Gemma mumbled and they disembarked down the stairs and straight into another, slick black car waiting on the tarmac.

And then they were off, through the streets of London. With Robbie being back at training early the next morning, they stopped quickly to clean up in the hotel room (after a quick

285

fumble and kiss, obviously) and went out for a posh lunch.

Robbie took her to another very expensive and fancy restaurant (Gemma was wearing one of Robbie's ridiculously expensive dresses that she could only wear in a place like that) where there were what felt like a hundred forks on the tables and very pricey wines. Gemma was poured a wonderfully crisp and refreshing white wine while Robbie was poured a very plain cola.

Gemma smiled as he picked it up in toast.

"I feel bad drinking this wine, which is ridiculously expensive I will add, and you only get that." She indicated the soft drink in the fancy glass.

"Well, you might as well still enjoy the wine, even if I can't."

"Not even one?"

Robbie shook his head. "I don't want to risk it affecting my play."

"And flying halfway up the country to collect your girlfriend doesn't?" Gemma joked, but her smile instantly faltered when she saw the seriousness of Robbie's expression.

"No," Robbie said firmly and Gemma swallowed. "*Nothing* is more important than that." He cleared his throat, obviously done with the serious tones and replaced it with a much lighter tone. "So, to you. Thank you for coming to support me."

"I wouldn't want to be anywhere else." That was true, in part. She would like to be alone with Robbie in that posh hotel room, but they did need some sustenance she supposed.

"Well, I wouldn't mind being back at that hotel room," Robbie murmured and Gemma's jaw dropped open. "What?" He asked.

"I was literally just thinking that," she said in disbelief. Gemma felt Robbie's foot rubbing alongside hers. She was wearing these absurd contraptions that were apparently shoes.

286

But they seemed to be more strappy strings than shoes. But it meant she could really feel Robbie's trainer rubbing against the bare skin of her foot. Thriving on a bit of bravery instilled by the delicious wine, she rubbed the tops of her toes across Robbie's calf, feeling the thrill of his jeans against her open-toed feet. Robbie's demeanour changed instantly and he was looking at her with a hot intensity that Gemma fought the urge to waft herself with a menu. She still couldn't believe how much he could do to her with just one look.

"I hope this food hurries up so we can go back to the hotel," Gemma said, blushing at the intensity of Robbie's hot stare.

"I'm not sure I'll make it until then."

Gemma looked at him, open-mouthed and wide-eyed. "We can't," she said, her voice very quiet and low. Robbie's smile that smile that turned Gemma's bones to water. But right then, the waitress came with their food and the intense atmosphere was broken. Though Robbie's eyes didn't leave Gemma, Gemma snapped her eyes from his to the waitress and then back to Robbie, blushing.

"The steak," she said jovially, putting the plate in front of Gemma, it smelt amazing. "And the salmon." She put the beautiful plate of food in front of Robbie. "Your sides are just being brought over."

"Thank you," Robbie demurred, his eyes still looking at Gemma with that burning expression. Gemma tried to thank her, she looked up but her voice was lost.

It didn't matter anyway, because the waitress was looking at Robbie with a look that made Gemma's stomach burn with jealousy.

She was trying to get Robbie's attention with her big, beautiful brown eyes.

"Um," she said and she looked adorably sheepish. That made Gemma even angrier. Robbie saw Gemma near enough glaring at the waitress, so he also looked up. He hadn't even realised she was still standing there. She was looking at him, biting her lip, obviously wanting to ask something. Gemma looked at Robbie and saw he was waiting patiently, but in his eyes, she could see something deeper.

Apprehension? Annoyance?

He seemed to know what was coming before she got the courage to finish her words. "Are... are you Robbie Wilson?" Gemma's heart sank. She was a fan apparently. Or if she wasn't a fan, she was a fan of his fame and good looks. Gemma ground her teeth as she watched them. Robbie smiled, again very politely and it was a smile that didn't reach his eyes. It wasn't a smile he ever showed Gemma. Gemma's heart swelled with pleasure at the fact that this girl, beautiful as she was, wasn't seeing the true Robbie.

Only Gemma saw that.

Her glare turned to a look of slight smugness as she continued to watch the waitress. Robbie glanced at her and his eyebrows raised, but Gemma just shook her head slightly and nodded towards the waitress who was still looking at Robbie (completely ignoring Gemma).

"Yes," he said, not harshly but definitely less patiently than before. There was an awkward pause and the waitress sort of fumbled on her words.

"Oh wow, I love... I'm so... Can't believe..." Robbie just watched, his face back to the mask of patience again. "Can... can I get a picture?" Robbie just smiled blandly for a moment, before he nodded and flashed her a charming smile.

"Of course." And he stood as the second waiter came with

the promised and almost forgotten sides. He put them down, without much of a second glance at Gemma either and took the phone of the waitress, who was holding it outstretched and waiting. He took a picture of the two and Gemma couldn't help but notice the waitress was pressing her body a little closer to Robbie's side. That prickled her jealously, but it was quickly diminished as she saw Robbie's stance was stiff and to himself. He didn't remove his hands from his front to wrap an arm around her shoulders and he barely tilted his head to the side she was standing. The waitress switched places with the waiter, as he asked for one also and after another quick snap, they thanked him.

The waitress was a lot more enthusiastic, she even was brazen enough to reach out and touch his arm. Gemma thought her teeth would grind to powder if anything else would happen. But they left and Robbie sat back down.

"Sorry about that," he said and he reached his hand across the table, palm up. Gemma smiled softly and took his hand and he squeezed it. "Comes with the territory."

She shrugged lightly. Robbie took her hand and kissed the back of it and held it to his face for a moment.

"It's definitely a mood killer, that's for sure," Gemma laughed and Robbie joined in. "It's probably best, to be honest, it was a little bit *too* risky given that you are everyone's favourite guy."

"Only during the World Cup and if I mess up I'll be everyone's *least* favourite guy."

Gemma frowned and squeezed his hand that was now resting on the table. "That's a little fickle of everyone. So you're saying if you don't win everyone will think it's your fault? That's a crazy amount of pressure for you guys to be under."

"That's football," Robbie shrugged, "as long as I am still

you're favourite guy, nothing else matters." And Gemma sighed dreamily, squeezing his hand again.

"Always." He squeezed her hand once more before releasing it and picking up his knife and fork.

"Good, now let's eat before it gets any colder."

Gemma nodded and picked up her cutlery and took a bit of steak. It was amazing. Gemma moaned and closed her eyes for a second, savouring the flavour. She heard Robbie chuckling and her eyes flew open.

"My goodness, I have competition... with a steak. I thought I could only get you to make those noises." Gemma's flushed and bit her lip as she saw his eyes smouldering her again.

"This steak is good... but it's not *that* good." Robbie's mouth opened slightly and she knew he had just sucked in his breath.

"Eat up," he said quickly and he continued eating with an increased pace. Gemma fought back a laugh as she watched him.

"Why?"

"Because," he said gruffly, "I need to get you out of here and out of that dress." Gemma bit her lip. "Eat, or we'll have to get it to take home." Gemma laughed and started to eat and eat quickly she did.

"And what if we wanted dessert?" she teased, chewing her steak with the same vigour as Robbie. Robbie swallowed his mouthful and his blazing eyes met hers.

"We will have dessert in the hotel room."

And with that, they finished the meals in record speed, paid and ran from the restaurant and into the car before the need became too much.

Their lips met and the outside world faded away, leaving just them and their bodies at the centre of their entire being.

CHAPTER NINETEEN

Gemma woke the next morning, blinking sleepily as she felt Robbie untangle himself from her arms and legs. She groaned groggily and tried to reach out and grab him. She wanted to pull him back to the bed, she wanted to call out but her voice was diminished with sleep. She groaned again and buried her head into the pillow. She could hear Robbie moving about the room and after a few moments, she found the energy to sit up and look around the room. She blinked and took in the messy room. There were clothes, pillows, shoes, cartons of ice cream and whip cream canisters strewed all over the room. Gemma blushed at the sudden flashback from the night before. It involved a lot of ice cream and whipped cream and no clothing.

Robbie came into the room then, dressed in an England tracksuit and looking *very* good in it. Gemma had to take a breath to try and calm her racing heart.

Was she always going to react like that every time he walked into the room? Even in years and years to come? She thought that she probably would, Robbie would always make her heart race.

"Good morning," Robbie said and he smiled and leaned down and kissed her quickly. He touched her cheeks and smiled slightly. "Penny for your thoughts?"

"They're not worth that much."

"Well, still?"

Gemma bit her lip and looked into those warm, brown eyes. "I was just having a little… flashback to last night." She nodded

291

to a nearby ice cream tub.

Robbie glanced at it and turned back to her, smiling and with a devilish glint in his eyes.

"Ah yes, I forgot how much I love ice cream and whipped cream." Gemma blushed again and Robbie chuckled. "But not as much as I love your blush." That made Gemma blush more and Robbie caressed her cheeks.

"What are you thinking about to make you blush so much?" he murmured, still caressing her cheeks. Gemma wanted to always be honest with Robbie, so with a deep breath and mustering a little courage, she spoke.

"I just can't believe it all. I can't believe this is my life. I can't believe how good it all feels. Everything. I've never felt so loved." Robbie smiled and then he brought her mouth to his quickly.

"I do love you." Another kiss before he broke away again, "And I will spend the rest of my life showing you that."

"I just can't believe it can be so good," Gemma muttered, her cheeks burning again.

"What?"

"You know…"

Robbie was confused for a moment and then the realisation dawned on him. He let out a short laugh and nodded enthusiastically.

"Yes, I didn't know it could be so good either."

"What do you mean?" Gemma frowned at him for a moment before continuing. "Isn't it always like this? I've only ever been with Matt and you know what he was like." Robbie's face darkened straight away.

"Yes. I know," he said curtly with his jaw visibly tight. "But no, Gem," Robbie said much softer, "It's not always like this. I have never experienced it like this. It's never felt so good to me either." Gemma couldn't help but suck in her breath and grin like an idiot.

"Really?"

"Oh really. Never… *ever*."

"Wow," Gemma said, shaking her head and staring off dreamily while she tried to process what Robbie said. Robbie's laugh brought her back to the hotel room and her attention was brought back to his tracksuit. "So back to reality again then?" Robbie nodded, almost sadly.

"Yep. I'm training all day today and preparing for the match. I should have been in my own hotel room last night."

"This isn't your hotel room?"

Robbie shook his head. "My room is downstairs with all the boys. It's sort of a tradition, if you will. We stay together the day and night before a match. To get us until the zone… or so the manager says."

Gemma nodded, trying to fight off the burning disappointment in her throat. She knew Robbie was going to have to work and that meant spending a significant amount of time away from her. Yet she couldn't help being upset. She just about fought off a pout and nodded, her eyes falling down to her lap. Robbie put his fingers underneath her chin and tilted her head upwards so his eyes met hers. "But I might be sneaking out and coming here. I'm sure Jake won't tell anyone." Gemma had to laugh at that. They both laughed and then Gemma wrapped her arms around his neck.

"Um, whose Jake?" Gemma thought about the other players and Robbie's teammates. She literally couldn't name a single one. She blushed, whenever she watched England playing, Robbie was the only one she would look for. Robbie chuckled, kissing her lips quickly.

"Jake Whittle, he plays…" He looked at her, with his eyebrows raised. Gemma's blank expression was evidence enough that she had no clue about the positions players played on the football pitch. "At the front with me," he added and she nodded, still not sure what "at the front" meant.

"Anyway," Robbie grinned and pulled her to him to his chest. "I have to go."

"No," Gemma sighed, tightening her arms around him. And she kissed him and they embraced for a couple of minutes when there was a beeping noise. Robbie pulled back and sighed, reaching into his pocket and pulling out his phone.

"It's my alarm. I got to go." Gemma sighed and nodded too. "But Marcus said he'll take you to see some of London sights today."

"Okay, that sounds lovely." She wasn't completely lying but she would much rather be with Robbie. And preferably in that hotel room…

"Right, have a good day. And I will see you later. I'll give you a call when I get a break."

"Have fun." Robbie smiled at her attempt at enthusiasm. He kissed her, then brought his lips to her ear.

"I'll see you in a few hours. Shhh don't tell anyone."

She laughed and nodded and watched him go. She sighed and laid back down on the plump pillows. The bed felt uncomfortably empty with Robbie gone, Gemma didn't think she'd be able to go back to sleep. She grabbed her phone and saw it was a little after seven in the morning. She suspected that Marcus wouldn't arrive for another couple of hours yet. So she decided to go through her social media and check her messages. She had neglected her phone for a couple of days. She had spoken to her mum quickly to explain what had happened with Matt and where she was, but other than that, she hadn't spoken to her.

She needed to check-in.

As it was early so she decided to send her a message. But there was already a message from her. It said:

How are you darling? Pub is fine so don't worry about anything. You're in the tabloids again. I don't think I'll ever get over seeing you in them in all honesty. Love you xxx

Gemma's eyes welled up, she was overcome with a rush of love for her mum. When the rush of emotion settled down, Gemma saw her mum had sent her another message which appeared to be an internet link. Her stomach dropped. She tended to ignore the media, her mum often would send links and she wouldn't look into them.

She found it easier to not look at what the media was saying about her. She didn't really care what they said, what she struggled with was seeing her picture plastered on every page.

Sometimes alone and other times with Robbie and she wasn't sure what was worse. They were always extremely unflattering angles and shots and when she was standing next to Robbie (who always looked great in all pictures) it was always a kick in the gut.

She didn't know what possessed her to open this link, but she did.

It was a tabloid newspaper and on the front cover were a couple of pictures of the England football team, a still of Robbie playing in the last game he played and a badly angled picture of both Robbie and Gemma from the previous night's meal. The headline read:

Football superstar, Robbie Wilson back from his unexplained absence and WILL be playing in tomorrow's semi-

final.

Gemma started to read the article, the first part of it was mostly about England's success during the World Cup thus far and a little about their opponent's journey to the semi-finals. Then Robbie is mentioned and they exclaimed how relieved they are that he is back at training and that there were fears he may miss the semi-final due to personal matters. They also spoke about how Robbie had returned to the capital yesterday via private jet (which was worryingly detailed in Gemma's opinion for a tabloid) and he was back at training the next morning.

Then Gemma got to the bit she knew was coming: a whole section on her.

Or *the nation's heartthrob's mystery girl* as the tabloid referred to her. They speculated who Gemma was, it was already known that she worked in the pub but they were hazarding a guess at *how* they met. There were a few suggestions but none knew the truth it seemed. That was a little comforting that they didn't seem to know *every* aspect of Gemma's life. Or at least, not when that article was published. Little comfort that was, as there was a detailed paragraph about Gemma residing in London to watch the remainder of the World Cup. There was even a lot of details regarding the meal they had shared the previous night. So detailed it even included what they ate for dinner and what Gemma was wearing.

The staff must have given over information for a little extra cash. Robbie wouldn't be happy.

Not only was it detailed, it was public.

Which meant anyone could know where Gemma could be. Anyone being… Matt.

Gemma sighed, she didn't want to send it to Robbie but she knew he would eventually find out about it anyway through his

PA team and it was easier to not keep it a secret from him. So, begrudgingly, Gemma sent him the link and added a little message with it.

Hope training is going well. I miss you. Mum sent me this and I thought you may want to know about it. Think your girlfriend from last night may have been gushing about you a bit too much. Love you xx

She sent the message and after a couple of minutes of scrolling aimlessly through social media, she could feel her eyelids drooping. She turned off her phone and put her head back on the pillow, letting the sleep take over her once more.

Gemma hadn't realised she had properly fallen asleep until a shrilling phone ringing woke her up. She jumped up, grabbing at the horrid phone with fumbling, awkward hands.

"H-hello?" she stuttered, blinking at the sudden assault of noise and light. "Good morning, Miss Walker, this is your wake-up call."

"M-my wake-up call?"

"Yes, ma'am. Mr Wilson said you would be needing one." Gemma glared at nothing in particular. He could have mentioned *something*. "He said to also say that your tour guides will be arriving in one hour from now."

"And… uh… what time is now, sorry?"

"Nine, miss."

"Thank you, I — hang on, tour *guides*? Who are they?"

"He didn't say, ma'am. Just to relay that message that they will be here in an hour… at ten, ma'am." He reiterated because apparently Gemma didn't sound very "with it".

"Okay, um, thank you."

"You're welcome, ma'am. Someone will drop off some breakfast in half an hour for you."

"Oh, thanks."

"You're welcome. Have a nice day, ma'am." And the phone went dead. Gemma put down the receiver and reached for her phone. There was a message from Robbie.

Leave it with me.

Did you enjoy your wake-up call? I thought it was extremely thoughtful of me, personally.

I love you xx

Gemma had to laugh and she shook her head. She replied.

Thanks for the warning. Took about ten years off my life. Also... guides? x

She stood up and stretched. Her body ached and felt stiff. It felt like she had done a very strenuous workout, which she guessed was kind of true. She smiled to herself as she dragged herself to the shower. It was heavenly, with massaging jets and hot water. She walked out of the bathroom, feeling very relaxed and refreshed, wearing the super soft towelling robe. She sighed when she saw the mess of the bedroom again. She supposed she should clean up; it was embarrassing enough when Marcus was in the background when they kissed. She couldn't cope with him seeing what they got up to in private. She ran around the room, picking up pillows and clothes. She threw away the old tubes of ice cream and whipped cream, her cheeks burning at the memories flashing back to her. When she was done, it wasn't neat, but it was much better.

Enough to not be embarrassed about. She walked over to her phone and saw another message from Robbie.

That's for me to know and you to find out... soon.

Gemma smiled.

Oh wow. Please don't say that again... ever.

She sent her reply and walked over to her bag and pulled out a pair of jeans and top. She wanted to be comfortable if she was going to be spending all day walking around London. She put her moisturisers on and dressed and dried her hair quickly.

She went to the mirror to check her appearance. She wasn't going to put on a face of makeup to just sweat it off around London. It was much hotter in the capital than back in Netherby, so her top was light and flowy. She had a pair of light, high-waist jeans (because even though it was warm, it was still England) and white trainers. Though she might not be dressed up with heels, jackets and jewellery, she still felt it was a step up from her usual extremely casual clothing. She actually felt pretty good.

She blinked at her appearance for a moment. She hadn't realised that lately she had felt so much more comfortable with her body. Yes, she still had moments of insecurity or self-loathing. But she realised at that moment, she had more good days than bad ones.

Was that to do with her relationship with Robbie? Could it be how tentative and affectionate he was with her that helped with her self-confidence? Had years of Matt's constant put-downs and controlling nature been the reason she hated herself so much? Yes, she had to admit, there were many reasons Gemma self-loathed and had very little self-confidence that wasn't all to do with Matt. Yet had coming out from under his control allowed her to gain a little more confidence and self-worth? Had it been that she had finally allowed herself to be happy and wasn't constantly riddled with the guilt of Abi's death?

There was a pang of sorrow through her heart and a ripple of guilt through her stomach. Okay, so she wasn't totally rid of that feeling. She gnawed at her lip as she thought about Abi, for the first time in a long while. How had she not thought of her? Surely, she had thought about her, even just a little, over the past few weeks?

Could she really be so shallow that whenever she was in Robbie's presence, she thought of nothing else? Then when she wasn't in Robbie's presence, she still thought of nothing else. Yes, she had decided to not let her guilt for Abi hold her back from her relationship with Robbie, but could she be so obsessed with Robbie that she totally disregarded her friend without a second thought the second a man came into her life?

What kind of friend did that make her?

Still trying to digest the guilt bubbling away inside of her, she was just about to turn back from the mirror when there was a knock on the door. She glanced at the clock on the bedside table. Half an hour had passed since her wake-up call, so she assumed it was the breakfast.

She opened the door and jumped at the sudden outburst of noise.

"Surprise!" Everyone shouted and Gemma literally screamed and fell back. That was received by a collective laugh from the group in front of Gemma.

The group consisted of Rose, Arty, Pip and Gemma's mum, Linda. Gemma could also see Marcus and a couple of security personnel in the hallway, looking up and down. Obviously with a group, they needed to increase security, so Gemma didn't know the names of the other personnel.

Gemma just stared open-mouthed at them for a moment. They were mostly (except her mum) all going to Robbie's match later that evening. But she didn't expect to see them all until much later, hence why she thought she was spending the day with Marcus.

"Are you happy to see us?" Linda gushed, stepping forwards

and bringing Gemma into a bone-crushing hug.

"Of course! I'm just surprised. I didn't expect to see you at all! And you," she looked over to Robbie's family, "I didn't think you'd be getting here until later on! I was going to meet you at the stadium!"

"Well," Rose said as she came in for a hug after Linda, "Robbie asked if we could come down earlier and surprise you. He didn't like leaving you alone."

"Aw, well this is a lovely surprise. So it's not Marcus taking me around London then?" She flashed a grin at Marcus and he nodded.

"I will be tagging along though if that's okay."

"Of course." After everyone had greeted Gemma and filed inside, they walked over to the sitting area of the extravagant hotel room. Before Gemma could sit though, someone knocked on the door again. This time, however, Marcus went to the door, first checking the peephole before opening it again.

It was the breakfast and if the breakfast had arrived before everyone Gemma would have been slightly offended. Robbie had obviously ordered enough breakfast to feed a few people, a few times over. So clearly, it had been arranged that everyone would join Gemma for breakfast. They filled their plates with perfectly cooked eggs, expensive sausages and bacon and freshly cooked bread. There were bowls of fresh fruit and yoghurts. There were cold-cut meats and cheeses. There was a teapot and one of the staff members (there were a couple) even took coffee orders so they could order a certain coffee to be brought back up to use.

"Wow," Gemma said about twenty minutes later when she had had some cook breakfast and sipping a barista-made coffee. "That was delicious."

"Robbie has spared no expense, that's for sure," Pip said,

patting her stomach (which was still flat) as if she were pregnant. "That was good. I'll have to thank him. Bet that wasn't cheap in a posh hotel like this."

"I wish he wouldn't spend so much money," Gemma sighed, picking up a piece of melon and forcing it down. "I always feel so bad when he spends money on me."

"Technically, he's spent it on all of us," said Rose, smiling over her coffee cup at her. "Yes, that is true. But this hotel room is just for me, which I found out this morning."

"Robbie wants you close," Linda shrugged, also picking at one of the fruit bowls. "It's only natural that he would. I'm personally glad you are so close to him, it means you are safer." Everyone collectively nodded and murmured their agreement.

"How are you?" Pip asked, reaching out and grabbing her hand. "Are you feeling okay?"

"I'm fine, honestly." And she was. It might be different when she wasn't with Robbie constantly, but she had only been out of his company for a couple of hours. Not long enough to feel scared about being alone. "I feel very safe. Marcus and everyone are doing a brilliant job watching over me." Gemma smiled at Marcus, who smiled and nodded back.

"It's a pleasure, Miss Walker, truly."

"Thank you and I'll forget this time that you still called me 'Miss Walker'."

"Apologies… Gemma."

"That's better. So, where are we off to first?" Gemma asked the group at large. And then their day of sightseeing began.

They literally saw everything, all the sights from Tower Bridge to Big Ben to Buckingham Palace to St. James' Park.

They stopped at indie cafés and had very tasty and expensive coffees with impressive latte art on them. They rode on the tube (much to Marcus's distress!) and got confused with the London Underground map.

Robbie had even arranged for them to have an open-top bus tour, for just them and booked them in for a high tea lunch at the Gherkin. They ate little sandwiches and scones and drank champagne and laughed until their bellies were sore.

It was the most spectacular day and with the match being an early evening one, they all returned to the hotel (they all had rooms there too, Robbie surely booked the entire place) fairly early and got ready for the match. Gemma was a little buzzed from the champagne and her whole body just felt light. She couldn't believe how wonderful the day had been and how much she truly missed spending time with them all.

It had been far, far too long.

Once she showered again, she changed into jeans and her brand-new England shirt, courtesy of Robbie. And when she checked herself in the mirror just before leaving to meet the group, she noticed something on the back of it.

It had Robbie's number on it, sixteen and his surname on the back.

She was wearing one of Robbie's actual England shirts that he played in. Gemma felt actually a little bit proud to be wearing this shirt, with Robbie's name on it.

Grinning like an idiot, she left, meeting Marcus outside who took her downstairs to the lobby where she met everyone else. It didn't escape her notice that there was also security in the lobby too, so it wasn't just Gemma under Marcus' watchful eye. They were taken down the garage and then got into a big SUV with seven seats, so they could all spread out. There was a little buzz of excitement in the atmosphere and also, some nerves.

Gemma hadn't spoken to Robbie all day. They had

messaged, but since her good-luck message an hour ago, she had heard nothing from him. She knew he would be getting into the zone and rallying with his teammates. Would he feel sick with nerves like she did? Probably not; this was his job and he was one of the best in the world at what he did. But Gemma felt so nervous for him. She had never watched him live, only on the screen at the pub. She would actually be in the stadium with him, shouting to him and knowing full well he wouldn't be able to hear her over the roar of the crowd.

When they arrived at the stadium, Gemma felt like she might throw up. They all got out of the car and were escorted to one of the stadium entries, which apparently was a more private door. Gemma could still see and hear all the fans around them and the atmosphere was pulsating with anticipation and excitement. Gemma felt slightly less sick (only slightly) and more energised. She bounced up and down as they waited for Marcus to talk to the steward and showed them their tickets. They were given passes to wear around their neck, each with their identification and picture on.

Gemma looked at hers and it almost looked like her driving licence or passport photo. It was obviously a photo they had on file or something. They were being escorted into the stadium by some sort of host. Though Robbie had obviously got them sort of box, they appeared to be being escorted to the actual stands.

"Where are we going?" Gemma asked Rose, who had been to all of Robbie's football games, near enough.

"To the stands," she said simply and looked at her as if she was simple.

"Well obviously," Gemma scoffed, "but I thought we had a box?"

"We do," Rose nodded, but then she scrunched up her nose

304

in distaste, "But you can't get the atmosphere from the box, so we also have seats in the actual stands so we can soak up the atmosphere too. We'll normally go to the box for drinks before and after the game. And sometimes at half-time as well. We're too late to go for any now."

"Oh! That's a good idea," Gemma nodded approvingly.

"Of course, it was mine," Rose said, holding her head up smugly, "He used to always put me in the box, with expensive alcohol and food but it just wasn't the same as being packed into the stadium, alongside real fans."

Rose was right, as soon as they stepped into the stadium, there was an instant electric atmosphere. The joy and elation were so contagious, Gemma almost forgot she was nervous. Only almost though, there was still a slight squirming in her stomach as she waited for the game. It was probably only about fifteen minutes in total that they waited, but it felt much longer. Even with the chants and songs from the crowds, the time seems to drag.

Finally, there was an announcement to say the players were coming out, so they stood. Gemma was slightly mortified that she didn't know any of the players apart from Robbie. She maybe thought she might be able to guess Whittle out of the line-up, but no others. These were Robbie's teammates, his closest friends. She needed to make an effort to try and know them. She made a mental note to ask Robbie when they were next alone.

If they weren't too busy, she thought shamelessly.

The music swelled in the stadium as the players, mascots, linemen and referees all filed out and stood in a straight line, facing the direction of Gemma and half of the stadium. Gemma could see Robbie clearly, they were close enough that if Robbie looked towards her, he could probably see her. Gemma didn't think he would, she thought he would want to stay in the zone. But she could see his eyes searching the crowd, until he found their party and moved along each face until he found Gemma's.

Their eyes met and Gemma smiled encouragingly.

Robbie visibly let out his breath, his shoulders sagging slightly before he stood up to his full height and looked up. Gemma followed his eye line and saw that two flags were descending from above. The two flags were in staggering contrast next to one another. The host country went first with the national anthem, so most of the stadium erupted in song. Gemma felt a sense of pride as she sang along, the music swelling and building to a crushing crescendo and huge applause. The second anthem was played in much the same way and when the song had finished, the players broke out of their straight line and began jumping and slapping each other on the back.

It was about to begin.

The players all shook hands with each other and the referees and Gemma saw Robbie go up to the other team's captain and shake his hand. They tossed a coin to pick a side, Robbie had obviously won because he pointed to the side he wanted and they all nodded and then the players got into position on the field, awaiting the starting whistle.

The cheers were colossal in sound and feeling. Gemma could feel their chants and songs literally pulsating through her entire body as she stood and kept her eyes trained on Robbie. Her stomach was twisting and turning and she wrung her hands, unable to remain still.

Finally, the whistle sounded. And the players all started to run.

Gemma kept her eyes fully on Robbie the entire time. Even if he didn't have the ball and he was just running along, weaving in between players and trying to get to the ball or goal. He was mesmerising. Gemma had obviously watched him play before, but never live and never so close. He was so graceful and moved with deadly precision. Everyone seemed to just swarm him whenever he got the ball. He was being tripped and tackled but he kept getting up. He kept pushing forwards but the other team were defending fiercely. They hardly pushed towards their own goal, they seemed to think the best tactic was just to keep Robbie and his teammates from theirs.

Before Gemma knew it, half-time arrived.

Gemma let out a breath she hadn't realised she was holding. She relaxed her hands from their claw-like grip around one another. Her muscles ached from the tense stance she'd been in for nearly fifty minutes.

"Come on," Rose said to her, "I need a bloody drink." So they moved from the stands, through a couple concrete walkways and reached a door which then led to the box. They entered and sat on the comfy chairs provided, no one speaking. A waiter came in and took their drinks orders and was back within a couple of minutes. Gemma took a big glug of her ice-cold cider and let out a sigh.

"How do you cope with this?" Gemma asked the room at large, mostly directing her question to Rose and Arty. "How do you cope with the anxiety and seeing him being knocked down constantly?"

"We're used to it," Rose said grimly.

"But he does seem to be being knocked over more than usual," Arty nodded in agreement. He sighed and rubbed his eyes with his fingers and pinched the bridge of his nose. "They just can't break through. They just need one break. I hate it when it goes to penalties."

"Me too, he beats himself up for days after them."

Arty nodded and then there was another silence. They drank their drinks with little or no talk, everyone sitting and thinking to themselves. And after a few minutes, they went back to the stands and Gemma resumed her stressed position with her hunched back and clasped hands. The second half was full of ups and down. England scored first and Gemma screamed so loud that her voice ripped through her throat and left her sore. She hugged Linda and Pip, who were standing on either side of her. Robbie had set up the goal, driving it forwards until just outside the box where he knocked it back to his teammate, milliseconds before an opponent took him out. There were boos and hisses at that, but it was soon forgotten when the England fans realised the ball hit the back of the net.

Their elation was short lived, however, as about three minutes after that, the other team scored. It was neck and neck and one all. If Gemma was nervous in the first half, it was nothing compared to the second half.

It was shot after shot after shot, from both teams. But neither managed to get the ball into the back of the net. It was approaching the final whistle, but if no one scored, it would be extra time and penalties. Gemma's nerves were shot and she couldn't sit (figuratively speaking as she stood the entire time, sitting would have been impossible) through another thirty minutes of play and then possibly penalties after that.

She thought she would surely implode with all the pressure.

It was looking like extra time was a real possibility... until the final two minutes of the game.

There had been an extremely close call at England's goal. It led to the opposition very *nearly* sending the ball into the back of the net, but luckily, the goalie (Gemma wanted to say his name

308

was Jameson, but in all honesty, she wasn't sure) did a momentous save. He kicked the ball right down to the other end of the pitch. Right into Robbie's teammate's chest. It was Whittle, Gemma knew that because he was Jake Whittle, the player Robbie was supposed to be sharing his hotel room with. Gemma had googled him that morning after Robbie had mentioned him. It had been Whittle who had scored the goal earlier in the half. Whittle had the ball and was weaving between the onslaught of blue shirts all sprinting towards him. His white shirt the only one in a sea of blue... which meant one thing.

Robbie had been left undefended.

Whittle had also noticed this and volleyed the ball neatly over the sea of blue shirts, landing it neatly at Robbie's feet.

Within seconds, Robbie was in position in front of the goalie, just as some of the opponents tried to shut him attack down.

It was too late, the ball had already left Robbie's magical right foot, sailing through the air. It was almost like slow motion.

The white and black ball flew, unsuspended in mid-air for what seemed like hours. It was as if it knew most of the world would be watching and it was taking its time, soaking up the limelight. Finally, it seemed to crawl its way to the goal. The goalie had dived towards it, his arms stretched out wide.

For a moment, it looked as if he was going to knock the ball right off course and protect the goal. But his hands seemed to dip, ever so slightly and the ball sailed neatly over his outstretched fingertips, passed its last defence and into the goal, shaking the net with a final quiver before it came to its final resting place, at the back of the net.

CHAPTER TWENTY

The stadium exploded.

Gemma screamed and cheered until no more noise came out of her throat. After Robbie had kicked the ball into the back of the net, he sprinted along the side of the pitch until he reached where Gemma and everyone was sitting. He looked up, his face alight with a cheer. He had his hand clenched and was shouting something at them and punching the air. His eyes were searching and his eyes moved along the line of supporters until his eyes stopped on Gemma's. He smiled even wider, if that was possible. He then brought his hands to his lips and blew Gemma a double kiss. He opened his arms and shouted something. Though Gemma couldn't hear him, he knew exactly what he said.

"I love you!"

Gemma felt her cheeks burning, but she smiled and shook her head at him.

She was going to kill him, but that moment was *his* moment. And Gemma couldn't stop smiling. Robbie deserved his moment and she felt honoured to share it with him. A second after Robbie had blown her a kiss, his teammates all leaped upon him and he was buried in a wave of white shirts. They all celebrated for a moment or two before they ran back to the field, Robbie turning as he ran and blowing Gemma one more kiss before he joined his team back on the field.

They readied themselves to start play again and they started off but within a couple of minutes, the final whistle sounded.

That was it.

England was through to the final of the World Cup.

"Oh, thank God," Gemma heard Pip sigh in relief and she turned to her and brought her in for a hug. "God, that was stressful," she said in Gemma's ear and she nodded in agreement.

"You're telling me, I don't think I relaxed a single muscle that entire game."

"Come on, let's get another drink and wait for Robbie." They waited for some of the initial traffic of bodies to move and then they made their way to the box. There were flutes of champagne and canapés waiting for them and Gemma went straight over and glugged some champagne. There was silence and everyone seemed to do the same.

"I don't know how I will cope during the final," Gemma said, her eyes glazing over as she focused on something insignificant in the distance. Everyone seemed to murmur in agreement.

"Wow, so this is my cheering squad?" A voice sounded from behind them and they all turned around to see Robbie standing in the doorway, in a fresh tracksuit. There was a general exclamation and cheer within the group as all raced over to congratulate him. Gemma let his parents and sister go ahead of her and she smiled and watched him hug his family. He kept catching her eye, and after a swift hug with them all, he crossed the room in a few long strides and pulled Gemma into his arms and spun around, laughing.

"You were amazing, Robbie," Gemma gushed and he put her down and kissed her quickly.

It was almost easy to forget the others in the room with them. Almost.

There was a little clear of throats and Gemma and Robbie looked to the rest of their party. There were four pairs of eyebrows raised.

"Wow, so what are we? Chopped liver?" Rose said, but she was beaming at them. "Doesn't want to know us any more, now Gemma's here." Robbie laughed and turned to walk back to them, grabbing Gemma's hand as he went.

"It's only because I've never been to one of his games before," Gemma said modestly, blushing and taking another swig of her champagne.

"So what's your schedule like now until the final?" Arty asked as Robbie and Gemma reached them again. Robbie grimaced slightly, glancing down at Gemma quickly before answering his dad.

"Think the manager is going to lock us down a bit, to be honest. We'll just be training and have the team for company. No outsiders allowed, I'm afraid." Gemma felt her heart sink slightly but tried to shake it off.

This was so important to Robbie and she shouldn't be selfish.

Robbie squeezed her hand and she glanced up at him. He wasn't looking at her, but he seemed to nod. Gemma had no idea what he meant, but obviously it was something he wasn't going to say in front of the others.

"Well done," said Rose and she was positively beaming. "So, so proud of you." She pulled him in, kissing his cheek and squeezing her arms around his waist. Robbie pulled her to his chest and rested his head against her head.

"Thanks, Mum." She pulled back, wiping tears from her eyes. Then each in turn gave Robbie a hug and congratulated him. "Okay," Robbie said once he hugged everyone else, "I'll have to go back for the quick debrief, but I'll meet you back at the hotel for dinner. Go and get some drinks and will see you there in an hour." He turned and kissed Gemma quickly on the top of the head before he left.

They finished their drinks and had a few nibbles while the stadium emptied. When it was emptied enough, Marcus and his crew escorted them back through the stadium and back to the car.

Back at the hotel, they all disbursed again and got ready for dinner. The hotel restaurant was much fancier than the jeans and England shirt that Gemma was wearing. So she found herself standing in front of the mirror once again, twisting and turning looking at the dress that was one of the few that Amy had brought for Gemma. It was much more fitting than Gemma would have ever picked for herself.

And red.

She would have never picked a colour so vibrant. She tended to stick to blacks, browns and navy blues. Those colours were apparently more flattering. Though it never felt flattering to Gemma.

But this dress… it seemed to suit her.

Amy had been in her room when she returned from the match with a selection of dresses. She even helped Gemma a little with her hair and makeup, though Gemma mostly did it herself. But the dress! Amy had well and truly outdone herself. It fitted her in the right places and hugged, sculpted and smoothed the places Gemma hated the most. Gemma's heart was thumping in her chest as she looked over at herself. She didn't know if she was brave enough to wear it.

She gnawed on freshly lipsticked lips as she had an internal battle. She could change quickly, she could pick something more flowy and less revealing…

Yeah, she would do that.

She turned (nearly stumbling in her high heels) and went to walk back to the wardrobe. But as she took the first step, there was a knock on the door. Gemma froze and looked at the door.

There was another knock, a bit more urgent the second time. Gemma groaned and walked over and peeked through the eyehole. It was Pip and she was bouncing up and down. She knocked a third time and Gemma pulled the heavy door open.

"I'm nearly ready—" Pip shot passed her with little speech. She said something about "toilet" and she slammed the door and Gemma heard her sigh in relief.

"Do you not have a toilet in your room?" Gemma heard the flush and the tap running and Pip came back out. She scoffed and shook her head.

"My room isn't as nice as yours. You're definitely Robbie's favourite."

"Well," Gemma said, smiling slyly, "I am the one who—"

"For the love of God, do *not* finish that sentence."

Gemma laughed. "Okay. Well, I was just going to change, then we can go down?"

"Change?" Pip turned to her and her eyes widened. "Why are you changing? Gemma, you look amazing!"

Gemma blushed. "Really? I thought it was a little tight and revealing."

Pip shook her head. "No! You look hot! Wow!"

"Stop it."

"Seriously, Gemma! Robbie is going to struggle to keep—"

"Now, *you* do not finish that sentence!"

"Hands! I meant his hands!"

"That's no better!" But Gemma and Pip were both laughing. When they stopped, Gemma took a deep breath. "Right, fine. Let's get going then."

Pip beamed at her, linking her arm with Gemma's and dragging her out of the hotel room before she couldn't change her mind. Marcus, who did a double take when he saw Gemma, of course escorted them down to the restaurant.

Gemma even got a "You look nice, miss" before he coughed and stammered forward. It made Gemma smile and made her feel kind of... nice. She wasn't often someone who was deemed attractive and was often overlooked. At the restaurant, they were shown to a private seating area where they were they met with Rose, Arty and Linda.

"Oh wow, Gem!" Linda said, her eyes sparkling as she gazed at her daughter. "You look beautiful!"

"Well, you have to say that, you're my mum. But thank you."

"I don't have to say it and I think you look smoking!" Rose beamed. "That dress is beautiful!"

"Thanks," Gemma mumbled, "It's one Robbie's stylist chose. She also helped with my makeup and hair a little," Gemma added pointlessly.

"Well, you look stunning," Pip said loyally and Gemma smiled weakly back at her.

"Thank you." To Gemma's relief, their drinks had arrived and the conversation moved on from Gemma and her little red dress. They discussed the football match, well, Gemma drank and everyone else talked. Gemma's heart was still thumping uncomfortably in her chest. She kept glancing at anyone who walked past or looked her way. She felt like there was a spotlight above her head and it was shining brightly upon her.

She felt her skin begin to prickle and she felt hyperaware of every lump and bump her body possessed. She tried to straighten up and lengthen her neck. She tried to pull in her stomach. She held her arms out so that the skin wasn't being pulled against the fabric on the shoulders.

She felt hot and uncomfortable and her eyes started to dart around the restaurant, looking for a bathroom. God, why had she

315

worn heels? She felt like an Amazonian woman compared to her party. She was the tallest of them all apart from Arty, but in heels, she matched his six-foot frame. She felt humongous in every way possible. She felt sick and her drink was empty. When did she drink that? She was going to have to go and get changed. She leaped up suddenly and everyone looked at her. She mumbled something about going to the toilet. Maybe she could splash water over her dress and come back and say she needed to go. She could run upstairs and change quickly before Robbie saw her in this dress. Or she could fake sickness or—

"Robbie!" Gemma's head snapped up, Pip had shouted him over and Rose rolled her eyes.

"Pip!" Rose hissed, embarrassed, "This is a posh place! Don't yell your brother's name."

"Well, I didn't think he could see us. Which is stupid, because look! He's only got eyes for Gemma! Jeez, we're only his family."

Gemma looked over her shoulder and she could see Robbie out of the corner of her eye. She turned slowly and looked at him. He was standing, suspended in mid-step for a moment as he gazed at Gemma. His eyes were warm and full and they were transfixed on Gemma. Instantly, at the sight of him, Gemma could feel her insecurities subsiding. They weren't gone completely, but she was feeling more comfortable in her own skin.

Robbie strode over to them, never taking his eyes off Gemma. He still had his mouth open slightly and he was gazing at her with a heat that made Gemma shiver. The initial shock and awe seemed to be replaced by something much hotter. His eyes were dangerously smouldering as she saw him look her up and down. It was a look Gemma was very familiar with and had seen many times. He fell into line beside her, his eyes still on Gemma. He stood there for a moment before he turned to everyone in turn, nodding and saying their name before he turned back to Gemma. He leaned down and kissed her cheeks before he whispered in her ear, "You look beautiful."

Gemma flushed and smiled goofily up at him. "What, this old thing?" she joked, smoothing her hand over the skirt. "I just found it lying around."

Robbie's eyes gleamed devilishly. "I can't wait until it's 'lying around' your hotel room again later on."

Gemma gasped and glanced around at everyone, who had moved to follow the waiter to the table.

"Robbie!" she gasped, "Stop it! Our family—"

"Are out of earshot." Gemma jumped as she felt Robbie's hand suddenly skimming up her thigh and over her bum. "This... is going to be a painful dinner," he murmured in her ear and Gemma shivered. She bit her lip and her eyes swept the now empty sitting room and she turned back to him.

"Painful? Why painful?" Robbie's hands moved to Gemma's hips and he pulled her to his chest so that her back was pressing against the length of him. Robbie's breath was hot on her cheek and neck and he kissed her exposed collarbone quickly.

"Robbie!" Gemma breathed, but she felt her resolve melting away. His hands moved down her hips, over to the front of her thighs and dangerously close to her centre. "R-Robbie..." He pulled her tighter against him and she could feel him pressing into her back.

"Can you feel why this is going to be a painful meal for me?" His voice was pure seduction and his lips only left her skin slightly as he spoke. His hot breath flittered across her bare skin and Gemma rested her head on Robbie's shoulder, melting into

317

him more. Gemma was shivering with anticipation. Gemma couldn't speak so she just nodded and Robbie chuckled against her neck. "So very painful." He kissed and grazed her skin with his teeth all while his hands trailed down to the edge of her skirt and he started to caress her thigh and lift her skirt up slightly.

Though Gemma could feel her restraint failing, there was a small part of her brain still working (barely).

"Robbie," she said, it was breathy but still stronger than before. "Our families are in the next room, waiting for us."

Robbie sighed, almost sadly. "I know," his hands flittered back down to her hem, pulling it back into place. His hand went to her cheek and he pulled her head to the side so his lips could meet hers for a passionate, quick kiss as he pressed himself against her bottom for a final, fleeting moment before he released her. He moved to her side and took her hand.

"But soon, and I mean *very* soon, I will be peeling that dress off you. I promise you that."

"I hope so," Gemma said and she glanced up at him again and had to stifle a laugh.

"What?" Robbie asked.

"You've got…" Gemma trailed off, reaching up and wiping his lip gently. "A little…" She rubbed off the red lipstick, but it still partially stained his lips. "I don't think I'll get it off," Gemma admitted. Robbie shrugged and pulled her to him quickly once more.

"It doesn't matter." And he kissed her again. "Robbie!"

"I won't be able to keep my hands off you anyway, so it's pointless." He grinned roguishly before he kissed her again. This one a little deeper and Gemma felt herself sighing and melting into his kiss. Robbie groaned and pulled back slightly, his eyes alight with desire. He groaned again, and finally pulled back but took Gemma's hand.

"Let's go. Before I throw you over my shoulder and ran back to the hotel room."

Robbie walked to the adjoining door, he opened it and stepped to the side to allow Gemma through first. As she moved passed, his hand skimmed her bottom one more time and Gemma glanced at him with raised eyebrows.

"It's a very nice dress. I think Amy needs a pay rise."

They entered back into the main restaurant and quickly found their table. Robbie pulled out a chair for Gemma and she slid into it.

"Thank you, how very gentlemanly of you." Robbie flashed her a crooked smile. "Always."

Pip scoffed next to Gemma and Robbie looked at her with raised eyebrows. "Pl-uu-eaase. You? A gentleman?"

"I am very gentlemanly actually."

"Right and I'm very ladylike."

"Well—"

"Children, children, children. Enough now please."

"Sorry, Mum." Both Pip and Robbie murmured and Robbie sat down at the last empty seat. The waiter walked over to Robbie with the wine menu. Robbie chose a bottle of champagne and though Gemma had never heard of it, Gemma knew it would be delicious and expensive. The waiter returned with the drinks order and all the champagne flutes were filled, they all raised their glasses in a toast. Even though Robbie didn't normally drink when he was playing, it wasn't every day you secured your country's place in the final of the World Cup.

"Congratulations, Robbie," Arty said, beaming with pride at his son. Robbie leaned back in his chair, resting his arm across the top of Gemma's and her shoulders. He had his glass raised and he smiled back at his dad. He squeezed Gemma's shoulder quickly and she looked up at him. His eyes were shining slightly and he looked back at his dad again. "We are so thankful for you sharing this with us all. No matter the outcome of Tuesday's match, we're so unbelievably proud of you. So, to Robbie." Arty charged his glass and toasted his only son. Everyone else around the table followed suit and toasted Robbie, murmuring his name before drinking the delicious and expensive champagne.

Robbie removed his arm from Gemma's shoulders, grazing his fingertips along her bare skin and moving his hand so that it rested on her leg, above her knee. His fingertips caressed her skin and tickled under the hem. Gemma looked at him, eyebrows raised but breathing much faster. He just looked at her, with those warm, big eyes and raised one eyebrow in return.

Gemma just looked away, biting her lip and trying to fight off the warm, flushed feeling that was tingling from Robbie's touch. The conversation moved from the upcoming match to London itself, all the while Robbie's fingers moved in tickling patterns up Gemma's thighs. He never moved to her core, he sometimes allowed his fingers to trace the sensitive skin of her inner thigh, but never further up. They were in the company of their family after all, but it was enough to make Gemma squirm and her breath quicken.

Robbie was right, this was going to be a painful meal. And he seemed to be making sure it was painful for Gemma too.

"And what was your favourite landmark, Gemma?" Robbie asked, flashing her another crooked smile. His fingers tingled her inner thighs and dipped tantalizingly close to her centre.

"The Gherkin," Gemma croaked out and Robbie laughed.

"Yes, it's an amazing view when you're on top of it." Nobody but Gemma noticed his underlying meaning, but the heat radiating off her was getting uncomfortable. She felt bothered and frustrated.

"Stop it." she whispered, almost hissing at him. She covered his hand with hers, stopping the caress. Robbie's eyes gleamed with a devilish look, but he stopped his hands from moving so far up her skirt until they rested again by her hem. Gemma didn't want him to stop, but they couldn't do that there. Not around everyone. They ordered their food and spoke about anything of little importance until the entrees arrived. They were eating in companionable silence when Rose suddenly spoke.

"So, I spoke to the doctors earlier." Everyone froze, except Rose, who continued to eat as if nothing was amiss.

"And?" Pip demanded, her smoked salmon suspended in mid-air on her fork. Robbie's knuckled turned white as he grasped his cutlery very tightly. Gemma placed a reassuring hand over his. She could feel him shaking so she squeezed it. She looked up at him. He was staring at his mother, his eyes tight and his jaw clenched. But he sideway glanced at Gemma and nodded once. He let go of his fork and grabbed her hand tightly. Everyone waited with bated breath as Rose chewed and swallowed her goat's cheese.

"For the love of God, Mum," Robbie spat out, "get on with it."

Rose chuckled, took a swig of champagne, dabbled her mouth with her napkin and looked at her two children in turn. Slowly, a small smile began to form on her lips and a weight seemed to be lifted off Gemma's chest, that she hadn't even realised was there.

"The removal was successful," she said, tears brimming in her eyes. "Obviously, it's still early days but things are looking really positive. A few more checks like that and I'll be officially in remission." There was a pause where no one said anything and then there was an explosion of noise. They all cried out, they all cheers and exclaimed. Robbie and Pip leaped out of their seats and moved to their mother, both of them hugging her together. Tears flowed freely down both their faces. Gemma got up and while Rose hugged her children, she hugged her mum. Linda was sobbing into her napkin and Gemma hugged her and kissed her. She then hugged Arty and when Rose was freed from her children's arms (they moved onto Arty and then Linda in turn) Gemma brought Rose in for a bone-cracking hug.

"Brilliant!" Gemma exclaimed. "I can't believe it! This is the best news."

"I love you, Gem," Rose said, her façade completely broken and she was full-on crying too. "I just wanted you to know that I love you like a daughter." Gemma was now crying.

"I love you too, so much." And when they pulled apart so that Arty could hug and kiss his wife, Gemma hugged a sobbing Pip quickly before Robbie literally snatched her away from Pip and pulled her to him. He wrapped his long arms around her, holding her tight and burying his face into her neck. She could feel the tears sliding down her neck as he cried. He held her for a couple of moments before he had to kiss her. It didn't matter that they were with family, Robbie needed to kiss her.

And kiss her he did.

It was a sweet, passionate kiss that left Gemma feeling dizzy and dazed when he pulled back. He rested his forehead against hers as his face shone with tears.

"God," Robbie whispered, trying to steady his breath from all the tears, "I love you so much, Gemma. You have no idea."

"I have some idea. If it's anything like what I feel for you…" And Robbie's face broke into the most breathtaking smile. He was so happy he was literally radiating it. He kissed her again, quickly before he pulled her into another tight embrace.

After some time, they all returned to their seats and toasted again. The second time, it was dedicated to Rose and her health, which was surely now going to be long and prosperous.

That night, was one of the happiest of Gemma's life.

They drank delicious wine, they ate delicious food and the laughed and hugged and cried and laughed again.

Bottles of champagne kept appearing at the table then quickly they emptied. Gemma felt light and bubbly and just... happy.

Hours passed and they were the last in the restaurant.

Robbie settled the bill, with everyone exclaiming to pay at least *some* of the momentous bill, but Robbie rolled his eyes and waved their shouts down. If Gemma was sober (which she most definitely wasn't) she would have shuddered at the final amount. It would have made her feel guilty and self-conscious about Robbie spending so much money on them, but at that moment in time, she felt nothing but joy. Their party broke apart, all stumbling off to their own rooms. Robbie had his arm around Gemma, walking her back to her hotel room. She swayed slightly and he was grinning slightly at her.

"What are you smiling at?" Gemma demanded and Robbie raised his eyebrows at her glaring expression.

"I'm surprised you noticed. I didn't think you could see straight," he joked.

"I'm not that drunk. Definitely tipsy, but not drunk *drunk*."

"Well, that is good news," Robbie murmured in Gemma's ear, pulling Gemma more tightly to his side. "I was planning to have my wicked way with you tonight." Gemma smiled but didn't blush. The champagne made her braver than usual.

"And what does my drunkenness or there lack off have to do with that?" Gemma raised her eyebrows daringly. They stopped walking and they were outside Gemma's room.

"I wasn't sure you were up for it."

"Oh," Gemma bit her lip and gazed up at him, "I am *always* up for it." And then Gemma turned her back to Robbie and pulled the key out of her bag and slid it until the lock. While she was unlocking the door, she bent herself a little more forward than she normally would have done. She glanced over her shoulder at Robbie.

His eyes were on her back and backside. They were hungry and hot, Gemma felt her breath catch in her throat and she felt her boldness falter. She straightened and turned back to Robbie.

She pressed her back against the slightly ajar door, her eyes locked with Robbie's. They stood there for a moment before Robbie closed the gap between them and pressed his body to hers, his lips finding hers. They stumbled backwards into the hotel room and with a click of the door, the rest of the world disappeared.

And it was just Gemma and Robbie, their lips and bodies entwined so tightly that they were one being.

So that night started with delicious wine and exquisite food but finished with lovemaking so superb, they both felt drunk with the ecstasy of the post-coition high. Their bodies were still wrapped tightly around one another that they seemed to breathe as one as sleep finally took them, some hours later.

CHAPTER TWENTY-ONE

When Gemma woke the next morning, it was safe to say her head was very, very painful.

Though she hadn't drunk enough wine to be considered drunk, it was still more than she was used to. And being wine (and the same for champagne), it seemed to render her with a much worse hangover.

"Argh…" she groaned and glanced at the clock next to her bed. It was still early; it was only seven in the morning. She groaned again and buried her face under her pillow. Another annoying thing about hangovers for Gemma meant early rising. Another good reason she never really drank much. Robbie's arm tightened around Gemma's waist, nuzzling into her hair and then kissing her between the shoulder blades.

"Good morning to you too," he whispered, his warm breath caressing her back.

"It's too early," Gemma groaned, squeezing her eyes tight. "No good morning yet. Sleep more."

Robbie chuckled and kissed her bare skin again, apparently trying to stir some life into her. It was working, but Gemma's head still throbbed. "Do you not have a hangover?"

Robbie squeezed her body to his and she felt him shake his head as he continued his attempt to stir her. "I didn't really drink. I only had a couple of glasses. Not," and Gemma actually felt him smiling against her skin, "that you noticed. You rather enjoyed the Bollinger then?"

Gemma groaned again. Just the name of the champagne was enough to make her feel slightly sick.

"I'll take that as a no then."

Gemma groaned again. "It was very nice yesterday… not so much the morning after." Robbie laughed and propped himself on his elbow, kissing Gemma's back and shoulders again.

"Mmm," Gemma murmured, feeling the start of desire stirring in the pit of her stomach again. "What do you think you're doing?" she teased, but she didn't want him to stop.

"Well, I thought that might be self-explanatory." His breath was hot and caressed her skin again, sending a delicious shiver down her spine. "I won't have a lot of time after breakfast, Whittle is already covering for me." A thought entered Gemma's mind.

"I should probably learn your teammates' names," she said, though a little half-heartedly.

Robbie's kisses on her back were very distracting.

"Right this second?" he said, but Gemma could hear the humour in his voice.

"When are we ever alone and not doing—"

Robbie kissed a particularly sensitive part of her lower back. Gemma shuddered and moaned. "You were saying?" Robbie cooed and Gemma looked over her shoulder and glared at his grinning face.

"I was *saying* that I don't know any of your teammates." Gemma rolled over so that she was on her back. Robbie grinned again.

"I can kiss your front as well."

"Robbie," Gemma warned lightly.

"Fine," he sighed and slid up her body so he was lying next to her. His hands still caressed her body. "What do you want to

326

know?"

"Are they your friends?" she asked, "or just work colleagues? Is there anyone you're close to, or any you don't like?"

"Look at you, trying to get the dirt on the England football team."

"I'm just trying to find out a little more about you."

"Okay, well. Jake Whittle is a good friend of mine, we've been together since the academy days and were signed together. He makes terrible mac and cheese though," Robbie added, flashing her a grin. Gemma looked at him confused for a moment before realising what he was referring to.

"Oh my God! Jake's mac and cheese! Jesus, I forgot about that." They reminisced for a few moments before Robbie continued.

"Luke Jamerson," he smiled at her blank expression, "the goalie," he added and Gemma nodded again. "Also plays with us in the premier league, so I am pretty close to him too as we train and play a lot together. The others," he sucked his teeth and shrugged. "Yeah, we get on. Yeah, we're close as a team. But it's like any other workplace, we just hang out at work. I mean, don't get me wrong. If we win the World Cup, there will be one hell of a party. But come August, when the premier league and all the other leagues start, we will be rivals again."

Gemma nodded, she understood what he meant. "They're just your work friends," she said simply and he nodded.

"Now, are we done discussing the team?" Gemma nodded again. "Good, now may we continue what we started?"

"I'm not sure I'll be able to participate as fully as I usually do." She raised her eyebrows at him.

"That's fine with me. Let me do all the work."

327

Gemma smiled as he propped himself up onto his elbows, so they were nose to nose again. He kissed her then, so deeply and passionately that Gemma pressed herself against him as the stirrings of desire started to fill her body once more. Robbie's lips trailed kisses down her cheeks and down to her jawline and neck.

"Can we go back to where we were before?" Gemma blushed, she felt so bold saying it, but she really did like the way Robbie's lips felt on her back. Robbie lifted his head up, smiling crookedly up at her.

"Okay," he said, looking at her with a fire that made her tummy flip. She rolled over again and buried her face into the pillows as Robbie started to kiss her back again. "But don't bury your head," he said softly against her and she lifted her head up to look at him over her shoulder. "I like seeing you." The tingles shot up her spine in a delicious shudder. Robbie just knew exactly where to touch and kiss that made Gemma squirm and clench with anticipation. And so they stayed there, entangled and entwined until they were spent and lying naked in each other's arms.

Gemma felt Robbie's pounding heart against her cheek as they continued to catch their breaths once more.

"I love you," Gemma said, kissing Robbie's chest where his heart pounded beneath.

"I love you too," Robbie returned, kissing the top of Gemma's head. "God, if the manager knew I have been sneaking into your hotel room... with the final in a few days..." He actually chuckled and sounded almost guilty. Like a school child who was in trouble but couldn't help but laugh.

"Why aren't you allowed to stay with me?" Gemma looked up into those warm brown eyes and sighed. "I wish you could."

"Me too. Trust me, it would be a lot easier if I wasn't sneaking back and forth."

"Suppose someone sane would argue that it was only a couple days and we should manage with without any... hanky-panky until then."

"Hanky-panky?" Robbie looked at her with raised eyebrows as she flushed.

"It's still a bit weird to discuss it... you know? Like I never talked about anything with Matt. I was never brave enough to suggest positions or try anything..." Gemma trailed off, Robbie's jaw was very tight. "Sorry, I shouldn't talk about it. It's just so different. Much better obviously! I feel so much happier and more comfortable with you that I feel like we can discuss things. Before, it was like a dirty secret or something. Like he was embarrassed by me."

Robbie visibly swallowed his rage, he paused for a couple of seconds trying to compose himself before his expression considerably lightened. "Sorry. I just hate that he... well... you know. He didn't treat you the way you deserve. But I am happy that you feel comfortable enough with me that we can discuss things. Try new things out." He flashed Gemma a devilish grin that made her heart skip a beat. "This is all new for me too. It's never been like this before."

Gemma swallowed her stab of jealously and smiled up at him. "Good, I'm glad." She paused, frowning slightly. "But you never said, how come you can't stay with me?"

Robbie shrugged his shoulders and rolled his eyes. "No idea. It's a stupid, outdated tradition. I mean, look at the semi-final. I played well that day and I spent the night before with you... and we," he flashed her that devilish grin again, "had plenty of hanky-panky that night too." Gemma blushed at the memories flooding back to her.

Robbie caressed her cheeks, a soft smile on his lips. "I love it when you blush," he murmured and Gemma felt her blush deepening further.

"I hate it. It's so embarrassing. I'm just an open book." Robbie leaned down and kissed her cheeks in turn.

"I think it's endearing," Robbie said, "I love being able to read what you're thinking." Gemma's stomach decided then to growl ridiculously loud, making her whole face burn with embarrassment. Robbie chuckled and planted a kiss on her nose quickly before he disentangled his limbs from hers. He reached for the phone on the bedside table. "I think it's time we ordered room service."

"You don't want to go down for breakfast with our families?" Robbie grimaced, almost like he had forgotten everyone else was there also. "They are going back home today until the final, apart from Pip," Gemma added.

Robbie groaned slightly and quickly turned and pulled Gemma to him for a fleeting hug. "I guess you're right. I just wanted to stay here for a bit longer."

"Me too, but we have got to say goodbye. Our parents are on the eleven-twenty back to Liverpool." Normally, if you wanted to actually get to Netherby's little train station in the sticks, it would be a further two and a half, even three hours after arriving in Liverpool. There was no direct line to Netherby, it involved many smaller, local lines and then a bus from Netherby station that only came every hour. Luckily, with Robbie having many drivers and the money to hire such services, a car would pick the parents up at Liverpool Lime Street and drive them the hour trip to Netherby. Even driving through Liverpool and on the M6, it was quicker than getting two trains and a bus home.

Robbie sighed and nodded, releasing Gemma once more and sitting up. He got out of bed and strode over to the wardrobe and pulled it open. He pulled on some boxers, jeans and a polo top before turning back to Gemma and raising his eyebrows at her. He had caught her watching his muscles tensing and taunting as he moved and got dressed.

Essentially, she was nearly enough drooling watching his fine form get dressed. "Can I help you?" he said, his voice as soft as silk.

"Just enjoying the view," Gemma said brazenly, biting her lip as she smiled at him.

"Then surely it's your turn to get dressed and my turn to enjoy the view?" Gemma laughed and shook her head, throwing her head back into the pillow.

"It won't be as good as what I've just seen." There was a pause and Gemma almost sat up and looked at Robbie again when his body was suddenly on top of her. Robbie was straddling her, his jeans and top grazing her bare breasts and belly as he placed his hands on either side of her head and looked into her eyes. His eyes were fierce as they glared into Gemma's.

"And that, my dear, is where you are wrong. It'll be a thousand times better. And I am thankful that I am the one that gets to see it. Now, if you please, stop putting yourself down. You are beautiful. And I would very much like to watch *your* fine form getting dressed. We are on a tight schedule, as you said."

Gemma's laugh was a mixture of nerves and disbelief. Robbie's eyes were so intent on hers; there was nowhere to escape. They gazed at each other for a long moment before Gemma finally whispered, "Okay." Robbie got off from on top of her.

Gemma rose slightly from the bed, naked.

She felt very bare as she crossed the short distance to the wardrobe. Gemma could feel Robbie's eyes on her as she grabbed the first pair of jeans, top and underwear her fumbling hands could reach. Gemma threaded her legs through her knickers and hoisted them up. They were much lacer and high cut than she would normally wear but she didn't want to change them. She put her bra on and she felt much less exposed. Finally, she braved a glance at Robbie and she felt her heart swell with emotion.

Robbie's eyes were warm and loving as he watched her. The instant their eyes met, Gemma felt instantly relaxed and comfortable under his gaze. Gemma felt a smile spreading across her face and the tension leaving away. She put her hands on her hips and looked at him with raised eyebrows.

"Can I help you?" she said and Robbie grinned like a cat in cream.

"Just enjoying the view," he said, his voice silky again. Gemma turned and pulled on her top and bent to pick up her jeans. Gemma jumped as she felt Robbie behind her. He had moved silently off the bed and his fingers traced the lace of her knickers.

"Oh my God," Gemma said, clutching at her chest. "You scared me."

"Sorry, I just had to get a closer look. I like these. Are they new?" His fingers trailed the lacy thong, tingling the skin beneath.

"They're courtesy of Amy and your wallet, yes," Gemma breathed, looking up at him. But Robbie's eyes were trained just on Gemma's new attire and bottom.

"Well, I think she needs a pay rise. I like these very much," his voice purred. He bent down and kissed the top of the band on her waist.

"Robbie..." Gemma sighed, leaning her head back and enjoying the heat of his breath for a moment. "Breakfast... parents..." It was a feeble attempt, but Gemma felt her resolve melting away. Robbie groaned and straightened, kissing her on the lips quickly.

"I know. But we'll have to come back here after." Robbie stepped back, handing her the jeans and turning away slightly. "Hurry up and get dressed. This is taking all my self-control not to throw you back onto the bed." Gemma laughed and slid her jeans on, she pulled the high-waisted jeans up and did up the button. She turned to the mirror and looked at herself. She turned this way and that, quite liking the jeans and nodded approvingly. She heard another groan from Robbie and she looked at him. His eyes were hungry and needed and firmly placed on her backside.

"Is something wrong?" Gemma asked, looking at her bum for any signs of damage to the jeans. There wasn't anything there. They hugged and cupped her bum flatteringly.

"The only thing wrong is that I want to pull them off you as well. You look very, very nice in them jeans." He placed his hand on her bum and squeezed slightly, testing the weight and shape of her in his hand. He groaned again, squeezing slightly harder. "Right!" he said suddenly, turning on his heel and stalking off to the door, swinging it open. "Let's go! The quicker we go downstairs and say goodbye, the quicker I can throw you back onto that bed!" He indicated with his head that Gemma should leave the hotel room.

With a laugh, Gemma quickly slipped on some pumps and a shirt and grabbed her phone and key before leaving the room. Robbie shut the door with a click and grabbed her hand, tugging her unceremoniously down the hallway to the lifts.

He jabbed the button and pulled Gemma to his side, wrapping his arm around her waist, as they waited for the lift. A few impatient toe-taps later (from Robbie), the lift arrived with a *ping* and Robbie pulled her into the empty lift.

There was an electric atmosphere humming between them as the lift descended smoothly. Robbie's body felt warm and pulsated against Gemma's side as she kept her eyes up at the sign that indicated the floor level. Out of the corner of her eye, she could feel Robbie gazing at her, but she kept her eyes averted. Knowing her luck, she would kiss Robbie (maybe even have a little fumble) and someone would step into the elevator. Gemma wasn't brazen enough for that.

After a couple of charged moments in the lift, it finally pinged again at their wanted floor. The doors slid open, letting the cooler air from the lobby flow into the lift. Robbie chuckled under his breath and took Gemma's hand again, leading her away from the lift and towards the restaurant. As he approached, the waitstaff all seemed to become flustered and excited. Gemma couldn't help herself, she rolled her eyes as all the staff near enough swooned at the sight of him, both the female and male waitstaff.

"Mr Wilson! Good morning, did you sleep well?" The hostess fluttered her eyelids at him, smiling broadly up through her eyelashes at him.

Robbie seemed oblivious to her flirty body language as he turned to Gemma and grinned suggestively at her.

"Didn't get much sleep, did we?" Gemma blushed as Robbie continued to smile at her with raised eyebrows. "But that's no fault of the hotel," he added, flashing a lethally charming smile at the hostess. "The room is beautiful and the service is excellent."

She flushed and stammered for a couple moments as Robbie smiled and waited patiently for her to gather herself again. "Yes, well," she spluttered, before picking up a couple menus and stepping away from the host stand and indicating that they should follow her. "Your table is ready, you are the first of your party to arrive."

Robbie sighed, sounding almost annoyed. "Typical."

"Why is it typical?" Gemma asked as they followed the hostess through the restaurant. "Well, two reasons. One, because we didn't need to rush and I could have enjoyed those lacey knickers a little longer before leaving."

"Robbie!" Gemma exclaimed, checking the empty tables around them.

Robbie ignored her. "Two," he continued, "now I have to wait even longer until I get to enjoy them." He sighed, shaking his head. "They better hurry up," he grumbled as he sat down at the table and took the menu handed to him by the hostess.

"Thank you," Gemma said to her, which was pointless as she was ignoring her and focusing solely on Robbie but Gemma couldn't be rude.

"Yes," Robbie said, as if realising the hostess was still there. "Thank you."

"Would you like any tea, coffee or any other drinks while you wait for the rest of your party?"

"Tea for me please," Robbie said and looked at Gemma.

"Flat white for me please."

The hostess nodded and left them. Gemma was looking at the menu, debating whether to go pancakes or full English when the rest of the party arrived.

"Finally!" Robbie exclaimed, standing up and kissing his mother and Gemma's mother on the cheek.

"Finally?" Rose asked, eyebrows raised.

"Well, we've been waiting for ages."

"Five minutes," Gemma said, shrugging and rolling her eyes at Pip.

"Well, you guys got your train to catch soon."

"In two hours?" Pip asked, eyebrows raised.

"And I've got to get to training," Robbie added lamely. "In three hours?"

"Fine, whatever! Just order your drinks will you? I'm starving."

Gemma smiled to herself as she glanced back down at the menu. Pancakes, she decided and she folded the menu and put it down on the table. Talk around the table was little. Everyone was obviously feeling the after effects of the alcohol. Robbie hurried them to order their food, which came pretty quickly and Robbie literally inhaled his full English with little or no chewing. Everyone around the table looked at him. Rose had her eyebrows raised, Arty looked amused, Linda frowned and Pip had her fork suspended in mid-air, staring open-mouthed at him.

"What?" Robbie demanded, looking at each of them in turn, his mouth filled. Gemma fought back a laugh, Robbie looked surprising like a hamster with his mouth so full. If hamsters were six-foot-two sex gods…

Robbie's eyes met hers and Gemma bit back a smile. He raised his eyebrows at her and she just shook her head, trying to keep the smile back.

"You just look like you've got somewhere to be," Rose said, still looking at him with raised eyebrows.

"I'm just hungry," Robbie replied gruffly, shoving another humongous forkful of breakfast in his mouth.

"Right," said Pip, shaking her head in disbelief.

The rest of the breakfast was passed in small talk and companionable silences.

The bill was settled after another round of coffees after the plates were cleared and they said their goodbyes. Rose, Arty and Linda went straight off to check out and went straight to the train station.

Pip went back to her hotel room to have another sleep as her hangover was a late bloomer. Robbie quite literally scooped Gemma up and ran back to her hotel room. He threw Gemma onto the bed, to have his wicked way with her, even before the door had clicked shut behind them.

The next few days passed with Gemma spending the days with Pip around London. They went to museums, art galleries, high tea lunches and sipping coffee in indie coffee places. The days were spent with Pip, filling the time, and the nights were Robbie's. Every night, after dinner, when they retired to their hotel rooms for the evening, Robbie would slip into her room. It was always a couple of minutes after Gemma arrived herself and he would leave before most would rise the next day.

Gemma's nerves started to build up and come the day of the final, Gemma thought she might explode with angst. Their parents had returned the morning of the match and they spent the day in the hotel spa and pool, trying to relax and calm themselves.

It didn't work.

Gemma felt sick with nerves and before she knew it, they were dressed and escorted to the car. No one really spoke, they were all squirming and twitching with nerves as the stadium approached. Again, same as the semi-final, they were escorted into the stadium through a VIP entrance and taken to a stand near the front of the pitch that linked in with all the other stands and seats.

The atmosphere was electric.

Upon entering the stand, Gemma felt her nerves tingle with some excitement (even though she was still mostly anxious) as she beamed around her. There were seas of white, grey, green and red shirts throughout the stadium. There was singing and shouting and dancing and chanting.

Gemma couldn't wipe the smile off her face and even though she was nervous as anything she was so thrilled and honoured to be witnessing it all first-hand.

There was the usual, almost pulsating atmosphere in the stadium as the players, referees, officials and mascots all filed out of the tunnels and onto the huge, neat pitch. The national anthems played for both teams before they all broke out of line to shake hands.

Gemma spotted Robbie instantly at the front of the procession, captaining the team. He shook hands with the other captain and referees before turning back to the other captain and flipping the coin. The coin landed on Robbie's predicted outcome, so he picked the side his team wanted to face and they shook hands again before he jogged back to his teammates for a final huddle.

The noise was still booming around the stadium and Gemma felt goose pimples breaking out in tingling waves over her skin. As the players broke their huddle and went to their allotted positions on the pitch, then there was a sudden silence.

Everyone seemed to wait with bated breath as the ball was brought onto the pitch and given to Robbie. Gemma's heart thudded against her ribcage as she watched him. His head was down as he looked at the ball under his foot.

Thump, thump, thump.

The atmosphere was thick with anticipation.

Gemma felt someone grab her hand and clasp it for dear life.

It was Pip. Her hand was cold and shaking, even though it was a warm summer's evening.

Gemma brought it closer to her as she grasped it too, not taking her eyes off Robbie.

Again, more slow moments ticked by, waiting for the dreaded whistle.

Finally, the whistle sounded. It was shrill and deafening compared to the loaded silence that was before it.

The game was intense, much like the semi-final. There were no goals during the first half as both teams defended their goals with serious force. There were a couple of tackles resulting in yellow cards. There were some really close attempts from Robbie and other players on the opposition's goal. Yet it seemed every time England attacked their goal, they picked it straight back up and attacked England's goal with frightening attempts at goal.

Half-time came and went and Gemma and everyone else didn't bother going to the box for a drink. It was like they were frozen stiff with nerves. Gemma found herself just staring at the pitch, eyes and mouth wide open in a silent scream. The time passed surprisingly quickly, Gemma didn't see the players file back onto the pitch and restart the match.

The cheers got louder and louder and the match proceeded without any goals. There was jeering when players were tackled, some roughly and others a little more dramatically than necessary. Robbie made a break for the goal in the eightieth minute that led to a rather rough tackle that made Gemma gasp.

There was uproar from the England supporters as they all shouted for a penalty.

Gemma shoved her hands into her mouth and bit down onto

her knuckles. She couldn't cope with penalties. She willed that Robbie would get one, take it and that would be it. But really, she should have known how the game would go.

The penalty, after much deliberation and VAR, was not allowed. There were groans, shouts and swearing from the supporters.

The play resumed, neck and neck once more.

The final whistle sounded about ten minutes after Robbie's tackle and there was a collective groan from the supporters and Gemma.

Extra time.

And after another thirty minutes of constant near misses and frighteningly close calls, the whistle sounded again.

Gemma's stomach dropped.

The boys from both teams started to huddle on the pitch with their managers and other coaches. Gemma put her hands over her face and sank into her chair.

Penalties.

England was known for their dismal history on penalties.

The opposition was known for their reliability in scoring penalties.

Gemma groaned again. She felt hands rubbing her shoulder reassuringly and she looked up. Linda's eyes were sparkling with unshed tears. She smiled but it was tight and restrained.

Gemma was clearly not the only one with crippling nerves watching this match. Gemma glanced at Pip, who was staring at the pitch with darting eyes. Arty was sat down, a mask of calm on his face while his leg twitched and jumped with nerves. And Rose, her big, brown eyes only for her son. She watched his every move with a loving and worried expression. If Robbie had looked at her, he would know what that expression was trying to convey.

It's okay, you've done us proud.

Gemma looked back at Robbie, standing from her seat once more. She found him, instantly. And he was looking for her.

Their eyes met and Gemma instantly felt calm.

It would be okay, regardless of the outcome they would all be okay.

"I love you," Gemma said quietly, trying to mouth the words so Robbie could lip read. His shoulders dipped again and he patted his heart.

"I love you," he mouthed and after a final glance at Gemma, he turned back to his team, who were huddling around him. They all looked to Robbie, their captain, for words of wisdom. Whatever he said, he said it animatedly because a couple of moments later, they were all pumped and slapping each other on the back and shouting. The goal was ready and it was Jameson in, swaying this way and that, watching the opposition as he walked towards him.

The stadium was deathly quiet. It was so still, it was as if everyone breathed as one.

There was a collective intake of breath and the player in green took a step back from the ball. He had his hands on his hips as he waited. He took a deep breath and took a few strides to the stationary ball. He brought his leg back in an elegant arch and swung it through, smacking the ball with power and precision.

The ball flew through the air and as Jameson threw his body in the direction of the ball. He was too late. The ball soared above his head and into the top right corner, shaking and quivering the net until it fell to the ground and went still.

There was nothing for a moment. Everyone, including the players, all seemed to stare at the shaking net. And then there was an eruption from the opposing fans and players.

Then it was England's turn. It was Whittle's turn.

Much the same happened as with the previous penalty. Jameson was swapped for the opposition's goalie and Whittle stood with his hands on his hips and he took a moment before he swung his leg back and sliced the ball through the air. This time, it went to the bottom left and literally scrapped the tips of the goalie's outstretched fingers as it crashed into the net, making it do that hypnotic quiver as it shook with the force of the ball.

Then there was uproar again.

Gemma screamed and clapped along with the rest of them, feeling a respite of relief before the nerves would surely take over once more.

Then it was the opposition's turn again. They missed.

England scored.

They scored; England missed. Both teams scored.

It all hung on the final penalty. If they missed and England scored, they would win the World Cup.

Gemma bit down on her knuckles so hard she tasted blood, but it didn't register because the opposition was taking their penalty.

Jameson looked so tiny in the goal and Gemma knew for a fact that he was six-foot-seven and built like an ox (fact-checked by google). He was definitely not tiny but in that moment he was. It was like the goal was growing around him, giving the opposition more net to score in.

The player in green seemed to be praying as he stood before the ball and goal. He kissed something around his chain and took a few steps back.

Gemma thought she would be sick.

Her stomach was twisting and turning with a ferocity that Gemma was sure the contents being churned up would make a second appearance. Gemma focused on not throwing up that she was shocked when the player suddenly pelted towards the ball, throwing his leg back in that same graceful arch. His foot met the ball and again and sent it shooting towards Jameson with a speed that Gemma doubted he could react to. It was heading for the top left corner, so cleanly that Gemma was certain it was in. But Jameson arched and twisted himself with a flexibility and agility that Gemma didn't think was possible for someone of his size and build. He stretched, flying through the air, reaching for the ball. He was closing in and it would be close. Gemma still thought it would shake the net and cause the fans to scream with joy.

But just as she thought it was going in, Jameson's fingers tips clipped it and he managed to smack it away from the goal. The ball went careening off target and shooting to the left, missing the goal by inches.

The England fans erupted with sound, literally shaking the stadium.

One more.

They just needed one more penalty.

And Gemma knew full well who would be taking the last one for England.

Robbie stepped out his team's line and walked purposefully towards the point where he needed to place the ball.

She knew he would take the last potential penalty.

It wouldn't be for the glory of potentially winning the World Cup for England, it would be in case he didn't win the World Cup for England.

Robbie knew the last player would have a lot more pressure than the others. He knew that a lot more would be riding on that player's shoulders. Though Robbie was still young at twenty- six, he was still one of the most experienced and eldest players on the

343

team. He didn't want his teammates to have to deal with the backlash that would come with missing a gravely important goal. That responsibility lay with the captain.

So Robbie stood before the huge goalie, hands planted on his hips as he looked at the grass that lay between him and the goal.

The deathly silence was back as everyone's eyes were trained on Robbie. No one uttered a sound. Gemma swore she could almost hear Robbie's breath as he sucked in a sudden breath. He swallowed that breath and looked to her. Their eyes met instantly, as if they were magnetically linked. Gemma felt that calming sensation spreading through her once more, as she realised that it would all be okay.

Regardless of if he scored or not, it would all be okay. So, Gemma did something that she had not be able to do throughout the entire match.

She smiled.

She smiled at Robbie, willing him to understand that it was okay. It didn't matter. Gemma loved him regardless of what happened in the next few moments. And Robbie knew that because he smiled back. He put his hand over his chest once again as he smiled at Gemma for a moment. He took a deep breath and turned back to the goal, his whole demeanour calm and in control. He looked up the goal, taking a final breath before he took two or three graceful leaps to the ball, moving his leg back and swinging it forward in one swift, motion he sent the ball spiralling through the air and towards the goal.

It sped across the space between him and the goal so quick, you could have missed it if you had blinked. It darted to the net with an attack like a predator attacking its prey. The goalie tried to bend and arch himself towards it, throwing himself to the ball's destination.

He stretched and reached and extended himself so that he could get his fingertips to the ball, but it wasn't enough.

The ball slid across the tips of his outstretched fingers, passed the goalkeeper's hands, past his flying body and into the back of the net.

There was a pause for a nanosecond as the ball crashed into the back of the net. Everyone seemed suspended, open-mouthed in a silent scream.

Then the noise erupted from all the fans. It was like nothing that Gemma had experienced. She literally felt the surge of noise deep down in the centre of her body. It was electrifying and Gemma felt like she was floating above the screaming crowd. Robbie had been running towards them but he was tackled down to the ground by his teammates and was buried in the sea of white and red jerseys. Gemma found herself laughing at them all piling on top of him. But then others joined them and it took a moment for Gemma to realise that they were fans.

Fans were spilling onto the field from every angle.

"Let's go!" Pip screamed and she grabbed Gemma's hand as she dragged her over the couple of rows of seats ahead of them. By the time her feet hit the pitch, there was a sea of supporters already surrounding Robbie and his teammates.

Pip and Gemma tried to weave through the crowd, but it was slow moving. They were hugged by random supporters, knocked off course by jumping fans and picked up and spun around by elated groups of fans. Gemma's smile was so big and she felt so carefree, she didn't care about strangers hugging her or picking her up.

She kept trying to move through the crowd. Someone picked Pip up and Gemma lost hold of her hand again. Then Gemma felt arms around her waist as she was left up and spun around.

She was put back down facing a different direction to where she was facing and she lost sight of Pip.

"Damn," she muttered, trying to look through the crowd and get her bearings. She was trying to lean around a particularly large fan when she felt arms around her waist again and she was lifted and spun. When she landed it was again somewhere different.

"Um, excuse—" but she was lifted again and spun, taking further away from the thickness of the crowd.

"Hey!" she said, but she was lifted and moved yet again. "Hey!" she said louder, trying to spin around and see who was lifting and dragging her away from Robbie and Pip. She wriggled out of this person's grip and tried to push away from them, but a voice sounded in her ear.

"Stop moving, don't make a scene," Gemma felt as if her whole body had plunged into ice as the familiar voice was hot on her neck and ear. It was a voice she had hoped to never hear again, a voice that sent fear pulsating through her entire body.

Matt's voice.

CHAPTER TWENTY-TWO

"Good girl. Do not make a scene. We are going to get to the side of the pitch and climb up the stand until we reach an exit tunnel. You understand?" Matt had got them to the edge of the crowd and set Gemma down. He wrapped his arm around her waist and led her to the small dividing wall between the stands and the pitch. "Over you go, Gemma." Gemma glared at him and glanced back to the crowd. "I wouldn't if I was you," Matt said, smiling slyly. "You see, my plan needs just one of Robbie's nearest and dearest. It doesn't have to be you, his sister would work just as well. Or even better, his mother." Gemma's heart dropped as she looked into those cold dark eyes.

"Fine," Gemma hissed at him and she climbed over the small wall. Matt was on her heels as she scaled the stand and walked along to the stairs that led to the tunnel exits.

"Good choice, Gemma."

Gemma didn't reply, but he kept his arm wrapped around her, securing her to his side. He didn't even do that when they were dating, so the fact that he was doing it now made Gemma feel even more uneasy than she was already feeling.

They reached the exit tunnel, which was empty due to the fans celebrating on the pitch. "Now, give me your phone."

Gemma frowned at him. "Why?"

"Just give it to me." He didn't want anyone to be able to track them. Gemma tried to think of a way to keep it, but it was useless. She reached into her jeans pocket and pulled it out. She passed it to Matt, who put it on the floor before he stamped on it, smashing it.

Matt continued forwards, tugging Gemma along with him and leaving her shattered phone behind. And much quicker than Gemma had expected, they were at the exit of the stadium. No one intervened as they calmly left the building. Matt led her out of the stadium and straight into one of the cabs waiting out front.

He opened the door for Gemma to climb in, which she did and he quickly followed. He gave the driver an address which sounded like some form of pub or B&B. Gemma was surprised that she wasn't more nervous. She knew Matt was crazy, but she didn't feel as scared of him as she used to.

She glared at him as the cab driver pulled away. "What—" but Matt cut her off.

"Shh, shh, all in good time." He put his arm around her shoulders and pulled her closer to whisper in her ear. "If you care so much about that future sister or mother-in-law of yours, then stay quiet and do what I say."

There was no mistaking the malice and threat in his voice. Gemma knew to take him seriously and though she wasn't as scared, he was unpredictable. So she sat there, looking out the front windshield and trying to take in where they were going. It was pointless because even though Gemma had been staying in London for a week or two, she didn't know the area enough to differentiate anything helpful. More than anything, she just wanted to keep her eyes averted from Matt.

She felt his fingers grazing at her temple along her cheek and jawline.

Gemma pulled back slightly, keeping her eyes averted and trying to not shudder at his touch.

"What to do, what to do?" he murmured, still caressing her

cheek with his rough, calloused fingers and palm.

"What to do?" Gemma asked, her voice quivering.

"Well, we can discuss that when we get there."

Gemma didn't speak again. Matt continued to stare at her as he traced patterns on her cheeks, then moved down to her neck and dipped his finger underneath the shirt collar to feel her skin beneath.

"Hmm," he said, as if debating something in his head. Whatever it was, Gemma would soon find out because the cab had slowed and parked. Matt paid the cabbie cash and grabbed Gemma's hand and pulled Gemma out. "Not much further," he said, wrapping his arm around her waist again and pulling her towards a seedy looking pub. It looked more like a hostel than a pub, but Gemma could tell it was a "pay cash in hand and no questions asked" place. Matt steered her towards to the entrance and walked straight past the small, dirty bar and straight up a flight of stairs opposite the door. The stairs led to a creaky, small hallway with a few doors on along both sides. Everything was so dark, the floor, the walls and the doors with flickering dim lights that threw shadows along the hallway. They stopped at a door and Matt unlocked the door with a key. He pocketed the key and pulled Gemma inside before turning and locking it from the inside.

Gemma glanced around the room.

It was small with a bed, small table and tea and coffee station. There was a door that was presumably a bathroom. Gemma wrapped her arms around her as she turned back to Matt. He was leaning against the door, smiling and watching her. Gemma kept his eye, trying to not convey any fear. She wasn't going to give him the satisfaction. He didn't speak and there was a lengthy, loaded silence. An infinite amount of time passed before Gemma couldn't stand it any longer.

"What do you want?" she asked and her voice was a little shaky but clear.

"Well, you see, I'm still deciding. Option one: I can leave you here, pick up a lump sum payment from your wonderful boyfriend and disappear into the sunset. Option two: I take you with me and still get your boyfriend's money. Decisions, decisions."

"Leave me," Gemma whispered. She didn't want Matt to get a penny of Robbie's money but she couldn't stay with him. If he left her and picked up the cash and fled, then he would probably be caught. If Matt took Gemma, Robbie would keep paying him. If he took her somewhere and wanted Robbie to drip feed the money, eventually Robbie would try and find him. Gemma couldn't risk that. Matt laughed and sneered at her, his dark eyes narrowed.

"Well, Gem," Gemma hadn't missed the change in nickname, "it's not up to you. You see, this was always the 'master plan' but then you messed it up."

"What could I have possibly done?" Gemma spat, glaring up at him. He strode over to her and he grabbed her upper arms, pinning them to her side. He bared his teeth as he glared down at her, looking at her with narrowed eyes.

"Well," he hissed, his voice was low and deadly. "You see, Gem, I knew Robbie was in love with you years ago. I saw how he looked at you. I saw how he watched you all the time. I saw it all. So I knew, when he finally grew some balls that he would come back. He'd come back for you. Grovel and beg until you opened your legs to him." He leered at her, leaning down until his nose was touching hers. "That didn't take you long, did it?"

Gemma swallowed but kept his gaze. She didn't speak but

350

she wouldn't show him her fear.

"Nothing? Hmm," he murmured before he continued. "He came back, like I thought he would. Then he started sniffing around you like a dog on heat. But then something funny happened. Do you know what happened then, Gemma?" His breath was hot on her face and Gemma fought back a gag. After a moment to regain her control again, she answered him.

"No, but I'm sure you will tell me." Matt smiled at that, if a leer could be a smile.

"Well, that lip is one of the reasons." He ran this thumb over her lip as he watched her mouth. "What happened was…" Matt hesitated, his breath catching in his throat as he continued to watch his thumb rub roughly over her lips. "I felt something, this need to have you. To make you mine." Gemma sucked in a deep breath and stepped away from him now he had freed one of her arms.

"Don't lie. You never loved me." Matt pulled her roughly to his chest once more, squeezing his hands on her upper arms again.

"No," he said coldly, staring into her eyes with a look of disgust. "I never loved you. Who could love someone like you?" he spat.

"Robbie does." Gemma's voice was firm and confident for the first time.

Matt threw his head back and laughed harshly. "He doesn't fucking love you. He's got a fetish with fatties. That's all." His words stung.

"Then why do you want me then?" Gemma spat back, lifting her head to look at him with as much pride and dignity she could muster.

Matt's fingers dug more painfully into her flesh. "I don't

351

fucking know how or why. But I can't get you out of my mind. You are *mine*."

"No, you want to control me. You can't stand that I stood up for myself and left."

Matt's nostrils flared and his lip curled over his teeth. He charged forwards, pushing Gemma back until he slammed her into a wall and pinned her up against it with his body. He held her jaw and cheeks roughly in one hand while he had the other entangled in her hair. He pulled her hair roughly so that she was looking up at him. Tears stung in her eyes with the pain of the slamming but she blinked them back.

"That fucking lip," he growled, his face so close to hers. "You don't talk to me like that. You are mine. And you will do exactly as I say, or I will make you pay." He let go of her hair and reached behind himself and pulled something out of the back of his jeans.

It was a gun.

Gemma felt him dig the end of it into her ribs. She gasped and watched his face break into a crazy and evil smile.

"Yeah, I'm not fucking around, Roly-Poly. You are *mine* and nobody else's. Do you understand?" Gemma couldn't speak, she looked into his eyes, wide-eyed and nodded. "Good. Now if you do anything to get back to your beloved boyfriend. I'll take this," he pressed it deeper into her side, "and I'll go find that little sister of his or his mum. Or even," his free hand gripped Gemma's jaw and cheeks again, holding her face while he lowered his face to hers more, "or even, *your* mum. I always liked Linda, even if she never liked me."

"I'll do whatever you want. Just don't hurt them. Please." He looked pleased with her begging, but she didn't care. Gemma needed to keep everyone safe.

"Good girl." He pushed back from her slightly, releasing her. She sagged against the wall slightly. "Now that's settled. Get on the bed." Gemma's stomach dropped. Gemma had been so preoccupied with Matt kidnapping her, she hadn't even begun to fear what he could do to her. "Now!" he roared at her and she stumbled over to the bed and perched on the edge. "Take off your jeans." He stalked towards her and his eyes racked over her as if she was his prey.

Gemma's entire body shook and she was frozen as she watched him stalk towards her. "Matt…" she whispered, not caring that she was pleading. "Matt… please."

"Take them off." His voice was low and deadly again.

"N-no." Gemma sat up straight, looking him in the eye.

"Now!" He strode across the room and closed the gap between them. His hands gripped her shoulders and Gemma shouted with the pain of his fingertips digging into her flesh.

"Matt! You're hurting me!" She wriggled and writhed, trying to loosen his fingers tips. But his grip was too hard. He was stronger than Gemma and he grabbed her arms as she went to push him away. He pushed her down onto the bed and pinned her down with his body.

"Don't fight. You are mine."

Gemma fought, trying to get her knees up so she could knee him and throw him off her. But she couldn't. Gemma's heart was thumping in her chest and her breath was coming in fast puffs. She was beginning to hyperventilate. She couldn't throw him off and she couldn't see how she was going to escape him. She was locked in a room with him and nobody knew where or if she'd been taken. She stopped fighting and stared at him. She hoped he would look at her eyes and be spooked by her expression but he just laughed a merciless laugh.

"Good girl. Stop fighting the inevitable."

"I will always fight you. I will fight you until my dying breath." And she bucked and threw her body around the bed. He wobbled and tipped to the side and she tried to make a break for the door but he managed to snake his hands around her arm and pull her back to the bed. "No you don't." And he mounted her again, grabbing her hands and putting them above her head again.

He leered down at her with an evil smile again. "You are *mine*," he hissed and he grabbed both her hands in his as he felt around for something in his pocket. Gemma's heart sank, she knew it would be a way to tie her hands together. As he was reaching into his pack pocket, a phone rung, sending a shrill noise through the silence between them.

"Damn it," he growled and sat back on her, still holding her hands with one of his and answering the phone with the other. It wasn't his normal smartphone. This phone was a small, cheap burner phone. "Wilson," he said stiffly and he looked down at Gemma, his eyes still hungry and cruel. "Impeccable timing… as always."

Gemma heard a muffled voice on the other end of the line, but she knew it was Robbie. And he was furious. "Oh she's fine… for now."

Robbie said another muffled reply.

"What do I want?" Matt's eyes turned from hunger to pondering. He seemingly decided because a smile started to spread across his face. "Two hundred and fifty thousand for the first sum, cash. Dropped at a location after this call in one hour." Robbie said a muffled reply again and Matt's face dropped slightly. "Fine," he spat and he got off her and walked away.

Robbie spoke again and Matt turned to Gemma. Gemma sat up and shuffled to the end of the bed quickly. "Fine, here she is."

He handed the phone out to Gemma and said, "Speak."

Gemma took the phone with both of her bound hands and held it to her ear.

"Robbie?" her voice cracked.

"Oh, Gemma," Robbie said, almost crying. "Are you okay?" Robbie's voice was thick with emotion. Gemma fought back a sob.

"Yes, I'm okay," she whispered and Robbie let out a gush of air in relief.

"Ha-has he done anything to you?" Gemma blinked back the tears in her eyes.

"Almost, but no." There was silence at the other end and when Robbie spoke again, it was a low growl.

"He swore he wouldn't touch you in any way. Otherwise, he gets no money. I will come for you, Gemma. I'm going to get you away from him. Very soon."

"Robbie. I love you."

"I love you," Robbie said in a much softer tone, "And I will get you back. I swear. Now, put me back on to Matt." Gemma held out his phone and Matt snatched it back. Robbie was talking to him and he was looking at her, his face emotionless.

"One hour, Wilson. Or I am taking what's mine. Tick tock." He hung up the phone. He turned to face her and the sneering returned. "Now," he said, "how shall we pass the time?"

The hour passed in relative quickness. It was filled with sneers from Matt, asking questions about her and Robbie's sex life. Gemma ignored them all. She thought it was better to not engage than rather anger him with details of Robbie as her lover. As tempting as it was to see his face go red or his fists shake with anger, she thought it best. Matt pulled out his phone, to check the time for the umpteenth time.

"It's time. The drop off should have taken place."

"Sh-shouldn't you go and get the money?" Gemma asked, confused why he was still in the hostel with her. Matt scoffed, rolling his eyes.

"You think I'm going to pick it up? Pfft. That'll be like having a target on my back. No, I've got someone to pick it up for me. Someone your boyfriend doesn't know."

"Who?"

"Do you really think I am going to tell you that? Divulge my secrets? No, I'm afraid not." He grinned cockily as there was a knock on the door. He walked over to it and Gemma tried to crane her neck to see outside, but Matt was blocking door. Gemma heard a familiar male voice and she tried to place it.

He was young, whoever his accomplice was. And Gemma had heard it before. With sudden realisation, she realised it was Ethan. Gemma felt a surprising anger welling up inside her. She couldn't believe that Matt would drag Ethan into this. He was just a kid with a young family. What had Matt got over him to blackmail him into this? Gemma knew that would be the only reason why Ethan was assisting Matt.

Matt was handed a duffle bag and he pulled it into the hotel room. "I'm done," Ethan said and his voice was cold.

"You're done when I say you're done." Matt closed the door in Ethan's face and locked it again. He walked over to the small table and pulled open the bag. He chuckled with glee as he grabbed handfuls of cash. "He fucking did it! That rich bastard!" He turned to Gemma and showed her a wad of cash and flashed her a grin. "Now for the next phase of the plan." He stuffed the money back into the bag and went over to Gemma and untied her hands. "Let's go."

356

"Where are we going?"

"Like I am going to tell you." He dragged her to her feet, walked over to the bag and slung it over his shoulder. He also picked up another large bag in one hand and he turned back and grabbed Gemma by her elbow with the other. Matt steered her towards the door. They left the dingy hostel room through the dark hallway and through the seedy looking pub below. They went outside to the street and into a waiting Uber. Ethan must have ordered them one before he left. Gemma's heart sank.

Matt really had planned their every last movement so they would be untraceable.

Gemma didn't even bother fighting him or making a break for it, she knew she couldn't escape. And she rather it be herself in Matt's grasp then Pip or their mothers. So she climbed into the Uber willingly and Matt climbed in after. The quiet, electric car took off silently. Gemma watched the roads of London pass by her out of the car window. After a stretch of time, Gemma realised they were leaving London. She turned to Matt, who was watching her with that horrifyingly hungry expression. Gemma's throat caught and she tried to push herself away in the small taxi cabin. But Matt slide closer and leered down at her.

"Where are we going?" But Matt shook his head slowly. "It's a surprise." His voice was oily and mocking.

"But—" But Matt silenced her with a finger to her mouth. Gemma jerked her head back from him. Matt bent down and whispered in her ear, his breath hot and uncomfortable on her face and neck.

"Stop asking questions." His tone was a warning. And so she kept quiet as she kept watching the streets of London disappear. He then kissed Gemma's neck, skimming his nose along the long arch of it, up to her ear. Gemma shivered, and not with pleasure.

"Hmm," he murmured against her neck, running his nose up and down. "I forgot how you smell."

Gemma didn't comment, she just held herself away from him as much as she could. It would do well to rile Matt while she was confined in the taxi with him. So she just bit her tongue and kept her eyes on the window. The further out of London and the longer they spent on the road, Gemma realised that she sort of recognised the route.

It looked a similar journey to what Robbie and Gemma had taken when they arrived in London. When they had used Robbie's private jet.

They were heading to the same private airport. He was taking her to the airport.

Tears pricked in her eyes. He had decided his plan and he had chosen plan B. To take Gemma with him, wherever he was going. You could get anywhere in the world with two hundred and fifty thousand pounds. With two hundred and fifty thousand in cash, and with more to come, Matt could pay for a private jet with no questions asked. Gemma's heart sank again, if they got onto that plane, she wasn't getting away from Matt. And Matt will constantly torture Robbie and take more and more of his money.

"Have you guessed where we're going?" Matt mocked, his dark eyes alight with malice.

"Yes," was all Gemma said, not rising to him.

"What? No questions? Guesses on where we will be jetting off to?"

"It doesn't matter."

"What?"

"It doesn't matter where you take me. Robbie will find me." Matt grabbed her face and forced her to look into his glaring eyes.

"No. No, he won't, Gemma," he hissed, "we will get on a plane and vanish forever. You are mine and only mine. Do you understand me?" He tightened his grip on her face. "Do you?"

"Yes," Gemma spat out, struggling to speak through his grip.

"Good. Now," Matt put his arm around her shoulders and pulled her near, "once we are out of reach of your boyfriend, I will make you mine again. Do you understand?"

"Yes," was all Gemma said, trying to pull her head away from his hot breath.

"Good. Now shut up." And they rode the rest of the way in silence.

They approached the junctions and roads leading to the private airstrip and Gemma's stomach turned. She couldn't see any way of getting out of it and as soon as she was on that plane, she would be stuck with Matt, and possibly for the rest of her life.

She blinked back tears again, it wasn't the idea of remaining with Matt her entire life. No, it was the idea of never seeing her family again. Her family and…

Robbie.

God, her heart felt tight and her stomach twisted in agonising despair. She didn't even get to say goodbye.

The Uber slowed down and parked outside the private airstrip and Matt got out of the car and grabbed a couple of bags out of the back. It was obvious now that Matt had planned to take Gemma all along. The bags were big enough to contain enough clothes for both Matt and Gemma. With a sinking feeling, Gemma realised Matt had probably broken back into the flat and stolen some of Gemma's clothes. Gemma waited by the Uber, glancing around. The private airstrip looked deserted, with nowhere for Gemma to run or hide. Matt's arm snaked around her waist before she could even think about taking a step forwards and he pulled her to him in an iron grip. He led them towards the small entrance and Gemma suddenly thought of something.

"I don't have a passport with me, how can we go anywhere international without one?"

"I've got your passport."

Gemma faulted her steps. "What? How?"

Matt didn't say anything as he led her to the front desk. Gemma looked at him and it suddenly came to her. "You took it. You've broken into the flat and took it didn't you?" Again, Matt didn't say anything. They walked into the small entrance and over to the welcome desk where a young man was sitting, looking rather bored and playing on his phone. He didn't realise that Matt and Gemma had approached the desk until the last moment. He suddenly jumped up, his phone crashing onto the desk with an almighty crash.

"Oh!" he said, fumbling around awkwardly, trying to pick up his phone and smiling fakely up at them. "My apologies, sir! We weren't expecting anyone today." Gemma glanced at his name tag and noted he was called Joey.

"I suppose everyone is busy with the World Cup," Matt joked jovially and Gemma stared up at him. How was he being so calm and normal about kidnapping her?

Matt didn't even joke with people in normal circumstances.

Obviously, having a bag full of Robbie's money was making him extremely happy. "Yes, sir. Did you watch the final?"

"We did, didn't we, honey?" Matt wrapped his arm around and placed a kiss on Gemma's temple. Gemma froze, keeping herself stiff and void of emotion. She needed to keep Matt happy if she had any chance of escaping.

"That Robbie Wilson," Joey shook his head in absolute

admiration. Gemma's stomach dropped at the mention of Robbie's name. "What a legend!" Matt's mouth turned up in a sly smile.

"Yes, what a legend." Gemma saw him tapping the bag of cash that was slung over his shoulder.

"What can I do for you today, sir? Ma'am?" Gemma swallowed back the bile bubbling in her throat. The thought that people would think Gemma and Matt were a couple again was a sickening thought.

"We would like to book a private plane, to fly to Spain. For as soon as possible."

Joey blinked, rather confused. Gemma noticed him glancing Matt up and down. He wasn't their usual clientele obviously. Joey put on a fake smile, going back to service mode.

"Of course, sir. The price region for hiring a private plane to go to Spain is around twenty-five, is that okay?" Gemma's mouth dropped open.

Twenty-five *thousand* pounds?

Matt must be desperate to get Gemma out of the country to spend that kind of money. But in the scheme of things, it was nothing compared to the two hundred and fifty thousand sitting in a sports bag slung over his shoulder. Plus whatever he was going to try and weasel out of Robbie in the future. Matt's face broke into a horrid, sly smile. Joey shrunk back from Matt's unnerving smile and Gemma couldn't blame him.

Matt looked seriously unhinged.

"That won't be a problem." He let go of Gemma and she debated making a break for it for a fraction of the second. Yet, it would be pointless. Matt would catch up with her in seconds. So she watched Matt put the bag of cash on the floor by his feet and he opened it and pulled out a few wads of cash. He slapped them down onto the desk and grinned at the guy again.

"Cash okay?" was all he said as he continued to grin strangely at Joey. Joey blinked, obviously surprised before he slapped on another smile. Gemma's heart dropped with disappointment. She was slightly hopeful that this boy would raise the alarm, but when someone paid cash, people didn't ask questions.

"Yes sir!" he said enthusiastically as he started to tap away on his computer. "I'll just need a few details and we should get the plane ready for you in half an hour. Would you care to wait in the lounge and I'll bring you some refreshments?"

"That would be delightful. Thank you, Joey." Both Gemma and Joey looked at Matt for his weird behaviour before Matt picked up the heavy sports bag and slung it back over his shoulder. "Come, darling." He put his other arm around Gemma and pulled her to his side once more. "Let's get you a nice glass of something, eh? To celebrate." He leaned down and kissed her on the cheek. Gemma just about fought back a gag as Matt began to steer her towards the lounge that was situated opposite the front desk.

They went into the deserted lounge and sat at the first table that Joey had indicated. He took their passports and drink order and after a few minutes, returned with a bottle of chilled champagne. He then returned to the desk to sort of the remainder of information needed to hire a private jet. Matt poured them both a flute of champagne (he had drunk both glasses that Joey had poured for them) and held his one in a toast to Gemma.

"To our new life in Spain." He didn't wait for Gemma to toast back, not that she planned to anyway, and he took a massive swig of the golden, bubbly drink. Gemma raised the cold, crisp drink to her lips too and took a sip. It did little to calm her nerves.

She was looking around, desperately trying to think of an escape route. Her eyes fell upon a sign in the far corner.

The bathroom.

If it had a window, perhaps she could climb out of it? It was worth a shot.

"I need the toilet," Gemma said suddenly, her eyes darting from Matt to the toilet sign, then back again.

"Tough, you'll have to wait."

"I haven't been since before you kidnapped me," Gemma hissed. "It's been hours and I can't hold it any more."

Matt glared at her, narrowing his eyes. "This attitude will have to stop."

"I've changed since we've broke up."

"And you'll be going back to the way you were. If you know what's good for you." They were locked in a silent argument through glares. When Matt didn't speak, Gemma did again.

"Regardless. I still need the toilet and we could be waiting sometime. So if you want me to wet myself in the middle of this posh lounge…" Matt bared his teeth in annoyance before he stood up and dragged her unceremoniously onto her feet.

"What are you doing?" Gemma asked, panicked.

"Taking you to the toilet." Matt bared his teeth in a smirk that looked pleased with Gemma's panic. "You didn't think I'd let you go alone, did you? Oh no, baby. Wherever you go, I go. Maybe we can even have a little reunion of own while we wait for the plane."

Gemma's stomach rolled with disgust. "But you told, Robbie—"

Matt turned on his heel suddenly and leered down at Gemma with his teeth bared. "Fuck Wilson. I am taking what's mine. He'll never catch us now. You're mine, Gemma, all *mine.*" His mouth stretched even wider in a toothy leer as he continued to bear down on her. Maybe it was instinct, or maybe just sheer stupidity, but Gemma acted impulsively.

With all her might, she pulled and turned. Catching Matt by surprise, she snatched her hand from his grip, spun on her heel and threw herself towards the lounge door.

"You bitch!" Matt yelled and tried to grab her before she reached the door. Gemma moved as quickly as she physically could. Matt wasn't far behind her but Gemma saw a gap as the doors seemed to have been left ajar. She stumbled and sprinted as fast as she could towards to the exit.

"Gemma!" she heard Matt shout, but she didn't dare look over her shoulder. She knew he was close on her heels. She kept her eyes trained on the exit. As she reached it, she chanced a glance over her shoulder but as she turned her head for a split second, she felt her body collide with another.

Her first thought was that somehow Matt had got ahead of her. But then his body didn't feel the same as Matt's as he was much bigger and stronger.

The next thought was Matt had employed some help to ensure that Gemma was captured and didn't escape. But if that was the case, these arms felt too gentle to be in capture.

A familiar smell filled Gemma's nostrils that made Gemma's whole body relax, even if her racing mind hadn't caught up with her body's response. Her head was still turned over her shoulder as this man held her, protectively in his arms. And then the man spoke and Gemma's mind finally caught up with her body.

Because that voice could only be one person, the person Gemma loved most in the world. It was Robbie.

CHAPTER TWENTY-THREE

"Gemma!" Robbie exclaimed, his body sagging with relief as he pulled her to his chest and crushed her to him. Gemma couldn't speak, she choked out a sob and buried her face into Robbie's chest. "Oh, Gemma," Robbie sobbed, burying his face in her hair and taking a deep, steadying breath. "Thank God." If possible, he seemed to squeeze her more to him. Robbie then pulled back slightly so he could look her in the eyes. "Are you okay?" He wiped away the tears streaming down her face. "Did he hurt you?" Gemma couldn't speak so she just shook her head.

"N-no. I'm okay, I'm okay now. Oh, Robbie!" She kissed him quickly on the lips and sobbed again. "You're here!"

"Yes, of course I am. Now, come on, we need to—" But he was cut off.

"Going somewhere?" Gemma felt like a stone of ice had slid into her stomach. She had quite forgotten she had been running from Matt.

"Get back, Clark," Robbie spat, pulling Gemma behind him so that his body was shielding hers from Matt.

"I can't, you've got something of mine. We had an arrangement, remember?" Matt pulled the gun out quickly and let it dangle at the side of his body, menacingly. There was a gasp from the desk situated just behind them. Gemma saw Joey throw himself to the floor, hiding behind the desk. Gemma hoped that he had an emergency button under there and had pressed it. Gemma turned her attention back to Matt, who had his head cocked to the side. He was watching Gemma intently and blinking innocently. "Or should I go get Pip instead?"

"You leave my sister alone," Robbie spat at him, still keeping Gemma protected behind him. "And she's not going anywhere with you. Take the money and go, before the police come."

"You and I both know they are already here. And the only way I am getting out of here free is with Gemma. You won't let anything happen to her, will you, Robbie?" Robbie glared at him and tightened his protective arm around Gemma. "It's a pity you weren't so caring about her best friend." Gemma eyes snapped to Matt, who was grinning malevolently.

"What are you talking about?" Gemma asked Matt, but she noticed that Robbie went stiff. "Oh? He's never told you? That's funny." Matt looked at Robbie with raised eyebrows, "You'd think that would be something you would have mentioned, considering you've been fucking her for the last few weeks."

"Watch your mouth!" Robbie hissed.

"Well, your boyfriend here and your best mate Abi, well, they didn't see eye to eye."

"What's he talking about?" Gemma asked Robbie. Robbie opened his mouth, but Matt spoke over him.

"They fought on that fateful night. Abi was coming back to make amends when she ran into Robbie. I overheard them arguing about you. They didn't agree about what was best for you and that's when I knew that our Robbie was in love with you."

"What's that got to do with Abi leaving?" Gemma asked

"Well, you see, Abi was coming back to make up with you. But our Robbie here" — he smiled and opened his arms to hold them out to Robbie, almost affectionately but the gun was still hanging loosely in his fingers; Gemma kept her eyes trained on

366

it as Matt waved it back and forth, nonchalantly — "told her to go. He told her you didn't want to see her. He told her that he was going to you instead."

Gemma's eyes snapped from the gun to Matt's sickening smile. He was grinning and nodding at her as Gemma's stomach turned with the memory of what happened that night. Robbie had found Gemma that night.

And they had kissed.

Gemma was suddenly overcome with flashing memories of that night. Of fighting with Abi, of Robbie's lips on hers, of being in Pip's bedroom as the New Year celebrations continued around them as they kissed.

Did Abi really come back to apologise to Gemma?

And while she wanted to apologise, had Gemma been in bed with Robbie? Kissing him and forgetting about her best friend?

Yet again, Gemma realised how terrible a friend she had really been to Abi. When they fought, Abi had thought about reconciling with Gemma. Whereas Gemma had only thought about one thing and it was the one thing Gemma only ever thought of.

Robbie.

How could she have been so fickle with her friend for a boy?

She looked up at Robbie, whose pained eyes were silently pleading with her.

And to know that Robbie had sent Abi away... how was that supposed to make her feel?

Gemma couldn't think and she couldn't feel. Gemma felt as if her whole world was vanishing. She wasn't standing in that small, deserted airport with Matt standing opposite and a gun in his right hand. All she could see was Abi's face, heartbroken and tear-streaked. Abi's round hazel eyes so wide and full of despair,

Gemma could only stare into them, her heart squeezing with guilt and pain.

"You're lying," Gemma spat, coming back to the present situation and glaring at Matt.

"Ah, but I'm not, am I Robbie?"

"That's not how it happened." Gemma looked up at Robbie and his eyes were on hers, pleading with her. Gemma stepped back slightly, looking up at Robbie. "Please believe me Gemma, that is not what happened. I will tell you everything, I promise. Just let me get you out of here, away from *him*." And then, Gemma knew that she had to hear Robbie out. Gemma nodded once and turned back to Matt.

"You're still going with him? After everything I've just said?" Matt growled, he stepped towards them, his eyes glaring at Gemma.

"Stay back!" Robbie said. "Now, we are going to go our separate ways, Matt. You can keep the money, get on a plane and get out of our lives. Or make a scene, the police come and put you away for a very long time. It's your choice."

Matt didn't do anything, he just glared at them both.

"Right, good choice. Let's go Gemma." Robbie started to turn, guiding Gemma along with him.

They both turned slightly, not fully turning their backs to Matt and made towards the exit.

They walked a few steps when a voice suddenly shouted from behind. "No!" Matt roared and Robbie and Gemma spun back around to face him. "You don't get to take her!"

Then, as quickly as Gemma thought humanely possible, Matt's arm raised in a flash, so that the barrel of the gun was pointed towards them. It was obvious that he was out of control. His expression was crazed and possessed and he only had

Gemma in his sights.

"If I can't have her…" he yelled and cocked the gun, he seemed to have uncontrollable tears cascading down his face as his eyes found Gemma's. The sudden slip showed Gemma a scared and desperate man, but as quick as the mask slipped, it was replaced with a hardened, brutal expression. Matt's face instantly still, becoming expressionless as he lifted the gun and pointed it at Gemma. "If I can't have her," he whispered again, "then no one can."

And he fired the gun.

He fired one, clean shot which exploded out of the gun and sliced through Gemma's core with a sudden, white-hot pain.

For a second, Gemma was suspended in mid-air, clutching at the bullet wound before she went ricocheting down to the floor with a bone-shattered thud. Gemma gasped, struggling to breathe through the pain and the odd sense of liquid flowing out of her midsection and soaking her shirt. Not even a second had passed since the bullet had sliced her insides then Robbie was at her side. He pushed his hands onto her wound and pushed so hard, Gemma thought she might shattered from the jolt of pain. She cried out but Robbie kept the pressure on the wound.

"Don't move, Gemma, I need to put pressure on it."

"It's hurts, Robbie, it hurts so much."

"I know, Gemma, I'm sorry," Robbie's voice cracked as his eyes found hers. "But I've got to stop the bleeding. Hold on, help is coming." More people were around them and from the shouts and demands, it sounded like the police had arrived and had detained Matt.

"Matt?" Gemma asked, lifting her head slightly but putting it back down as the room spun.

"Don't move," Robbie said gently but firmly. "They've got

him, Gemma, he won't hurt you again. I swear." Gemma couldn't speak for a moment, she closed her eyes and focused on her breathing, trying to steady her erratic heart. "That's good, Gemma, nice deep breaths. The paramedics are on their way."

Gemma could hear the sirens and knew he was telling the truth.

"You've got to make it, Gemma, you need to be okay. Please." Robbie's voice was pleading and desperate now, Gemma opened her eyes and looked into Robbie's deep brown eyes. They were tear-filled and panicked. Gemma swallowed and lifted her hand (which was covered in blood) and touched his cheek.

"It's okay, Robbie."

"It's not, Gemma, I've got so much to say, so much to apologise for. About Matt and Abi." His voice cracked and he fought back a sudden sob. "We need more time."

"We will have it. It's taken ten years for us to be together, you aren't getting rid of me that easily." Then blackness started to fill Gemma's vision and Robbie's face, the sound of the sirens and the whole world seemed to slip away and Gemma felt herself vanishing into the blackness as well.

When Gemma awoke an indefinite time later, she was somewhere completely different and completely alone. Truth be told, she wasn't even sure where she was or how she even came to be there. She was lying on the floor, or at least what she thought was the floor. The whole space around was plain, shapeless without anything of any particular matter. Gemma thought she was laying down, but then suddenly, she was standing, looking around the shapeless space. After a few turns of her head this way and that way, Gemma decided to call out. It was a relief when she heard her own voice leaving her mouth. Wherever she was, she still had the ability to speak.

"Hello?" Nothing.

Nothing but a deafening, pulsating silence.

"Hello?" Gemma tried again, a little more desperately.

"Hi, Gem." A voice came from right beside her and Gemma leaped back, her scream of shock reverberating off the surrounding nothingness. Gemma turned to the source of sound her eyes scanning her almost smoky surroundings. Her eyes fell upon a figure. She was standing there, her face warm and full of love, beaming up at Gemma with those stunning hazel eyes.

"Ab-Abi?" Gemma croaked and Abi broke into a tearful beam and raised her arms out to Gemma, nodding.

"Yeah, Gem. It's me." Gemma ran to her and wrapped her arms around her, burrowing her face into her neck and inhaling familiar florally smell. She hadn't inhaled that scent for so many years, she almost felt drunk breathing it in.

"Abi, I can't believe it." Gemma cried, pulling back and stretching out her arms to look into the face of her best friend. "You're exactly the same," she whispered, shaking her head in disbelief.

"And you're so grown up. You've become a beautiful woman, Gemma."

"An old woman, you mean." They laughed and Gemma shook her head trying to think through all the emotions of seeing Abi.

But was she seeing Abi?

The Abi in front of her was still exactly the same as the Abi she had known ten years earlier. She still had the small, slight body of a teenage and hadn't fully grown into a grown woman.

"You're exactly the same," Gemma repeated quietly, the

sadness obvious in her voice. "You haven't grown up. Is this a dream? Or am I...?" Gemma's eyes met Abi's. They were much wiser and seemingly so much older than her youthful appearance.

"Dead?" Abi asked with raised eyebrows and a slight smile.

"It's not funny," Gemma whispered.

"It's a little funny." Her face softened and went more serious again. "No Gem, you're not dead. "

"How are you here then?"

"I have always been with you, Gemma, I never left."

Gemma's eyes swelled with tears and she blinked through them. "So am I dreaming? Is this like in the movies when they're working on the patient and they're having a vision or dream?"

Abi actually laughed. "You watch too much medical dramas. It's probably more like an epiphany that you're having."

Gemma frowned and took in her words. This was all happening inside Gemma's head? She wrapped her arms around her middle. It took a moment for her to realise there was no wound there.

"I survived the gunshot?" Gemma's mind was suddenly full of the memory of the airport, Matt, Robbie and the gun. "Is Robbie okay? Did Matt shoot anyone else?"

"No, no. Everyone is fine. It's you we're all worried about."

"Is it bad?"

"Well, you were shot."

Gemma rolled her eyes. "Yeah, thanks for the reminder. But am I going to die?"

"I think only you know that."

Gemma just looked at Abi for a moment.

"Wow." She finally said, "That was incredibly vague and unhelpful." Abi flashed her a grin and Gemma couldn't help but smile back. They were silent for a moment and Gemma looked around for a chair for them to sit on. And as if the realm that they found themselves in were listening, a small, wooden bench appeared. They sat without talking until Gemma final spoke. "There's so much I've wanted to say, for years, Abi. But now you're here, I don't know where to start."

"I know, Gem, there is something I would like to say to you too."

"What?" Gemma's lips went uncomfortably dry and her breath became more rapid.

"I want to say, there is nothing to forgive, Gemma." Her voice was loud in the silent surroundings and seemed to reverberate and bounce off the nothingness that surrounded them. Gemma's breath caught as she stared into the face of her best friend. Her best friend who she missed more than anyone in the world. Her best friend she would give anything to see again. Perhaps, even Robbie. Gemma swallowed and looked down at her lap. Her hands were folded together and resting in her lap.

Would she give up Robbie? It was easy to say that in that moment when she was there with Abi. But could she have a lifetime without Robbie? She wasn't so sure.

"You don't have to pick between us," Abi said gently, putting her small hand on top of Gemma's folded ones.

"I do. I can't be with him without feeling guilty."

"You deserve to be happy."

"No," Gemma said firmly, ripping her hands away and standing up. She paced back and forth, wringing her hands. "No, I don't, Abi. I don't deserve to be happy while you aren't."

"I am happy if you are." Gemma's head whipped around to look into Abi's kind and loving face.

"You can't be happy here."

"This is an epiphany remember?" Gemma rolled her eyes

again at Abi's slightly joking demeanour.

"Please be serious."

"Okay," Abi sighed and stood up to join Gemma. "Seriously now, Gemma," Abi grabbed Gemma's arms and held her in place in front of her. Her big, hazel eyes looked up at her and she smiled softly. "Robbie makes you happy. You have been the happiest you have ever been the last few weeks than you have ever been."

"But you're not there," Gemma said quietly. "How can I be fully happy when you're not there?"

"I said it before Gem, I am always with you." She reached out and squeezed Gemma's hands, bringing them to her chest. "You need to forgive yourself Gemma, what happened was nobody's fault. If it's anyone's fault, it's the man who got drunk and drove home that night."

Gemma met Abi's eyes, tears streaming down her face. Abi grabbed her face and smiled softly again. "It was not your fault, Gemma. Or Robbie's for that matter. You both deserve to be happy and forgive yourselves. Just be happy, Gemma, be with Robbie. Marry him if you want. Have lots of sex and babies. Go to university and get out of that pub. Just do what makes you happy. That's all any of us want." Gemma blinked through the tears. As she blinked more and more, she realised it wasn't the tears clouding her vision but a brightening of everything around her.

"Wh-what's happening?"

Abi just kept smiling softly while the brightness seemed to grow and almost softened her silhouette. It was as if Abi was fading into the brightness. "Abi!" Gemma called out, clutching at her. But her hands grabbed nothing but thin air.

"I love you, Gemma, please be happy," Abi said and Gemma

374

felt herself being pulled away from her. "I love you, Gemma," Abi said one last time before the brightness shone so bright that everything else was washed away in a sea of white.

"Abi!" Gemma cried out, but there was nothing there. "Abi!" But Abi was gone and Gemma was fading as well. Fading away into the whiteness, into the light and into nothingness once more.

CHAPTER TWENTY-FOUR

When Gemma awoke the first time, she wasn't fully lucid. She could hear loud beeps and there were blaring lights as she blinked, trying to gauge her surroundings. She blinked and shook her head at the sudden assault of light and noise. A groan slipped from her lips and she felt a hand on her shoulder, squeezing it.

"Gemma?" A hoarse and quiet voice asked and Gemma thought it was her mother's voice.

She groaned and tried to clear her throat. It was dry and scratchy and was hard to form words. "M-Mum?" She finally managed.

"Yes darling, I'm here."

"R-Robbie?" But where Robbie was, Gemma never found out because as suddenly as she had awoken, she fell back into a dreamless sleep once more.

When she woke up the second time, it was sometime later. Gemma was much more coherent the second time, however. She slowly blinked, taking in all the surrounding stimuli. It was stark white, with loud beeps and bright lighting. Gemma was lying in a crisp, cold bed that felt clinical. She turned her head to the side and could feel tubes pulling from her nose as she moved.

"Argh," she groaned, reaching up to pull the tube feeding into her nose. She realised then that there were many other tubes attached to her hands and arms. "Argh!" she complained again, slightly overwhelmed by the sheer number of tubes. She didn't know which one to pull out first. She went to reach for the one on the top of her right hand when a much larger, tattooed hand reached out and suddenly covered hers.

"Don't you dare," said a low and gravelly voice.

Gemma's eyes snapped up to the owner of the hand and her eyes met familiar warm brown ones. She felt instantly relieved when she looked up into his worried face.

"Robbie!" she cried out and she reached out to wrap her arms around him. He leaned forwards so Gemma didn't have to stretch so far and she buried herself in his warm, strong chest. "Oh Robbie, thank God you're okay."

"Thank God *you're* okay, Gemma. You really scared me there for a moment." Robbie's long arms wrapped around her, pulling her tighter to his chest as he buried his nose into her hair.

"What happened?" Gemma asked suddenly, remembering Matt and the gun. "Are you okay? What happened to Matt?" Gemma felt her heart starting to beat unevenly and the heart monitor she was plugged into seemed to convey that with ferocious and erratic beeping.

"Shh, Gemma, it's okay. Everything is okay," Robbie soothed and both Gemma and Robbie turned to the monitor for a moment and watched Gemma's heartbeat steadying slightly. When it went back to a semi-normal rhythm again, Robbie continued. "The second you passed out, the ambulance and the police arrived. Matt had tried to run off, but he was caught not long after."

"Not long after?" That was fairly vague.

"Well," Robbie said squeezing Gemma's arms as he pushed her gently back to a laying position. "I was a little preoccupied you see."

"With me?" Gemma asked sheepishly and Robbie nodded.

"Yes. I didn't know what was going on in the world, all I

377

could see was you. And it scared the hell out of me seeing you like that." Gemma smiled weakly at him, but he didn't return the smile.

"Robbie?" Gemma asked and she saw him taking a shaky breath. Gemma sat up slightly, as much as she could manage in an awkwardly low-laying hospital bed. Robbie didn't speak for a moment so Gemma persisted. "Robbie, what's wrong?"

"I was so scared, Gem," he said, so quietly, Gemma struggled to hear him over the annoying beeping of machines around her. She reached out and took his hand once more.

"I know, Robbie, but everything thing is okay now. Matt is locked up…" Gemma thought for a moment before glancing up at Robbie. "Right?" He nodded and Gemma sighed with relief. "So, he won't be able to hurt anyone else."

"He hurt you, Gemma," he said in a low, deathly voice. Gemma looked into his suddenly hardened face with his flaring eyes and locked jaw. "And I swear, if he'd… he'd… I would have…" Robbie was so furious; he couldn't even finish his threats. Gemma's heart swelled and tears pricked in her eyes. She reached out and touched the side of Robbie's tight jaw and weakly pulled him towards her. He understood what she was trying to do, so he leaned down so that his face was close to hers. They looked into each other's eyes for a moment before Gemma sighed and closed her eyes, resting her forehead against his. Gemma felt Robbie sigh and relax under her touch. She pulled him closer until her lips could press lightly to his for a moment before she sighed again.

"Gemma," Robbie whispered, his voice low and breathy.

"I'm okay, Robbie." And Robbie's shoulders relaxed a little more. He kissed her again, this time with a little more firmness as he held her face in his hands. He was kissing her lips, her nose, her cheeks, her forehead. Gemma's heart monitor began to beep noisily and erratically (Gemma would have been horrified if she wasn't so lost in Robbie's kisses) but they both ignored it.

"I don't know what I would have done," he was saying in between planting kisses on every inch of Gemma's face. "And after what Matt said about what happened that night." Robbie pulled back and looked into Gemma's eyes with such pain and fear. "If you'd never talk to me or see me again, I'd... I'd understand. It would kill me, but I would stay away. If that's what you wanted, Gemma."

It was Gemma's turn to grab Robbie's face and hold him steady as she peered into his eyes. "Robbie," she said and her voice was firm. "Stop this. I don't blame you for what happened."

"But—"

"It wasn't your fault. I was the one that fought with her. I was the one that turned her away. I was the one that didn't go after her. I am the one who should feel guilty." Gemma's voice cracked as Robbie went to speak but she shook her head. "No, I need to say this, Robbie. I will always have that guilt. It will never go away. But..." And Gemma surprised Robbie by smiling slightly. "I think she would have forgiven me. She would have forgiven me because she would have wanted, more than anything, for me to be happy. So even though I am always going to have that guilt whenever I think of Abi, I am not going to let it hold me back. Abi wouldn't have wanted that. She would have forgiven me. She would have forgiven *us*, and she would have supported us. You make me so happy Robbie, it's the happiest I have ever been."

Robbie caressed Gemma's cheek and rested his head against hers. "You make me happy Gemma. So unbelievably happy. I didn't think it could happen, that I could feel so much love and happiness."

"Me too. So I think we should be happy, Robbie. It's what Abi would have wanted."

Robbie's expression changed and he suddenly gripped Gemma's face with his eyes gazing intently into hers.

"Really, Gemma?" Gemma nodded.

"Really. We both deserve to be happy. After all these years and—" But whatever Gemma was going to say, was lost as Robbie brought his lips to hers roughly. He kissed her with a renewed enthusiasm that left Gemma's head dizzy and the heart monitor beating frantically as Gemma tried to catch her breath.

"I love you, Gemma," Robbie said against her lips. Gemma just about managed to reply with a "love you too" as Robbie's lips reclaimed hers and he kissed her again. It was some time before they stopped kissing and holding each other close. The doctors came back around sometime later in the afternoon, when Robbie and Gemma reduced their affection to hand-holding and eye-gazing.

The doctors were happy with Gemma's recovery, but she still needed to remain under their care for a few more days while they ensured her vitals were completely stable.

She had taken a bullet to the abdomen after all.

Robbie visited every day, along with her mother. When she saw Gemma awake the first time, she nearly squeezed the life out of her once more in a deathly embrace. Rose, Arty and Pip visited also, but when it became clear that Gemma would make a full recovery over a few days, her visitors became just Robbie and her mother.

Gemma was released a few days later and once they had returned back up north, Gemma stayed with Robbie so he could ensure her recovery was continued. She wasn't allowed to work, so Gemma found herself constantly being propped up in Robbie's huge bed, resting. It would have been rather boring if Robbie hadn't been present in the bed with her. So, Gemma suffered through her recovery, with Robbie's body (more often than not) wrapped around hers.

Things fell nicely into place.

Gemma continued to work at the pub, but with the help of Robbie as an investor, became more of a manager. They could hire more staff with the pub's increased popularity, so Gemma and her mother could still work but also found themselves with a better work-life balance. Gemma even decided with her free time she would looking into becoming a therapist again. Starting off with part-time college courses and finally taking the leap to go to university.

The day she received her acceptance to Abi's dream university, Liverpool, was one of the happiest in Gemma's life. That one was for Abi.

Rose was in full remission and she and Arty even allowed Robbie to treat them to a travelling trip around France, Italy and Greece where they could drink a lot of wine and eat a lot of delicious food.

Pip finished university and landed herself a job in the local primary school, which meant Gemma was able to see much more of her.

Matt was sentenced to a hefty prison sentence which ensured that he wouldn't be able to cause any more problems for Gemma or Robbie for many, many years.

And Robbie continued to excel in his footballing career, playing for his childhood team, which thankfully, was close to her university.

There were days when Gemma felt so guilty about what had

happened with Abi, that she thought she didn't deserve to be happy. There were days were Gemma couldn't stand to look at herself in the mirror. There were days were Gemma dreaded Amy leaving her new clothes to try as she couldn't bear it if she didn't fit into them. But those days were much less common as she spent more and more time with Robbie.

Mostly, Gemma was so unbelievably happy and in love with Robbie that she forgot about anything else. Robbie made her feel light, free, sexy and so loved that it was nearly impossible to feel down about much. Of course, it was an ongoing battle for Gemma but having Robbie and their families around her made it all just that much easier to get through those tougher days.

So, finally, after so many years, Gemma and Robbie finally did get their happily ever after. Together.

EPILOGUE

Robbie

Bollocks. He was going to be late... again. Steve was going to have his head... and his nuts probably. But he didn't care because he just couldn't leave Gemma. He couldn't stop the smile forming on his lips as he ran through the stadium. He couldn't stop thinking of her, even after all these years. For years, he'd seen her completely stripped bare, he had kissed every inch of her body, done all the things (and more) he had been dreaming about for all those years. And yet, he just couldn't get enough of her. Even when she felt fat with her swollen belly and ankles, in her ninth month of pregnancy, Robbie thought she was absolutely beautiful. Even then, as he ran towards changing rooms, Robbie thought back to a couple hours earlier.

He was just getting ready to leave when Gemma walked (well, perhaps waddled was more accurate) into the kitchen, huffing and sighing uncomfortably.

"I'm so huge," she had complained, looking truly fed up.

Robbie closed the fridge door that he was still holding. Every time she entered the room, Robbie found he would just stare at her for a moment and forget completely what he was doing.

"You're beautiful," he said, smiling softly at her. Gemma scoffed and rolled her eyes because Robbie *always* said that.

No matter what.

"It's true," he said and he placed the sports drink down on the counter that he was holding and crossed the large kitchen to her. He took her hands and brought them to his mouth, grazing

383

her knuckles with his lips.

Gemma's eyes opened wide and her lips parted slightly with a rush of air. Robbie smiled again, this time a little more suggestively. He loved that she reacted to his touch that way.

It was like she couldn't get enough either. Good.

Robbie had pulled her to him before turning her around so her back pressed against his front. He wrapped his arm around her large belly, placing one hand on her hard stomach and the other on her thigh. He pulled her more urgently against him, pressing himself more into her backside.

"Oh, Robbie," she had murmured, as Robbie's mouth found the spot on her neck that always sent shivers down her spine. "Again? You're going to be late," she moaned again as he kept kissing her neck, groaning against her skin.

"I don't care."

"He'll be so angry," she whispered, but her attempts to sway him were futile. She didn't want him to stop either. Robbie moved his hand that was gripping her thigh to in between her legs and whatever Gemma was trying to say was lost completely. She arched herself more against him and Robbie decided she had far too many clothes on. He grabbed the hem of her flowing dress and whipped it off, throwing it to the floor before getting started on her underwear. Soon, she was standing naked before him and he paused to admire her once more.

"So beautiful," he murmured and he pulled her to him again, pressing her to him as much as he could with her pregnant belly.

"I'm fat, too fat for this," she breathed, but he knew she was only half-heartedly saying it. She wanted Robbie to continue and continue he did.

"Think of it as I am helping you," Robbie said, grinning at her as he led her back to the bedroom and soon he pulled her to his chest yet again and felt the entire back of her body pressing against his front.

"Helping me? How?" Gemma breathed and Robbie couldn't help but smile as she closed her eyes and threw her head back onto his shoulder.

"Helping you trigger labour. You said you wanted this baby out. I'm just helping my beautiful wife to not be so uncomfortable any more."

"If that was true, I wouldn't still be pregnant, would I?" But she was smiling, melting into his chest and arms. Their bodies were moving to the sensual rhythm and Gemma was putting her head back, moaning into Robbie's ear while he kissed...

"Wilson!"

Robbie was suddenly jolted into the present day, in the smelly changing room as opposed to in his bedroom, with Gemma, naked and entwined...

"For God's sake, Wilson! Stop thinking about your bloody wife and focus."

There was a murmur of good-natured fun-making from his fellow teammates and Steve held up his hands and everyone was instantly silenced.

Even after years of marriage, years of holding her in his arms, she was never out of his head. He was always thinking about her, was it normal to think about your wife so much? To think about her naked and pregnant in their bed? He felt like he was a horny teenager. It wasn't always sexual (mostly, yes, he'd have to admit) sometimes he would just think about her, asleep next to him or when she was concentrating on a TV programme. The way he'd smile watching her face twist and screw as she tried to hide her confusion because she wasn't following the documentary because she was looking at her phone instead. The way she—

"Now," Robbie again was thrown back into the present day, back into the changing room with his team, "if you're quite finished about thinking about your wife's…" he trailed off and Robbie glared as there were a few wolf-whistles and Steve laughed, "All right, sorry. But now I've got your attention, can we focus back on the game?"

After that, Robbie tried with his entire might to focus just on the game and not on Gemma and her naked body or smiling face. But try as he might, his thoughts always drifted back to her, naked or not.

"Everyone clear?" Steve shouted and there was the usual rumble of agreement from the lads as they all riled themselves up, ready for the imminent match. Out of habit, Robbie checked his phone to send Gemma a message as he usually did before the match, when he saw a missed call. His stomach flipped because it was from Gemma.

Gemma never called him on a match day, which could only mean something was wrong.

He rang her and after a couple of rings, there was a "Hello?" on the other end. But it wasn't Gemma, which panicked Robbie even more.

"Linda? What's wrong?"

"Nothing love, don't panic. Gem's just been having some contractions—" Robbie cut her off, now fully panicking.

"What? Is she okay? I'm coming home."

"No, no Robbie. I'm sure we have some time. She says she's been having this on and off for a few days, hasn't she?"

"Yeah, the midwife said something about early labour?" It was all gibberish to him. But he hated when she would go quiet and withdrawn and he could see she was in pain. "Linda, is she

386

in pain?" he asked quietly, feeling slightly sick.

"Robbie," she sighed and he knew the answer. "She's not comfortable, but she's okay. She's just trying to have a bath to help ease some of it. She doesn't want you to worry, I'm just updating you."

He nodded, then realised she couldn't see him. "Right, well, I'll tell Steve. Just in case, I'll give my phone to someone and ring it if you need me."

"We will, honestly, Robbie, it could be hours yet, if anything will happen."

"Okay, tell her I love her okay?"

"I will, talk soon, Robbie. Good luck." The phone line went dead and Robbie tried to swallow the sickly feeling bubbling up in his stomach and throat. He took a few deep breaths and went to Steve, who was still standing and looking at notes in the changing room.

"Steve?" Steve looked up from his notes and nodded to Robbie. "Yeah?"

"I've just had a call about Gem," and his face changed.

"Everything—?" but Robbie cut him off.

"I don't know. Her mum just called and said she's having contractions, but they think it can hours yet. Just wanted to let you know and wanted to give this," He held up his phone, "to someone in case she has to call again."

"Yeah, yeah of course." He held out his hand for the phone, "I'll give it to Michael." Michael was the assistant coach, "And he can tell me straight away if anything happens. Do you want to play?"

He nodded, playing would help keep his mind at ease. Steve didn't question him, he just nodded and pocketed the phone. But he could still see Robbie's distress.

387

"She'll be okay and they're probably right. It does normally take hours. My wife was the same with our first."

"I hate that she'll be in pain," he murmured quietly, unable to stop himself.

"I know," he said quietly, nodding. "And I'll not lie to you, it's horrible seeing them go through it, you feel so helpless and give anything to take that pain away. But when it's over and you see them with that baby, you won't believe how wonderful it feels." Robbie nodded, unable to speak. "Right," and he slapped him on the shoulder. "Let's get going, in the tunnel." Robbie jumped to attention and took a few deep breaths.

Gemma would be okay, she had to be, because life without Gemma...

He didn't let his thoughts go down that path. He gave himself a little shake before making his way to the tunnel to head the team out.

The match started off well and it did distract Robbie significantly. They were two-nil up and it was the eighty-fifth minute before Robbie had any inclination that anything was amiss. Oddly, Steve had requested a team change. That wasn't in the game plan at this stage with a couple goals under their belts and when Robbie saw it was his number being swapped out, his stomach dropped instantly. He ran, as hard as he possibly could, forgetting all fatigue of the match and running on pure adrenaline.

He knew it had to be Gemma; he knew that her mum must have called.

Robbie couldn't see or hear anything, he just ran. He couldn't even hear the thousands of fans calling out confused and upset shouts. He slapped his teammates hands, he couldn't even recall who it was in that moment and turned to Steve who handed him his phone.

"Linda called, she's in the hospital. You need to go, things are happening quick."

His stomach dropped and his throat felt tight.

"Is Gemma…?"

"Look, she's okay. She's in labour, so in pain, but you really need to get going. It's happening very quickly, apparently."

Robbie nodded and took off running as fast as he could.

He didn't remember running through the stadium, going to his locker and getting his keys and getting into his car.

He didn't remember taking off so quickly, that he would leave tyre marks on the car park.

He didn't remember weaving in and out of the light traffic and arriving at the hospital much quicker than Gemma would have approved had she been present too.

He didn't remember racing through the doors, running straight for the delivery suite and bursting through the doors.

He didn't remember yelling Gemma's name at the receptionist and her telling him the instructions.

He didn't remember bursting through the door and hearing Linda crying out his name as she held on tight onto Gemma's hand as she lay on the bed.

He *did* remember seeing Gemma for the first time. He would never forget the feeling of pain tearing through him at the sight of her. She was sweating and clearly, in an immense amount of pain.

It wasn't like the movies, where the woman looked a little sweaty and pushing when the midwife was telling. She kept arching off the bed, trying to hold back a scream and it almost looked like she couldn't control the pushing.

"Well done, Gemma, after this contraction, I'm going to check you again. But I think you're almost ready."

"No," Gemma cried, "No, it wasn't supposed to be like this. I'm not ready. Where's Robbie?" And the sound of pain in her voice as she asked after him awoke Robbie. He moved to her side and grabbed her hand and the side of her face.

"I'm here, Gem," he said, trying to hide any fear and pain in his own voice. He had to be strong for her. He needed to be strong for Gemma when she was so scared.

"Robbie!" she cried and her beautiful blue eyes flew open and looked into his. It was physically painful to see the pain and fear in her eyes, but it was slightly comforting to see how some of it was elevated slightly when she realised he was there. "Robbie, you made—" but she couldn't finish, she seemed to be overcome with pain and the effort of pushing. She screamed and held onto Robbie tight.

He couldn't do this, Robbie thought instantly, he couldn't do hours of watching her like this. It would kill him.

"Okay Gemma, listen to me," The midwife called, looking back up at Gemma. "You are ready. You are ten centimetres. On the next contraction, push. Don't scream. Push like you need the toilet."

"Oh God," Gemma cried, "I can't do this. It's happening so quick, I can't."

"Gemma," Robbie said and he took her face in his hands, "Gemma, look at me, you can do this. You've done amazing. You're so close. I love you." She looked into his eyes and calmed down a little, taking deep breaths. Not even a second had passed and the pain was ripping through her core again. She cried out and her eyes closed so tight as she pushed with all her might.

"Keep it going, keep it going, keep it going!" The midwife

was shouting and Gemma kept pushing and exhaled with the exertion when the contraction was over. "Perfect, Gemma! That was perfect! Keep doing that! I can see the baby."

Robbie kissed her hand as it slacked slightly, but for only a few seconds before she was pushing again.

The noises that were coming from Gemma were horrific. It was like taking a knife through his chest, squeezing the air from his lungs.

"Dad, do you want to look?" the midwife called, looking up at him from between Gemma's legs. Robbie's stomach lurched, it was bad enough watching Gemma at the top end.

"No thanks," he said quietly and she laughed.

"Yeah, it's not for everyone. Look down here though," She indicated the spot on the bed between Gemma's legs. "You won't see anything other than your baby. I promise." Robbie nodded and glanced at the bed, full of these bed pads, that had a strange beehive pattern on them. Robbie barely had time to wonder why that pattern was there when Gemma screamed again and this time, Robbie knew something was about to happen.

"Good, Gemma, good pushing. Right. Now you're going to have to hold your baby there, I know it burns, but you've got to keep them there. They can't slip back or you've got to go again."

Gemma was squeezing and grunting with the efforts of whatever she was doing and Robbie dreaded to even imagine what the midwife meant.

On the next contraction though, Gemma let out an almighty scream and Robbie really did think he would scream as well.

"What—" Robbie started angrily at the midwife, but when he turned, Robbie could see a head and all his words were lost.

"Well done, Gemma!" the midwife shouted, "Well done, that's the head, now we just need the shoulders," Gemma

391

screamed again as a shoulder was visible.

Robbie couldn't believe what he was seeing. He was just staring at this tiny person coming out of the person he loved. He almost couldn't see all the gory side of it, he was just totally amazed by Gemma.

She was superhuman.

"Oh my God," he was saying, "Gemma! Gemma! You're doing it! You're doing amazing! Keep going, you're almost there!"

Another shoulder and with one final heave from Gemma, a baby quite literally shot out, onto the beehive bed pads. The midwife seemed to scoop them up, pat them down and suddenly, all was quiet.

Just for a moment, before the scream filled the room and everyone seemed to breathe a collective sigh of relief. The midwife seemed to literally chuck the baby onto Gemma's chest and Robbie caught a glimpse of the gender.

"It's a girl! Gemma! We have a daughter!" Robbie hadn't realised he was tearing up, his throat felt thick and he blinked through watery vision at Gemma. Gemma cried as she held the baby tightly to her chest, she looked up at Robbie her face equally exhausted and elated.

"I did it!" she sobbed and closed her eyes taking some deep breaths. "I did it! I can't believe it."

Robbie let out a sob that was in his throat. "You did it, Gemma, you did so amazingly. I can't believe it. I love you so much." And he leaned down and planted a sloppy, tear-stained, kiss on her lips. "So amazing, I can't believe it."

"You did do amazing, Gemma," Linda wept and Robbie had quite forgotten she was there. "So strong, you are amazing." Gemma cried even harder at their praises and kissed her mother before turning and looking at the little baby clinging to her chest. She wasn't crying, her eyes were open as she was taking in the scene around her.

"Is she okay?" Gemma asked and the midwife nodded.

"She's brilliant, she's just a little surprised. As we all are. Well done, Gemma, you did amazing."

"I can't believe it," she said, still staring at the baby the moments before was still curled up inside her. Robbie kissed her forehead as they both gazed down at their daughter.

"I can," he said as he wrapped his arms around them both. "I never doubted you, you are the strongest person I know." Gemma beamed up at him before looking back down at their daughter.

"She's so beautiful. Oh, Robbie, I can't believe she's ours!" Robbie's eyes welled with unshed tears as he watched his wife and his newborn daughter.

"She's just like you, Gemma. She's so beautiful." He kissed Gemma and kissed their daughter again, bringing them into his arms and holding them to his chest.

Another thing that movies don't tell you about when you give birth, is the afterbirth and stitches. Poor Gemma had about five minutes to gaze lovingly at their baby before midwives were pressing onto her stomach and she was contracting again.

Robbie thought he might punch the specialist that came in not long after that. He examined Gemma, who was in apparent agony as he was trying to assess her tears and whether she'd need stitches.

Robbie yelled, "Just give her some pain relief!" as he clutched at Gemma as she cried as he examined her. Once she had been numbed, she was back to sitting quite serenely as they stitched her and she snuggled their newborn daughter.

"Do you have a name?" the midwife asked as Gemma was

brought back to her feet after her stitches and led to the shower. Robbie was sitting in the armchair, gazing at this little girl who had stolen his heart. Robbie looked up to see Gemma and the midwife smiling at him, obviously waiting for his input in their conversation.

"W-what? Sorry, I just can't believe how beautiful she is. I love her so much." Robbie gushed as he looked back down at the bundle of blankets that housed half of his heart.

"Abigail," Gemma said softly, smiling back at Robbie and baby Abigail who was still too smitten with each other to notice anything surrounding them. "Abigail Rose Wilson."

Robbie looked up at Gemma, his whole heart bursting with joy and love, he thought he might simply explode from all the joy.

"Abigail Rose Wilson," Robbie agreed, looking back down at her. And just when he thought he couldn't love anyone as much as he loved Gemma, she came into the world and made his heart double in size.

He now had two beautiful girls that he loved more than life itself.